More praise for Dewey Lambdin and his hero, Alan Lewrie

"I am such an enormous fan of the informed, superbly paced, witty adventures of Dewey Lambdin's Alan Lewrie, who is no better than he should be, that I found myself at a bookstore trying to plunk down cash for the next in the series six months before it was to be published."
—GREGORY MCDONALD
Author of *Fletch*

"We get a great taste of British naval life and some marvelous combat on the high seas. . . . Alan Lewrie [is] a raunchy hero who always fights the great fight and escapes death to swashbuckle another day. . . . No doubt he is on his way to an admiralship in future books, but it is enough to take them one at a time and follow this boy's career. Hornblower he ain't, and thank goodness for that."
—*Lincoln Journal-Star*

"Fascinating . . . A salty, bawdy sea story that will delight fans of the historical action novel."
—*Library Journal*

THE KING'S PRIVATEER

Dewey Lambdin

FAWCETT CREST • NEW YORK

A Fawcett Crest Book
Published by Ballantine Books
Copyright © 1992 by Dewey Lambdin
Excerpt from *The Gun Ketch* copyright © 1993 by Dewey Lambdin

This novel is a work of fiction. Names, characters, places, and incidents are either the product of the author's imagination or are used fictitiously. Any resemblance to actual events, locales, organizations, or persons living or dead is entirely coincidental and beyond the intent of either the author or the publisher.

http://www.randomhouse.com

Library of Congress Catalog Card Number: 95-96177

ISBN 0-449-22451-1

This edition published by arrangement with Donald I. Fine, Inc.

Manufactured in the United States of America

First Ballantine Books Edition: August 1996

10 9 8 7 6 5 4 3

Belated thanks too many years too late to:

Major Tom "Commander" Harris at Castle Heights Military Academy, who helped me learn to fly a plane and recognize good writing when I stumbled across it;

And to his sister Dr. Elizabeth McDavid at Cumberland College in Lebanon, Tennessee, who made me keep on scribbling until I got it right.

I only wish they were still around to see that they could like my books, because they were the first ones who told me I could do it if I wanted to.

Full-Rigged Ship: Starboard (right) side view

1. Mizzen Topgallant
2. Mizzen Topsail
3. Spanker
4. Main Royal
5. Main Topgallant
6. Mizzen T'gallant Staysail
7. Main Topsail
8. Main Course
9. Main T'gallant Staysail
10. Middle Staysail
11. Main Topmast Staysail
12. Fore Royal
13. Fore Topgallant
14. Fore Topsail
15. Fore Course
16. Fore Topmast Staysail
17. Inner Jib
18. Outer Flying Jib
19. Spritsail

A. Taffrail & Lanterns
B. Stern & Quarter-galleries
C. Poop Deck/Great Cabins Under
D. Rudder & Transom Post
E. Quarterdeck
F. Mizzen Chains & Stays
G. Main Chains & Stays
H. Boarding Battens/Entry Port
I. Cargo Loading Skids
J. Shrouds & Ratlines
K. Fore Chains & Stays
L. Waist
M. Gripe & Cutwater
N. Figurehead & Beakhead Rails
O. Jib Boom
P. Bow Sprit
Q. Foc's'le & Anchor Cat-heads
R. Cro'jack Yard (no sail fitted)
S. Top Platforms
T. Cross-Trees
U. Spanker Gaff

THE KING'S
PRIVATEER

I

"Go, mount the western winds and cleave the
  sky;
Then with swift descent, to Carthage fly:
There find the Trojan chief, who wastes his days
in slothful riot and inglorious ease—
bid him with speed the Tyrian court forsake;
with this command, the slumb'ring warrior
  wake."

Aeneid, Book IV
—VIRGIL

Chapter 1

"Shortest damned commission in naval history, I'll be bound," Alan Lewrie commented to his dining companions at Gloster's Hotel and Chop-House in Piccadilly.

"Oh, God, is he on about that one again?" The Honorable Peter Rushton, one of his old friends from his brief term at Harrow, almost gagged. "Give it a rest, will you, Alan? There's a good fellow. It is a wonder you don't still wear blue exclusively."

"Can't dine out on yer little bit o' fame forever, ye know, Alan," Clotworthy Chute, Rushton's constant companion, agreed round a bite of steak, and sloshed a sip of wine into his mouth to clear his palate to go further. "Bloody war's been over nigh on a year, don't ye know. You're home, well set up, got oceans o' chink to spend. Oceans o' mutton to bull. What man has need of anything more?"

"Well, it's not exactly oceans of guineas, Clotworthy," Alan pointed out. "More like a trickle of 'yellowboys' than a proper shower."

"But didn't Granny Lewrie just finish visiting?" Peter Rushton asked. "I'd have thought she'd have refilled your coffers to overflowing."

"So that's why you two bade me dine with you this evening," Alan said with a leery expression. From the first time he'd met them, neither Rushton nor Chute had had two pence to rub together. Chute's parents had gone smash and only provided him a miserly hundred pounds a year. Rushton's poppa, Lord George Rushton Baron of Staughton, had scads of loot and rents, but limited The Honorable Peter to a mere thousand guineas a year—it should have been enough for anyone, but young Peter had always spread himself a bit wider than most, and loved the gaming tables a bit too much. Both of them could be downright abstemious with their own funds, but could happily spend some other young fool's money in the twinkling of an eye.

"You use me ill as so many bears, sir!" Peter shot back as if he had been stung to the uttermost limits of his personal honor, but then gave a sardonic bark of amusement. "The thought had crossed my mind, damme if it hadn't, Alan, but we'll go equal shares on the reckoning tonight, so there. I believe we're flush, hey, Clotworthy?"

"Flush up to the deck-heads, as our Alan would say," Clotworthy agreed, smacking like a contented porker over some recent change in his fortunes. "And how was old granny? Still prosperin'?"

"Nigh onto seventy, and spry as a hound," Alan marveled. "And none too fond of my living arrangements, let me tell you. Spent most of my time over at their lodgings getting preached at."

"Glad my father's off in the country most of the time, too," Rushton commiserated. "Leastwise, there's my younger brother should I have a bad end. Title's safe. Lord, parents do have such *vaunting* expectations, don't they, though? Wasn't enough I got through Harrow *and* Cambridge, now he wants me to amount to something! I ask you, *me* amount to anything? Just let me inherit."

"And who were those rustics I saw you with on the Strand, Alan?" Clotworthy teased. "New companions?"

"The cousins, damn 'em." Alan winced. "I'd hoped no one would know me. Had to take them everywhere, see and do everything. Except anywhere near a good tailor or dressmaker. Following fashion is sinful extravagance to their lights. Just about everything back in old Wheddon Cross is perfection, to hear them tell it, and everything in London is like a German wood-cut engraved Hell."

"Wheddon Cross. Wherever the devil's that?" Clotworthy asked.

"Devon, near Exeter."

"Ah, damn dreary, I should think." Peter Rushton shivered.

"You'd think right," Alan agreed. His post-war visit had been the most boresome two weeks of his life. The Nuttbush cove his granny had married to transfer the Lewrie estate to his coverture, so his father Sir Hugo couldn't lay hands on it, was a dour old squire, not much taken with him from the first, no matter his repute as a sailor-hero, and had made it perfectly clear than Alan should harbor no hopes of getting his sinful little paws on a farthing of the new Nuttbush estate. He'd also made it pretty clear that the farther such a rake-hell was from his own kith and kin the better, no matter what his grandmother wished.

"Old granny still dotes on you, don't she?" Clotworthy asked further. "He hasn't turned her off you, has he?"

Clotworthy was one person Alan would never discuss money with. He'd started out school days a living sponge, just borrowing at first, but had graduated to a higher calling of criminal endeavor lately.

"Aye, she slipped me a little on the sly. Not much, mind." Alan lied. Actually, his grandmother had done him rather proud: a purse of bank notes worth an hundred extra pounds above his two hundred a year remittance. And she'd gone shopping and had outfitted his suite of rooms with a new Turkey carpet, a handsome wine cabinet and desk, and a new set of chairs for his second-hand dining table. She'd also provided a new lock-box for his chocolate, tea, sugar and coffee, and, while strolling with him through one of the Academy exhibits at Ranelagh Gardens, had purchased a nautical painting he'd taken a fancy to which now hung over his sitting room fireplace mantel.

"Ah, well," Clotworthy sighed in slight disappointment, knowing he couldn't hit Alan up for a loan, not right then, at any rate. Alan was surprised Clotworthy Chute had even agreed to go shares on their supper. Usually he lived on someone else's dole like a Roman client, when he wasn't bamboozling some idiot out of some ready pelf.

Must have found a new fool to bilk, Alan decided.

"They were the most peculiar lot, Peter," Clotworthy said, laughing.

"So tha'ss t'Strand, coozin Alan?" Alan mimicked. "Go' blessus, hi'ss *wide*, ahn't eet? However ye geet 'cross t'street 'ere in Loonun, me dear?" Which caricature set his dining companions off in mirth. "I tried to take 'em to my usual haunts, but they weren't having any of it. Coffee houses were nests of idleness. They'd be happier in a *counting* house, where people do productive work. Covent Garden, Drury Lane, I do believe shocked 'em to their prim souls. Got an hour's rant about sin, fornication, the low morals of theatre people . . ."

"They're right on that score, thank the Lord," Peter said, giggling.

"Lord's Cricquet Grounds . . . that was acceptable to 'em. The banks, the palace; the 'Change you'd have thought was Westminster Abbey," Alan went on. "Couldn't even get 'em enthused about a raree-show. Suggested watching a hanging; thought that'd buck 'em up, but it was no go."

"Speaking of actresses and such," Peter Rushton sighed. "How does a run over to Will's Coffee House in Covent Garden sound? I feel like putting the leg over some nubile young thing."

"Topping idea, Peter," Clotworthy said in his best toadying style. Evidently, Chute had gulled some other young wastrel earlier, and for once had his own cash to go on a high ramble.

"And just who was it this time, Clotworthy?" Rushton asked him, much amused by his schoolmate's new trade as a "Hoo-Ray Harry," one of those "Captain Sharps" who could decypher to the penny how much someone's inheritance was worth at first sight, and could also discern to the shilling just how much of it he could abscond with in his role of guide-amanuensis to the pleasures of London life.

"The Right Honorable Mathew Jermyn, Viscount Mickleton," Clotworthy boasted. "Poor little shit. Twenty years old, just down from the country. Rich as Croesus now he's inherited. Must have led a damned dull life up to now. Like Alan's cousins, he wants to go everywhere, and do everything. So far, I've shewn him a decent tailor . . . you can't believe how 'Chaw-Bacon' he looked when he got down out of his coach. Had suiting I'd not give a starving Irishman. With a *tricorne* on his head, don't ye know, haw haw haw!"

"That wouldn't be your own tailor, would it, Clotworthy?" Alan asked, pouring them all another glass of burgundy and waving for the wine steward to fetch another bottle.

"Made the man an easy three hundred pounds in an afternoon, with enough overage to pay my bills off. And finagle a new suit for meself out o' the bargain!" Clotworthy tittered. "Oh, we've had some fine times, I tell you. The old family equipage just wouldn't do, so I steered him to a carriage maker of my acquaintance. Over to Newmarket for four fine horses. New hats at Lock's, and a brace for me as well. I've got him ensconced in a town-house of his own in Old Compton Street, close to all the action. There was an extra two hundred for me on the deal. Introduced him to all the people who matter, don't ye know. Got him invitations to just about everything."

"What's he worth, do you reckon?" Alan asked, grinning in spite of himself. Clotworthy could sell roast pork to Muslims, and convince them to eat it with avidity.

"There must be fifty thousand pounds a year due the young clown. And if I don't end up with ten percent, I'm a bare-arsed Hindoo."

"He'll tumble to you sooner or later, you know," Alan said.

"Aye, but by then I'll have got mine, so what care I?" Clotworthy boasted. "Ah, another bottle, just in time, too. Peter, you must meet him. He knows nothin' about cards. You could skin him for a few hundred to tide you over, I should think. And you, as well, Alan. You cut a dashing figure about town."

Lewrie preened a little at that remark. Poor as his purse was, he had his stolen guineas from the French War Commissary ship *Ephegenie* to call upon, plus his two hundred pounds a year, and what the Navy laughingly called half-pay, which with the various deductions came to a miserly eleven pence a day. But he could still afford to wear the outer attributes of a stylish young gentleman about town with the best of them.

Styles had changed drastically since he'd been dragooned into the Navy in 1780. Cocked hats and tricornes were out; wide-brimmed, low-crowned farmer's styles or narrow, upwardly rolled brimmed hats with truncated, tapering crowns were in. Long waist-coats were horribly passé; short, double-breasted styles were all "the go" now. Sensible shoes with sturdy heels and soles had been replaced by either two-toned high boots or thin-soled slippers little more solid than a ladies' dancing shoe. No one carried a sword anymore unless out after dark in the worst neighborhoods. Now one had to sport a cane or walking stick with an intricately carved handle.

And suits: the finery of a long, full-skirted coat had been out for some time and those of Society with the proper *ton* now favored those coats drastically cut away from the legs in front.

Alan was sure he looked as acceptable as any other follower of popular fashion. It was dangerous in London to look too odd; the Mob had been known to throw dung at people who looked foreign or too out of style. Following fashion was cheaper than the cleaning bills!

"Think there's a penny in your cully for me as well,

Clotworthy?" Alan smirked. "You know I don't gamble deep anymore."

"Might be some wine and entertainment, anyway," Clotworthy promised, his round, cherubic face aglow. Damme, Alan thought, but he looks so innocent butter'd not melt in his mouth. "Like Peter here, you know everyone of note. An invitation or two'd not go amiss to bedazzle our calf-headed innocent while I skin him."

"Damme, who'd a thought you'd end up a swindler, Clotworthy?" Alan marveled. "I'd have put you down for nothing higher than *amuser* back when we were caterwauling in '79."

"Might as well be a pickpocket or a handkerchief snatcher," Clotworthy sniffed. "Never steal out of need. Amusers blow snuff in some cully's eyes, beat him up into the bargain, and elope with what they can get. Now a true artist, such as I, only accept payment for my services. That's not true stealing. I mean, damme, Alan! What good's an education if you can't use it fer yer own improvement?"

"And since you did so poorly in school . . ." Rushton supplied, waiting for the expected tag line that was almost Chute's *cri de coeur*.

"A man's got to be good at something, don't ye know?" Chute bellowed, and shook with amusement at his own well-tried jape.

"Well, the last of the last bottle," Rushton said, sharing the last of the wine into their glasses. "Port, cheese, the house's specialty sherry trifle? Or should we just pay up and head for the nearest *bagnio* and get ourselves stuck into some bareback riders?"

"I must confess I'm most pleasantly stuffed," Alan replied, with not an inch more room for dessert or cheese and biscuit.

"Too much food stifles the blood's humors," Clotworthy added, burping gently. "Let's pass on dessert and stroll supper off. Time enough for a cold collation after the whores."

"Afraid you'll have to roister without me tonight, gentlemen," Alan said, waving for the waiter and digging for his purse.

"Ah, an assignation, is it?" Rushton teased, digging him in the ribs. "Who is it tonight, then? Lady Cantner, or the lovely and so-edible Dolly Fenton?"

"Now that would be telling." Alan grinned with an air of mystery. Besides half-pay and prize money from his naval service, he could always count on the generosity of women whose husbands or keepers were too busy about their public affairs to pay proper suit to their private amours.

Tonight it was to be Dolly Fenton, who had been his mistress at Antigua for a few delicious weeks after he'd gone into the *Shrike* brig. She'd gone back to England on the packet once his ship had been transferred to the Jamaica Squadron, but she was still half in love with him, even if she had gained herself a wealthy City magistrate as a patron and lover. The man had to spend time with his wife and family, which left Dolly bored and lonely. She was to come to his lodgings for a few hours of bliss, and he was going to be a trifle late if he didn't stir his young arse up and hurry home.

Dolly was a few years older than he, but that hadn't been a detriment so far. Alan had solved her financial difficulties after her husband left her a penniless widow on Antigua, by the simple expedient of pointing out to her that instead of whoring of even the most genteel sort, she could sell the late Captain Fenton's commission in the Army to a richer junior officer of his unit who wished to buy his way up in rank.

Tomorrow, though, he would have to devote all his time to Lady Delia Cantner. When Alan had been a midshipman aboard the small dispatch schooner *Parrot* in 1781, she and her husband had been their passengers. In the midst of an outbreak of Yellow Fever among the crew, Alan's insubordinate actions had burned a French privateer to the waterline, a ship that had appeared like the last act of a capricious God to torment them in their already dire peril.

Lady Delia was years younger than her husband, the ancient squint-a-pipes Lord Cantner, who was most conveniently crossing over to Holland to transact some business, and would be gone for some time.

Where Dolly Fenton was green-eyed and blessed with hair the color of polished mahogany, with a slim young body, Lady Delia was dark, like a Spanish countess. Black hair, smoky brown eyes with a lazy, sensuous cast and a bountifully soft and round form with the biggest bouncers Alan had ever doted upon. He would be hard put to choose exactly which of the pair he'd prefer, if he had to give one of them up.

And with two such lovelies in his life, both so eager to be rogered to panting ruin as often as possible, the idea of going on a rut among the drabs was less than appetizing. At least with Dolly and Lady Delia, he didn't have to worry (much, anyway) about catching the pox and suffering the dubious, and painful, mercury cure.

They paid their reckoning, gathered up their hats and cloaks, and headed out into a bitter night. Sleet was falling. The streets and walks were already glazed with a rime of slush half-frozen into ice, and a brisk nor'westerly wind would harden that into a proper snowfall before dawn.

"Nasty bloody weather," Clotworthy grumbled from the depths of his three-tiered cape-collared overcoat.

"Who'd be a sailor on such a night," Alan sighed, wishing just once more for the sort of balmy warmth he'd experienced in the West Indies, and shrugging deeper into his dark blue grogram watchcoat, part of his uniform he'd never expected to use.

"Damn your invigorating stroll, Clotworthy," Rushton said. "Let's whistle up a coach. Here comes one now."

A coach and four was indeed trotting up to the doorway of Gloster's, the horse's hooves splashing and skidding a little in the muddy slush of the roadway. A postillion boy muffled to the eyebrows in yards of scarves jumped down and opened the door to hand out the occupants, as Clotworthy arranged a fare for Drury Lane.

There was something familiar about the bleak, almost harsh-faced young man who was alighting from the equipage. Snapping hazel eyes, ash-blonde hair and a certain, stiff, almost military manner in which he carried himself. Alan's face split in a grin of recognition. And when the second young man with the same features alit, he stepped forward and extended his mittened hand in greetings.

"Governour Chiswick, is that you?" Alan demanded.

"What the devil . . . Alan Lewrie!" the elder Chiswick brother boomed out loud enough to startle the horses. "Give ye joy, sir! Caroline . . . Mother! See who's come to meet us!"

Chapter 2

"I declare, Mister Lewrie, London must be the world's largest *little* city," Mrs. Chiswick stated over supper. "Once we left Charleston and sailed for home, we lost all track of you, and then, up you pop like a jack-in-the-box!"

Alan had debated whether to beg off and run home to his set of rooms to Dolly, or stay and catch up on old times with the Chiswicks, whom he hadn't seen since Yorktown and the evacuation of Wilmington, North Carolina. It was Caroline Chiswick who decided the matter for him. She had blossomed from a gawky and almost painfully thin young girl of eighteen to a lovely young lady of twenty-one, his own age. She was still slimmer than fashion dictated, and was taller (or gawkier) than most men preferred, at a bare two inches less than Alan's five foot nine. But the hazel eyes of the Chiswicks were like amber flames into which he was drawn with the certainty of a besotted moth. Her light brown hair glittered in the candlelight as though scattered with diamonds. And her delectable mouth beamed the fondest of smiles at him from the moment he had helped hand her out of the coach. The cheekbones were high, still, the face slim and tapering to a fine chin. Her eyes still crinkled at the corners, and formed little folds of flesh below the sockets of a most merry, and approving, cast, as they had that last day on deck when she and her parents had been sent ashore at Charleston.

The way she laid her gloved hand on his coat sleeve and gave it a squeeze, and the pleading, wistful, way she had gazed at him as she had said, "Oh, please sup with us, do, Alan!" had knocked all thoughts of Dolly Fenton from his head.

Alan had had to introduce Peter Rushton and Clotworthy Chute to them. And when Clotworthy had learned they were in

London to seek out some position for the younger brother, Burgess, it was all Alan could do to drive Chute away from the possibility of a few hundred pounds. Thankfully, the weather had driven his friends into the relative warmth of the carriage, and the Chiswicks into Gloster's, before Clotworthy could offer his "good offices" and connections with the influential of the town on their behalf.

"You can't imagine what a pleasant surprise it was for me, as well, Mistress Chiswick," Alan replied in turn. "Last I heard of your family, you were considering taking passage for Eleuthera in the Bahamas to try your hand at farming there."

"Land's too dear in the Bahamas," Governour stated. "For cotton or sugar, you need slaves, and slaves cost too much, so we didn't have the wherewithal to start over out there. There's been some talk of a compensation treaty, so the Rebels may someday make restitution to all the Loyalists who had to flee. But I'd not hold my breath waiting for a penny on the pound of all that we lost."

"We're in Surrey, near Guildford, with our uncle Phineas, now," Burgess Chiswick, the younger brother stated. "Cattle, sheep and oats. Some barley and hops, too. You must try our beer and ale! It'll never be like the Carolinas. Never be like our *own* place, not really, but . . ." He shared a glance with his mother, shrugged and shut up.

"Governour manages the estate for Uncle Phineas," Caroline said to fill the awkward gap. "He was most kind to help us with our passage, and to give us a place to live. And although it is nowhere near as grand as our former home and acres, it is a solid enough croft."

"Aye, it is," the mother agreed firmly. "We've a roof over our heads, a tenancy with enough acreage for a good home-farm. Rent-free, may I remind you, Burge. 'Tis more than *we* could have hoped for, and a deal greater than most could ever dream of in these unsettled times."

"And Mister Chiswick?" Alan inquired. "He is well?" The last time Alan had seen their father in Wilmington, he'd been daft as bats.

"Improved most remarkably, sir!" Burgess was happy to relate. "He does for our acres wonderfully well. 'Twas amazing what a piece of land and herds did to inspirit him after all those trying months."

"Indeed, you would not know him now, Alan," Caroline chorused. His feebleness had been embarrassing to her. "Now, he's ruddy and hale, out in all weathers with the flocks and herds like a man half his rightful age! Dealing with the crofters and the lesser tenants."

And a tenant himself after all these years, Alan thought glumly. No matter they've food in their bellies and a dry hearth, it must still be a mortifying come-down from being Tidewater planters along the Lower Cape Fear.

"I'd think there'd be work enough, Burgess. Or do sheep put you off your dinner?" Alan teased.

"God, I hate the bloody things!" Burgess burst out, which set them all laughing. "And . . . well, I don't know if you have any interest in things agricultural, Alan, but what with Enclosure Acts being passed every session, and with the changeover of crops, there's little to do. The poorer crofters have been run off the common lands, and gone to the cities and mills for work, and there's no need for a large tenantry, no permanent laborers anymore. Which leaves little for me to do, either," he concluded with a wry shrug.

"We were hopeful of an Army career for Burgess here," Governour said as their food arrived. "Uncle Phineas can't extend his generosity so far as to buy Burgess a set of colors, but we both know he's an experienced officer. He made lieutenant with our regiment of volunteers before the war ended."

From the tone of Governour's voice when speaking of generosity from their blood relation, it was a slim sort of beneficence, and most like as cold as charity. It would cost this uncle Phineas nigh on four hundred pounds to settle Burgess as an ensign in even a poor regiment, and that with no support to maintain himself in the mess later, either, if the man was as miserly as Governour hinted. He didn't sound like the sort who'd spend money just to get young Burgess out from under foot, not unless there was a satisfactory return on his investment.

"If not a regiment, Burgess had a decent education, Alan," Caroline told him, drawing his attention most willingly back to her. "There must be something clerical for him to do. He knows lumber from our mill before the war. Horses. Trade. I've come to learn it's not socially acceptable to admit to a career in trade here in London, but there surely is something he could do to earn his way in life."

Law, Parliament, the Church, military service, banking or such careers were for the upper crust, Alan knew. Burgess was too old at twenty-one to be 'prenticed out to learn a trade, and it sounded as if farming was out, too. What little was left for him? That this spectacular specimen of mankind would grub away his days in some counting house, clerking and writing for a bank or mill owner? It was a ghastly thought. And, with the country inundated with veterans returned from the war, jobs were scarce as hen's teeth already, with a hundred queuing for every opening, and a thousand more tramping the roads from one rumor of employment to the next.

"Bow Street Runners!" Alan spoke up with sudden inspiration. "You know, that Fielding fellow's watch service. Replacing the parish Charlies with a police force. It's a bloo . . . a devilish un-English idea if you ask me, having a police force like the Frogs over in Paris do. Might as well declare martial law and have done, but they'd look kindly on a well set-up young fellow with military experience. I've read he hires ex-servicemen, sergeants and corporals, mostly. Good men handy with a staff, who can take care of themselves. Surely, they'd need someone like you, Burgess. You could show 'em what Red Indians fight like."

"It's a good idea, Burge," Governour opined heartily. "Not too much different from the Army, I suppose. Get in on the ground floor, so to speak. And with your education, and your skills, you'd move right up quickly."

"Aye, it's a thought," Burgess piped back, but Alan could see, even if the others didn't, that his heart wasn't exactly in it. From their time at Yorktown, besieged by the Rebels and the French, and in their daring escape after being blown down-river in those damned barges the night before the surrender, Alan was pretty sure being a constable of the watch was not the career Burgess Chiswick would care for.

He was a strange young fellow. So woods-crafty, so in control of his troops by an almost natural sense of superiority. Yet down in his depths, Alan had always caught an inkling of fear, of uncertainty. God knew, Alan had seen enough war to make his own knees knock every time he heard a cannon go off, and he still couldn't quite credit the Navy with making him a Commission Officer and giving him command of a ship of war, even one so small as *Shrike* in the closing weeks of the war—he of all people by God knew uncertainty like a close relation! But with Burgess, he felt a . . . softness. A nature too soft for the slings and arrows of life, like setting foxes to outfight hounds. And yet the ember of ambition burned within his breast, the wish to do great things perhaps beyond his measure.

"Who knows?" Burgess went on between bites of his fish course. "There's always the sea, like you. Or the East Indies. I've heard officers with 'John Company' come home at least a chicken-nabob. Fifty thousand pounds in diamonds and rubies'd suit me right down to my toes."

"I pray not, Burge," Caroline said, frowning. "So far away, so harsh and hot. Why, they die like flies among the Hindoos, do they not, Alan?"

"So I've read, Caroline," Alan replied, and was rewarded with another of those deep gazes, and a slight touch of her hand on his in thankfulness for backing her words. A touch that struck a spark between them as remarkable as their first timid kiss on the *Desperate* frigate's midnight quarterdeck two years and more before.

Why'd I act so miss-ish with her before? Alan wondered. I even entertained a thought of marrying her, even if she was poor as a church-mouse. 'Course, that was back when I still had hopes of Lucy Beauman and her daddy's guineas. Any other girl, I'd have bulled her aft by the taffrail and damned anyone in the watch who'd interfere. Governour or Burgess would have called me out and skewered me for it, though. Maybe that's why I didn't. Maybe that's why.

"It would be a capital way to renew the family fortunes," Burgess insisted. "To get on with 'John Company.' Even as a clerk to some trading house out there would put me in the way of money beyond measure. And it wouldn't be but for a few years."

"Your friend Mister Chute intimated he had influence, Alan," Governour said. "Perhaps he could suggest something."

"I'd not trust him any farther than I could spit, Governour," Alan replied. "I knew him at Harrow, before I was expelled. He still owes me half a crown for tatties and gravy after all these years, and devil a hope I have of ever being repaid. He makes a career of making efforts on people's behalf. But he charges a pretty penny for it."

"Ah, that kind." Governour scowled again.

"And I thought after Mister Richardson's novels about such doings, they'd be a law to stop such as he," Mrs. Chiswick all but cried in alarm. "Harrow, though. A good school, for all I've heard tell. And what did you do to get yourself expelled, Alan?"

"Tried to blow up the governor's coach-house. And his privy," Alan was forced to admit. "Come to think on it,

Clotworthy Chute and Peter Rushton were both in on it with
me, and left me holding the bag. Or the wick, in this case."

The food had been swill, the new governor of the school
had strict ideas about discipline, and most schools were run by
terror, anyway, with the students ready to riot at any provoca-
tion. Just before term ended, when parents came to fetch their
children and saw the one instance of decent victuals (put on for
their benefit and not to be seen again), they had decided to do
something grand. A small keg of gunpowder had been procured, with a length of slow-match. It had been only extreme
bad luck that the governor had been on his way to the privy
behind the stables when the charge went off.

The intent had been to destroy the man's splendid coach and
let him know how reviled he was among the students. But the
measure of powder was a lot more than it ought to have been.
Alan had lit the slow-match and run back away from the stables and coach-house what he thought was a safe distance to
watch the show, and Clotworthy, Peter Rushton and a couple
of other young scamps had hidden in the box hedges, tittering
with anticipation.

The roof had been blown off. The doors and windows disappeared in a *whoof* of flame and smoke, and the carriages inside had certainly been turned into heat and light. But the
horses had panicked and broke free from the stalls, and ran all
over the county as the barn caught fire. Everyone had run for
his life, and Alan had had the misfortune to choose the wrong
direction, had not thought to put down his port-fire and had
collided headlong with the governor, ramming his head right
into the man's stout stomach and nightshirt, which abrupt collision had addled both of them, and Alan was last to his feet,
with the incriminating evidence by his side.

"I could have tattled on the others, but I didn't," Alan said
in conclusion of his tale, "and he *still* won't pay me for those
tatties. Or the beating I got, either."

"Were I your father I'd have tanned your bottom, sir!" Mrs.
Chiswick declared, swooning with laughter with the rest. "No
wonder a career at sea, where you could indulge your passion
for explosives, resulted. Oh, what a scamp you were, sir!"

"And still is, I'll be bound," Caroline added fondly. "I can
see where your sense of adventure comes from, Alan."

"And where is your father, now, Alan?" Governour asked.
"In London as well?"

"Last I heard from him," Alan lied smoothly, "he went to Portugal. Something about the wine trade, I believe."

Such as getting closer to the source of his sherry, Alan told himself, hoping they wouldn't pursue the topic any further. By the time he'd brought *Shrike* back to pay her and her crew off at Deptford Hard, his solicitor, Mr. Matthew Mountjoy, who had been pursuing a suit against Sir Hugo, had told him he'd fled to the Continent, leaving a host of creditors behind, and was rumored to be living in Lisbon where even the impoverished could scrape by, as long as one did not upset the church authorities and the Inquisition by one's behavior.

"Even so, he must indeed be proud of you, sir," Mrs. Chiswick continued. "To become a Sea Officer in only three years."

"Well, there was the war, ma'am. They were pretty desperate, you know." Alan chuckled in mock deprecation.

"Yes, tell us what you did after we lost track of you, Alan," Caroline urged, totally ignoring her portion of Dover sole and wine.

"Um, Battle of St. Kitts under Hood. And then our ship *Desperate* fought a French twenty-eight-gunned frigate and took her as prize the same day," Alan said, sounding as if it was nothing much to take note of, but secretly glad to have a chance to boast. He'd had few enough in the last months—half of London had tales of battle and bravery and the populace was heartily sick of hearing them by then. "Passed the examination board right after, and was made first lieutenant into the *Shrike* brig. Made a nuisance of ourselves along the Cuban coasts . . . took a fair amount of prizes. Ran guns to the Creek and Seminolee Indians. Ended up *anhissi* to the White Clan . . ."

"The devil you say!" Governour burst out. "Of their fire, ey?"

"Took a Foreign Office party up the Ochlockonee and the Chatahootchee to get the Indians to side with us against Spain if we landed troops, but nothing came of it," Alan said, frowning between sips of wine. "Got ambushed by the coastal Apalachee. Had an exciting hour or so, 'til the Seminolee showed up and rescued us. Then we got stuck in at Turk's Island in the Bahamas to retake it from the French. That didn't work, either. My captain was wounded pretty sore, and Hood gave me command temporarily, really. The war ended two weeks later, and we brought her home to pay off with the first batch of ships."

"You actually commanded a ship!" Caroline exclaimed. "Alan, I cannot imagine! You remember, mother, how masterful he was, how nautical, the morning we sailed down the Cape Fear? 'Quartermaster, half a point to'—to what-you-may-call-it—'helm up and hands to the braces'? Lord, Alan, I knew you were a competent sailor even then, as a master's mate. But to run a ship of your own, well!"

"For the shortest commission in naval history, I expect," he replied, almost glowing inside on the warmth of their regard. "But I also expect Governour and Burgess have more interesting adventures, and I'm dying to hear them. Allow me to sport us all to another brace of this rather good wine, and tell it all to me."

He stayed long past his intended departure time, partly because the Chiswick brothers indeed had exciting tales to relate. Of how they had used the remnants of their North Carolina Loyalist Rifle battalion alongside depot troops and recovered sick from Simcoe's Queen's Rangers around New York for a few months as scouts and raiders to keep the Rebels on the hop, then had been trans-shipped to Charleston to defend the approaches to the city from Rebel probes. Partly because he was with Caroline Chiswick, who had been beautiful before, but was now so incredibly, deliciously handsome.

"And you stay in London how long?" Alan asked as they stood on the icy street once more, whistling up another coach to take them back to their lodgings.

"We may spend two weeks at the outside," Governour informed him. There probably wasn't money enough to allow them to rent rooms and buy food for longer. Burgess would have to be settled in that time, or he would have to return to Guildford and take what little the countryside had to offer.

"We must see each other again, sir," Caroline insisted, from the frame of the same dark red velvet, hooded traveling coat she'd worn in Wilmington in 1781. It was a little shiny in places from too much wear, but still presentable enough, and it made Alan feel an urge to buy her a new one, a cloak fine enough to suit her, and what he felt she deserved from life.

"Call on us, do, Mister Lewrie," Mrs. Chiswick agreed. "We lodge in St. Clements Street. Oh dear, I forget the house number, but it's a decent enough house, I'm told. Governour knows it."

"Panton Street for me," Alan said. "I'd never be able to afford it but for Admiral Sir Onsley Matthews and his wife. You remember I wrote of them, Caroline."

He and Governour exchanged addresses while Burgess managed to flag down a coach, one of the few that would still risk horses on the streets that were now icing over under the constant drizzle of sleet. Caroline and her mother huddled for warmth to one side by the door.

"Goodnight, and thank you for the wine, Alan. Do call on us!"

"Aye, I shall," Alan told Mrs. Chiswick again, then turning to Caroline, said, "We have so much to catch up on."

Which sentiment Caroline agreed with heartily, and gave him a last smile of invitation, and a firm nod of her head as they said their goodnights as well. Then the coach trundled off, leaving Lewrie to trot home on his own, swaddled up in the voluminous dark blue watchcoat he'd never thought he'd find a use for back in the West Indies.

His lodgings were one pair-of-stairs up from the main floor in the front of the house. Once a substantial mansion, Lady Maude Matthews had turned it into sets of rooms to let. For a very decent fifty guineas a year, about half what Lewrie suspected it was really worth, he got a sitting room with fireplace and mantel, and two whole windows—the Window Tax be damned—that overlooked Panton Street, a fashionable address for foreigners, secretaries and under-ministers to overseas embassies, well-heeled younger blades such as himself; home, too, to a regiment of mistresses. The set of rooms bent in an L, with a bed-chamber to the rear along the outer wall, and from a tiny window, in that room, he could look down upon Oxenden Street, and farther down to the Haymarket and St. James' Market. It was inclined to be a trifle noisy in the mornings, but he'd learned by then to sleep through almost any din, as long as he wasn't at sea. Civilian noises and alarums meant nothing to a weary sailor who'd developed the habit of trotting (or crawling) up his own stairs at "first sparrow-fart" every morning and caulking like a sodden log until noon.

He stepped into the sitting room, where a small sea-coal fire burned in the grate, and the embers and flames were reflected into the room by a brass back-plate. It was the only light in the room until his manservant Cony woke up at his entrance and used a paper spill to light him a candle or two.

"Mistress Fenton still here, Cony?" Alan asked as he

shrugged off his watchcoat and went to thaw out before the fire.

"No, she ain't, sir," Cony was forced to admit. "She did come, but when the church bells went ten o' the clock, she went on 'ome, sir."

Cony shyly handed Alan a folded and wax-sealed letter that had been waiting on the silver tray by the door.

"She lef' ya this, sir," Cony told him. "I 'spect you'd be wantin' a brandy'r somethin' warmin', sir?"

"Aye, thankee, Cony. I'd admire that," Alan said, drawing a well-preserved William and Mary chair he'd found at a second-hand shop closer to the fire to read it. Alan Lewrie had gotten too many notes or letters from women to imagine that it was good news. Which explained his waiting until he had a brandy in hand and one sip in his belly for fortification before he broke the seal and unfolded it.

"Ah," he said after a first, quick, perusal. Cony was thankfully busy in the other room, putting a warming pan into his bed and building up the fire in the second fireplace so Lewrie could retire and undress without turning blue from exposure.

If it had tears splashed on it, it couldn't be more plaintive. This wasn't the first time Alan had so shamefully ignored her, he read, and he had to admit Dolly was right. There were so many other things to do in a city as great as London. So many interesting people to hear speak, edifying exhibits to visit. Theatres, dramas and comedies to gawk at. Oranges to be bought and hurled at poor players. So many young women to bull.

She is getting a little long in tooth, Alan told himself. His putative mistress was getting on for thirty. There were the first hints of wrinkles around her mouth, kissable as it was. The first crow's feet around her peculiarly dark green eyes, bright as they were still. Or perhaps, it was because she was available for his pleasure so little of the time.

In the beginning, when he'd run into her at a supper dance back in the summer, it had been intriguing to have her again, to pick up where they'd left off on Antigua. And having her free, with another man to pay her keep, and enjoying her between the magistrate's visits, with one ear to the hallway and the latch was exciting, too.

"Just as well," Alan decided. "Come to think on it, I was getting a trifle bored with her."

"Yew say somethin', sir?" Cony asked from the other room.

"Just maundering, Cony; pay me no mind," Alan called back;

"Aye, sir."

Dolly had been so grateful for his assistance, and his money which kept her during the war. She'd made a real shore home for him, an activity he strongly suspected she'd want to do again, if he had enough money to support her as he once had. Dolly Fenton was at the upper end of marriageable age, and her magistrate wasn't doing her much good in that regard. Only the most fascinating widows ever got a second man to take them on, he knew. The best Dolly could hope for was someone incredibly rich to keep her on the side, as her magistrate did. Someone titled, who could keep a mistress openly, care for her all his life and leave her well provided for when he turned up his toes.

Damn hard lot for most women, Alan thought, folding the letter up with a sense of finality. Wonder what Caroline Chiswick's lot's to be? American Loyalist, not a hundred pounds for her "dot" if she did marry. Country girl, even lovely as she is. Service with some family around Guildford? Married to some pinchbeck "Country-Harry" and up to her ankles in dirty children and sheep the rest of her life? God, what a thought, he shivered with more than cold.

"That be all, sir?" Cony asked.

"Aye, Cony. You go caulk."

"Tomorrow's me day off, sir," Cony reminded him. "If there's anythin' you'd be a'wantin' afore I go in the mornin', sir?"

"Hmm," Alan pondered, tossing Dolly Fenton, and her letter, on the coals. "I'll have a couple of letters for you to run about the town. One to St. Clements Street, to the Chiswicks."

"The Chiswick brothers 'ere in London, sir?" Cony brightened.

"And the mother and Mistress Caroline, too. You tell 'em I sent you, and I expect you'd want to visit them as well after all we went through during the siege."

"That'd be wondrous fine, sir! I liked the Chiswicks!"

"And there'll probably be a dram or two in it for you, and some of the mother's ginger snaps. I'll leave the letters on the tray by the door," Alan promised. "Tell one of the housemaids to do for me, so you can depart early as you like."

"Aye, thankee, sir."

"And I expect you'd be needing some cash, hey?" Alan teased his longtime hammockman, wardroom and cabin servant. "Can't make a grand show with the young ladies without a shilling or two."

He dug out his purse and gave Cony his four shillings.

"Thankee, sir, thankee right kindly, sir," Cony said, pocketing the coins and almost skipping down the hall to his own bed belowstairs with his week's wages ready to burn a hole in him.

"Damme," Alan spoke to himself aloud (a habit he'd developed in those few weeks he'd inhabited the captain's great cabins aft in *Shrike*), "I don't believe I've been home this early in weeks. And by myself, at that. What a novelty it is!"

He trailed into the bed-chamber and shucked his street clothes for a silk nightshirt, and a dressing gown thick and heavy enough to serve as a horse blanket. Sleet rapped on the panes, and the glass was frosted almost opaque as a muscovy-glass lantern on the windows.

Alan surveyed his little kingdom, the first home of his own he had ever had that the Navy or his father hadn't provided. He'd had it repainted a cheery pale yellow before he moved in, with snowy-white wood trim. The mantel and hearth were milk-veined grey marble—the genuine article instead of some painted slate most builders tried to foist off on the unsuspecting. There were some nature scenes hanging on the walls, the anonymous sort of thing sketched on some aristocrat's Grand Tour of the Continent. Roman ruins, Greek temples, viaducts with tall poplars lining narrow roads, almost awash in happy peasantry and well-rendered animals of indeterminate breed—cattle, mostly. There was a copy of some Frog artist's imaginings of a Sultan's harem, though the women weren't as Junoesque as the classics depicted them. Alan suspected the copyist had used some slimmer Covent Garden whores as models. And he wasn't so sure but that the one reclining on the couch in the foreground wasn't 'Change Court Betty, who had been one of the first whores he'd ever sprung money for. Once he saw it being loaded into a cart to be auctioned off with the rest of a household's belongings, he had to have it. Besides, the painting was so inspiring, and a harem had been one of his favorite fantasies since puberty.

A portrait of his mother Elizabeth hung on the inside wall of the sitting room near the door, over the sofa. His granny had given it to him on his visit to Wheddon Cross. A portrait of himself as a naval lieutenant hung beside it. He'd had one done for his granny, and had thought a second copy could always come in handy as a present for some future amour.

The furnishings were quite good—half London was always selling up and moving to stay a step ahead of creditors, or buy their way out of debtor's prison, so the selection had been quite varied. Deep blue velvet, sprigged with bright vines and flowers, covered the sofa and two upholstered high-backed chairs. The tables and exposed wood shone with bee's wax and lemon oil, and no one hardly ever noticed the odd nick or scratch the previous owners had caused. And he had the bench before the fire, and the two side chairs as well. The dining table, sideboard and wine cabinet made the far end of the room a cheery, cozy place to eat or play cards. Cards, mostly. The most fashionable young men dined out at clubs or chophouses, sending down to an ordinary for meals if at home. And if he did have to entertain and feed guests, he could send Cony out shopping, and trust the kitchen in the basement of the lodging house to come up with something presentable, though he did it seldom.

He could maintain this lifestyle for some time yet, if he was careful with his money. Three hundred pounds a year had been enough to keep a single gentleman in *style* before the war, and with no need for a horse or coach of his own, and only the one servant, two hundred would do now. He could not purchase every book that struck his fancy. Could not entertain lavishly. Would have to watch for bargains instead of spending like a lord on the Strand.

Oh, he'd had to buy plates, saucers, silverware and serving utensils for the first time. Stock that wine cabinet. In his reverie of accounting his possessions, he opened it and poured his glass of brandy back up to full. Yes, it could be a good life, he decided. Best he'd lost Dolly Fenton, after all. She'd have turned expensive.

"Speaking of Dolly," he said aloud again with a weary mutter.

He had notes to write. One to Dolly, a parting shot to salve his ego. One to the Chiswicks, and Caroline, laying the ground for a proper reunion with her. And one to Lady Delia, to let her know she could expect him by early afternoon, if the weather would allow.

Chapter 3

Mwack. A carping little sound, half trill in the back of the throat. Then the rustle of cleverly parted bed-curtains, and a heavy weight hitting the mattress down near the foot of the bed.

Mwack, again. Something stalking up the side of the bed to the pillows. Then a leap from one side to the other that for one moment put all four paws in an area no larger than a pocket watch. Right in the center of Alan's belly.

"Oh, for Christ's sake," he groaned, opening one eye.

He was confronted by a round, furry face, and two yellow eyes staring back at him somberly from three inches' range. *Mwack!* More petulant, louder this time. William Pitt had his best pout on.

"And what the hell do you want, you little bastard?"

William Pitt had been the best mouser aboard the *Shrike* brig, a ship absolutely infested with the creatures—his former captain, Lieutenant Lilycrop had adored the little beasts—the king ram-cat and the one with the worst disposition of any feline even Lilycrop had ever met. Why he, at long last, took a liking to Lewrie (who had always thought a cat was better drowned at birth), no one could ascertain.

He'd moved into the great cabins once Alan had gotten command. More than that, William Pitt had startled the officer initially appointed into *Shrike* at the entry port and sent him crashing back into the longboat to break his unfortunate skull before he could even introduce himself.

They'd paid off at Deptford Hard, laying *Shrike* up in-ordinary, and sending the crew off to civilian pursuits. Somehow, he'd followed Alan's belongings down the gangplank at the stone pier, and into the coach. The cat had an open door to

24

depart anytime he felt like it, but so far, had shown no signs of taking advantage of it, other than a stroll out into the back-gardens, or sunning himself when the miserable London weather allowed. There were queens enough in the neighbor-hood for him to roger when they came into heat, and Alan grudgingly let the cat be fed in his apartments.

Pitt slept near the hearth, either in the below-stairs kitchens where the housemaids and other servants slipped him some tucker on the side, or in the bed-chamber. William Pitt wasn't picky. Nor was he of a disposition that doted on much affec-tion from humans, so he could be tolerated most of the time.

Alan put out a hand and rubbed the top of the cat's grizzled head. Pitt allowed himself to be greeted, then shook his head vigorously and sank down on his haunches to scratch at his of-fended ears with a back paw. One did not make the mistake of touching Pitt more than he liked more than once. Not if one enjoyed having fingers.

"How'd you get in here, anyway?" Alan mumbled, sliding up to the headboard and plumping up his pile of pillows.

"Mornin', sir?" a tentative voice called from beyond the bed-curtains. "Your man Cony said to come wake you, sir? 'Tis Abigail, I am, sir?"

An "Abigail" named Abigail, Alan grinned lazily. How rare.

"Aye, I'm awake, thankee, Abigail."

Alan slid the bed-curtains on the inner side of the room back to let the heat of the fireplace in. The room was cold as charity.

The girl was kneeling down by the grate, dropping fresh coal on the embers and stirring them up with a poker.

"Hollo, you're a new 'un, ain't you?" Alan commented.

"Started las' week, sir," the girl said, turning to give him a grin. She was a lovely little thing with new-penny coppery hair and blue eyes, not a minute older than fifteen or sixteen, he noted. "Your man already done took your letters, sir. But he says to me on his way out, he says, I'm to wake you, an' ask you for your key so's I can make your tea, sir?"

"Ah, right," Alan said. "In my waist-coat pocket."

She passed out of his sight to the foot of the bed and he heard something rustle as she picked up his clothes from the floor where he'd dropped them. Then she came back to the open side of the bed.

"This be it, sir?" she asked him. Close to, he saw that she

had a dusting of freckles across the bridge of her saucy, up-turned little nose.

"Aye, that's it."

"An' what'll you be havin' this mornin', sir? Tea? Coffee? Chocolate?" she asked.

"Do you make good coffee, Abigail?" Alan asked her, sitting up higher against the pillows. "I mean, really good coffee?"

"I reckon I can, sir," she replied, a trifle dubious.

"Grind the beans fine as corned gunpowder. Use a heaping spoonful per cup, mind, don't scrimp," Alan instructed. "Water hot as the hinges of Hell, none of this tepid water. And let it steep and drip until all the water's gone down into the pot, or the cup."

"Aye, sir, I'll do it, s'help me, though I know nothin' 'bout gunpowder, sir," she promised earnestly. "Toast, too, sir? Or d'you want me t' go out an' get some rolls for you?"

"What sort of a day is it, Abigail?" Alan asked.

"'Tis that cold, sir, t'would make a stone cupid shiver," she informed him. "Snow up t' the bottom steps already, an' ice under. An' more comin' down, sir, like there's no tomorrow."

"Toast, then, from the kitchens. No sense slipping and breaking your pretty young pate for my pleasure," Alan said, grinning. "First, I need a kettle of hot water for shaving, and then the breakfast."

"I'll do her, sir!" Abigail said as she curtsied her way out.

Alan steeled himself, then slid out of bed and toe-walked to his stockings and slippers on the icy cold floorboards. He stripped off his nightshirt and bundled it into the armoire, donned a clean pair of white canvas slop-trousers from his sea-chest, and the heavy dressing gown.

He went to the living room window and rubbed the glass clear of fog and frost on the inside to look out. The semi-translucent view he had of the street reminded him more of the Arctic wastes he'd seen north of Halifax and Louisburg than London. The girl had stoked up the sitting room fire as well, so he sat close to it as he waited for his shaving water.

Abigail was back with a large copper kettle, using a thick rag and both hands to hold it away from her so she wouldn't sear herself on it. "Your man Cony says t' me, he says, sir, that you likes plenty o' hot water o' the mornin's, so I brought ya a full gallon measure."

"Topping!" Alan cried in appreciation. "Wash-hand-stand's

in the bed-chamber. Lay me out a fresh towel and I'll attend
to my shaving things, Abigail. Here, let me take it. It looks
heavy."

"Yessir, it is, sir, but I can manage, sir. No bother."

She poured the bowl full, set the kettle down by the hearth,
and handed him a towel on the way out. Alan hummed to himself as he unrolled his "housewife" and stropped his razor. It
wasn't too long before he'd not had to shave every morning,
and that only for Sunday Divisions aboard ship, at that. But
Delia Cantner appreciated the lack of stubble to irritate her
more private parts. If he was to keep his tryst with her that afternoon, he wanted to please.

Once shaved, he fetched out a washcloth and began to
sponge himself down from neck to ankles with hot water and
a precious bar of scented Italian soap, a present from Lady Delia (one of many she'd given him over the last few months).
To do so, he had to drop his slop-trousers.

Ohpe! came a small gasp from the door to the sitting room.
The young maid Abigail had come back with his coffee and
toast, and was standing in the doorway with the tray in her
hands, ready to drop it in shock at seeing him standing there
with his robe open and his trousers down around his ankles.

Before he could say a word in explanation, she was gone,
and he could hear the tray and the items on it rattling as she
set it down on the table and began to lay them out.

Alan grinned to himself, finished swabbing himself dry and
belted the robe about himself again, neglecting the slop-
trousers.

"Ah, hot as the very devil," Alan said after his first sip.
"Abigail, you simply don't know how bad coffee usually is
here in London. Tepid muck, too weakly brewed, looks about
the color of China tea. Worst excuse for a beverage I've ever
seen."

The girl was blushing a furious red from her startled embarrassment still, and only nodded and avoided his eyes as she
finished bustling about with his breakfast things, her hands
trembling a little.

"They brew it much stronger and thicker in the West Indies," Alan went on. "The way I'm used to it. This is good.
Very good. You could show my man Cony a thing or two, I'm
certain."

"Thankee, sir," she replied, losing her shocked color at last.
"I'm that glad you likes it. Jam for your toast, sir? Black cur-

rant's the only sort we had below-stairs this mornin', sir. Or I could fetch you up some treacle."

"No, this black currant'll do right nice, thankee anyway, Abigail," Alan replied. The girl had looked so abashed a moment before he suspected she'd drop dead of apoplexy, but now, she was grinning again in her shy little way, eager to please with an errand. "Care for some toast, Abigail?"

"Ah, I couldn't go . . ." She blushed again. "I've had me breakfast hours ago, sir, an' there's so much work to be doin' . . ."

"Do you work for another of the lodgers, or for the house-keeper, hmm?" Alan asked to keep her in the room. She was incredibly pretty in her own way. "And how much work is there, really? Fuss and clean the lodgings after the occupants are off at work? Upstairs maid, or maid-of-all-work, are you?"

"Maid-of-all-work, sir," she admitted. "An' I does for that Mistress Harper on the third floor, too, but it's little enough there is to do for her, her bein' out on the town so much, you know, an' she with her own maid already."

A bell tinkled downstairs and the girl was off like a hare, suspending any further conversation. Alan smeared butter and jam on his toast, spooned sugar into his coffee, and began to munch, missing his newspaper. Usually, he arose late, as he had that morning, had his sparse breakfast and hit the streets, making for a coffee house where he could borrow the house paper and converse with others of his sort. He could not re-member the last time he'd stayed in his lodgings this late in the day with nothing to do, long after all the others had de-parted for their daily chores or rounds of visits.

There was a rap on the outer door, and Abigail was back once more, wiping her hands on her apron so as not to soil the letter she bore in her hands.

"Iss note come for you, sir," she squeaked, in awe of the crest and the quality of the paper, and the liberality with which it had been sealed in blue wax. "From a great lord, I thinks. The footman come in the downstairs parlor grand as a lord his-self, he did."

Alan opened it and read that, due to the weather, Lady Delia Cantner would not be receiving that day. She wished his com-pany, but not at risk to life and limb from the slippery streets, nor the risk of sickness at being exposed to such cruel cold. Besides, her previous guests were staying over because they couldn't get home, and his presence would not go down all that well. Tears, unrequited passion, etc.

"Ah, well," Alan sighed, folding it back up and tossing it aside, thinking that he'd not had much luck lately in notes from women. "So much for visiting friends for cards this afternoon," he explained. "Lord and Lady Cantner. Knew 'em in the Indies. Saved their lives a few years ago."

"Ah, did you, indeed, sir!" the girl gushed. "Your man Cony, he told me, he says to me, how you were a Sea Officer, an' how many adventures you've had, sir. Yorktown, an' Red Indians, too!"

"This was before I met Cony, before I joined the ship he was in. Oh, sit you down. Ever had coffee, Abigail?"

"Lord, no, sir! 'Tis dear stuff for the likes o' me back in Evesham."

"Have a few minutes to spare from your work?" Alan cajoled. "Have a chair, pour yourself your first cup of coffee and see if you like it. And I'll tell you all about how I made the acquaintance of Lord and Lady Cantner."

"Well . . . just for a few minutes, sir," she replied shyly, casting a glance toward the hallway door. "The housekeeper, she'd turn me out if she thought I was shirkin'.'"

"Tell her you're doing my rooms while my man Cony is off. That I asked you to do it," Alan coaxed. "Have a slice of toast, too."

Undermaids usually were run ragged from sunrise to long after sundown for little more than six pounds a year, and not a full day off to themselves. And most were half-starved teens down from the country whose stomachs growled loud as a midshipman on short commons. The offer of a second breakfast, some quiet time away from the demands of the housework and a tale of derring-do alone with a gentleman were too much temptation. She plunked herself down in a chair, snatched toast and knife in a twinkling and laid to with a will.

"Oh, 'tis bitter," she said of the coffee, but liked it a lot better with sugar in it—another luxury most servants never tasted except when allowed. And for a few blessed minutes, she sat on the edge of her chair, gasping here and there, uttering an occasional "my stars" or "God bless!" at his saga of desperate danger, as though it were a play she was watching from the cheapest seats in the back.

"Why, sir!" she exclaimed in a soft voice when his narrative was through, "I do believe your man Cony was right!

You're a true English naval hero, that you are, sir, if I may be so bold as t'say so!"

"You're too kind by half, Abigail," Alan replied, patting the back of her hand, to test the waters. If Dolly Fenton was on the outs with him, and Delia Cantner was saddled with unwanted house-guests, the day would not have to be a total loss, he decided. He admired the way Abigail's chest had heaved with emotion.

"You'd not be knowin' it, sir," she said, dropping her voice to almost a whisper once more and averting her eyes, "but the first time I clapped eyes on you, I said t' myself, I says, there goes a fine gentleman. So dashin' an' brave lookin'. I . . . sort of . . . well, talk gets around below-stairs, from one servant t' the t'other, and I heard tell you was a sailor back from fightin' the King's enemies an' all? But Cony didn't tell me the half of it, he didn't!"

She didn't stiffen up as he massaged the back of her hand, nor did she quail as he turned it over and held her small, work-roughened hand in his. He pulled her gently to her feet, towards him as he pushed back his chair. She leaned forward even before he could rise, and in a moment, she was seated on his lap and he was raining kisses on her slim young neck, on her cheeks, and their lips met in a first, clumsy little maidenly kiss. He put a hand to the back of her neck and she opened her mouth to his pressure, slipping her arms about him, warming to his play quickly. Too quickly for the shy maiden she seemed.

"Lor', they warned me 'bout London, they did, sir," Abigail chuckled softly between kisses. "Weren't no diff'rent than any house a girl could work for in Evesham nor Birmingham, neither."

"At least the men are gentlemen, Abigail," he whispered. "The game's the same, city or country."

"I can't afford t' lose my position, though, sir," she complained gently as he slid a hand under her skirts and stroked his hand over her warm, incredibly soft and slim young thighs. "If'n I get turned out with no ref'rence, they's not a house in London'd hire me, 'cept a bawdy-house."

"You do for me, like you do Mistress Harper, then," Alan said, thrilling to the way she was shifting her slight weight on his lap.

"She gives me two shillings a week," Abigail suggested coyly.

"I'll match it," Alan promised. "And on your next day off, I promise you a pretty new hat. A ride in a coach, a grand supper."

"Like a real lady, sir?" she sighed, parting her thighs so he could stroke her downy groin. She leaned hard into him in passion.

"One day a week, you can play the lady," Alan swore, too afire at that moment to care. "As long as we may play."

"You will be careful, won't you, sir?"

"Go lock the door," he ordered.

She was too young to need a set of stays, and had only thin, unsupported linen petticoats on under her sackgown. Alan had but to unbutton her down the back and gather her dress around her waist, and he was rewarded with soft, warm, tantalizing flesh under his hands and lips. Smooth young legs wrapped around his hips under his robe as he spread it to cover both of them. Pert young breasts that stood up proud as islets even flat on her back.

"Got t' hurry, sir, before the missus . . ." she pointed out as he licked and kissed and stroked her into flames, taking time with her mounting need as most would not. Pretty young house-servants were fair game for the sons, the fathers, the butlers and footmen. Too poor to be able to complain they were, mostly. Or too willing for the game to continue, as long as they didn't get caught, or turned up with a jack-in-the-box. Town servants would be turned out come summer, anyway, to spend several months trying to eke out an existence on what pitiful few pence they'd managed to save, until their families returned from summer homes in the country. London was full of part-time courtesans, willing servants such as Abigail. Some like Abigail, indeed, who were more than willing, if they could make some extra money on the side from it, get enough to eat for once, be rewarded with gifts of nicer clothing than most housekeepers begrudged them.

It was a quick, furtive sport, for the most part, done at the top of the stairs, across an unmade bed, in a rarely visited garret storage room. Fast, furious and rapidly over: that was what Abigail had grown used to. Not this langorous, incredibly sensuous stroking and kissing. Hands and lips touching her in places she had never known. Her breath came fast as she swooned with anticipated pleasure, with restless want, fear of discovery a spur to her abandon.

He entered her at long last, his member sheathed in a sheepgut condom, and she bit her lips and turned her face to cry out into the pillows. Experienced she might be at house-games, but still young and snug, reminding Alan of his tempo-rary "wife" among the Creek Indians, Soft Rabbit. She'd been that hot and moist, that firmly gripped around his engine. And that wildly exuberant.

I may be Hell's own bastard with the women, Alan told himself as he drove deep into her and reveled in how she heaved her hips in synchronicity with him. Them that want to play. But never let it be said I left the little dears wanting for anything!

He held off his own explosion as Abigail clung to him like a squid, buried her face into his neck and squawled and mewed in climax, wishing she could scream out loud in ecstasy. Then she fell away limp and dragged him down atop of her, show-ering his face with weary kisses.

"Lor', sir, you're a terror," she shuddered, weak as a kitten. "Thankee ... for takin' time, an' all? Can't say when I cared so much for it last. Oooh!"

Alan rose up on his hands to loom over her, and began to stroke into her once more, long and slow, delighting in her sur-prised look.

"Don't you be teasin' me, now, sir," she whispered, beam-ing an expectant smile up at him from the pillows. Her red hair had come half unpinned from under her mobcap, and she swiped a tress away from her face. "An' did I please you, too, sir?"

"Not yet, Abigail," Alan grinned, punctuating his remark with another, deeper and firmer thrust. "But you will."

"Oh, darlin'!" She gaped at his meaning, lifting her knees once more. "Hurry! Gallop away, fast as you like! I ... oh ... it feels so good! So ... bloody ... good!"

An hour later, she came back, asking if he wanted some more coffee brewed, since he could not go out for it. That was an excuse for another bout of "the blanket hornpipe." Nothing shy about this time, and they were bouncing across the bed and giggling in covert joy almost before she could set the tray down.

She returned in mid-afternoon with tea and a Cornish meat pasty, and had at each other again. It was too cold to go out for a meal at a two-penny ordinary, she assured him. They snatched another fifteen minutes of utter bliss, with her sprawled face-down on the side of the high bed and her skirts thrown up over her back.

It was almost a relief for Cony to come back from his day off and putter around the rooms, ranting happily about how grandly he'd been received by the Chiswicks when he visited them. Cony was the one to brave the cold and fetch a meal from the handiest ordinary, though Abigail assisted in laying the table, and gave Alan a most fetching smile or two while Cony had his back turned.

"Wind's come more sou'westerly, sir," Cony opined finally as Alan prepared to turn in early that evening. "Snow stopped, an' h'it's turnin' t' rain, looks like. Be thawin' t'morro', thank the Lord."

"Filthy streets," Alan yawned, nodding by the fire with his feet up in the second chair and a blanket over his lap while he read a book about the recent war that was as factual as a Turkish rug merchant. "I'll try getting out to visit tomorrow. Set out my boots, if you would, and give them a daub or two of blacking. We'll coach where we're going as well.

"Aye, sir. That be all fer the evening', then, sir?"

"Yes, you turn in early, Cony. Enjoy a yarn or two with the rest for a change."

"Thankee right kindly, sir, that I will. Goodnight, sir."

All in all, a grandly satisfying day, Lewrie thought smugly as he drowsed by his fire with a book in one hand and a brandy in the other. His personal chronometer read eleven, the one he had "borrowed" from a Spanish brig off Cuba. Time to turn in, he decided.

There was a soft scratching at the door.

"Surely not," Alan whispered in delight, rising to open it.

Abigail slipped in and shut the door softly behind her, opening her arms to be enfolded and lifted off her feet. Her slippers fell off, and under her thin flannel bedgown, she was as toasty-warm as a bed of coals.

"Just wanted t' stop by an' see if you needed anythin' more tonight, sir," she said grinning. "Turn your bed down? Warm the sheets for you?"

"Off for the night, are we, you little minx?" Alan chuckled, carrying her toward the bedchamber.

"If you wants, I am," she suggested, bolder with him now.

"I wants," Alan agreed. "'Deed I do!"

Chapter 4

"So you see, Sir Onsley, I thought it best if we came to you for advice regarding Burgess' future," Alan told his host. Admiral Sir Onsley Matthews was all tripes and trullibubs, fat as a porker before slaughter when Alan had served on his staff at Antigua, and now he'd been retired by a supposedly "grateful" Admiralty, had put on enough weight for three all-in wrestlers. He'd never been blessed with the brains God promised a titmouse, but he knew just about everybody who counted, and even in retirement controlled bags of patronage and "interest," the lifeblood of a successful career.

"Damme, Mister Lewrie, but yer concern for the welfare of a colleague does ya credit," Sir Onsley heaved with deep breaths as he lolled in his wing chair, one foot up on a hassock—a foot wrapped in hot, damp cloths, to alleviate the agonies of the Admiral's latest bout of gout. "And these *bona fides*, Mister Chiswick, sir, shew much the same enterprise and pluck as I've come to expect from our Alan. Like bookends, you are, lads. Hewn and carved from the same hearty oak!"

"You're too kind, Sir Onsley," Burgess remarked, sitting prim and nervous on the edge of his chair by the roaring fire. He wore his best pale blue "ditto" suit, with a plain, long-skirted older waist-coast, and clutched a black cocked hat across his knees. His own glass of brandy sat untouched on the side table.

There hadn't been much enthusiasm shown for his efforts to get a position so far, and the Chiswicks had prevailed upon Alan to see if he had any influence with anyone at all, a task Alan had happily undertaken because it would allow him to see Caroline almost every day.

"Devil I am, young sir, devil I am," Sir Onsley maundered.

"I say no more'n the plain truth. I'm a plain old tarpaulin hand meself, not given to pissin' down some young'un's back for no cause."

Oh, spare us, Alan almost groaned! Sir Onsley's flagship *Glatton* hadn't stirred from her moorings once in a full three years' commission, and had been rumored to be hard aground on a reef of beef bones. It had been his small ships and tenders to the flag that had done the dirty work against the French, Spanish and Dutch and had reaped Sir Onsley a princely one-eighth of their prize money, which had sent him home rich as Croesus to a place on the Board of Admiralty, where he'd drowsed the last three years of his career away.

Still, he was a useful old stick, Alan thought, and kept his expression respectful and admiring. Who knows, Alan might actually have need of his good offices in future, slim as that chance might be now there was peace, and nine-tenths of the Navy laid up to rot.

"Been to Sam Hood about this yet, Mister Lewrie?"

"Not yet, Sir Onsley," Alan replied. "I did write to him, just a short note. No reply so far. I doubt he recalls me, fond as he might have seemed after Turk's Island. I'm sure he passed it off as one more half-pay officer looking for employment for himself."

"There's devilment afoot still in this world, young sirs," the old admiral warned them, laying a thick, be-ringed finger to the side of his rather large and drink-veined nose. "Losin' this war's encouraged the Frogs no end. Their Navy showed rather well in the East. I know not why the nation feels so secure. All I hear up in the House of Lords is deficits and bankruptcy, hand-wringin' and budget-cuttin'. Meantimes, they're over there on the Continent just diggin' like the furtive rats they are, looking for an openin' to throw us over for good and all, damme their blood. And heroes such as you pair sit on the beach, twiddlin' your thumbs, instead of being allowed a chance to stop their frightful business wherever it emerges."

Alan stifled a yawn, covering it with another sip of brandy. He paid court to the Matthewses at least twice a fortnight when they were in London, to keep his low rent on his set of rooms, and to lay his ear to the ground for any hint of great affairs that could help him prosper. He'd heard this screed, chapter and verse, too many times before to rise to it this time. He nodded sagely, though, which Sir Onsley took for much the same hearty approval as earlier.

"Lewrie there's a nacky one, the sort of young feller who knows I speak the truth," Sir Onsley pointed out to Burgess. "By God, Mister Chiswick, sir, if Alan'll speak for you, that's good enough for me. I can't promise you an easy place. I'll not say more now. Too many plans afoot at the moment. But a place, I can promise you, and there's my word on't for sure!"

"That's marvelous, Sir Onsley!" Burgess gasped. This interview had seemed the last slim thread of hope to save him from bringing in the sheaves for his uncle Phineas, and Alan had privately assured him it was bound to be disappointing at the end, but suddenly here was this word of assured employment. "As a serving officer, sir? Pardon me if I inquire at least a little."

"With the East India Company," Sir Onsley nodded. "I'm on the board. I'm privy to certain . . . nay, it'll be discovered to you later. I should think at least as a lieutenant, Mister Chiswick. Tell me now, and tell me true if you're a mind for it. And a heart for it. It'll be damned hot and dusty duty, halfway round the world and like as not it'll be sickness, bugs and flies, and God knows when you'll lay eyes on your dear family again in this life. But 'tis a duty like as not'll confound our foes better than anything you'd accomplish in a lifetime of regular soldierin'. Are you game for it?"

"I am indeed, Sir Onsley!" Burgess piped up. "Lead me to it!"

"Toppin'!" Sir Onsley shouted back, wincing a little at the end as he moved his gouty foot and suffered a spasm of agony. "I'll speak to the Board tomorrow. Leave me your *bona fides* and all that to show them. Irregular . . . skirmisher . . . Indian fighter. Just the sort of lad we need. Mister Lewrie, I do believe Fate sent you to me with young Mister Chiswick's plaint at exactly the right time."

"And grateful I am you could do my friend a service, Sir Onsley," Alan replied, flat aback at this energetic development. He had not seen the old twit that bombastic, or awake, in years. And Alan could hardly wait until they could get back to St. Clement Street to tell the rest of the Chiswick family. Most especially Caroline. She would be impressed to no end that it was *Alan's* influence and connections that had turned the winning trick for her brother.

It would disappoint her, though, that he would have to sail around the world, into that land of pagan Hindoos she had feared so much, where Burgess would be exposed to so many cruel diseases and chances to die a young, untimely death. Matter of fact, Alan wondered if he'd done Burgess much of a favor at all. Sir Onsley was sober enough to not let slip what sort of devilish danger this new duty was, but it didn't sound like anything Alan would want a part of, not if he had at least five minutes' warning, and a head start. Some new wrinkle on what Lieutenant Lilycrop of *Shrike* had termed "war on the cheap," dreamed up by some crystal-ball gazer, map reader and quill-pusher who had no idea about what life was like outside his own doorway, much less how deadly it could be for the men on the shitten end of the stick a world away.

"Mum's the word, my lads, until you hear from me by letter," Sir Onsley cautioned. "But stand ready to shift yourselves at a moment's notice. No man is to hear word of this appointment."

"You have my solemn oath, Sir Onsley," Burgess promised proudly, which oath Alan had to chorus as well.

"Damme, but Caroline is going to kill me," Alan sighed once they were in a hired coach on their way home. "I had no idea things would turn out like this, Burgess."

"I shall be forever in your debt, Alan," Burgess assured him, taking his hand and giving it a hearty squeeze of gratitude. He was all but piping his eyes in joy at his sudden salvation from civilian dullness. "Don't fear what Caroline thinks."

"Well, he didn't make it sound like Canterbury Fair, you know. God, what have I gotten you into? If anything happens to you, and it sounds hellish like it might, I'll never forgive myself. And neither would your dear sister," Alan objected.

"You've given me the world, Alan!" Burgess said with a catch in his voice, his face aglow like a martyr promised crucifixion before sunup. "Oh, 'tis fine for Governour to farm and pore over the accounts. He's set up with a vicar's daughter in the county. But for me, Alan . . . you remember when you took me aboard your frigate during the siege as a guest of the wardroom? Just the smell of a ship . . ."

"Foul as they smell," Alan drolly pointed out.

"The smell of distance," Burgess waxed lyrical. "Of adventure in faraway places. Hemp and tar, salt and spices . . ."

"Pea-soup farts and rotting cheese," Alan said, scowling.

"To lay eyes on the East Indies, to live a life of new things to taste and smell, my God, how wondrous it's going to be!"

Burgess went on in his rapture. "Oh, it'll be hard, I know. And it'll like as not be dangerous. But the chance for glory! More'n most people'd ever suspect! You must know, I'm not cut out to be a farmer. Before the Revolution, I'd half a mind to run off and trade with the Cherokee over the Appalachians. To see what there was to see, cross mountains and rivers, all the way to the other ocean. And now you've given me my chance, Alan. I'll break free. Now I'll know what you felt as a sailor. You do not know how much I've sometimes envied you your life as a Sea Officer."

"Just as long as you do come back a chicken-nabob," Alan said, realizing there was nothing he could say to dissuade Burgess from making a total fool of himself. "And when you do fetch home all those diamonds and rubies, better tote along a small sack for me as well. I mean, damme, who'd have thought old Sir Onsley would have a place for you? I warned you going in, it was a slim hope, a clerking position at best. This, though . . . well, maybe you should think about it . . ."

"I'd have never forgiven you, for certain, if that was all I could aspire to," Burgess cracked, thumping him on the knee. "Damme, you should be glad for me, Alan. Glad as I am."

"Well, if it pleases you, Burge, there's nothing more I can say," Alan surrendered. How could he tell him he thought the lad was not cut out for desperate doings, any more than he was cut out for farming? How do you tell a friend you think him too starry-eyed to prosper?

"Alan Lewrie, I should despise you!" Caroline hissed at him harshly, once the celebration had begun. She took him by the hand and led him to sit with her on a ratty older sofa away from the others, who were singing and mixing a large bowl of lemons, sugar, hot water and gin for a gala punch.

"Caroline, I swear I had no idea . . ." he began. It was the first time he'd ever seen her angry at anything or anyone, and it was most disconcerting to be the target of her anger.

"This . . . this hush-hush adventure you've gotten poor Burge into," she whispered. "No word of what it was? No inkling of how much danger there'll be?"

"None. Only that he's to keep mum and be ready to be received in a few days, one way or another," Alan told her sadly, feeling just a trifle sheepish under her hot glare. "I was all amort that the old fool'd offer anything at all, much less something like this, I tell you truly. And Burgess didn't have to accept it so quickly, either. He could have asked for a few days to think it over, but *no*, he had to just leap up and go all shiny-eyed over it. Don't take it out on me, I beg you, Caroline. I did what Governour and your mother bade me. I used what influence I could. How was I to know it'd turn out like this?"

"But so far away from us," Caroline insisted. "With the chance we'll never see him again in this life! Oh, I know it isn't your fault, Alan, but . . . you must see how frightened I am for him. He's always been so . . ."

"Unprepared for how cruel life can be?" Alan whispered back.

"You recognized it, too?" she gasped, taking his hand and wringing it like a washcloth, pressing his hand to her troubled breast, surely unaware in her bereavement of what she was doing.

God Almighty, Alan thought, feeling his innards lurch at the touch of her. I could spend the rest of the day like this!

"He'll go under, sure as Fate, I know it," she said, weeping softly.

"It's what he wants, Caroline," Alan told her. "Better one chance at an adventurous life than drudging on a farm and feeling trapped. He told me as much. God pity him, he envies me all the shit . . . sorry . . . I've been through. All the exciting and exotic places I've sailed. And he may prosper. I've seen others do so, in the Navy. God help me, I prospered, and I didn't know a futtock shroud from a horse's fetlock when I first began."

"But you're the sort of man who *does* prosper, Alan," she told him, lowering her hand, and his, to her lap before her mother noticed. "If only I knew there was someone as courageous and steady as you to look after him out there in India, or wherever he's going to be."

"Me?" Alan tried a smile. "Mine arse on a bandbox! I'm not as steady as you think. No one is, outside their memoirs."

"Well, I think you are," she whispered. "So sure and capable. As you were when I first met you. When you organized us into your ship to escape Wilmington. Momma in her vapors and poor Daddy half out of his mind with grief, and poor me so weak and helpless."

"I never thought you weak and helpless," Alan assured her. "I have always considered you the most resourceful and clever of females, Caroline."

That softened her up right smartly.

"Say you forgive me. Please," he beseeched.

"Oh, Alan, I do forgive you," she relented, and gave him a wee smile, sad and wan though it was. "He'll not have to purchase this commission. Which shall please Uncle Phineas. If it comes to fruition. There is a possibility it may not, isn't there? There's many a slip t'wixt the cup and the lip. Pray God they may choose a more experienced officer in his stead!"

"Which would crush poor Burgess, though," Alan sighed. "And he'd be right back where he started. I know you can't stay in London hoping much longer. He'd be back to counting sheep. It would kill him."

"No, we can't," she agreed. "I must own to you, Alan, that I hoped you would be here. That we might regain our acquaintance. Your letters meant so much to me. Your . . . memory. Oh, pray do come to see us down in Surrey! Now that we have had a chance to speak almost daily, and to be together like this, I remember all over again how much I have delighted in your companionship. I would so enjoy you being our guest in the country. When the weather is better. And we could write each other in the meantimes. Could we not, Alan?" she suggested sweetly.

"Nothing would give me greater delight as well, Caroline," he told her. "I've never known anyone I like talking to more than you."

"Come take a cup of cheer, you two!" Governour ordered from the far end of the room. There was no more privacy for them. Caroline wiped her face quickly with a handkerchief from her sleeve and put on a happy expression for her family.

"We must dine together tonight," Mrs. Chiswick insisted, half gone on a large glass of gin punch already. "It'll be sad even so, knowing my little Burge will be going off among the heathens, but we'll know he's doing something for King and Country. As he did so nobly during the Rebellion." She stifled her fears—almost.

With your shield or on it, like the Spartans, Alan thought grimly. Why don't they all fall down bawling instead of acting so proud, he wondered? God knows, *I'd* be into the sackcloth and ashes by now.

"And our benefactor, Alan Lewrie," Governour proposed. "He must be guest of honor tonight!"

They raised their glasses and toasted him, making him feel even more a total fool than he had a moment before.

"Make no fuss over me," Alan suggested. "And I wouldn't

feel right, anyway. Spend your time with Burgess. Sir Onsley didn't say when the summons would come. Besides, I cannot."

"Alan!" Caroline cried in sudden disappointment.

"I have a dinner invitation already that I cannot break," he told them, setting his glass down. "But I hope you shall let me treat you to supper another night, once we've learned what Burgess is down for. Would you allow that?"

Caroline saw him down to the first floor, and dismissed the house's servant to help him on with his watchcoat herself, tugging his collar snug about him and smoothing the fabric to lie flat.

"I wish you could have stayed, Alan. I begrudge every minute you are away from ... from our family, now we're reunited," she said, with a hitch in her voice. "I ... we feel so much gratitude, and admiration for you, for so many things you've done for us."

"I could not, not tonight, Caroline. I fear for him, too, and I couldn't have sat there with him."

"I understand," she replied softly. "I shall do my weeping in private, too."

She raised her arms and he took her in his arms, holding her snug and safe, stroking her back as she almost gave way to her emotions, whispering "there, there" to comfort her if he was able and secretly enjoying the closeness, and the feel of her slimness against him. How tiny her waist was, how neat her breasts felt. How sweet and clean she smelt: her hair and her slight hint of Hungary Water scent.

Caroline peeked over her shoulder to see if any of the servants of the lodging house were about, then turned her face up to his and closed her eyes. With an offer like that, Alan could not turn it down.

He kissed her. As gently and as shyly as he had just that once years before. Her lips parted just a little and her clean breath mingled with his. Then her eyes flew open and her arms locked behind his neck, pulling him down to her and there was nothing shy about it.

"I must ask your forgiveness once more," Alan muttered, shaken to his core by this entrancing creature all over again as she fell away slightly, dropped back from tiptoe and leaned back to regard him with such a smile of wonder and delight.

"Mine arse on a bandbox, Alan Lewrie," she said, grinning, and then whispered with secret glee, "Between us, I pray there shall never be anything to forgive."

"My God!" he gasped.

"All the English ladies tell me it's most improper to be quite as forward as I am," she added, laughing. "I'm but a crude rustic from America, don't you know. Do sup with us tomorrow. And the day after. And the day after that. Spend your every waking moment with us. With me. I would enjoy it so awfully much, before we're parted again."

"You'd be scandalized," Alan gawped. "Governour would run me through!"

"I trust to your gentlemanly nature, Alan. And to your sense of decency. What harm to my good name could you ever do me?"

God help the poor mort, Alan thought. If you only knew I *had* no sense of decency, you'd run screaming behind your momma's skirts!

"Lord knows, I'd think of something. Sooner or later," he admitted at last. He tried to pass it off as a jape.

"I would trust to the affection you already show for me," she said with such a solemn little face it almost made his ears ring. "As I trust how admirable I hold you in mine."

One more quick kiss, and then he had to go, out into another freezing cold afternoon, but warmed right through by her regard and the feel of her lingering upon him.

"Damme, she's the sweetest, dearest young thing!" he said to himself as he trudged along the street, dodging darting youngsters, mongers and traders. "Oh, if only . . . what? Christ on a cross, Lewrie, you're cunt-struck! Next thing you know, you'll be thinking of asking for her hand! And haven't I done enough to her family already?"

"Dear Alan," Lady Delia cooed as he entered her morning room and took the proferred hand to kiss. She stroked his face with a hot-house rose she'd been toying with.

"Delighted to see you again, milady," he told her soberly.

"Do be seated and break your fast with me, sir," she said. She turned to her servants and told them they could depart on their errands. Once the door was shut, she was out of her chair in a twinkling, into his arms and raining kisses and endearments upon him. Devil a bite of roll or sip of tea he got until they had fallen into a swoon across her soft bed in the other room, strewn their clothing to the winds and slaked their lusts with the frenzy of rutting stoats.

Lewrie lay back on her soft pillows, panting and grinning,

so pleased with the world in general, and his lot in it in particular. A young girl in love with him he'd half a mind—merely half a mind so far—to pursue with fantasies of wedded bliss, tender and succulent young Abigail to roger all over his suite whenever he wanted her, and Lady Delia Cantner to top the bargain off. For as long as his luck was in, he'd not shed a tear.

Of course, if he went down to Surrey and pursued Caroline, he would have to give up all this, he pondered as he got his breath back. Well, Abigail was merely a convenience, nothing more, and her delight was in her obvious hero-worship and her talented young body. She'd play the game with another lodger, get her couple of shillings for her troubles from another man. Lady Delia, though. That was fun, he had to admit. Part of it was the covert glee of covering old Lord Cantner's lawful blanket, sneaking and taking their pleasure as they just had, with the servants out of the way, and playing the "Merry Andrew" the next moment, a devoted family protégé when the stupid old colt's-tooth was around. Nothing lasting there, either, ecstatic as it was. He knew if he begged off, Lady Delia would have another admirer gnawing on her magnificent breasts as quick as she could change her dress. There were legions of them waiting in line for a chance at her. Affectionate as their relationship was, it was not love, not the sort of love that Caroline's eyes promised. And he was getting a little jaded with simple sex, Alan thought. Once his grandmother died, and he inherited, he'd have enough to care for the lovely Caroline in the manner she deserved.

"I have seen so little of you these past few days, my chuck," Delia crooned, sliding a thigh over him. "Those beastly friends of yours have kept you from me."

"I believe you just made up for it, m'dear," Alan chuckled.

"Not a jot of it," she promised. "And did you secure your friend a place at last?"

"That I did," Alan replied, expressing his doubts he'd done Burgess any favors. Lady Delia had put out some feelers for him as well, though with his lordship out of the country, there was little direct she could do without his presence.

"So the task is ended." She beamed. "And you may begin to pay attention to me again. How delightful. It's rare enough to have Roger out of the house, much less over in Holland, so I may be with my darling lad. I thought I would die of happiness to know that we'd have so much time free of interfer-

ences. Then the weather, and those Chiswick people . . . Did
you miss me, Alan? Tell me you did. Tell me how much you
did," she teased lazily.

Her long raven hair spilled over his chest and his face. Her
large, firm breasts mashed down onto his chest as she rolled
astride of him and held herself on knees and palms, breathing
on his neck and into his ear, rocking back and forth, from side
to side maddeningly.

"Better I show you instead," Alan laughed deep in his
throat, taking hold of her bouncers and squeezing them, kissing
her neck in return, eliciting her deep groans of impending
bliss.

"Ummm, yess," she muttered, shaking with husky amusement as well. "Devour me, Alan. Ooooh, yess! Ummmm!"

Tumescent as a belaying pin, he slid back into her for the
second time in half an hour, and she leaned back and flung her
arms to the ceiling to ride St. George on his member, grinding
her hips down against his, clasping him with her thighs and
moaning with heartfelt abandon as his hands kept possession
of her heavy breasts, leaning forward into his grasp with her
hands clawed into his shoulders and grinning and crying out,
wincing with each thrust and movement. Panting and grunting
as their pace quickened.

She looked magnificent, perspiration sheened on her body,
her nipples hard and rasping on his hungry palms, her soft
thighs clasping and slipping with sweat and her heels under his
buttocks to drive him deeper. Her hair was matted and a stray
lock clung to the corner of her crumpled mouth as it hung
open. Hot, burning dark eyes glowed down at him, urging him
on, begging him for more . . .

"Well, damme!" a petulant voice interposed.

"Sufferin' shit!" Alan gasped, looking toward the door to
espy a very thin, reedy Lord Roger Cantner standing in the
doorway.

I think I've been here before, Alan thought sadly. Christ,
this time I'm going to get my young arse killed!

"My dear," Lady Delia said, looking back over her shoulder,
calm as you'd like, "you're back early."

"How . . . how dare . . ." Lord Cantner sputtered. "That
young swine, behind me back, you whore!"

"Surely you must have known, Roger dear," Delia replied,
still astride and making no moves to break away. "If not about
Alan, then about any of the others." She did pull up a sheet to

cover herself, Alan included, for which he felt only slightly grateful.

Get the fuck off, you cow! he screamed mentally. Let me get on my feet and out of here! I need clothing, and a head start!

"Me own wife!" Lord Cantner tried to howl in outrage. But it came out little more than a petulant screech.

"In name only, Roger, as we both are well aware. A wife may expect conjugal relations now and again," Delia said, smiling wickedly. "Of a successful, and pleasing, nature, *n'est-ce pas?*"

Lord Cantner put a hand to the hilt of his smallsword, and Alan gulped in total fear, his suntanned complexion turning white as Delia's flesh.

But Lady Cantner only chuckled deep in her throat at that threat. "Would you run me through, dear Roger? Or Alan? That's murder, you know. Too public a thing to share with the Mob. And you might swing for it at Tyburn, even so."

Alan couldn't credit it. Under the secrecy of the sheet, she was stirring her hips once more, as if she wanted to torment the old cuckold into mayhem! And, God help him, what should have shriveled up like a deflated haggis was now hard as a marlinspike inside her!

God, I promise you, let me get out of this with a whole skin and I'll be good, I swear! he prayed silently. I'll marry Caroline Chiswick, I'll be monogamous as a bloody swan forevermore!

"Or would you rather go to Pickering Place and duel for your honor, my dear," Delia almost snickered. "Come slap him if you wish. I'll hold him down for you."

"For God's sake!" Alan finally gave voice.

"You little bastard!" Lord Cantner rasped, his sour little mouth working around what was left of his teeth. "Should have known when I come in on ye an' this bitch aboard that schooner, you all snivelin' on her tits, oh, I knew then ye were spoonin' her yer cream-pot love even then! One o' me own I praised t' the skies!"

The hand had, however, dropped away from the sword hilt and both were wringing themselves in quandary. Alan felt a moment of hope.

"Murder, then, Roger dear?" Delia sniffed at her husband's indecisiveness. "A challenge to a duel? No? Then please be good enough, after the fruitless years we have spent together, to go away and make up your mind and leave me to my pleasures."

Lord Cantner stamped one of his little feet and gave out with another feeble bleat of displeasure. "Bedamned to ye, ye bitch! And Goddamn yer traitorous blood, *Mister* Lewrie! I'll see the both of ye in hell, I swear I shall. You'll pay. Oh, my yes, you'll pay. I'll have both yer heart's blood, ye see if I don't!"

But, amazingly, the old man quavered out another unintelligible warning, and doddered out the door, slamming it behind him!

"Well, I'm damned!" Alan gasped, going limp as Italian pasta against the pillows. "Christ, that's torn it! He'll have me dead!"

"He won't, dearest," Delia cooed, stirring her hips to revive him as coolly as if one of the servants had dropped off clean towels and departed.

"Easy for you to say!" Alan raved, after drawing a deep breath.

"Alan, don't flatter yourself; you're not the first," Delia said, giggling. "We've slept in separate rooms almost from the wedding night, and he knows his limitations at his age. Would he take the risk of dueling my darling lad? He shakes too much to hold a pistol, and the weight of a sword is quite beyond him for more than a minute. He's too stubborn to die and leave me everything. And too proud to ask Parliament for a bill of divorce. He's known about you."

"Then how could he play cards with me if he did? How could he stand to have me eat his fare?"

"What he knows is one thing," Delia grinned, leaning down to him once more. "What he wants others of his circle to know is quite another. They believe him capable in bed, and I give no sign he's not. I brought enough money to this miserable marriage to walk out anytime I cared to. So far, I have not. My family was rich Trade. He was respectable aristocracy. So we have no heir as of yet. Before he dies, I shall present him with what he wants most. Had he his wits about him, he'd have sent word on ahead from Dover he was returning. I expect the sea voyage upset him, poor thing."

"By God, you're a cool 'un!" Alan marveled. He'd thought he'd met some crafty, scheming women in his time, and had suffered at their hands more than once. But he'd never seen the like before. Even Mrs. Betty Hillwood back on Jamaica hadn't been this icy.

"If he hadn't been addled by *mal de mer,* I'd have known when to receive him back, and you would not have been in this predicament. We'd have been sitting around the card table, or truly having breakfast, when he arrived," she went on. "He'd have known what we'd been up to in his absence, but he'd have been spared the actuality."

"Well, he wasn't," Alan said, trying to lever her off him so he could get dressed and obey his instincts to take a *long* vacation in Scotland. Perhaps change his name and herd sheep with the Chiswicks down in Surrey until Lord Cantner had the good grace to die. "And he's *seen* the actuality. You said he has his pride. That means he'll get even, no matter what you think he'll do. You heard what he said. He'll hire himself some dockyard toughs to stop my business!"

"I give you my best assurances, dearest, sweetest, Alan, that he shall do no such thing," she said, laughing, hugely amused. "You don't know what a relief it is to end this pitiful *charade* at last. Just like that night he retired early, remember? Oh, I surely do. And we sat up playing backgammon until he was fast asleep?"

"Yes." It had been one hell of a night, sneaking into her chambers trying not to make a sound, tumbling onto the carpet before a ruddy fire, all the while the old man had snored in the room next door, and all night long, they had lurched fearful between strokes each time he'd coughed, muttered or turned over, only to begin again.

She pressed back down on him, trying to revive his flagging interest in the proceedings.

"I shall most like have to get out of town for a while," Alan told her. "I mean, I can't just trail my colors in his face, can I?"

"Oh, do spend some time in Bath! Warm spa waters, gambling in the Long Rooms. Beau Nash is dead and it's getting more lively now he isn't there to demand decorum," Delia enthused. "I could join you there for a couple of weeks if you wish."

"Let's not press our luck, hmm?" Alan snapped. "Don't rub salt in the wound. I'll be an old hound, too, one of these days, and I'd surely kill the first young pup that sniffed around *my* wife!"

"How possessive you suddenly are!" she pouted. "Darling,

if we must indeed be parted ... give me something to remember you by."

"In for the penny, in for the pound?" he scowled.

"Something like that," she teased.

"Sorry, m'dear, I'm off like a bloody hare!"

"Cony, pack a bag for me," Alan said, back in the safety of his lodgings. "I feel the urge to take the waters somewhere."

"We goin' t' Bath'r Brighton, sir? Ahn't never been!"

"Somewhere. Anywhere. No, I'll need you to take this note to Coutts' for me. I'll pack myself. Post some letters for me after. And get us a couple of horses," he added. "And make sure they're the fastest ones alive."

"Fer in the mornin', sir?" Cony asked in all innocence.

"Ah ... hmm," Alan replied. "I should think *tonight* would be devilish fine."

"T'night, sir? If'n ya want, sir. 'Course, hit'd be 'ard t' find a decent inn that late on the road. An' the country a'swarmin' with 'ighwaymen now the vet'rins is outa work."

"We'll go well-armed," Alan told him. *Count* on being well-armed, he thought. He had a Ferguson rifle from his time with the Chiswicks, a saddle musketoon, his brace of naval pistols and another brace of dragoon pistols, his hanger, and there was a cutlass around somewhere for Cony to wear as well. Damned *right*, he'd go armed! He wouldn't put it past Lord Cantner to raise a battalion of pursuers, no matter what Delia thought, with a hundred guineas for the man who harvested his liver?

Cony went off with a note for the bankers, and Alan wrested a traveling valise from his armoire and began cramming things into it any-old-how. But he was interrupted by a scratch at the door.

"Ah, Abigail, my little chuck," he said, not pausing in his haste.

"I gotta talk to you, sir?" she said, tremulous as the first time he'd clapped eyes on her. "You packin' t' go some'r's?"

"Just for a couple of weeks." Alan shrugged it off.

"Alan," she drawled out, and he stopped packing long enough to take her in his arms, give her a fond kiss, and set her down out of the way.

"Be back sooner or later. We'll have more fun, hey?"

"Don't know as I'll be here when you gets back, Alan me love."

"Oh? Why?"

"Well, the housekeeper'll prob'ly turn me out without no ref'rence," she intoned with a hard gulp.

"Did she discover about our little arrangement?" Alan asked, abandoning his packing once more. "How'd it happen?"

"I think I'm gonna have a baby, Alan," she managed to say, her lower lip quivering, and tears starting to flow from her eyes. "Yours."

"Well, shit, what next?" he sighed, and sat down at the table with her as her face screwed up and copious tears bubbled out.

"Alan!" she wailed. "Wha's gonna *happen* t' me? I can't care for a *baby!* I'll be out in the streets, an' no house'll take me on, not with a littl'un comin'. Alan, you gotta *do* somethin'!"

I knew it was too good to last, I knew it, I knew it! God, he thought miserably, remember that promise about swans? I think I meant it this time!

"Umm, are you sure, Abigail? Absolutely sure, I mean . . ."

"Hadn't had me courses this month. An' I get sick as anythin' o' the mornin's, I do! My stomach feels a little hard, too. Here, feel of it. Don't it feel diff'runt to you? I can't have no baby, an' me a spinster girl, Alan. Parish'll turn me out an' tell me t' move along t' the next. Same with that'un, too, I reckon. I seen it before, I have, back in Evesham. Girls havin' t' run off t' Birmingham, an' nothin' good at the end of it. But if I was t' be married, I could cry widow, blame it on a farmboy . . ."

"What? Married?" Alan exclaimed in shock.

"Yes," she bawled, putting her face down on the table and blubbering fit to bust. "Say you will, jus' t' let me have the record for the parish! I'm sorry! I thought we was bein' so careful, you with your cundum an' all. Don' let me be rooned, Alan, if you love me . . ."

In the middle of this, while Alan was trying to think of some way to escape being bound to the little mort for all eternity, there was another scratching at the door.

"Wait your bloody turn, damn yer eyes!" Alan barked with his best quarterdeck rasp, which startled Abigail into a fit of hiccups. "What?" he demanded, flinging the door open.

"Lieutenant Alan Lewrie, Royal Navy?" The messenger from the Admiralty sniffed at his unexpected greeting. He took in the bawling girl at the table, and gave another audible sniff.

"I am."

"Then this is for you, sir. If you will be so good as to sign here to shew I have delivered it to you? I have a stub of pencil, sir. No need for a pen," the old pensioner intoned with all the hauteur of a flag officer. "I was instructed to await your reply, sir."

Alan scribbled off his name and slammed the door in the man's face. He broke the blue wax wafer on the parchment and opened it to read it.

"Bloody, bloody, flaming Hell!" he muttered.

"Sir;

Our Lords Commissioners of The Admiralty have seen fit to offer you an active commission, the exact nature of which we shall be glad to discover to you should you deem yourself able to accept immediate Employment. You shall be appointed 4th Lt. into a Ship of the Line, the 80-gun 3rd Rate *Telesto*, now lying in-ordinary in the port of Plymouth, for three years' Commission in foreign waters.

Please communicate to us your Availability, or state reasons why you cannot fulfill a term of active service, pursuant to the customary usages such as loss of half-pay, reduction in seniority from the roll of commission Sea Officers, etc.

Yr obdt srvnt,
Phillip Stephens, Sec. to Admlty"

"God, I meant that bit about the swans, but this is a trifle extreme, don't you think?" he said to the ceiling.

"Wot?" Abigail hiccuped.

"Not you. Look, my girl. Marriage just ain't in the cards, see?" Alan told her matter-of-factly. "Yes, I'm going away. I've been ordered to go to sea. I'll give you some money to take care of you, and to see to your lying in. That's the best I can do."

"Oh, my God, you heartless bastard," she wailed.

"Twenty pounds to see you through, Abigail. And another twenty pounds so the baby's looked after. Tell people whatever you like. I can't marry you, and you know it. I'd make you bloody miserable."

"Miserable's I am now?" she spat, changing emotions quickly.

"Worse, most likely," he replied, trying to gentle her. He knelt down next to her and put an arm around her shoulders, and held her even as she tried to shrug him off. "Look, girl, I'm fond enough of you. You're a sweet little chit, that you really are. There's plenty of homes would like a healthy baby, if you don't want to keep him, or her. You'll have about six years' wages for food and lodging, if you don't squander it on foolishness. And there are houses that'll have you. I'll write you a letter of reference if you want. I'll say you worked for me. Blame it . . . blame it on some sailor who took advantage of you on your day off. Tell the parish you were raped by some sailor you never saw before or since. Long's you have money to keep yourself, and you're not on their Poor's Rate, they won't care a whit."

"But you won't marry me," she sobbed, quieter now, and put her arms around him sadly.

"I'm going to foreign waters, Abigail. Three years and more. Dry your eyes, now. Call me a bastard if you like, but I'll try to do right by you, as much as I'm able. But marry you . . . I'm sorry."

He shooed her out, scribbled a quick acceptance letter for the Admiralty messenger, who fled before his old soul was corrupted any more than it most probably was, and sat down to relish a huge glass of brandy. God knew, he needed it about then.

Chapter 5

The more he thought about the arrival of the Admiralty's offer of immediate employment, the better he was resigned to it. A commission in foreign waters, far away from Lord Cantner's wrath, and any hulking minions he might hire, was probably the best thing. It also got him out of London, out of England, so little Abigail could not cry "belly plea" on him before a magistrate if she found his terms of settlement unacceptable, once she had a chance to put her little brain to work on them.

Surprisingly, Cony had seemed suddenly eager to go to sea with him as a seaman and cabin-servant as well. The Matthewses said they'd store his furnishings in the garret of his lodgings on Panton Street, though Sir Onsley had been mystifying as all Hell about why Fate had chosen that exact moment to bless him with active service. The old Admiral had made offers before, but nothing had ever come of them, and after three years' privation in the Navy, Alan was not exactly "cherry-merry" to go to sea again, though he showed game enough when Sir Onsley talked about the possibility.

There had come another letter from the Admiralty before the week was out, though, delivered by the same pensioner porter, and this one had advised him to travel to Plymouth at once, in *civilian* clothes. What had been the point of that, he speculated? At least, his route took him through Guildford, where the Chiswicks resided. It was the final disappointment to his feelings to learn that they were not at home. He sighed heavily, left a letter for Caroline with their housekeeper and got back on the road.

"I thinks they's a rider comin' up a'hind of us, sir," Cony warned. Once leaving Guildford, they had taken the coast road for Plymouth, from Dorchester to Bridport and Honiton, skirted south of Exeter for Ashburton across the southern end of the Dartmoor Forest. Highwaymen were rife with so many veterans discharged with nothing but their needs, but so far they had traveled safely enough in company with other wayfarers.

Ever since leaving their last inn that morning, they had seen no one, though when they stopped to rest their horses they had thought they could hear one, perhaps two, riders behind them. The wintry air was chill. Snow lay thin and bedraggled on the muddy ground like a sugar glacé on soaked fields. Rooks cried but did not fly in the fog that had enveloped them. It was thinning now, not from any wind but from the mid-morning sun, and sounds carried as they do in a fog, easy to hear from afar but without any true sense of which direction they came from.

They were two men on horseback, with a two-horse hired wagon to bear their sea-chests, driven by an ancient waggoner and his helper of about fourteen. They had gotten on the road just before dawn, and now stood listening, about halfway between Buckfastleigh and Brent Hill. A lonely place. A perfect place for an ambush, Alan thought. He cocked an ear towards the road behind him, trying to ignore the creaking of saddle leather and bitt chains.

"'Ear 'em, sir?" Cony whispered. "Sounds more like two now."

"How far to South Brent from here?" Alan asked the carter.

"Jus' shy of a league, sir," the grizzled old man replied, looking a trifle concerned. "Maght be an' 'ighwayman, ye know. Lonely stretch o' road 'ere'bouts. 'R could be trav'lers lahk y'selves, sir."

"Let's be prepared, then," Alan ordered. The carter and his boy had bell-mouthed fowling pieces under their seat, and they took them out and unwrapped the rags from the fire-locks. Alan drew one of his dragoon pistols, checked the priming and stuck it into the top of his riding boot. That pistol's mate went into the waistband of his breeches. Finally, he freed his hanger in its scabbard so it could be drawn easily.

"'Tis two men, sir," Cony muttered cautiously as two riders hove into sight on the slight rise behind them like specters from the mists. They checked for a moment from a fast canter, then came on at the same pace.

"Stand and meet them here, then, whoever they are," Alan ordered. He reined his mare out to one side of the wagon, while Cony wheeled his mount to the other side. The old carter kept his fowling-piece out of sight, but stood in the front of the wagon looking backward, with one hand on his boy's shoulder to steady him.

But once within musket shot, the two riders slowed down to a walk and raised their free hands peaceably. Alan kept his caution—they looked like hard men. One was stocky and thick, tanned dark as a Hindoo, and sported a long seaman's queue at the collar of his muddy traveling cloak. The second was a bit more slender, a little taller, though just as darkly tanned. He seemed a little more elegant, but it was hard to tell at that moment as he was just as unshaven and mud-splashed as his companion.

"Gentlemen, peace to you," the slender one began, halting his animal out of reach of a sword thrust. "We've heard your cart axle this last hour and rode hard to catch up with you. 'Tis a lonely stretch of road, and that's no error. Fog and mist, and I'll confess a little unnerving to ride alone on a morning such as this."

Alan nodded civilly but gave no reply.

"Allow me to name myself," the fellow went on. "Andrew Ayscough. And my man there, that's Bert Hagley. On our way to Plymouth to take up the King's Service. You going that way as well, sir?"

"The road goes to Plymouth eventually, sir," Alan replied.

"Then for as far as you fare, we'd be much obliged to ride with you, sir," Ayscough asked, "if you do not begrudge a little company on the road, sir? Four men are a harder proposition for highwaymen than two. Our horses are fagged out. Being alone out here made us push 'em a little harder than was good for them. That and having to be in Plymouth by the first bell of the forenoon watch, sir."

"You're seamen, the both of you?" Alan asked, losing a little of his caution.

"Aye, sir," Ayscough admitted. "Down to join a ship. I've a warrant to be master gunner, and Bert there's to be my Yeoman of the Powder Room."

"Already down for a ship, hey? Not just going to Plymouth to seek a berth?" Alan queried further. The man looked like the sort to be a warrant master gunner. He even had what looked to be a permanent tattoo on one cheek from imbedded grains of burnt gunpowder. "I suppose there'd be no harm in you riding along for as far as we go. What ship?"

"*Telestos*, sir," Ayscough replied evenly.

"Alan Lewrie," he said with a relieved smile, untensing his body and kneeing his horse forward to offer his hand to Ayscough. "That's my man Will Cony. Cony, say hello to Mister Ayscough and Mister Hagley."

"Aye, sir," Cony intoned, still a little wary.

Near to, with his hands empty of weapons, one hand on reins and the other groping like a sailor out of his depth on horseback at the front of the saddle, Ayscough appeared to be a man in his late thirties to early forties. The hair was salt and pepper, worn long at the back in sailor's fashion. The complexion matched as well; scoured by winds and sun, and pebbled with smallpox scars. But the man's speech was pleasant, almost gentlemanly, and the eyes were bright blue and lively.

"*Telestos*, did you say?" Alan said as they began to ride along together, smirking a little at the man's unfamiliarity with the Greek pantheon. "What do you know of her?"

"She's an eighty-gunned, two-decked Third Rate, sir. Bought in-frame at Chatham in 1782." Ayscough chuckled as they headed west. "Completed but never served, she did. By the time she was launched and rigged, the war was over. And you know how eighties are, sir. Too light in the upper-works some say. Snap in two in a bad sea, some of 'em did. But *Telestos* had her lines taken off a French line-of-battle ship. Laid up in-ordinary for a while, then just got sold as a . . . trading vessel." Here Ayscough tipped him a conspiratorial wink. "Now she's to fit out as an Indiaman."

"For the East India Company?" Alan asked, a little confused. If he was to join *Telesto* as a Navy officer, what was the need for subterfuge about being an Indiaman? And Ayscough said he was in possession of a warrant for a King's ship.

"That's all they told me, sir," Ayscough commented with a shrug.

"*Telestos*," Alan said, feeling cautious once more. "That's Greek, is it not? I read a little Greek. Horrible language."

"Why, I believe 'tis one of Zeus' daughters, sir. The ancient goddess of good fortune," Ayscough replied brightly. "A favorite of mine, sir. She's always treated me well. Do you know, sir, you have the look of a seaman yourself, you and your man Cony. Might you be on your way to join a ship as well?"

"Only going to visit relations near Plymouth," Alan lied, not knowing quite the reason why he did so. "I know little of the sea. Nor do I care to, sir. Life is brutal, short and nasty enough on land for most people, is it not?"

"Ah, I thought you to be, sir," Ayscough said, frowning. "After all, you have what looks like seamen's chests in your cart. Why, at first, I fancied you to be a sailorman, sir. Perhaps even an officer. I've heard tell of an Alan Lewrie. A Navy lieutenant, I believe."

"Lots of Lewries here in the west, Mister Ayscough, but thankee for the compliment," Alan replied, now chill with dread. "One of my distant cousins, perhaps. My family is from Wheddon Cross. The Navy? God no, not me!" He pretended a hearty chuckle. "I mean, who in his right mind would really be a sailor?"

"I see," Ayscough said, pursing his lips. He put both hands on the front of the saddle and frowned once more, as if making up his mind. "Bert!" he shouted, digging under his cloak for a weapon!

"Ambush!" Alan screamed, raking his heels into his horse's flanks and groping to his boot-top for his pistol. He sawed the reins so his horse shouldered against Ayscough's as he tried to thumb back the hammer of his pistol.

Ayscough got a weapon out, a pistol, though he was having trouble staying seated. Alan lashed out with his rein hand, kicked Ayscough's mount in the belly, making it rear, and shoved hard. The other horse shied away, and Ayscough came out of the saddle to tumble into the slushy road.

There was a loud shot and a million rooks stirred up cawing. Time slowed down to a gelatinous crawl. Alan jerked the reins to turn his terrorized horse, saw Ayscough rolling to his knees to free his gun hand and begin to take aim. Alan's muzzle came up and he fired first. Missed! Thanks to the curvetting of the damned horse! Alan dropped his smoking barker, clawed at his waistband to get its twin, all the while looking down the enormous barrel of Ayscough's gun. There was another loud shot, another angry chorus from the wheeling rooks, and Ayscough grunted as the air was driven from his lungs. He pitched face-down into the slush, the mud and the stalings from myriad animals, his pistol discharging into the road with a muffled thud, his cloak flapping over his head like a shroud. The back of it had been rivened with a positive barrage of pistol balls.

"Cony?" Alan shouted from a terribly dry mouth, wheeling around to face the next foe.

"Ah'm arright, sir, no thanks t' the likes o' this'un!"

"Jesus!" the waggoner's lad said, trembling, in awe of having killed his first man. "Jesus, Mary and Joseph!" It was his shot from that fowling-piece that had taken Ayscough down: a mix of pistol and musket balls, bird-shot and whatever else looked handy.

Alan dismounted, handed the reins to the boy and pulled Ayscough's head up out of the mud, but the man was most thoroughly dead. So was Cony's foe, run through by his seaman's knife.

"Wot yew suppose t'was all about, sir?" Cony asked, dismounting and coming to his side. They were both shaking like leaves at the sudden viciousness of the attack, at how quickly two men had died and at how easily it could have been them soaking in the snow and mud.

"Something about that ship we're joining, I think," Alan said. "They must have something on them, some kind of clue. You search that one yonder."

"Bloody 'ighwaymen," the old carter grumbled as he got down from the wagon seat and began to strip off Ayscough's high-topped dragoon boots. He tried one against the sole of his worn old shoes to see if they would be a good fit, and grunted with satisfaction. "Wot'iver 'appened t' 'stand an' deliver', I asks ya? They wuz gonna kill ever' last' one of us'n, I reckon, an' then rob the wagon, too."

"Pretending to be honest seamen," Alan said shuddering. "Our lucky day you and your lad were so quick on the hop, sir. Cony and I would have ended our lives here if it hadn't been for you."

"Why, thankee, sir, thankee right kindly," the old man preened.

Alan found a purse of gold on Ayscough's body: one and two-guinea coins, along with a goodly supply of shillings—nigh on one hundred pounds altogether! There was also a note written on foolscap, in a quite good hand. It described Lewrie and Cony, gave a hint of what route they would be taking, the name of the ship they would be joining, and an assurance that they would be staying at the Lamb and Flag Inn in Plymouth!

"Your lucky day, too, sir," Alan said, once the old carter had his new boots on and was stamping about to try them out. Alan counted out a stack of coins and gave them over. "I put a high price on my hide, and they'll not be needing these where they're going."

"How'd yew know, sir?" Cony asked, once he had turned Hagley's pockets inside out and helped lumber the corpse into the back of the wagon.

"Ah, well, you see, Cony," Alan sighed. "Ayscough there said the ship's name was *Telestos*, not *Telesto*. He claimed to have studied Greek, but he called her Fortune, one of Zeus' daughters. But it's common knowledge her name translates as Success, and she was one of Ocean's daughters. And Hesiod's *Theogony* is almost the first thing one reads in Greek, so he couldn't have been a real student."

"Oh, I see, sir!" Cony said, in awe of his employer's knowledge.

"And he mentioned our sea-chests, trying to confirm if we were sailors on our way to Plymouth, and if I was the Alan Lewrie that was in the Royal Navy. While he swore he was a master gunner with a warrant for our ship, you see. But where were *their* sea-chests?"

"Sent on ahead, sir, by coaster?"

"And what sailor would ride a horse when he could coast along with his chest, Cony?" Alan drawled, at his ease once more, and with his nerves calmed down to only a mild after-zinging. It wouldn't do for Cony to know that he suspected that it was Lord Cantner who had sicced these bully-bucks on them. Or too much of the *why*.

Had to be him, no question, Alan thought as he retrieved his dropped pistol, cleaned it and reloaded. The old fart wants me dead, and he swore he'd have my heart's blood! I can't remember mentioning Plymouth, and I didn't tell Cony I don't think. The talk around my lodgings was I was going to sea again. But Lord Cantner could have snooped around—he knows everyone worth knowing back in London. He could have found where I was going easy enough. But what's this about this Lamb and Flag Inn? I've never even heard of the bloody place. And I'd have gone direct to the ship to report aboard. I just hope there's no more of these murderous bastards on my trail, he thought grimly.

By the time they got the bodies to South Brent and whistled up the magistrate, their own mothers would not have known them. The carter and his boy had outfitted themselves in their hats and cloaks and shoes, putting their old castoffs on the corpses, which made them appear even more the very picture of desperate highwaymen. The magistrate had not even opened more than one eye from a mid-morning snooze to adjudge the matter. Perpetrators dead, hoist by their own petard. No one local, from the looks of them to stir up more trouble. All they needed was burying. Case closed.

"Lieutenant Lewrie, come aboard to join, sir," Alan said to the officer on deck once he had gone up the gangplank to the quarterdeck.

"A little bit less of it, if you please, Mister Lewrie," the officer in the plain blue frock coat told him. There was much about the man that bespoke a naval officer—the way he held himself erect, the hands in the small of the back and the restless grey eyes that cast about at every starting. But instead of naval uniform, the man wore dark blue breeches and black stockings, and there was nothing on his cocked hat or his coat sleeves to show any indication of rank.

"Sir?" Alan replied, taken a little aback. Although he had obeyed the strictures of his letter from the Secretary to the Admiralty, Phillip Stephens, and worn a civilian suit, he had expected a nicer welcome than that. "I'm at a loss, then, sir," he admitted. "And you are . . . ?"

"I am captain of this vessel. Andrew Ayscough," the older man informed him, civilly offering his hand.

It was not the first time that Alan Lewrie had been totally stupefied in his life—certainly it was not going to be the last—but the way his jaw dropped, and the ashen pallor which claimed his phyz did much to convince his new captain he was dealing with a slack-jawed fool.

"Are ye well, Mister Lewrie?" Ayscough asked.

"I would be a lot better, sir, if I hadn't seen you dead in the road east of Ivybridge," Alan finally stammered.

To make matters worse, there was a superficial similarity to the dead Ayscough. This living version had salt-and-pepper hair, eyes of a most penetrating nature, a seamanly queue of hair over the collar of his plain blue coat and the same weathered face, though the man that stood before Lewrie bore the unconscious, outward *ton* of command that the other had not.

"My cabin, Mister Lewrie," Ayscough suggested with a harsh rasp.

"Aye, sir."

They made their way aft from the starboard gangway to the

quarterdeck, then under the poop. Aft of there were many cabins usually not found on a man-of-war, before they reached the captain's quarters right aft. There was no Marine sentry, no one to guard the lord and master's privacy. And as Alan had observed, even in his present confused state, no inkling of Navy anywhere aboard *Telesto*.

"Now what the devil is this?" Ayscough asked, flinging his hat across the cabins to hook onto a peg with a practiced motion.

"Sir, I should like to see some *bona fides* that you are who you say you are before I say another word," Alan finally managed.

"Piss on what you want, you impudent puppy!" Ayscough rapped back. "Prove to me you're who you say *you* are first."

Alan dug into his coat and drew out his letters from the Admiralty, laid them on Ayscough's desk and let the man peruse them.

"Alan Lewrie, to be fourth officer, right," Ayscough allowed grudgingly. "Here." He produced his own papers from a drawer in his desk, a drawer that he had to unlock first.

"Post-captain, Royal Navy," Alan read aloud. "Very well, sir. I shall have to take on faith that you are a commission Sea Officer."

"Now what the devil is this tale of yours?"

Alan repeated his assertion, and filled the man in on what had occurred on the forest road. He produced the note, and what was left of the guineas in the purse.

"We found nothing else on them, sir," Alan concluded. "At first, I thought it might be . . . well, something of a personal nature. Someone trying to gain revenge for an incident that happened in London before I departed. But the coincidence of the name, well . . . now I wonder."

"What sort of an incident?" Ayscough demanded, mollifying his tone and his suspicious glower enough to trot out a squat leather bottle of brandy and offer Lewrie a glass.

"Um, it was a lady, sir. Her husband . . . names aren't important, surely, for the lady's sake. Now, the gentleman was quite old, unable to duel, but he swore he'd have my heart's blood." Alan tried to quibble around the meat of the matter.

"He had suspicions you were tupping his wife?"

"A little stronger than suspicion, sir." Alan shrugged, feeling as at-sea and cornered as he had during his first interview with his captain aboard *Ariadne* back in 1780. Ayscough raised his eyebrows and almost unbent from his stiffness for a moment.

"Not *flagrante delicto*, surely," Ayscough finally asked.

"Well engaged, sir," Alan said, nodding in affirmation.

"Damme, what sort o' sailors they going to send me, then?" the captain barked. "Can't even manage a boarding action without witnesses. Yes, I can see why you thought it might be personal, except for the following facts: one, this assassin used my name; two, he knew the name of this ship; three, he knew you were to join her; and, four, he knew the route you were taking. Daddies trying to head off their daughters on their way to Gretna Green to elope with some smarmy bastard have *less* information. I don't like the smell of this, Lewrie. I want you to go ashore and take lodgings for a couple of days until we have more of our people assembled. The Lamb and Flag is good."

"Not there, sir." Alan protested, "The man knew that, too!"

"Goddamn my eyes!" Ayscough roared, slamming a tough fist on his desk, hard enough to make the deck quake. "There's a spy about. Back in London, unless I miss my guess. I know it involves the honor of a lady, Lewrie, but just who was this son of a bitch you think was behind your attempted murder?"

"Lord Roger Cantner, sir."

"Hmm." Ayscough pondered, drumming fingers and staring at the overhead beams, dropping out of his energetic anger in a flash. "No, I've never heard of *him*. And surely, it wasn't anyone at the Admiralty."

"Pardon me, sir," Alan interrupted Ayscough's musings. "But if I might inquire . . . what the hell am I doing here, and what the devil is this commission all about?"

"They told you nothing."

"No, sir, only that it would be discovered to me after I got to Plymouth," Alan confessed.

"Why, Mister Lewrie, we're off to the East Indies!" Ayscough replied, snapping erect and pacing his spacious cabins. "Off to see elephants and *fakirs*, Bombay, Madras, Calicut. We'll not be allowed to carry trade from there to England, no, that's for the Honourable East India Company—long may Leadenhall Street and India House stand—but we'll be engaged in the country trade, just one more Interloper in a whole bloody fleet of them. Up and down the coast, over to Siam, to Canton in China and back during the trading season."

"Sir, I thought we were a warship," Alan protested, beginning to get a sinking feeling. Had Sir Onsley Matthews gotten an inkling of his affair with Lady Delia—was this his way of ending it?

God help me, is this part of the same mad scheme poor Burgess Chiswick was saddled with, he wondered, starting with an audible gasp.

"If needs be, we are, Mister Lewrie," Ayscough chuckled. "I have it on good authority that you're good with artillery, with small arms. You've done some hellish desperate deeds ashore, too. Yorktown, was it? On the Florida coast? Well, you'll get your chance to shine, let me tell you! *Telesto* will be well-armed, just like an Indiaman. Twelve-pounders on the quarterdeck and the fo'c'sle for chase guns. Eighteen-pounders on either beam on the upper gun deck. We'll turn the lower gun deck into quarters and cargo hold, with a few thirty-two-pounders hidden away just in case. Thirty-two-pounder carronades for you to play with."

"I don't understand, sir," Alan said, shaking his head, still in a fog. "We're armed, but we're not a warship?"

"Officially, we're the only vessel of a new trading company in the East Indies, what the nabobs of 'John Company' call a country ship," Ayscough continued in a softer voice, leaning back onto his desk conspiratorially. "You'll have no need for your naval uniforms. We'll have a letter of marque from the Admiralty, and from 'John Company,' so we may pass as a privateersman, if needs be. Hmm, might as well reveal all, now I've your rapt attention. Shut your mouth, Mister Lewrie; you catch flies like that."

"Aye, sir."

"There's a section of the peace treaty ending the last war that allows us, the Frogs, the Dutch and the Spaniards, only five warships in the Great South Seas," Ayscough muttered softly, pouring them some more brandy. "And none of them will be anything larger than a Fifth Rate frigate or a Fourth Rate fifty-gunned two-decker, see. But the Frogs ... aye, the bloody Frogs; it's always them, isn't it? We got wind they were putting ships like us out in the Far East, based out of Pondichery and the island of Mauritius. Shadowing the China trade, the round the Cape trade. Laying low until the next war, innocent as you please ... for now. And what's worse, stirring up the local pirate fleets. Giving them modern arms. Creating native levies for the next war. Only so much our five obvious ships can do about it. But, what a private vessel, out on her lawful occasions may do is quite another."

"So we're to lay low out there 'til the next war, sir? Stir up levies of our own? Arm pirates against the French trade as well?"

"Not quite that far. Confounding the French will suffice," the captain replied, smiling bleakly. "For now, I want you to act a role for me. As a half-pay lieutenant, a little short of the wherewithal, and . . . God bless me, what a wonderful *charade* your recent troubles are . . . you're fleeing a step ahead of an angry husband! So you're taking a berth in merchant service for your prosperity and your health. . . . it's perfect!"

"And the crew, sir?"

"We're all Navy aft, except for a few gentlemen whose expertise in the East Indies is vital to the venture. And our two super-cargo. Our putative owners, d'you see. Navy down to our bones," Ayscough said, thumping the desk once more, this time more softly—covertly. "Warrants, mates, quarter-gunners and gun-captains, yeomen and all are in on it. The ones we thought we could trust have brought friends from other commissions. We know who to look for at the Lamb and Flag. Ordinary seamen, landsmen, idlers and waisters; we can pick up reliable hands enough. Long as the pay's good, most English seamen don't care much what the job is, long's they get their merchantman's pay and decent tucker."

"And a hearty rum ration, sir." Alan smiled for the first time.

"That's the truth, by God it is, sir!" Ayscough barked in glee. "Well, I thank you for your information about this false Ayscough. I have a feeling you'd have been replaced with a fake if he'd succeeded. And thankee for the word on the Lamb and Flag. Somebody knows a little too much for my liking, before we even got the sails bent onto the yards. Too many coincidences to think it a personal *vendetta* against you. No, I think someone in the pay of a foreign power wanted to delay our sailing. Eliminate one or more of our key people and keep us in port until we'd whistled up others. You come highly recommended, Mister Lewrie. It's only natural some Frog spy would want you dead."

"I see, sir." Alan preened a little. It never hurt his feelings to have a little more praise heaped on. "A little daunting, though. To think that somewhere out there in Plymouth, there's a Frenchman just waiting to put a knife between my ribs. Perhaps I should stay aboard ..."

"No, we'll have to act natural," Ayscough said, waving off his suggestion. "Watch your back for the next few days, though. Don't travel alone. There's some good mates already aboard who'll do for keeping you alive, real scrappers if it comes to a fight—men from my last ship. Take them along on your errands."

"Um ... doesn't it strike you, though, sir, that if someone is on to us already, and tried to put me out of the way, that the whole gaff is blown?" Alan pointed out. "We might as well sail into Bombay flying battle flags, and we won't know which French ships are our enemies."

"As far as I'm concerned, *every* French ship is a foe," Captain Ayscough snarled. "And there's a good chance we may nip this in the bud, before we sail. There weren't half a dozen people in London who know about our existence. We're being paid for out of private funds. East India Company, Crown general funds, Admiralty Victualling Board and Ordnance Board. Nothing anyone may trace. But somebody talked out of turn. Or someone is in the pay of the French. We shall find out who, and when we do, that bastard'll wish he was never born!"

That was all Ayscough could, or would, impart. Other than the fact that to the Admiralty, Alan would remain listed as a half-pay officer, with a note for him not to be called up, as if there were a black mark against him. He would receive no more than regular Navy pay from their purser, and his half-pay would not be disbursed or saved for him. Until he returned to England, there would be no official record of this service. That was galling, and a little disconcerting. After all, he had made a good record, and now, for the sake of secrecy, he had a big question mark about his abilities or suitability for promotion or service in his records, even if it was a sham. How easy would it be for a clerk to get befuddled, and that would stay with him for the rest of his life? I mean, damme, he thought: the bloody Navy's the only thing I ever stand a chance of being really good at!

Lewrie strolled to the quarterdeck bulwarks to look down on the bustling wharves and warehouses next to which *Telesto* was tied up. The stone dock teemed with seamen, carters, chandlers, stevedores and mongers of every gew-gaw, trinket, notion and edible known to man.

I'm half a civilian, Alan thought gloomily. I suppose I should act like one. He stuck his hands in his breeches pockets and leaned on the bulwark, something he'd not done since his first day of naval service so long ago (and had almost gotten caned for it, then) and slouched.

Damme, I'll *have* to go ashore, just to buy plain coats and a hat or two, he speculated. Most of my kit in my sea-chest will do, once we're out at sea. Why, oh why, didn't anyone take the trouble to tell me all of this before I left London? Probably didn't think I could be trusted. Probably thought I'd beg off if I knew how bare-arsed an adventure they'd dreamed up. And I would have, too, Lord Cantner and his bully-boys be damned. Trot this lunatick idea out in the comfort of a club chair and I'd have been halfway to Liverpool before they could even begin to think of trying to catch me!

" 'Scuse me, sir," Cony said, coming to his side. "I checked in with the pusser, an' 'e gimme your cabin, sir. Got yer kit stowed away ready for ya. Yer on the upper gun deck, starboard side, third cabin forrud o' the wardroom table. Tried fer larboard, sir, but h'it was no go."

"What's the difference?"

"I heard tell from a mate o' mine in *Desperate* all the quality goes larboard east, starboard 'ome, on an Indiaman. The shady side, I 'spects, sir, an' the sun out there can be fierce, I've heard."

"Well, thanks for trying, Cony. How about you?" Alan sighed, wishing he'd gotten packed and out of his lodgings before that messenger caught up with him.

"The pusser figgerd I'd make a cabin servant for wot passengers we get, sir," Cony replied, sounding almost fiendishly cheerful. "I'll still be yer 'ammockman and man-servant, sir. Beats turnin' out on a dark night t' 'all Hands aloft an' reef sail,' it do, sir."

"That won't last longer than your meeting with the first mate," Alan gloomed, perking up a little at taking Cony's expectations of an easy job down a peg or two.

"Well, won't be the first time I went t' sea anyways, is it, sir?" Cony almost cackled.

"My God, but you're in a particularly good mood!"

"Sorry, sir." Cony sobered up. "H'it's just . . . well, London was beginnin' t' get a little . . . boresome I guess ya could call h'it, sir. I got right used t' bein' a seaman an' all. An' if I'd stayed, well . . . t'was best when ya got yer letter an' I could

come away with ya, Mister Lewrie, sir. I . . . I know yer a fair
hand with the ladies an' all, sir. An' I know h'it's not my place
t' say anythin' 'bout wot ya do. But I got meself in a deal o'
trouble from messin' where I oughtn't. I was gonna ask ya
what I should do 'bout it, you bein' a fair hand, as I said . . ."
Cony began to blush and stammer, turning his gaze to the
sanded plank deck. "An', uh . . . uhmm . . ."

"Oh, for God's sake, Cony, how bad could it be?" Alan demanded. Will Cony was probably the last of God's own inno-
cents, though how he managed that feat being around Lewrie
for very long, was anyone's guess.

"Well, t'was that pretty little Abigail, sir, the one who done
for ya when I 'ad me days off, sir? Well, uhm . . . some nights
below-stairs, sir. *Lord*, sir, I . . ."

"Have I been a bad influence on you, Cony?" Alan smiled.

"Well, sir, when I seed all them pretty lasses ya spooned
on, h'it set my 'umours t' ragin' more'n a night'r two, an'
. . . well, me an' Abigail . . . I guess ya could say we sorta . . .
indulged ourselves a time'r two, sir, on the sly."

"I would have been even more amazed if you hadn't,
Cony," Alan told him gently, trying to find a way not to burst
out laughing in the poor man's face. "She *was* a lovely young
girl, and you're a fine figure of a young fellow yourself. Only
natural."

"Well, sir, h'it felt natural as all *get-out*! Until she *tol'* me,
right a'fore we packed up an' come away t' Plymouth, sir, that
we was gonna have a baby."

"She never!" Alan gaped.

"Yessir, she did. My get, sir! I didn't know what t' do 'bout
h'it, sir, so I give her what little I'd been able t' save from my
prize-money an' all. Twenty *pounds*, sir," Cony wailed in conclusion.

"Ah," Alan intoned, turning away to look out toward Rame
Head and the harbor mouth before he began cackling like a de-
mented cuckoo.

It was all a lie, damn her little black heart, he giggled inside.
Goddamn, I've been had! If she truly is "ankled," I'll lay any
odds you want half London is trembling in their boots and
paying up their fair share! Oh, she played me perfect! Goddamn my eyes, what a little scamp! She ought to marry
Clotworthy Chute and bilk the *rest* of England! And poor
Cony, he thought. What to tell him?

"I'm sure you did the right thing, Cony," he told him. "You

can do a lot better should you ever decide to settle down and marry. Sweet girl and all, pretty as a pup, but . . ."

"I was sorta sweet on 'er, sir," Cony objected. "Iffen h'it weren't for the baby comin' s' soon, I mighta . . ."

"But awfully young and . . . you need someone a little closer to your own age, Cony, someone who's had the rough edges knocked off first. Somebody who'll be a real helpmate to you when you settle down. Some girl not so . . . flippant, I suppose. You did come away, though, didn't you."

"Yessir, I did." Cony mooned about, almost shuffling his feet together. "I suppose yer right, sir. Come a toucher o' stayin', though, that I did. Did I do right, sir?"

"You've provided for her and your babe. And you can look her up when we get back to London, if you've a mind. She might be more settled, more mature and suited to your nature by then. One never knows."

"Aye, I 'spect yer right, sir," Cony said, brightening a little.

"And in the meantime, I'll make up what she cost you, Cony."

"T'ain't rightly the money, sir, what was botherin' me, but I thankee kindly."

"And remember, we're on our way to the fabulous East Indies," Alan said, trying to cheer him. "*Nautch* dancers, girls in veils so thin you can count their freckles! China, and almond-eyed darlings the Tsar of all the Russias can't have, no matter how rich he is! It's a big, wide, exciting world, Cony. Take joy of it!"

Alan spread his arms and beamed a hopeful grin at his servant, and Cony began to chuckle. Then Alan looked over the bulwarks as a coach clattered up and Burgess Chiswick climbed out and looked up at the quarterdeck and the boarding ladder to the starboard gangway.

Oh no it ain't a big world, Alan cringed. It's too damn small and getting smaller all the time! Goddamn, we're part of the same hare-brained terror I tried to talk him out of! Is it too late to break my leg or something?

"Uh, ain't that young Mister Chiswick, sir?" Cony asked.

"It is, indeed," Alan almost moaned as Burgess espied them and waved gaily, pantomiming that he'd be aboard as soon as he paid off the coachee and got his chest up the gangplank.

"Er . . . wasn't you worried 'bout what 'e was gettin' 'isself into, sir?" Cony inquired with a worried note to his voice.

"That I was, Cony."

"Godamercy, Mister Lewrie, sir!" Cony blurted in alarm. "Ya don't think that we ... 'im an' us'n ... that same thing I 'eard ya goin' on about?"

"Looks devilish like it, Cony," Alan groaned.

"Godamercy, we're fucked, ain't we, sir?" Cony whispered.

Chapter 6

"Of all the luck," Burgess Chiswick opined, draped across the transom settee in the officer's wardroom, a warming mug of "flip" in one hand and a long church-warden clay pipe fuming in the other.

"Yes, wasn't it," Lewrie agreed in a sarcastic drawl.

"Sorry you missed us on the road, though," Burgess went on, oblivious to Alan's disgruntled feelings. "You must have been out of your lodgings like a race horse, soon as the letter came. We left London behind you. Went by Panton Street but they told us you'd already gone. Would have been nice to have coached down together."

Alan had been barred from discussing the murderous incident on the road, so all he could do was nod in agreement.

"And then to find you'd stopped off at the farm and gone on," Burgess told him, experimenting with blowing a smoke ring. "Caroline was very disappointed she'd missed you."

"Was she well?" Alan asked, abandoning his put-upon sulking.

"My sister is very fond of you, Alan. As is mother. Thinks you hung the moon. Or at least helped out. She's a fine young lady."

"Well, that's moot for three or four years, ain't it?" Alan sighed.

"Hope you didn't mind, but she adopted your cat."

"She did?"

"Didn't know you were fond of 'em," Burgess marveled. "Still, I can see the attraction. Affectionate old thing. Purred away like anything, soon's she picked him up, and rode in her lap all the way to Guildford in the coach. Thought he'd be happier on the farm. And ... well, he's a part of you, d'you

69

see, Alan. She said to tell you she'd take good care of him until you got back."

"Yes, I suppose that's best," Alan agreed, trying to picture *anyone* picking William Pitt up and trying to dandle him. "After a warship, he'd enjoy terrorizing a herd of sheep. Devilish good mouser."

"More a lap-cat the last time I saw him," Burgess chuckled.

Shoes thundered on the double companion-way ladders from the upper deck, and their attention was drawn to the newcomer. The sight drew both of them to their feet, for its novelty if nothing else.

A man stood there, a man with skin the color of a cup of cocoa. Fierce dark eyes glared under thick brows—the rest of the face was hidden behind a greying beard and a thick mustache that stood out stiff as the cat-heads up forward that held the ship's anchors. The man was dressed in sandals over thick woolen stockings, loose knee-length trousers, a long-skirted coat that buttoned from waist to chin with a glittery multi-colored silk sash about his waist, a burgundy colored old-style frock coat over that for warmth—and a turban.

"What the devil?" Burgess muttered.

"Namasté, sahib," the apparition said, putting both mittened hands together and bowing slightly to both of them. "Meestair Twigg *sahib*, want speech with Elooy *sahib*."

"I think that might be you, Alan," Burgess told him.

"Yes, but who the devil's this Twigg?" Alan wondered.

"My master, Elooy *sahib*. Kshamakejiye . . . excuse me . . . I am being Ajit Roy. You come, *jeehan?* Yes?"

"Yes," Alan replied. "Is he ashore?"

"Naheen, sahib," Ajit Roy told him, pointing upwards. "Is here on ship."

"Keep the flip warm, Burgess," Alan said to his companion. "And if I'm not back soon . . ."

The servant padded back up the companion-way to the upper deck cabins under the poop, where the captain usually had his quarters. There were other cabins forward of his that Alan had thought might be reserved for passengers. Ajit Roy rapped on one door, and someone inside bade him enter. The servant swung the door wide and stepped aside to let Alan in.

It was a fairly spacious cabin, considering. About twelve precious feet long bow to stern, and ten feet abeam. Piled as it was with chests, it seemed more like a storeroom, though, or a rug merchant's tiny stall. Or an opium den, Alan thought, sniffing the air.

"Achh-chaa, Roy-ji . . . Kuchh der men vahpasahiye'."

"Jeehan, Twigg-*sahib,"* Roy said, bowing himself out.

"Lewrie, I'm Zachariah Twigg," said the man, who had been sitting on the bunk, as he unfurled himself to his full height. This Twigg was tall and lean, almost impossibly lean: all arms and legs. He was dressed all in black like some dominee.

"Your servant, sir," Alan replied automatically, still befuddled, and thinking that he would most likely remain in that condition for some time to come.

"Sit," Twigg commanded, pointing out a chair with the flexible tube he held in his hand. "Captain Ayscough has related to me the peculiar circumstances of your incident. I want to ask you more about it."

"And you are, sir?" Alan demanded as Twigg perched himself cross-legged on the bunk again and began to draw from the tube, which Alan now saw was attached to a tall glass hubble-bubble pipe. In the faint gloom, illuminated by only a single lantern placed on one of the crates, Twigg resembled some kind of bird of prey. The face was all hollows—in his cheeks, behind his eyes, on either side of his temples. And his eye sockets were deep and pouchy. He wore his own hair, combed back thin and close to the skull, and a prominent peak jutted like a cape between receding temples. And Twigg's nose was long, thin and narrow, like a raptor's beak, until it reached the nostrils, where it flared out into a pad of flesh and cartilage an adult walrus could have envied.

"Let us just say that Captain Ayscough answers to me. As do you, Lieutenant Lewrie," Twigg told him with a brief, damnably brief, glint of humor. With the mouthpiece of the hubble-bubble pipe out of his mouth, the lips were caricature-thin, and pursed flat against each other in an expression of perpetual asperity. "I and my partner, Mister Wythy, are ship's husbands, and the . . . owners, let us say. We were the ones bought her, raised the capital, and bought the cargo. Should anyone ask, you were here to discuss lading with me, as the fourth mate of a trading ship ought. Now discover everything to me."

It was not a request. Alan stumbled out the story of his attempted murder, and the reasons he and Ayscough thought might be behind it.

Alan supposed England had spies. Any sensible nation did,

and he gathered that Twigg and his partner were the front men for the adventure, the plausible story that would hang together should anyone become inquisitive. The prime movers of this subterfuge.

"Doesn't make any bloody sense." Twigg snapped after a long silence. "Not to take anything away from your abilities, Lewrie, but you're a rather small fish to fry, if someone was intent on delaying our departure. If it's murder they'd stoop to, better me and Tom Wythy, or Ayscough himself. Better a fire in the hold than slay a junior officer. Might have even done us a favor. Given us time to find a more seasoned mariner than you. I've read your records, Lewrie. You've come up hellish fast, considering."

"If I do not please you, sir, perhaps you should," Alan snapped back. It ain't like I'm talking to an admiral, he thought; he's no patron of mine whose back I have to piss down. They can send another man down from the Admiralty and I can hide out in Wheddon Cross with granny for a while until Lord Cantner cools off. Boring as that would be. Maybe coach back to Guildford and stay with the Chiswicks.

"I would, but for the fact that you rose without *too* much 'interest' from those above you," Twigg allowed, acting as if he was amused by Alan's irritation with his remarks. "You're not the run-of-the-mill place-seeker, Lewrie. And you have this fascinating talent for snatching victory from the very maw of defeat. For survival. I value that, more so than I do dull-witted competence. It's a talent rarer than pluck and daring, or bravery. Any fool can be brave."

"I see, sir," Alan said, wondering if he had been complimented or insulted. Either way, he was still part of this lunatick venture, it seemed, down for three years of naval service unless he begged to be dismissed.

"We'll get to the bottom of this before we sail, at any rate." Twigg shrugged, and sucked deeply on his hubble-bubble pipe, caving in those already cadaverous cheeks even more. "Stores to be loaded on the morrow. Furniture, light artillery, military supplies for East India Company. Luxury items for our people out there as well. I expect we'll be awash in beer, ale and wine. You'll see to keeping the crew out of it, that it's locked up securely. Bring a fortune in Kalikatta once it's landed."

"They can't brew their own, sir?"

"Muslims won't drink spirits of any kind. Hindoos have their own muck that'd flatten an Englishman, he were fool enough to partake." Twigg frowned. "Water can't be drunk in the East unless it's been boiled and let cool in a clean vessel. Case of wine that'd cost you three shillings the bottle in London will go for five times that, *and* it's safe to drink. I expect our cargo will pay for the purchase of *Telesto*, and her outfitting. First cargo to China with Bengali cloth and spices will defray the cost of our first year of operations."

"My God," Alan gaped, trying to total that sum in his head. A 3rd Rate ship, even with half the artillery landed ashore, would go for at least twenty-five thousand pounds, and their profits would cover *that?*

I've been in the wrong bloody profession! he told himself.

"As Captain Ayscough instructed, not a word of this incident with your fellows in the wardroom. Show me your plan of lading after breakfast. I'll have nothing broken, mind."

"Aye, sir."

"And keep in mind we'll put in at Oporto or Vigo, maybe touch shore at Madeira as well, for passengers and more spirits. Save some cargo space in the deep hold for that. That'll be all for now, Mister Lewrie. A pleasant night to you."

"Er, aye, sir," Alan was forced to say, rising to leave.

"Ajit?" Twigg called out.

"Jeehan, sahib?" the Indian servant said through the closed door.

"Idhar ahiye'! Mujhe' sahib Wythy *se' baht karnee hai,"* Twigg ordered. "Have an ear for languages, Mister Lewrie?"

"Not much of one, really," Alan confessed, wondering if his lack of fluency in anything but English would suddenly, blissfully, disqualify him from this goose-brained voyage.

"You'll pick it up. I just told Ajit to come here, that I wanted him to bring Wythy to talk with me. There's enough bearers in Kalikatta who understand a little English, and if you pick up a word or phrase or two, you can stagger by. Bring this, fetch this, yes, no, too hot, too cold. You'll sound like a monosyllabic barbarian to the Bengalis. But then, that's pretty much what we are to them."

"Kalikatta," Alan assayed.

"Bengali name for Calcutta, up the Hooghly River. Where we're going," Twigg rasped out.

"I thought it was Calicut, sir. That's how Captain Ayscough said it."

"Then he's as big a noddy as you are," Twigg snapped.

"Goodnight, sir."

"Namasté."

"Um, right. *Namasté.*"

Whatever the hell that means, he pondered as he got out of Twigg's sight as quickly as dignity allowed.

Fortunately, in the next week, he had little to do with Twigg or his partner. He was busy being the most junior office aboard, working with the master's mates and the purser in stowing cargo in the holds, and on the orlop deck above the bilges. Hundreds of kegs and tuns of spirits, salt-meats, crates of broadcloth and ready-made shirts and breeches. Uniforms for the East India Company's native Bengali troops. Weapons and accoutrements. Books, and a printing press. Blank ledgers for the writers and clerks to fill up with numbers in their counting houses and trading factories. All those items of English life so sorely missed by the English in India, and the luxuries that made life worth living in an alien land.

And there were ship's stores to be piled away as well, to feed and clothe the officers and crew. A second complete set of sails and spars, replacement masts, miles of variously sized cordage for the standing rigging and the running rigging by which the sails and yards were adjusted. Powder and shot for *Telesto's* guns. Spare hammocks, bag after bag of ship's biscuit, holystones to scrub the decks with. Pikes and muskets, bayonets and cutlasses to repel any pirates hand-to-hand.

It all had to be wedged in tighter than a bung in a barrel, and gravel ballast had to be packed in between the heaviest items lowest in the holds, cut firewood and kindling jammed between, so that nothing could shift an inch once *Telesto* was out at sea, pitching and tossing and rolling at the whim of the sea. Once out of harbor, it was life or death, and could not be redone if a storm overwhelmed them.

Alan had to admit *Telesto* was an impressive ship. Compared to any other he had served in, she was massive—1,585 tons of oak and iron, 180 feet long on the range of the gun deck, 155 feet long at the keel and in the hold, and that hold was 20 feet deep, and 50 feet wide at her widest point, with a pronounced tumble-home to her upper deck that narrowed the quarterdeck and poop. Broad and bluff in the bows, gently tapering narrower aft like the head and tail of a fish, that shape adjudged best by naval architects to swim the seas of the world. An eighty-gunned 3rd Rate was the biggest ship in the Navy that could mount two decks of guns and not "hog" or strain down at both ends and break her back. The Royal Navy had not been lucky with them, since they were too light in the upper works to keep them from snapping like a twig in heavy seas, but *Telesto* was patterned upon the French *Foudroyant* after it was taken as prize in battle and had its lines taken off by the Admiralty to study and copy.

She was as long and beamy as a one-hundred-gunned 1st Rate flagship of three decks, as if she had been "razeed," shaved down by one deck to make her faster and lighter. And as with French ships, in Alan's experience, she was a little finer around the cutwater at the bow, and in her entry. She promised speed, and with so much cargo aboard, would ride out a gale of wind without as much angle of heel as other ships, even counting the wide span of her yards and upper masts for propulsion.

New as *Telesto* was, her hull was still golden under the preserving oils, not yet baked almost black. Her two rows of gunports were painted with twin stripes of bright red paint. No one was going to spring good money to fancy her up like a flagship, so the usual gilt trim around the entry-port gates, beakhead, taffrail carvings and the walkways and windows of her three stern galleries had been omitted, and a light yellow lead paint had been substituted.

"She'll fly like a seagull," Artemus Choate, her first officer predicted happily. "You take passage on a 'John Company' Indiaman, it's six knots when the sun's up, and they reef in and wallow slow as church-work, sundown to sunrise. Don't want to upset the passengers, I suppose." The tow-headed man in his middle thirties grimaced at the habits of civilian seamen. "Four months to round Good Hope and another three to the Bay of Bengal, if the seasonal winds are with you."

"It's five shillings a day for an officer, too, sir," Alan pointed out. "Who'd be in a hurry at that rate of pay?"

"Ha, you've a point, Mister Lewrie, 'deed you do. But we'll drive this ship like Jehu drove his chariot, weather permitting."

Telesto sometimes felt Navy in the way things were run even in harbor. But of an evening, she was as much a merchantman as any Indiaman. Ayscough and Choate, and Tom Wythy, the other partner, liked music, so *Telesto* had a good selection of bandsmen: fifers, fiddlers, drummers and the unheard of luxury of a bellows pump-organ—that mostly for the passengers' amusement. She also had six men in the crew who doubled as bagpipers, and most evenings would perform a con-

cert on the upper gun deck up forward by the forecastle and
the belfry. Alan wished they wouldn't, but Ayscough was some
sort of Lowland Scot, and doted on them. It irritated Lewrie,
and put the milk cow off production. The sheep, pigs, goats
and chickens in the manger didn't care for them much, either.

As for passengers, there wasn't much joy there. Alan had
fantasized about a few English females taking passage to India,
but no such luck. Their forty or so paying guests were all solidly male, all fairly young and just a trifle seedy in appearance.
Clerks and writers-to-be, young tradesmen who'd finished their
apprenticeships and were heading out where the competition
wasn't so fierce. Some men like Burgess of limited means who
would take military service in "John Company" as subalterns.
Not one sign of a "Mother Abbess" and her brood of whores
to service all that emigré masculinity out in the Indies, either.
God help him, they all looked so "skint" and short of money
even a card game would be unproductive.

They warped *Telesto* away from the stone docks on 4 February, sent the temporary "wives" ashore the next day and put
the crew back into discipline. Alan got to go ashore just the
once, to pick up his last personal stores and purchases to complete his kit, and almost drowned in the rough harbor waters
out and back in a ship's boat under lug-sail that tried its best
to capsize or pitch him out.

On the dawn of 7 February, the winds came fair, and the
weather moderated. *Telesto* sailed.

"Anchor's in sight!" Alan bawled to the officers aft from his
place on the forecastle.

"Heave and in sight!" Choate urged his crew on as they
tramped in a circle round the massive capstan on the lower gun
deck.

"Bosun, hands aloft there! Lay out and make sail!"
Ayscough bellowed loud as a steer. "Mister Lewrie, hoist away
jibs forrud!"

"Murray, hoist away, flying outer jib and fore topmast
stays'l! Chearly, lads!" Alan ordered. "Anchor's awash! Ready
with the cat to seize her up, there, larboard men."

Telesto paid off from her head-to-weather anchorage, free of
the last link with the land. They backed her jibs to force her
bows around to face the harbor entrance as the large spanker
aft on the mizzen filled with air and made the noise of a gun-
shot. Canvas boomed and drummed and rustled in the mid-

dling winds. Standing rigging that held the masts erect and properly tensioned creaked and groaned as a load came on them. Blocks squealed and sang as hands on the gangways and upper decks hauled away on lifts, halyards and jeers to raise her massive yards up from their resting positions. Drummers drummed on snares and bass, fiddlers and fifers gave the tune and the pace and the hands chantied.

> "We'll rant and we'll roll
> like true British sailors,
> we'll rant and we'll roll all across
> the salt seas,
> Until we strike soundings
> In the Channel of Old England
> from Ushant to Scilly is thirty-five leagues!

"Braces, there! Brace her in!" Ayscough almost howled.

"Ease your jib sheets," Alan ordered. "Walk 'em to the larboard side, Murray. Trim for starboard tack."

"Aye, sir! Walk away wi' the larboard sheet!"

> "So let ev'ry man raise up his full bumper,
> let every man drink up his full glass.
> For we'll laugh and be jolly,
> and chase melancholy,
> with a well-given toast to each true-hearted lass!"

"Anchor's catted, sir," one of the hands told him.

"Well, the cat. Ring up the fish," Alan said, leaning over to see how the hands over the side on the rails were doing after being dangled to seize the hook in the ring of the anchor to cat it. If nothing worse than a good soaking had occurred, it was a good day—handled badly, anchors could kill those poor men. Very few sailors of any navy knew how to swim, Alan Lewrie least of all, and going over the side for any task was enough to shrivel any seaman's scrotum. Those men came scrambling back up to the deck, up the heavy chain wale and beakhead rails almost on the waterline, soaked to the skin and turning blue from the frosty air and waters. One had to stay, hung in canvas hawse-breeches, to hook the fish onto an anchor fluke to swing it up parallel with the bulwarks. His bare legs trailed in the ship's now-apparent wake, and he shrieked as the icy waters surged as high as his waist.

"Oh, be a man, Spears!" Murray the fo'c'sle captain told him.

"'Nother dunkin' lahk 'at an' me man'ood'll be froze off!" the man shouted back. "Got it!"

"Haul away on the fish-davit! Ring her up!"

"Let fall courses! Starboard division, hands to the braces!" they ordered from back aft.

There was enough labor for a warship's crew of 650 men usually allotted to such a vessel. With the lower deck artillery mostly gone, *Telesto* had more a frigate's complement of 250, and everyone had to bear a hand to see her safely out of harbor. Had she truly been a civilian ship, she would not have carried 100 all told, and some of her men would already have been ruptured.

So it was half an hour before they had her put into proper order, with one reef in the courses on the lowest yards, one reef in the topsails, the royals raised at two reefs on the fore and main-mast, and the spritsail under the jib boom and bowsprit set to take advantage of the northerly wind. Gradually, the confusion shook down to a pull at this, a tug on that, and the rat's nest of heavy running rigging was coiled up, flaked down, hung on rails in giant bights and out of the way. Already the galley funnel was smoking as the first meal at sea was being boiled in the steep-tubs.

"Starboard has the watch. Dismiss the larboard watch below!"

Alan gave everything a last once-over and went aft along the starboard gangway to the quarterdeck.

"Oh, for God's sake, gentlemen, please!" he shouted to the passengers and landsmen of the crew, who were experiencing their first bout of seasickness as the ship began to feel the Channel motion. "If you have to spew, do it to larboard, over there. Downwind so it won't blow back on you, hey? Downwind so I won't have to send you over the side to scrub off your breakfasts. Oh, not on the deck, you oaf! Sorry, Burgess. Didn't recognize you with your face that particular shade of green."

"Oh, God, I'm so ill I think I could die," Burgess wailed in his misery as Alan tried to help him to his feet.

"You won't die of it," Alan offered. "You only wish you could."

"You heartless bloo . . . bloo . . . burgck!" Chiswick retched, and cast up more of his accounts on the starboard bulwarks.

"Were you ill when you sailed back from New York to Charleston? From Charleston to England?" Alan inquired.

"N . . . no," Burgess sighed as Alan led him to the larboard side of the ship, across the quarterdeck to the lee rail.

"Well, you're going like the town drains now, I must say," Alan said cheerfully. "Tell you what. Send down to the passengers' mess. Get a brimming bumper of hot rum. Stay up here on deck. The cold air will brace you right up. For God's sake, don't watch the ocean close-aboard! Stare out at the horizon. Think pleasant thoughts," he added in closing, unable to help himself and trying hard not to grin.

"Bastard!" Burgess hissed.

"I'm on watch, so I'll leave you to it for now," Alan sighed. "Steward?"

He went aft to stand by the sheltered double wheel, where four quartermasters threw their weight on the helm as *Telesto* butted her way through the off-shore Channel chop. There was now and then some hint of the Atlantic to come, a long roller cross-set to the chop. The wind, once out of shelter of the coast, was a live thing that tried to throw the ship's head down southerly for the coast of France, requiring those four men's strength to hold her course. Captain Ayscough took a last look around, nodded to the second officer, Mr. Percival, and took himself aft under the poop into the passageway to his great cabins right in the stern. Percival strolled up the canted deck from amidships to the windward rail, taking a look at the compass card and grunting his satisfaction in passing.

Alan didn't think he was going to like Percival. The man was one of those massive beasts, all chest and arms, with a neck like a breeding bull, and a heavy jaw. Percival had the brow ridge of a mountain gorilla, and looked to be the sort who could break oak beams with his bare hands.

He was certainly the sort of fellow who had grown up being the biggest and toughest of his playmates, the one who enjoyed being the top-dog in the pack, and would fight anyone to keep his status. In the last week, they had sparred, verbally so far. Even asking for the jam pot was a challenge to Percival's dominance.

"All prick and no personality," Alan muttered to himself, and one of the quartermasters grinned at the comment as he shifted a quid of tobacco from one cheek to the other. "West sou'west, half west, as she goes."

"Aye, sir."

Other than Percival, the wardroom was a fairly decent gathering. There was Choate, bluff and steady, glad to have active employment now the war was over. He had a wife and family in Harwich, and was more in need of full pay than most. The third officer, Colin McTaggart, was one of Ayscough's protégés, a slim and wiry young fellow of twenty-five or so. He had black hair as curly as a goat, dark eyes and a pug nose. Being a Scot, he was better educated than most young men who joined the Navy, and was enjoyable to converse with. So far.

To make room for their super-cargo (Twigg and his mostly unseen partner Tom Wythy) the sailing master, one Mr. Brainard, had been shifted below a deck to the officers' wardroom. He was another of those mysteries, like Ajit Roy— brought in on account of his familiarity with Asian waters. He was also, like Twigg and Wythy, civilian in origin, never having served in the Royal Navy. Brainard had a civilian's usual disdain for the Navy and its way of doing things. A sneer here, a lifted eyebrow there and a heavy sigh or two of exasperation met any evolution that differed from merchantman practice.

Brainard was as roly-poly as a Toby jug, but held no cheer, and sheltered his past, and any conversation, behind an aloof air of duty. He was as weathered and dried as a piece of hawse-buckler leather, baked to a permanent brick color. So far, he had not been seen to imbibe anything but water or small beer, or crack the slightest smile in the mess. Indeed, it would have been hard to determine if he had any facial expressions at all, since he swathed himself in the heaviest grogram watchcoat even below decks where a small coal-fired stove attempted to warm the wardroom. It seemed a chore to remove his mittens so he could partake of his meals. And the one time Alan had peeked through the opened door of his cabin as one of the ship's boys cleaned it, the bunk had been mounded with no less than four blankets.

One thing Alan had learned in his Naval service, though, was that even the worst messmates could be abided. He hadn't expected the voyage would be all "claret and cruising." People gave others personal space, as much as was able, and ignored the worst offenders, limiting their exchanges to professional work.

Far enough off the coast now that England was an indistinct smear of headlands almost lost in low scudding clouds, the ship was going like a hobbyhorse in a playroom. Alan clung to the weather shrouds on the starboard side of the wide deck and began to wonder why he had thought *Telesto* a big ship. The open Atlantic rolled and heaved up in dully glittering hills before them, shrinking the massive ship to a toy that groaned and creaked as she rolled and pitched with a slow, ponderous gait. Soaring up as the scend of the sea deigned to raise her, cocking downward as the waves receded behind her. One moment *Telesto* was elevated high enough to expose miles and miles of ocean to Alan's view, the next sunk down into a trough, sliding forward as though she would butt into the next wave and shatter, but always riding up and away from danger. And at those times, he could see no farther than the creaming tops of the wave-crests that hillocked like frothy ink on either beam as high as the weather deck.

"Going like a race horse," he muttered aloud, feeling *Telesto* as she trembled up from keel to oaken decks below his shoes. She was, indeed, riding the sea and careering forward at a wonderfully prodigious pace.

"Mister Hogue?" he called for one of the master's mates in his watch who was secretly a senior midshipman enlisted in their adventure.

"Aye, sir?"

"Cast of the log, if you please. I doubt very much if we'll get a decent sight for our position today. And I'd not like to set her on Ushant before the voyage is even begun."

"Aye aye, sir."

Hogue came back several minutes later, his watchcoat and hat speckled with drops of seawater, and his mittens soaked. "Nine and a quarter knots, sir," Hogue said proudly. "She's a fast 'un, no mistake about her, sir."

"Indeed she is," Alan said, grinning. He climbed up onto the mizzen shrouds for a better view with his telescope. "I make that to be the high point just west of Looe, just aft of abeam now. Where would that put us, were you navigating, Mister Hogue?"

"Allow me to fetch my sextant, sir."

Every time the ship rose up on a surging billow of ocean, they took a land sight, comparing compass bearings, trying to compute on a slate how far offshore they were, if the high ground west of Looe was known to be 387 feet high, and only subtended a degree or so above the indistinct horizon.

"Then on this course, allowing for *Telesto* making a certain amount of leeway to the suther'd, we'll fetch Lizard Point with at least ten miles of sea-room," Alan stated finally.

"If the wind stays fair, sir," Hogue commented, more sage than his scant eighteen years might allow. "Bound to come more westerly as we leave the Channel."

"A hard beat, then, but with the tidal flow, not against it, until at least midnight."

"Else we'll have to tack and fight the tides, losing everything we've gained, sir," Hogue warned. "Inshore in the dark."

"Thankee, Mister Hogue," Alan said, rolling up the chart Mr. Brainard had left on the binnacle table.

And if that happens, Alan thought lazily, it'll not happen on my watch, thank the good Lord. He strolled back up to the windward side and took out his pocket watch to take a peek at the time. Three hours to go until his watch would be dismissed below.

He threaded an arm through the shrouds once again and shivered in his thick clothing. The wind was wet and a little raw, a live thing out at sea, a continual noise that a landsman would never notice above the murmurs of the ship.

If the winds did come more westerly, they could harden up to close-hauled and beat within six points of its origin, he decided: just enough to keep *Telesto* in mid-Channel, well clear of the Lizard, and a safe twenty leagues or so from the rocky coast of France. He debated with himself if it would be worth it to tack north'rd if it really came foul—embay themselves south of Falmouth, then tack once more due south to clear the Lizard?

He turned his face to the raw wind and felt its strength on either cheek, sniffing for the source of all that awesome power that moved their ship. Still well north of west, and not so strong they'd have to take another reef aloft just yet.

A gaggle of passengers came boiling up from below, reeling in another bout of illness, and Alan smiled as they staggered down to the leeward side to spew. So far, his own stomach was showing its cast-iron consistency. And, he realized with a start, his sea legs were returning, those sea legs that in the beginning he had never even had the slightest desire to achieve. "Not so bad once you're in," he mused aloud. "Like Young Jack told his first whore."

Depriving and dull a voyage might be, but it was something he had become somewhat good at. His ability to shrug off the natural reaction to the ship's motion and spew his guts out, or reel like a sot as she pitched and rolled beneath him, was pleasing to his pride. As was his ability to decypher their rough position with the briefest of clues from the coast. And didn't *Telesto* ride well, he thought. She was a true thorough-bred, properly laden and ballasted, with as much canvas aloft as she could bear for the moment—slicing through those hummocking seas with a sure-footed neatness of motion that gave him a thrill of . . . dare he call it *pleasure* . . . with every swoop and rise?

"Damme, this feels good!" he declared to the winds and seas.

His first watch ended at four in the afternoon, and he headed below, face and hands raw with the wind and chill, eager for warmth, for a seat near the glowing stove and a glass of some-thing cheerful. But he was delayed from those simple pleasures by the sight of Tom Wythy, their other "owner."

"A word with ye, Mister Lewrie?" the man beckoned. Since Wythy had been pretty much an unseen presence so far, it was more curiosity that led Alan aft to the doorway to the passage that led under the poop to the super-cargo cabins.

"Aye, sir?" Alan replied, and followed the rotund man into his cabin across the passageway from Twigg's. He hoped he'd get some liquid refreshment, at the least.

"Tot o' rum?" Wythy offered once the door was shut. Wythy took up most of the cabin—he was rounder and heavier than even Mr. Brainard the sailing master, his face hidden be-hind a thick greying beard, and that in an age when most fash-ionable men shaved closely. There was a red-veined doorknob of a nose, ruddy cheeks round as spring apples and bright, glit-tering eyes lost in the pudding face the beard most likely con-cealed.

"I've made some inquiries about yer little excitement," Wythy told him, rubbing the side of that bulbous proboscis with the side of a thumb as thick as a belaying pin. "Took this long t' get even a fast rider t' London an' back. An' I asked about ashore. That's what's kept me busy an' out o' sight so far, so this is our first opportunity to make our acquaintances. Hope ye'll forgive me that."

"Of course, sir," Alan told him. "And what have you found?"

"Oh, we've stirred up an ant-hill, no error." Wythy grinned, baring a rather sparse, but strong set of teeth—those remaining in his head, at least. "Even caught us a French spy or two."

"So it was the French, sir." Alan enthused at the proof of a devilish conspiracy, the rum racing in his veins and warming his chill belly.

"Nothin' t' do with *ye*, sir," Wythy informed him, turning the broad smile off. "We winkled a brace o' informers out o' the woodpile, but that was more serendipity. Ye've been a bad boy, Mister Lewrie, 'deed ye have. A very bad boy."

"Was it anyone *I* told, sir?" Alan cringed, waiting for the thunderstorm of rage he imagined would follow.

"I was thinkin' more o' yer taste for married flesh, Mister Lewrie, not yer indiscretion," Wythy said, glaring at him. "Imagine it for a moment. Us expectin' the worst. Word o' our venture leakin' to our foes 'cross the Channel. No end o' shite-storm as our people trace back every man in the know, ye included, t' see if someone's blabbed in his cups'r whispered in the wrong wench's ear."

"But I knew nothing to 'blab' before stepping on board, sir," Alan replied, springing to his own defense out of long-established habit. He'd gotten rather good at it—had to have gotten good at it—since he'd been breeched. "Sir Onsley only said Burgess Chiswick would be going to the Far East on some vital mission but I had no idea I had any part of it until the old fool . . . until I received my letter from the Admiralty. And I didn't connect my appointment into this ship with him until Chiswick came aboard, either, sir."

"Ah, but yer patron, Sir Onsley could," Wythy hissed evilly. "What's more natural among gentlemen in their clubs'n t' answer an inquiry 'bout where ye are, lad? Under the rose, as it were. Well, let me say, yer *former* patron. Sir Onsley's stock 'round Whitehall's not so high anymore. Find another, 's my advice t' ye."

"But . . ."

"Had ye not been swivin' with another man's wife, he'd not have set henchmen on ye to kill ye," Wythy drummed out, beating Lewrie on the head and shoulders with harsh words. "We'd not have turned all the south of England arsey-varsey lookin' fer spies, not have spent over a thousand pounds o' Crown money to do it, either. Had ye the *slightest* bit o' sense, ye'd never been caught tuppin' her in the first place!"

"Lord Cantner?" Alan burst out in a near-screech of surprise.

"Aye," Wythy snarled. "Funny what a man'll stand for, long's he don't have t' be confronted direct. Funny the things a man'll stoop to once he is. *Two* brace o' murderers, one pair t' Wheddon Cross if ye'd gone there. T'other pair ye and yer man did for, all scum from a rookery who smuggled brandy an' lace for your Lord Cantner from the Continent. Seamen, might o' been in league with Frogs who supplied 'em. First pair come t' Plymouth an' nosed about, asking a lot o' questions. Even tried t' sign aboard this ship. Hah, ye didn't know that, did ye, now? Lucky we were a full complement when they did. Couple o' people in the pay o' the French got wind o' it. Began t' wonder what so many Navy hands were doin' signin' aboard *Telesto*. Never had a clue, 'less ye hadn't stirred up the waters, Mister Lewrie. Well, we stopped their bloody business. Stopped the business o' those hired killers, too. Dead bodies floatin' in a seaport town'r nothin' much t' get exercised about."

"Jesus." Alan gulped at the calmness with which Wythy spoke of having four human beings dispatched. He took a pull on his tot of rum.

"One o' our people had a little chat with yer Lord Cantner as well," Wythy went on. "Pity ye ain't back in London t' console the poor widow. She's become a dev'lish *wealthy* widow, of a sudden."

"You . . . you had him *killed?*" Alan shuddered.

"Expired on his own, damn his blood!" Wythy spat, as though he would have relished throttling the old colt's-tooth. "Right in the middle o' bein' told we had him dead t' rights for attempted murder. An' how vexed the Crown'd be with him. Apoplexy, they say."

"God's teeth!" Lewrie chilled, raising his tot to drain it dry. Well, at least that was behind him. He'd not have to fear any more attempts on his life from Lord Cantner, anyway, though he wasn't sure as to Wythy's or Twigg's intentions. "Hold on, now, sir. You said that you made inquiries. Did you ask of the Chiswick family? Did you pester them? Did you harm them in any way? By God, if . . ."

"Discreet inquiries, nothin' more," Wythy assured him. "I'm told the lass's prettier'n springtime. Soft on her, are ye? Well, she an' her family weren't run through the Star Chamber. And, ye'll be happy t' know that little servin' wench isn't truly 'ankled.' My word, but ye're a *busy* boy, ain't ye, now, Mister

Lewrie? But d'ye see just how much trouble that wayward prick o' yer'n has caused us?"

"Aye, sir," Alan replied, as abashed as a first-term student.

"And ye'll not breathe a bloody word more'n 'pass the port' t' anyone, long's yer aboard this ship. Long as this venture lasts, eh?"

"Indeed not, sir," Alan said, meek as a pup.

"And ye'll not go dippin' yer wick 'less I or Zachariah Twigg give ye leave, now, will ye, Mister Lewrie." It was not a question.

"I should think," Lewrie had to grin, getting his spirit back, "that that would not be a problem for the next six months, Mister Wythy."

" 'T'isn't funny, boy. Ye have need o' swivin' once we're in Calcutta, with our leave, mind ye, ye'll cleave yer tongue t' the roof o' yer mouth," Wythy whispered. " 'Cause if ye can't, if we ever suspect ye of *any* indiscretion that'd jeopardize this expedition, 'r risk men's lives, then God have mercy on yer miserable soul! Do we understand each other . . . *Mister* Lewrie?"

"Aye, sir!" Alan answered quickly, suddenly realizing just how dangerous this mission was. "Indeed we do, sir! I give you my solemn oath we do."

Christ, would these ghouls kill me? Yes, I think they just might! Goddamn me, what sort of a pack of monsters have I been caged up with? These . . . these blackamoors work for the Crown?

"Good. Ye may go, then. By the way . . ."

"Yes, Mister Wythy?" Lewrie said, damned eager to get out of the door, but held mesmerized like a bird by a snake.

"Seems that Lord Cantner might o' died happy in one respect," Wythy allowed. "The latest jape runnin' round his circle back in London's how he finally fathered an heir, and the effort killed him."

"Lady Delia?"

"Bakin' *some* young buck's bastard, aye," Wythy noted, grinning briefly.

"Seems to be a lot of that going 'round, sir." Alan grimaced. "May I go, sir? Is that all you wish of me for now?"

"Aye, Mister Lewrie, that'll be all," Wythy said, retrieving the glass from Alan's nerveless hand. "And I *do* mean all!"

II

"The nature of things is in the habit of concealing itself."

—HERACLITUS

Chapter 1

Falconer's Marine Dictionary, by now well-thumbed and stained with tar, proved prophetic on the subject of winds when Alan referred to it. Running down past Portugal, one hundred leagues offshore, they had reveled in the expected nor'east gales, from 28 degrees to 10 degrees north. Then, with winter waning, they met the southerlies south of 10 degrees north, against which they beat hard to make forward progress. And below that latitude, when the winds did indeed come more easterly, they brought gloom and heavy seas in the region known as The Rains, where *Telesto* was sometimes becalmed, sometimes boxing the compass in slight, vexing airs to the fourth degree of north. Then had come stronger easterlies, ferocious gales accompanied by chicken-strangling rainstorms and lightning displays worthy of the first portals of Hell to blow them south.

And once round the Cape of Good Hope, it was hard gales, black clouds and rain like buckshot, *Telesto* shrinking from fifteen hundred tons or so to the burthen of a rowboat, pitching and swooping like an errant water butt. It was sometimes reassuring that *Falconer's* consoled him in Item the Tenth under Winds that

> "Between the fouthern latitudes of 10 and 30 degrees in the Indian Ocean, the general trade wind about the S.E. by S. is found to blow all the year long in the fame manner as in the like latitudes in the Ethiopic ocean; and during the fix months from May to December, thefe winds do reach to within two degrees of the Equator; but during the other fix months, from November to June, a N.W. wind blows in the tract lying between the 3rd and 10th degree of fouthern lat-

itude, in the meridian of the north end of Madagafcar; and between the 2nd and 12th degree of fourth latitude, near the longitude of Sumatra and Java."

Lewrie was a bit leery, though, of the footnote from *Robert's Navigation*, that "the fwiftnefs of the wind in a great ftorm is not more than 50 to 60 miles in an hour; and a common brifk gale is about 15 miles an hour." He saw winds greater than that daily.

Once far enough north, they found the tract of wind which Falconer mentioned that ran like a racecourse between Madagascar and the African coast, fresh from the south sou'west, which at the Equator changed to the west sou'west.

And then came the Monsoon winds, which at that season of the year, were out of the sou'west in the Gulf of Bengal, none too gentle, either, as the late-year nor'east Monsoons would be. All in all, it was a horrid voyage for the most part. Captain Ayscough lit a fire under everyone's tails, and drove *Telesto* like Jehu drove his chariot, skating the ragged edge of being overpressed by the winds all the way, beating their way southerly along the coast of Africa below the Equator instead of taking the easier way over toward the Brazilian coast, as most Indiamen did.

Duty, sun sights, baking or boiling in tropic heat, shivering by turns in fear and cold, drenched to the skin in easterly gales and the air and water hot as a mug of "flip," sweltering in tarred tarpaulin foul-weather gear—weary enough to use his fingers to keep his eyes open in the middle watch, which was his by right of being junior-most officer.

"If I ever get back home, I'm going to become a farmer," he kept telling himself.

They smelled it before they could see it, even with a wind up their starboard quarter, in the last few hours of darkness before the sun burst above the horizon like an exploding howitzer shell. For a change, the winds were light, the seas calm and barely ruffled, barely heaving—more like lake sailing. *Telesto* gurgled and soughed instead of roaring and sloshing, her forefoot and cutwater under her bows parting almost still waters in a continuous, lazy surge.

"What the hell is that?" Lewrie wondered aloud, wiggling his nose like a beagle on a puzzling new trail. After six and a half months, barring the occasional port-call when they broke their passage at Oporto, Madeira and Table Bay at Capetown for hurriedly laden galley fuel, water and cargo, his olfactory senses had been brutalized by the stench of Ship. Tar and salt, fish-room, rancid cheeses and butter, salt-meats fermenting in brine, livestock in the manger, the odors of his fellow travelers below decks.

"Land, sir?" the middle watch quartermaster speculated from the huge double wheel, which now could be held and spun one-handed in the light airs.

Yes, there was a hint of coastline: rotting seaweed and the fishy aroma that most people called an ocean smell. But there was something else peeking from beneath that. A hint of cinnamon, pepper, coriander, almost like a Hungary Water that ladies dabbed on—perfume! First a tantalizing fantasy, then a real whiff.

"Flowers!" Alan yelped in glee. "Lots of green plants. And flowers! Ahoy, bow lookouts! See anything?"

"Nothin', sir!"

"Mister Hogue, leadsmen to the fore-chains. I think we're in soundings. Boy!" He directed the sleepy cabin servant–ship's boy on deck to turn the watch glasses on the half-hour bell. "Go aft and inform Captain Ayscough we're in soundings."

"Wake 'im oop, zir?" The boy yawned, stirred from his nap.

"Hell yes, wake him up. Witty, take a telescope and go aloft. It lacks two hours 'til sunrise, but you might be able to see something even so."

"A good morrow to you, Mister Lewrie," a voice called in the darkness. There was but a sliver of moon to see by, but Alan knew Ayscough's stern tones well by then. "Soundings, is it?"

"Smells hellish like it, sir. I've sent a man aloft with a glass, Mister Hogue, the master's mate, and hands to the forechains with the deep-sea leads. Last cast of the log showed just at five knots."

Ayscough came close by his side, clad in nightshirt and his watchcoat, his hair tousled by sleep. By the faint glow from the binnacle lanterns Alan could see him close his eyes and sniff deep.

"*Patchouli,*" Ayscough muttered, smiling fondly. "Perfumed tresses. Perfumed mustaches. Cooking *ghee*. Jungle forests and a million flowers opening. Charcoal-burners, garbage-middens, sacred cow and elephant dung. Exotic attars and shite. India, at last!"

"Hun-drayed faa-thim!" a leadsman in the chains sang out slowly. "One hunn-drayd faa-thim t' this liine!"

"Six and a half months," Alan chuckled. "A damned fine voyage!"

"A dam' fast voyage, you mean," Ayscough commented, leaving his pleasant reverie. "T'only joy of it was passing those 'John Company' Indiamen like they were anchored fast in the Pool of London! Still, it had its moments. Proper navigation cut weeks off it. One thing I picked up from an evening with Jemmy Trevenen and Captain King of *Resistance* during the war."

"I met King once, sir, at Turk's Island."

"Did you indeed? Clever men. Most masters would stagger from landfall to landfall, you know," Ayscough mused. "Way over to here, double the distance of their passage, just 'cause that's the way they learned how to do so. But, with a reliable chronometer, the skills at plotting position, one may cut the odd corner now and then, taking the unknown shorter way. Most of 'em'd be satisfied if they could hug the coast. Like breaking across the Atlantic to the West Indies. Know that ninety percent of the ships still fall as far to the suth'rd as the latitude of Dominica, then cross due west to make their landfall? Just 'cause Dominica's peaks are a sure seamark one cannot miss. When the Trades are the same south of Cape Verde, and one could scuttle across diagonally and save a week. A week, sir!"

"As we have, sir," Alan agreed, toadying a little.

"Hope you learned a little, then, Mister Lewrie. Something to consider on future commissions. Boy, go run and wake the master Mister Brainard," Ayscough directed. "Tell him, my compliments, and we're in soundings of the Hooghly Bar. Hundred fathom now, and I desire his expertise before the coast begins shoaling."

" 'Iss, zir," the boy replied, a trifle dubious he could remember all those "break-teeth" words in one sitting.

"Fiive an' ninety faa-thim!" a leadsman crowed loud as single rook on a foggy moor morning. "Fiive an' ninety faa-thim t' this line! Bott-tim o' grey mudd!"

"Grey mud, aye," Ayscough grunted in familiar pleasure. "Just what I'd expect. Hmm, five knot y'did say, Mister Lewrie? Pipe up to six by sunrise, if I'm any judge of these waters. Have the bosun pipe 'all-hands' at the change of watch. We'll take in t'gallants and feel our way in gently same time's we scrub decks. Coffee?"

"I'd admire some, yes sir."

"I'll send you a mug once my steward's brewed up a pot for me and Mister Brainard," Ayscough said as he was leaving. "Good thinking on the leadsmen and the overhead lookout, Mister Lewrie."

"Thankee, sir," Alan replied to the departing back. Ayscough was not lavish with his compliments. To earn even that slight, grudging notice was as much approval as most men would get from him in a full three years' commission. Indeed, a red-letter morning for him!

Low marshes. Swaying oceans of reeds straggling off to dryer ground. And heat. Harsh, crushing, damp heat worthy of a washerwoman's boiling, steaming tub of laundry water and the fire that stoked it, the sort of fire that could melt iron and forge artillery.

Once past the Hooghly Bar and into the river proper, Lewrie envied the hands aloft, up where the wind still filled the sails. On deck, it was hot as the hinges of Hell, and the pounded tar between the deck planks softened and ran sluggish and shiny as treacle.

"My God!" he cursed, mopping his face with a sleeve. Under his cocked hat, his hair was plastered to his head with perspiration, and sweat glued his shirt and breeches to his body.

"Serge or broadcloth!" Brainard sniffed, taking a rest from dashing about the decks from one beam to another to take sights on distant spires or landmarks, from tasting and sniffing at what the waxed plumb of the sounding lines brought up. "You dress like you was paradin' on the Strand in all that heavy clothin', you'll be dead as mutton by sundown, mark my words, sir. Think you have to look like an officer all the time? Think the hands wouldn't recognize your phyz by now? Shuck or die."

"Gladly," Alan agreed, doffing his blue wool officer's coat and serge waist-coat. They collapsed in wet bundles on the baking deck where he threw them—almost left puddles, he imagined. He tore his neck-cloth loose as well. And almost shivered with relief as a puff of wind touched his skin.

"Once we're anchored, there's ten thousand good tailors ashore glad to run you up some lighter clothes. Duck or serge de Nimes. I prefer the lightest Madrassi cotton, meself. You and your man hire a *darzee*. Won't cost more'n a half a crown for him to run you up a coat. Waist-coat, too, if you really feel you need one. But I tell you I'd not wear one before sunset," Brainard cautioned.

Twigg and Wythy were on deck, taking their ease in canvas chairs atop the poop, screened from the sun by an awning below the boom of the spanker. The servant Ajit Roy was now bare from the knees down, clad in only a loose pair of *pyjammy* trousers, a sleeveless white cotton shirt that billowed free round his waist and his turban. He was trotting out fresh lemon-water, while another man they'd hired off a passing native boat, as flimsy an excuse for a craft as Alan had ever seen, worked the rope of a *pankah* to fan them and keep the flies off.

"We've made good progress, even so," Alan said, unbuttoning his shirt down to his navel to let the light winds play with him.

"Aye," Brainard sighed, wiping his own face. "Quarter-point to larboard on your helm, quartermaster. 'Less things have changed much, there's shoals yonder I'd admire we didn't strike. Ah, there! D'you see that lump of reddish rock yonder? Looks like a squashed anthill?"

"Aye, sir," Alan replied, raising a telescope. Just over the tops of the trees, he could barely make out something more substantial than the foetid coastal lowlands and marshes.

"Fort William. Be anchored by sunset, if the wind holds," the sailing master told him. "Pity the poor Frogs. Their Bengal trading factory is far up-river from ours. Chandernargore. Even worse a sail to get there. It's a wonder they kept it after the last war."

"Hello, here comes somebody," Lewrie said, pointing to a small ship that had appeared in mid-channel, shimmering like a mirage in the heat waves. "On her way down to the sea. What is she, sir? Venetian?"

"Ha, appears to be! Local built. Good God! Haven't seen a ship like that in a long time." Brainard laughed. "Most country ships out here are built outa good, hard teak wood. Lasts forever. Seen a well-cared-for ship last a century out here, whilst good English oak rots away in five years. She's like an old Venetian caravel, she is. Mighta been felucca or dhow-rigged once. See, below the crossed spars? How she carries fore'n'aft sails on lateeners? Good to windward this time of year. Probably started life as an oared galley God knows how long ago, and got rebuilt over the years."

"I don't recognize the flag, though, sir."

"Ah, hmm. House flag. Part Portugee, part Parsee. Sharp businessmen, they are. Sort of Arabs." Brainard sighed wistfully.

Old and shabby she might be, Alan thought, but she was definitely exotic. Exotic in the extreme, just like everything they had seen in the last two days on their slow passage up the Hooghly. There were people working in fields in turbans and *dhotis*. Oxdrawn carts with only one axle and squealing, ungreased wheels one could hear nearly a mile away, with loads piled prodigiously high swaying along slowly. *Dak bungalows* here and there, a day's slow bullock-cart travel apart.

Elephants bathing and splashing mud on their broad backs on the river bank, their *mahouts* watching for snakes and crocodiles. Women in *sarees*, long head-cloths or cotton shawls out pounding clothing on the banks. Occasionally around some larger town or village, there were men doing the same labor, the *dhobees* from a prosperous house.

A rare Buddhist priest in a saffron robe and his begging bowl. More often Hindu priests. A local *rajah* or rich trader with his procession of loaded *gharies*, his retinue of gaudily dressed mercenary soldiers on horseback. Curtained sedan chairs borne by sweating lower-caste men that might contain a *babu*, a fat native clerk, or a *patchouli*-scented courtesan. And once, to Burgess Chiswick's delight, a column of infantry on the march. Exotic, they were, too, to one used to the sight of an English regiment. Red coats, white *pyjammy* trousers, white cross-belts, sandals and *kurtaa* shirts. Brown Bess muskets held at shoulder arms, cocked hats with neck-cloths bouncing against their necks to keep off the fierce sun and not a stitch more of European clothing on their backs. But they were well-closed-up and marching to fifes and drums, their English officers riding stocky native horses with their bearers trotting alongside.

And India did smell, as Ayscough had said: smelled powerfully. Flowers, green sap, perfume and spice—cooking aromas that made the driest mouth water. And rot and corruption, too. There was nothing about the place that could be considered a halfway measure. It was a place of strong, almost violent contrasts, and they hadn't even set foot ashore yet to discover one percent of them. Try to acclimate on the last stretch of the voyage as they could, the first sight of Calcutta set everyone's mind into a hopeless spin.

The harbor and the city banks were as busy as the Pool of London, with hundreds of ships anchored, everything from stately "John Company" Indiamen to ancient copies of galleons, from the largest to the smallest riverine trading ships. Hide-built coracles and rowing boats worked in a plague from the *ghats* built up along the river bank. Warehouses and docks stretched as far as the eye could see, with reddish Fort William brooding over it all, and behind the *ghats* there were pleasure gardens as gay as Covent Garden or Ranelagh, spacious as St. James' or Hyde Park, where in one moment rich men rode in their carriages or strolled slowly, and the next, a lower-caste *mehtar* would dash by carrying his bucket of excrement to be dumped. Behind the European quarter, the cantonment where it was adjudged safe to live, there were native quarters, teeming with life crowded elbow to elbow from sunrise to sunset, except in the hottest parts of the day. Sacred cows strolled oblivious through the greenest, lushest cricket pitch anyone had ever laid eyes on while the players waited for their bearers to shoo them away, gently and without offense. Native markets hummed and buzzed with commerce, and smoke rose from cooking fires, fires where brass and bronzeware was molded and hammered, where hides were tanned or clothes washed. It was all of London crammed into half the area, still huge enough to daunt almost all of them from going ashore into such an exotic alienness.

They found a safe anchorage where *Telesto* would have room to moor, and dropped the best bower anchor. The sails were clewed up to the yards, then brailed up and secured with harbor gaskets for the first time since Capetown. Yards lowered slowly, and squared away Navy fashion. A stream anchor was lowered from the stern and rowed out to keep her from swinging afoul of another ship. The sun awnings were rigged across the decks, and, unlike Navy fashion, would be left deployed day and night, instead of being taken in each day at sundown, for they provided some protection from the rains that would come during this season.

"Very well, Mister Choate. Dismiss the hands," Ayscough said after the last bit of tidying and straightening had been done to his, the bosun's and the first officer's satisfaction.

"Um, the matter of shore leave, sir," Choate ventured.

"Firewood and water first, Mister Choate. Ready the ship

for sea should it become necessary, then we'll consider it," the captain grunted, though his own nose was twitching to get ashore.

"Bosun, watering party!" Choate yelled.

"Excuse me if I suggest something," Twigg interrupted, coming down from his regal perch on the poop deck with his servant in tow. "You'll want to rinse out the ship's water barrels, of course. I'd suggest boiling water for that."

"Er, they are a bit foul, sir, even being sluiced at Capetown not so long ago," the purser chuckled. "A bit on the *tan* side, our water is."

"Yes, see to it. And from *my* prior experience, all the water we take aboard should be boiled first. Else it'll come out of this river," Ayscough harrumphed. They had all seen the garbage floating in the Hooghly, the excrement dumped, thankfully downstream from the city and their anchorage.

"You read my mind, sir," Twigg replied with a slight bow and a twitch of those tight lips of his. "Further, though. It is *my* experience in Asian waters that thin gauze should be procured for insect netting, if not for each hand to swath about his hammock, then at least for the hatches that lead below. I do not know why, nor do any physicians of my past acquaintance, but the incidence of *malaria* is much reduced if this is done."

"As long as it does not come out of ship's funds, though . . ." the purser objected. "Why, the Navy Board's . . ."

"Silence," Twigg snapped, raising a hand in warning. "And I tire of reminding you, sir, that I and Mister Wythy are funding this vessel? You may not care about the health of the men in your charge, but I do. If only for the inability to find trained seamen enough in India to replace the ones who die. And die they will, in job lots, no matter what precautions we may take."

"I merely meant . . ." the purser stammered on, red-faced.

"I'll speak to you in my cabins later, Mister Abernathy," the captain snapped. "Do what . . . our *owners* suggest."

After witnessing that entertaining exchange at the expense of "Mr. Nip-cheese," as Abernathy and most pursers were termed, Lewrie went to the larboard bulwarks to stare at the *ghats* that led down to the river in terraced steps. He'd seen insect netting used before in the West Indies, and sickly as that region was, he'd expected nothing less of the East Indies. Besides, he consoled himself, I've had the Yellow Jack once before, and everyone said back on Antigua that once you survived it, you couldn't get it again. He rubbed the top of his left arm where the family surgeon had punctured him over and over and made him howl with pain and terror even before he was out of nappies, to inoculate him against the smallpox. There were two major risks of the tropics taken care of. As for the rest, he was young, healthy as a rutting yearling bull, wasn't he? He was well-off financially, an established English gentleman—his kind was bloody immortal!

As for other diseases, he'd sleep with the nets, drink nothing but imported wine or ale, make sure his water was boiled first should he be forced to drink such a dull beverage—perhaps nothing but tea, he speculated. One had to boil tea-water if one wanted a decent pot.

Food could be washed in boiled water, he supposed, and anyway, there was salt-meat to fall back on. And he would take his sheep-gut condom ashore with him, should he ever be allowed ashore. Twigg and Wythy hadn't snarled at him in the last two months, so he supposed he had outlasted their anger at him. He'd not been allowed ashore at Oporto, Madeira or Capetown. Surely, he'd touch land—and a few other softer things—here in Calcutta!

Chapter 2

With so many hired stevedores, and those working for less than anyone could credit, the cargo was finally landed in their warehouse and factory ashore. Twigg and Wythy went with it, thank the good Lord, to establish their putative trading firm. *Telesto* rode higher out of the water. Firewood and water were brought aboard and stowed away. A distillery was established at the factory to supply them daily. Crates of chickens, small flocks of goats and sheep were hoisted aboard for fresh meat. The crew complained about the lack of juicy fresh beef, no matter the explanations that cattle were a protected species to Hindoos. The passengers had left the first day, Burgess Chiswick included. They'd shared one last bumper of claret and then he was off to Fort William for his assignment with the East India Company's army. There were some more chores that Captain Ayscough wished performed before shore leave would be allowed. The ship was smoked and scoured below decks, the bilges pumped clean and the many rats that had come aboard with the cargo hunted down and dispatched, or at least thinned out. Rigging had to be re-rove to replace spliced or storm-raveled cordage; sails had to be patched. Cosmetics about the look of the ship could go hang for a while, but she must be made ready in all respects to go to sea at a moment's notice before the hands were to be allowed a monumental rut or two.

Finally, after six days of labors, Ayscough summoned all hands aft and announced that he was pleased enough to let them have leave.

"Now this is a *rupee*," Tom Wythy said, counting out coins on his desk in the factory offices ashore, while Alan fidgeted and wriggled with impatience. "Worth about fifteen *rupees* to the pound sterling. You run across a gold coin, that's a *mohur*. Same as a guinea."

"Aye, sir."

"Think of a *rupee* as a strong shilling. Now these are *annas*. Like pence, but sixteen to the *rupee*. Have you got that so far, sir?"

"Aye, I think so, Mister Wythy," Alan almost groaned.

"And *pyce* are like ha'pennies—four to the *anna*. You'll be amazed how cheap things are here in Calcutta."

"How much—I say *kit nah*?" Alan recited. "*Bahut mehanga* is too much. God help me if the bastard wants to haggle, though, I'm flat out of the lingo."

"Round the port, Fort William and the European canton-ment, ye'll find enough *bazaar-wallahs* and *bunniahs* who savvy English," Wythy growled. "Their stores and stalls'd die if they couldn't. Mind now, ye'll be safer not goin' into the na-tive quarters without a guide or bearer. *Yih achcha jaga naheen, sahib!* A no good place, 'specially for a *feringhee* such as y'self. End up with yer purse lifted, poxed to the eyebrows by some *cutch*-whore, or knifed in an alley by some *bud-mashes*."

"The third officer and I, and my man Cony, will go together, sir," Alan assured him. "Swords for all, and a pocket pistol each."

"Good thinking," Wythy allowed. "Well, ye're on yer own, God help ye. Enjoy."

Enjoy, Alan did! Though for the first few minutes, he wasn't sure he could walk. He'd not been off a ship's deck for over six months, rocketing from beam to beam in storms, perma-nently heeled over in strong winds, and used to the motion of a ship. Even during their brief port stays, *Telesto* still snubbed at her cables, lifted and rolled gently to tide or off-shore breezes, and heavy as she was, was never still.

Once outside, they'd headed up one of the major thorough-fares, aiming for a grove of monstrous trees they couldn't rec-ognize, anxious for some shade, but they simply couldn't attain them.

The land was so still, yet it seemed to heave and roll, to yaw to windward like a ship with too much weather-helm! Alan found himself paying off to leeward, staggering and shambling as if he'd just put down half a dozen bottles of wine. Colin McTaggart and Cony were not much help, either. Either they were staggering on the opposite tack, crossing under his hawse and threatening to trip him up, or they were bearing down on each other in collision.

Holding on to each other to raft up for mutual support wasn't such a good idea, either, for they tugged in opposite directions even standing still!

"God, 'elp me, Mister Lewrie, sir!" Cony wailed. "H'an't nivver been *land*-sick afore, but h'it's acomin' over me 'ellish strong, damme'f h'it h'ain't!"

"Perhaps if we closed our eyes," McTaggart suggested, his dark tan turning very pale. "Noo, that's nae the way."

Alan had tried that, but as soon as he did, the canals of his ears began to swirl like milk in a butter-churn, making him feel as if he were spiraling out of the sky like a well-shot duck!

"Can't be the cholera, or *malaria*, could it?" Alan paled.

"Nae sa soon, surely not!" McTaggart sighed. "An ale shop up yonder. Let's hae us a sit-doon, for the love o' God!"

A few milds, and some time safely ensconced in solid chairs seemed to help abate the reeling.

"Looks as if we're not the only ones suffering," Alan pointed out. Three hands off another ship were short-tacking up the walks in front of the European shops on the far side of the street, careering from storefront to the verge of the curbing in a series of short tacks from beam to beam quick as a regatta of tiny pleasure boats on the Thames. One grizzled bosun followed them; older and wiser to the predicament, he trailed the fingers of his right hand along the buildings for a reference point, groping like a blind man.

They espied several others who did not suffer *mal de terre* as badly, these bucketing along normally as any other pedestrian, but with the rolling gait of a long-passage sailorman.

Once the symptoms abated somewhat, they found their tailor, a *darzee* named Gupta, who measured them and ran up their requirements. Light, locally loomed cotton shirts, duck waist-coats light as number 8 serge de Nimes sailcloth for use in the softest weathers. He could supply *cummerbunds* to wrap about their waists, which he assured them was a healthy thing to do, purvey hats in European styles made of tightly woven straw that let their scalps breathe, but kept off the cruel sun.

Alan fingered a bolt of cloth, a very light, almost metallic mid-blue fabric that shone richly as the light struck it. Gupta went into raptures, assuring him it would make a coat as fine as any *rajah* wore, rich as the Great Moghul himself in distant Delhi, and only *"paintis, burra-sahib!"* Only thirty-five *rupees*, heroic as Alan's stature was. Brass buttons extra, of course. Alan knocked him down to thirty *rupees*, and fabric-covered buttons, and ordered more in silver-grey, and pale blue. Two pounds sterling each for a coat, he marveled, that a titled lord would gladly shell out fifty guineas for back in London, if he could get it!

He outfitted Cony with a straw hat, *cummerbund* and lighter cotton shirts, and a dark blue duck jacket to take the place of his wool sailor's jacket. Brass buttons one *rupee* extra, of course.

Then they were off for a tour of the *bazaar*.

"My God, it truly is Puck's Fair!" Alan exclaimed. It was as grand a sight everywhere he looked as the most intriguing raree-shows he had ever paid to see back home in England, and it was all free to the eye here!

There were rickety stalls spilling over with flower garlands and necklaces, with bundles of blooms the like of which he had never seen or smelled. There were ivory carvers to watch, wood carvers to admire. Strange, multi-armed little statues in awkward dance poses to haggle over. Rug merchants and weavers sewing *dhurries* from Bengali cotton, or imported fur. Persian or Turkey carpets down from the highlands of the northwest with their eye-searing colors and intricate designs.

In another corner were grouped the brass and copper wares: here gem cutters, there gold and silversmiths. In between were stalls heaped with fruits, vegetables and livestock. Now and then, there would be a cooking stall with the most enticing steams and spices wafting into their parched nostrils. Doves and snipe, ducks and wild fowl, chickens flapping as they hung upside down by one leg from overhead poles prior to sale.

There were pet birds in cages, colorful and noisy. Monkeys on leashes. And there were elephants actually being ridden by a man! Some working-plain, but a rare few painted with symbols and caparisoned as rich as a medieval knight's steed, adrape in silks and satins, real gold tassels and silver medals, brocades with little mirrors winking from knitted rosettes, and crowned with feathered plumes and bejewelled silk caps. And camels swaying under heavy loads!

There were sword-swallowers and sword-dancers beguiling the shuffling throngs for tossed money. Snake charmers tootling on flutes as they swayed in unison with deadly cobras. There were jugglers and acrobats, magicians and dancers, some young boys as beautiful as virgin brides who pirouetted to the enthusiastic clapping and cheers of a circle of onlookers, ankle bangles and bells jingling, with their eyes outlined lasciviously with *kohl*. There were girls in tight bodices and loose, gauzy skirts with their midriffs bare, the skirts and the gauze head-dresses flying out behind them as they danced, showing more to the amazed and love-starved eyes of him and his companions than most husbands would ever get to see of their wives back home in England!

There were puppet shows, the *rajah* and *ranee* version of Punch and Judy. There were groups of singers, street-theatre troupes up on flimsy stages ranting some historical or religious dramas. Or they might have been comedies—Alan couldn't tell.

And India wasn't all of a piece, either. Calcutta was a rich trading town. So down from the mountains inland, there were Afridis and Pathans, Nepalis and ancient Aryans, Persian-looking Moghuls, all with their *pyjammy* trousers stuffed into ornamented boots with love locks dangling from beneath their *puggarees*. They bore curved swords and knives with little bells jingling from their hilts. Poor *zamindars* in town to sell their produce, rich landowners shopping for bargains among the imported European items. Hindoos and Muslims, Jains, Sikhs, Parsees and the rare Buddhist. In time, Alan might learn to tell the difference between them, as well as the difference between the Bengali majority and the visiting Dravidians, Mahrattas, Dogras, the people from Assam and Nagaland to the east, the Tamils of the southeast and the harsher people who hailed from the Oudh north of the Vindhaya Hills, the great dividing line between permanently conquered India, and semi-autonomous India that the Aryans and the Moghuls had never been able to rule for long.

"Worth the voyage, I swear," Alan exclaimed as they sat in the shade of a tree, munching on dates, sugared almonds and pistachios.

"Aye, 'tis a rare land, I'll grant," McTaggart agreed as he essayed his first banana, after watching the natives to see if one took the bright yellow husk off first, or ate it entire. Colin was Calvinist-Presbyterian dour most of the time, over-educated like most Scots compared to their English counterparts who thought that too much intelligence was a dangerous thing, but could be nudged to enthusiasm now and again, enough to prove that he was human. "But with food sae cheap, how do ye explain sae many mendicants?"

Besides the exotic pleasures of the *bazaar*, there was the irritation of seeing so many poor, so many beggars minus a limb, an eye, covered with running ulcers. So many people barely clad in a ragged, filthy *dhotee* and *puggaree* who couldn't even afford the cheap but well-made sandals the *mochees* nimbly cut from their sheets of leather.

"Speaking of mendicants," Alan said, sighing, as a pair of beggars appeared near them, one limping grandly on a crutch, one leg gone, and the other sightless—one eye rolling madly and the other flat gone, with the empty socket exposed.

"*Naheen*, yer buggers!" Cony snapped, feeling protective of his people. "*Juldi jao!*" And the beggars sheered off. Under the amputee's robes, Alan could almost spot a leg and a foot, bound to the man's backsides. "Fakin' h'it, Mister Lewrie. Fakin . . . 'r maimed o'purpose."

"God's teeth, Cony, where'd you pick up such mastery of the language!" Alan marveled.

"Been talkin' t' that servant, Ajit Roy, sir," Cony replied, flushing. "Y'pick up a word'r two 'ere an' there, ya do, sir. An' Ajit done warned me h'about some o' the shams they kin get up to, sir. Lame their own kiddies t' make 'em look pitiable, worse'n Midland gypsies."

"But what did ye say ta them?" McTaggart inquired.

"*Naheen*, that's 'no,' plain as day, sir. *Juldi jao* is kinda like 'bugger off,' sir," Cony replied, getting sheepish.

"Ye'r a man o' many parts, Cony," McTaggart said, praising with an appreciative chuckle. "Lucky our Lewrie is, ta hae yer services."

Long as I don't have to pay him more than I do already, Alan thought, chiming in with verbal appreciation as well.

Cony's paltry vocabulary came in handy once more on their way back to Fort William's wide *maidan*, the drill ground, and the quieter regions of the European quarter. Frankly, after wandering about the *bazaar* and its many twists and turns, they were lost.

They could see one of the fort's ramparts down the length of a narrow, meandering lane of small two-story mud houses, and decided to take a shortcut. Music was more prominent in this quarter. *Sitars* and flutes, palms beating alien rhythms on *madals* that Alan couldn't quite get the gist of no matter how hard he tried. The music was mildly irritating to a European ear, but oddly pleasing after a little while. One more wonder to be savored of this grand experience paid for with so much labor, terror, drudgery and misery at sea—savored for its difference even if it had been noxious.

Several girls leaned out of doorways along the narrow street and came out to greet them, making the two-handed gesture of greeting and bowing gracefully to them.

"Namasté, burra-sahibs. Namasté!"

"Namasté," Alan replied, feeling foolish giving them the two hands at brow level just to be polite, encumbered as he was with his little basket of nuts and fruits.

*"Hamare ghalee ana, achcha, din,"** one lovely maiden intoned, giving him an appraising grin. Milk-coffee brown, not a minute above eighteen or so, bounteous breasts bound in by a snug sateen minijacket, bangles on her wrists and ankles, midriff tapering to tininess above taut but womanly hips contained in a sash and series of gauzy skirts. Her hair was long, loose and fly-away-curly under a gauze *chudder* head-cloth that hung to her hips, weighted down with little gold coins. *"Meré sath chalenghé, burra-sahib?"*† she cooed.

"Good God, Lewrie, ye dinna think . . ." McTaggart almost strangled in shocked prudery as the girl and her equally lovely compatriots wriggled their hips slow and sultry, comfirming their suspicions.

"Whores, aye they are, Colin. Bit broad in the stern-quarters for my liking," Alan replied, appraising them coolly. "And damn near strangle a man with those stout little legs of theirs. Suppose it's the fashion in the East. Still . . ."

"Man, ye canna be considerin' . . ." McTaggart gargled, turning red as a throttled turnip.

"Saat rupee, burra-sahib," the girl whispered invitingly.

"'A's seven o' them Hindoo shillin's, sir," Cony supplied in an even voice, feeling in his *cummerbund* for loose change between the folds. That little maid back in London had had a powerful effect on him. "Might be a bit steep, sir."

"And peppered wi' the pox ta her very brows!" McTaggart gasped. "Ye may count on it. Tell her 'No thank ye'!"

"Ham bahut kaam hai, girl," Cony told her. "We're busy, don't ya know? But . . ."

*"Good day, come into our street." Traditional whores' greeting.
†"Will you come with me, great lord?"

"Not to my taste, Cony. However, she might be to yours," Alan allowed. "We could meet you at the *darzee*'s."

"Thankee, sir," Cony replied, brightening. "*Main phir laut kar ahoongaa.* Be back later, girl. *Teen rupee?* Three, darlin'? Make it easy on a poor sailor."

"*Chha rupee,*" the girl demanded, and she wouldn't go any lower than six, much as Cony wheedled "*panch*" or "*chaar*"—five or four.

Cony finally sighed and they proceeded on down the street, accompanied by the derisive shouts of the spurned girl. "*Cutch-admi! Banchuts! Sastaa banchuts! Jahntee!*"*

"None too thrilled, sounds like," Alan said with a grin, enjoying himself hugely.

"What's she saying?"

"From the sound of it, I'd say it's something close to 'cheap bastards,' Mister McTaggart. Right, Cony?"

"Ajit, 'e didn't learn me none o' that, sir," Cony admitted. "'Spect I'd better 'ave me another lesson'r two."

They got back to the docks and the factor's offices just after midday, glad for the coolness of the mud-bricked walls and thick tile roof. Wythy had told them most white men took up the practice of napping through the heat of the afternoon and not stirring out until the sun was beginning to descend below the lowest yard-arms. To one so lazy as Lewrie if left to his own devices, it sounded like a marvelous invention. He had just found a bale of cotton on which to doze off when Burgess Chiswick came to look him up.

"Damme, but you look hellish dashing," Alan said in greeting. Chiswick was now clad in a red serge coat with broad white turnback lapels and cuffs, the uniform coat of the East India Company, with many figured buttonholes and brass buttons. A gorget of officer's rank hung on his upper breast, and each shoulder bore a silvered chainmail patch of rank, which could also turn a swordcut from above. "An ensign in 'John Company' now, are you?"

"A captain, no less, Alan!" Burgess preened. "In charge of the light company of our battalion. Can you imagine it?"

"By God, how bloody grand for you!" Alan laughed, shaking his hand warmly. "Here now, do I dine you out tonight in celebration, or is it your treat to 'wet down' your promotion?"

*"Poor [excuses for] men! Scum! Cheap scum! Oh, one pubic-hairs!"

"Oh, I've already been dined in at our mess," Burgess replied, fanning himself with his black cocked hat. "Good bunch of rogues, they are, let me tell you. Settled into my quarters. Been swotting up my Hindee with my bearer, Nandu. I'm the only white officer in the company, you know. Rest are natives. God, you should dine at my *bungalow*. My own private bloody house, if you can feature it! And cheap at the price, too. Whole squad of servants. Well, I share it with another officer, but it's so damned huge! You must see it. Had a chance to get leave yet?"

"Just this morning, and more to come once the sun's down tonight. Cony and I spotted a little street near here full of whores. Thought I might go back . . ."

"*Cutch*-whores," Burgess sniffed, having picked up the language awfully fast, a lot faster than Alan had. "Fessenden, the other captain I share the house with, has three native girls in his *bibikhana*. His own bloody harem! Rent clean un's cheaper by the month than an hour or two with the public girls! Or just buy 'em outright."

"By God, I could get to love the East Indies!" Alan exclaimed in delight, knocked back on his heels by the possibilities.

"But, why I'm here. Met my battalion major when I was dined in, and he's asked me to supper at his *bungalow* this evening. And he extends an invitation to you as well."

"Now why the devil would he do that for me?" Alan wondered.

"I mentioned your name whilst I was giving my record," Burgess replied. "That business at Yorktown, the siege and our escape in those barges you cobbled into sea-worthy boats came up, and once he heard your name, he was dead keen on hearing the whole thing, start to finish. And when I told him you were fourth officer in the ship that brought me out here, he perked up sharp as a fox-hound, damned near ordered me to bring you round."

"Stap me if that don't sound hellish like somebody in this world thinks I'm famous for something," Alan exclaimed, beaming, still a little bemused by the whole thing, but eager for a chance to shine with his betters—*and* a shot at free victuals. God knew he'd had little of either in the last year. "So who is this fellow?"

"Major Sir Hugo Willoughby," Burgess informed him. "He was once in the 4th Regiment of Foot, the King's Own.

Knighted after Gibraltar in the Seven Years' War. Can you imagine a hero such as he taking service with 'John Company'?"

"Oh," Alan replied weakly, positively shivering with dread. No, it can't be him, not out here, he thought.

"Heard of him, have you?"

"We've met," Alan allowed, turning pale. Has to be some imposter using the name, some *poseur* who can pull the sham off for a safe, profitable billet out here in the back of the beyond.

"Back in London, or during the war in the Caribbean?"

"London," Alan admitted.

"Know him well, then? I say, Alan, you look a trifle . . ." Burgess pried, his suspicions aroused by Lewrie's sudden discomposure.

"Well enough, I suppose, Burgess," Alan confessed. "See, unless there's two of 'em in this world, he's my bloody father."

Chapter 3

The old boy ain't done half bad for himself, Alan had to admit as he partook of their regal meal. Officers of the East India Company, military or civilian, had to provide their own quarters unless they lived in collegiate commons in the rougher posts such as Bencoolen on Sumatra, or some tax-gathering fort far inland. And cheap as things seemed to be so far in India, the house must have set him back a pretty penny or two.

They were dining on the second floor in a great room that ran the entire length of the building, and overlooked the huge courtyard where the horses were stabled and the carriage was kept, a courtyard aromatic with flowering bushes and trees. The lower level was kitchens, guest bedrooms, office and library. The *bungalow* was large enough for a rajah's palace, Hindoo-Moghul style, more like a fairytale Persian fortress, set in a plot of ground that would have served for a small park back home. The floors were highly polished teak on the second floor, up where the breezes were, tile and marble on the lower level. The furnishings were a mixture of transportable military-functional, or Chinee filigreed mahogany, much like the Chippendale styles that were growing popular back in London just before Lewrie left.

Sir Hugo's *major-domo*, an older Bengali in full regimental fig—obviously his personal bearer as well—stood by the sideboards to oversee the meal, while younger males, some no more than stripling lads, neatly dressed in native styles, served as *khitmatgars* to wait on table, one for every two guests. Silver candelabras, bowls and serving plates for the removes and made dishes made a parade up and down the long table, alongside the brass-ware. The plates were also Chinee in the latest Canton export pattern.

109

They dined—they being Sir Hugo, Alan, Mr. Twigg and his partner Mr. Wythy, Captain Ayscough and Burgess Chiswick—on a pleasing mixture of the familiar and the novel. They had started with a rich oxtail soup, just like they would have back in England. But that had been followed by a spicy chillie omelet, then a prosaic fish dish. The *khitmatgars* next trotted out *jangli murgee* and *teetar*, jungle game hens and partridge, baked *tanduri* style, with removes of mashed curried peas and carrots, fried "lady-finger" okra and *pulao* rice. They had the traditional beef course, though stringy and hard to chew, possibly a recently expired munitions *tonga* ox.

But then had come *shami kabab*, thick coinlike slabs of highly peppered minced mutton, with lentils, and instead of the thick, soft spade-shaped *nan* bread, the servers passed *chapattis*. And then came the last dish, the goat curry, with the *sambals* of blanched, slivered almonds, shredded fresh coconut, mango and coconut *chautnee* and a dozen more things Alan couldn't identify, but made such a pleasingly hot, sweet, crunchy blend of textures and flavors.

Since they were in Calcutta, in the middle of Bengal with all its sugarcane, they had a choice of desserts fetched out on a teak and silver cart. Alan opted for *khir*, a thick white milk and rice custard, flavored with a glutinous sugar and lemon juice syrup.

Finally, the tablecloth was removed, the port and cheese and extra fine biscuit set out, along with a silver bowl of assorted sweet or salted nut-meats, and the servants left.

"Sorry if I turn this splendid occasion into a *durbar*," Twigg began, sighing in ecstasy as he eased his waistband and *cummerbund*. "But I thought a conference in social settings might be less noticeable than something more formal at Fort William or aboard ship. Do you know if any of your house-servants speak English, Sir Hugo?"

"Chandra, my personal bearer, no others," Major Willoughby replied. "And that, only a few phrases."

"Excellent!" Twigg barked, obviously much happier with native foods in his belly, and a superior port making the rounds. "Well, I suppose you must have been wondering why your regiment was chosen to deal with us."

"Obviously, Mister Twigg, you wish military forces that can cross the *kala panee*, the ocean, without breaking their caste," Major Willoughby replied. "Something involving your trading ship, the *Telesto*. You're not really a country ship, are you?

Else you'd not have had Warren Hasting's ear over in Fort William and gotten 'John Company' to cooperate with you. So this is something *palatikal*. And, I trust, secret, hmm?"

"Well, I'll be blowed!" Tom Wythy rasped out, his face red as a beet from the heat, the meal, and the cargo of wine he'd already put below decks. "Hope you're the only one that can puzzle us out so easily."

Never knew the old fart was so smart, Alan mused to himself. Damme if he ain't smart as paint! The old bastard.

"The *gup* making the rounds is you're something under the rose," Sir Hugo went on, his face wearing a pleased expression of being more in the know than he was supposed to be, that same look of smug self-satisfaction Alan had quailed at when he was living under the same roof with the man. When Sir Hugo got pleased with himself, it usually meant a spell of the dirty for somebody else, and it was best to make one's self scarce as hen's teeth. "But, the other traders'll keep mum. Really now, gentlemen! Don't look so confounded! Big ship like yours, armed to the teeth, overmanned even by East India standards. And you arrived with a cargo that the Company snapped up at premium prices soon's it hit shore, for which I say thank God, for I bought more'n my share of it, and welcome your wines and brandies are out here. You're almost too late to make Canton for the trading season, September to March, even so, but early enough to keep an eye on all those Indiamen anchored out there in the Hooghly, loaded to the deck-heads as they are with *taels* of silver to trade for China goods."

"Well, I'm blowed," Wythy reiterated, mopping his face clear of moisture from the afterglow of a hearty, spicy supper.

"I see where your boy Lewrie gets his canniness, Sir Hugo," Twigg nodded somberly, his thin lips pressed together so snugly between sentences they almost turned white, and one could not have shoved a slim nail between them. Veins on his temples pulsed, betraying the obvious agitation he felt. "Aye, we are *palatikal*. And we do have to get to Canton. Or at least, to Lintin Island, before September."

Where the hell was this Lintin Island, Alan wondered, a little disappointed that he might not see the fabled Canton after all. He poured himself another glass of port as the bottle made the rounds, and munched on a handful of salted almonds and cashews. After six months of dull ship's fare, there was a gulf inside him that a week's suppers such as this one could only begin to fill.

"Lintin Island," Wythy grunted. "A right pirate's nest, aye."

"But what better place to search for French pirates?" Twigg commented. "They have as much need for deniability as we. So their ship, or ships, involved in this blood-thirsty trade among the native pirates have to be country ships like us, and need a place to unload their ill-gotten gains. English goods, looted from murdered crews. English ships disappeared, with no sign of their fate."

"Six, we were told before we sailed from Plymouth," Wythy said.

"More since," Twigg went on. "Governor Hastings told me today the count is up to ten. Well-armed ships, too. Indiamen, country ships, and the latest an Indiaman, the *Macclesfield*. Crew of nigh on two hundred, twenty-four guns, thirty super-cargo passengers. And over two-hundred-fifty-thousand pounds sterling to pay for teas and silks."

"Good God!" Sir Hugo paled. "I knew one of her officers. Gone, didje say?"

"Last reported passing through the Malacca Straits," Twigg told them. "Spoke a patrol cutter working out of Bencoolen not twenty leagues north of the Johore Straits where she would turn east into the South China Sea. Never reached Macao or the Pearl River estuary."

"Malay pirates," Sir Hugo suggested. "Or some Dyak head-hunters from Borneo."

"Usually we could assume that, or some nautical disaster. Fire, a dismasting gale, sir"—Twigg frowned even deeper than his usual wont—"but the weather was reported mostly fair, and no Indiaman'd get so close inshore she'd be prey to coasting *praos*. And even a lightly armed Indiaman in the open sea is more than a match for a fleet of pirate *praos*. Wythy?"

"Balignini pirates work out of Borneo. Swords, spears, blowguns with poison tips, some poor bows and arrows," Wythy informed them knowledgeably. "If they have cannon, they're old stone-shooters and slow to load. *Cutch*-powder, too. A nuisance, they are, mostly. Know better'n tangle with a proper European vessel lest they catch her at anchor. The Borneo princes subsidize 'em for loot and slaves. East of Borneo ye'll find the Moluccas, cross the Makasar Strait and the Celebes. Maluku pirates work from there, but it's a long reach to place 'em in the Johore Strait. And they're even worse equipped than the Balignini. Now there's the Sea Dyaks that work out of the Seribas and Skrang rivers. Might be a possibility, except I've never known a European they'd trust, or not turn on whoever gives them anything sooner or later. And, being fairly close to the Malay princes, who mostly stay on decent terms with 'John Company' because of trade, I can't see them doing it."

"Chinese, then, sir?" Alan dropped into the speculations.

"I'd rather hope so," Twigg sighed. "Else it's the Lanun Rovers. Pirates of the Illana Lagoon on Mindanao. Worst of the lot."

"Big *praos*, pretty well-armed, too. Go off on three-year raiding cruises like Berserker Vikings," Wythy agreed with distaste. "The Spanish can't do a thing with 'em. Last expedition from Manila to Mindanao got cut up pretty bad, so I hear tell. Yes, they could sail or row—they have what amounts to slave-galleys—anywhere they want. South China Sea, Malacca Straits, Gulf of Siam, Gulf of Tonkin and use the port of Danang among the Annamese if they've a mind."

"Bencoolen's done a fair job of suppressing Malay and Dyak piracy off Sumatra and in the Malacca Straits," Sir Hugo mused as he filled a church-warden pipe. "The Dutch keep a sharp eye on the seas to the west, I'm told. So, it's either the Chinese, or these Mindanao pirates."

"Perhaps a combination of both," Twigg rasped. "But, once we tangle with them, we'll know. By their weapons. Some booty they've taken from an English ship in their treasure-trove."

"Then we'll know whom to chastise," Captain Ayscough promised. "And chastise them, we shall. To the last root and branch."

"Take a fleet to do that, Captain Ayscough," Twigg said, turning to gaze at his captain. "Hard as it may be on your soul, 'tis not our brief to completely stamp out piracy in these waters."

Thank bloody Christ for that, Alan thought; sounds like one of Hercules' twelve damned labors. And poison arrows? Poison blowguns? Damme if I signed aboard for that, either!

"We're sure it's not the Dutch, nor would the Dutch turn a blind eye to someone encouraging and arming pirates," Twigg added. "Spain? Weak, plagued with problems in the Philippines as it is, their ships as much prey to these savage beasts as anyone. With more to lose, let me remind you. Without the annual treasure galleons, Spain suffers. I'd not expect a lot of help from them, but to sanction piracy? Not them!"

"That leaves the French!" Ayscough harrumphed, clawing the idle port decanter to him and pouring a crystal glass to knock back without tasting. Whatever drove him, Ayscough's hatred for the Frogs was hot as a well-stoked forge.

"Cunning bastards," Sir Hugo rumbled. "Had my fill of 'em in the last bit of the war out here. Helping Hyder Ali and his son Tippoo Sultan, skulking behind the scenes and urging them on to fight us, but never having the nutmegs to take us on in a real fight!"

"Aye, Sir Hugo, you find skullduggery in this world, and I'll lay you any odds you want, it'll be some modern-day *Richelieu* behind it!" Ayscough agreed hotly, spitting out the name of the old cardinal-schemer like a sour turd he'd dredged up in his soup. "The first to claim their superiority in this world like they're the Chosen People, but they're sneaking, low, vile, torturing monsters under all their silks and lace, their gilt and be-shit manners and their honeyed words! Oh, aye, 'tis sharper than a serpent's tooth, they are!"

"We shall find these pirates, Captain Ayscough, let me assure you." Twigg prophesied grimly, reaching out a hand like a taloned paw to pat the man on the shoulder. "And they will lead us to the Frenchmen behind this hideous plot. Then we'll have revenge enough for all."

After Ayscough had calmed down from his sudden fit, Sir Hugo blew a lazy cloud of smoke at the ceiling and refilled his brandy.

Ah, that's more like my old father, Alan thought—can't stir his arse up without a snifter in his hand!

"So you wish me to supply troops from my *pultan*, my regiment, for this expedition against the pirates, sir?" Sir Hugo asked.

"Yes," Twigg nodded. "They're low-caste, did you say?"

"The Nineteenth Native Infantry are mostly Bengalis," Sir Hugo informed them. "Not a bad lot of scrappers, though. No *brahmin*, no *kshatriya* and damme few *vaishya* caste. If any were, they were damned poor merchants, 'cause they came into the battalion with nothing but the clothes on their backs. No, they're almost all *sudras*. Serfs. *Ryots* or *zamindars* at best. Well, needs must in wartime, when we recruited anyone. And I suspect I've an Untouchable or two lurking 'mongst 'em, but that don't signify, long's they may form line and fire three volleys a minute. There's even some Goanese, some half Portugee mixed in, from our being down south toward the end of the war out here. No, they'll go across the *kala panee* for you and not worry about breaking their caste. When and where do you need 'em, sir?"

"A half-company now aboard *Telesto* for our voyage. The rest transferred to Bencoolen on Sumatra, to place them closer to the action until we need them."

"A damned unhealthy place," Sir Hugo replied, shivering.

"My God, where out here ain't?" Alan muttered. "*Yih achcha jaga naheen*, eh, Mister Wythy? Like you said this morning."

"Sicklier'n most, young sir," Wythy assured him.

"Yes, sicklier in fever, heat . . . and in morals," Sir Hugo went on. "Anyone sent there is sure to be peppered to his eyebrows with the pox. Regiments serving there go down like flies. Pox, drink . . ."

And just when did Father ever worry about morals, Alan thought.

"The death rate among even native levies is nothing short of extermination, sirs," Sir Hugo complained. "Not to mention the effect the utter anarchy of Bencoolen exerts upon troop discipline. Had you the Brigade of Guards in Bencoolen, you couldn't put a half-battalion on parade fit for a day's march a month later, and those'd be so raddled and debilitated, so mutinous, you'd not be able to turn your back on 'em for a second."

"I'm sure your colonel would disagree with me, Sir Hugo," Twigg replied, his voice calm and reasonable, but Alan had seen that thin-lipped asperity often enough to know he was on the verge of an explosion. "Besides, what good do your troops do us if we needs must return to Calcutta to fetch 'em on short notice?"

"We do not *have* a colonel for this regiment," Sir Hugo admitted. "He died. Of cholera. And for your information, the Nineteenth N.I. is only six companies, only a little better than a half-battalion to start with. It was never more than a one-battalion regiment, anyway."

"The hell you say, sir!" Wythy burst out, covertly restraining his senior partner before Twigg blew up at being sassed.

"As I said, we saw a lot of action down south against Hyder Ali and Tippoo Sultan," Sir Hugo told them. "We suffered more than our fair share of casualties. And when the war

ended, more than a few of my men 'cut their names' to take
their small pensions. I doubt I could muster three hundred men
this moment, including officers, the band and the color-party.
And *that*, sir," Sir Hugo huffed with a cruel grimace at Twigg's
discomfiture, "is why this battalion was made available to
you. We are all that may be spared. Trouble west and north in
the Oudh, trouble with the Mahrattas west and south. Trouble
on every border of the Bengal Presidency. If you transfer us
now, with no chance to recruit, well . . ."

Sir Hugo blew a smoke ring, which seemingly mesmerized
Twigg.

"We're fit for garrison duties only, now, and there's not
money enough to flesh us out. Send this battalion to Bencoolen
at its present strength, equipped as we are, and one might do
my *sepoys* a better kindness by simply shooting them here in
Calcutta," Sir Hugo related with a sad smile. "We've one foot
in the grave already. For what you want to do, we're a broken
reed. At present, that is, sir."

"Well, damme," Twigg sighed at last, leaking air and authority like one of that Frenchman Montgolfier's hot-air bal-
loons. "Would it be possible to recruit the Nineteenth here in
Bengal before we sail?"

"Assuredly, sir!" Sir Hugo beamed. "There is the matter of
pay for the men, though, the joining-bounty. Uniforms, muskets. And if we become a full-fledged ten-company battalion
once more, the Nineteenth would have need of a colonel once
again."

That last made Twigg smile bleakly. Even after being ordered by the East India Company to comply with Twigg's
desires, Sir Hugo was angling for a promotion to lieutenant-
colonel! Alan raised his brows at what his father was hinting
at. No one else on the face of the earth would have the utter
cock-a-whoop gall to do it, he thought!

"What have you now, Sir Hugo?" Twigg inquired.

"A grenadier company, light company and four thin line
companies, Mister Twigg. Had to combine a few to even field
that."

"And artillery?" Alan asked. "Two six-pounders, I'd imagine?"

"At present, yes, son," Sir Hugo replied, eyeing him with a
quirky, bemused expression that had his dander up. Son, indeed!

"We might need more'n that," Wythy opined. "If we're gonna go up against pirates ashore."

"Ship's artillery, with suitable carriages," Twigg agreed.

"Excuse me, sir," Lewrie interjected. "The pirates will live in jungles, around lagoons with lots of sand? Then better we have lighter guns, on light carriages. Three- or four-pounders. Perhaps even some two-pounder swivels. Or do we expect stone fortresses to be battered down? In that case, some heavy guns would come in handy."

"Yes, more artillery. Light guns."

"Something like Gustavus Adolphus' light horse-artillery guns." Sir Hugo pondered, going for the brandy decanter again. "Easier to man-haul through swamps and jungle. I'd suspect a full battery, six pieces, too. Half battery for each wing should we encounter a whole village of pirates. But that would take skilled gunners. More than are available here in Bengal. Most of the native artillery's a poor joke, and the good artillerymen are mostly English. Already spoken for, I might add. I could procure the guns and carriages, and I might find natives who've been around cannon. It would help immensely, though, if some of your gunners could be seconded to my command. To train and stiffen my lads."

"I couldn't spare many," Ayscough squirmed. "Why, if we're to trail our colors looking for pirates, or run up against these French privateers, we'll need every skilled man on my great guns! Surely, Mister Twigg . . ."

"We could consider it, Sir Hugo," Twigg allowed, and Lewrie thought he could hear the man's teeth grinding all the way across the table. "Now, how long do you think it would take for you to raise the Nineteenth Native Infantry to full-strength, and train them properly?"

"Well, should Hastings approve the expense this very instant, I'd expect I could put ten companies in the field, well-trained as an English battalion, in four months. More like six, really, if you want 'em steady," Sir Hugo informed them.

"Damme, sir, I thought we were to be given full cooperation by 'John Company,' " Ayscough carped. "We need trained troops now, do we not? Better we should go back to this fellow Hastings and tell him the Nineteenth won't suit! Surely, there's another unit that could take ship earlier than that. We could find these buggers in the next two months, and then we're hamstrung without sufficient force!"

"Caste, Captain Ayscough," Twigg snapped. "This lot are

the only ones available who could cross the 'black water' without breaking their bloody caste."

And, Alan suspected, Twigg couldn't even dare go back to see this Hastings fellow over at Fort William. He had *requests* from the Crown in his pocket, not orders. From his fellow midshipman, Keith Ashburn, whose family was high up in the East India Company, he had learned long ago that out here in the Far East, and most especially in Indian matters, "John Company" was a law unto itself. Right now, they had a lot more on their plate than this one expedition, no matter that it was East India Company ships being taken as well as country ships. They'd much prefer a navy of their own than have to run to HM Government for help, or let Parliament get a finger-hold on their affairs. What aid Twigg had been offered, unsuitable as it was, was all he was going to get from the Company *nabobs*. And Sir Hugo knew it!

"And then," Sir Hugo went on blandly, "there is the matter of how much all this is going to cost. Arms, uniforms, accoutrements. Pay. Passage to Bencoolen with all rations and supplies. What's more, just who exactly pays for it, Mister Twigg?"

"Partly from Crown funds," Twigg harrumphed, looking like he'd been robbed at knifepoint. " 'John Company' will contribute their fair share. And"—here the grinding teeth could be imagined once more—"partly from the proceeds we gain in our guise as merchants."

"Well, if all's been approved so far"—Sir Hugo smiled once more—"then I'd better be about beginning, shouldn't I? If we are agreed, in *all* particulars, hmm? The Nineteenth to recruit to full muster. Light artillery to be procured, and carriages built. Troops to be trained for action somewhere in the Far East. Transport to be provided to Bencoolen once they're ready. Of course . . ." He paused.

"Yesss?" Twigg drawled out, his face flushing with restraint from mayhem upon Sir Hugo's grinning phyz.

"It strikes me as how you shall have a half-company detachment of my light company, sir," Sir Hugo sighed. "And one of my white officers and an experienced native *subadar*. Perhaps I should recruit to flesh out the existing light company in their absence, and add a second light company for skirmishing, 'stead of another line company. That will put us over our usual troop allotment, but under the circumstances, it seems reasonable. And in jungle conditions, they might prove more useful. Or do you not think so, Mister Twigg?"

"Do what you think best, within *reason*, Sir Hugo," Twigg replied, "I cannot profess to proficiency in the *arcana* of soldiering. But," he said with one of those bleak little smiles, "let us say that we load cargo for Canton, beginning tomorrow. We may be in the Pearl River by the beginning of the trading season, or slightly before, late August. We may stay the entire six months in Canton, we may not, depending on whether we discover the identity or presence of those French pirates who have been preying upon English vessels. We may need your troops earlier than March of '85. So once you have recruited, and trained your *sepoys* to a fair level of competence, you will take ship to Bencoolen on Sumatra, the problems there notwithstanding, and continue to train in jungle conditions, awaiting our summons. The transport will stay with you, so you might practice embarkation and amphibious landings in ship's boats. I do believe we are agreed in all particulars now, Sir Hugo? And I am sure that your brevet to lieutenant-colonel shall be forthcoming, if you satisfy my desires, hmmm?"

"I believe we understand each other completely, Mister Twigg," Sir Hugo smiled back. Of course they did, Alan thought! His father had just picked Twigg's pockets, gotten himself a boost in rank and had the man over a barrel. Twigg had to give in, or have nothing to fight pirates with. The deployment to Bencoolen was Twigg's only sop to his ego. Sir Hugo would pay that price for everything else.

"This'll be expensive," Wythy sighed. "Thank the good Lord cotton an' opium's dead-cheap. We'll still have a full cargo for Canton."

"Opium, Mister Wythy?" Chiswick asked, breaking his long junior officer's silence. "That's some sort of medicament, is it not, sir?"

"An' a most powerful one, sir," Tom Wythy beamed. "The Chinee desire it more'n anything we could haul from England. Their mandarins'd cut your head clean off yer shoulders for smugglin' it, but the profit's so great, they can't stop the trade. Ye smoke it, sir, smoke it an' see the dragon! Bliss of heaven in a little pill of it rolled up in a pipe. Hard as life is for the Chinee, they need it. An' once they try it a few times, they need it even more, until they pay any price t' get it. The Co Hong merchants won't touch it, but their creatures or the mandarins'll slip down t' Lintin Island or Nan'Ao an' buy ev'ry scrap we may carry. Pay good silver, too. *Taels* o' silver . . . *lacs* of the stuff. See, 'tis the only goods we have so we may get silver to support the China trade, or we'd bankrupt the Treasury back home, else. Country ships sell opium for silver, the silver goes t' the East India Company for our legal cargoes, and they use the silver t' purchase teas, silks, furniture an' such. We make a profit on the opium, the Company makes money, too."

"Couldn't make a farthing on the China trade without it, Captain Chiswick," Sir Hugo added. "The so-called Celestial Empire turns its nose up at most English wares. Oh, some Berlin goods, some English woolens go down well. Clocks, expensive gew-gaws and toys. But for bulk trade, as I'm sure Mister Twigg will agree, there's little we may offer they would buy. Arrogant bastards."

"Gangetic opium, Bengali and Madrassi cotton from which they weave nankeen," Twigg added lazily, with a wave of one lean hand. "I lay you any odds, sirs, that whatever Frenchmen are behind this nefarious business will be deep into the opium trade as well. So what better cargo for us, the profit besides? The stuff's cheap as dirt, and goes for its weight in silver, damn near. From which profits, we shall outfit Sir Hugo's battalion, and confound the plans of our foes. 'Tis only fitting, if one thinks about it for a moment."

"To opium!" Wythy proposed, raising his glass. "Opium, and lashes of silver!"

Once they had drunk the health of the humble poppy, Twigg rose. "Well, that should do it for this evening, sirs. Sir Hugo, my thanks to you for a splendid repast. Whilst back in England, I despaired I'd ever eat as well as ever I did in India, and your *khansamah* is worthy of the Great Moghul's. Should you tire of having to beat him when he goes *ghazi* on you, I'd admire to hire him as my personal cook." Twigg didn't even sound half disgruntled at being had.

"So happy you enjoyed it, sir," Sir Hugo replied courteously, knowing it was pretty much a gilt and be-shit compliment that Twigg was offering his hospitality, a covering for the bile he really felt.

They filed down to the first floor entry hall to reclaim their hats, swords and canes prior to departure.

"If you travel so well-armed, sir," Sir Hugo seemed to come upon like an idle thought, "your ship *Telesto* stands a much better chance of making Macao than most. Your talk of opium

. . . to enter better into the spirit of your venture, what would you say to allowing me to round up a few pounds of my own to purchase a few crates, to go with your cargo as well? Full charge on the carrying fee, of course."

"A few crates, aye, Sir Hugo," Twigg smirked, and Alan suddenly realized why his father had seemed so pale and upset by the news about the Indiaman, the *Macclesfield*, disappearing. He'd probably had a ton or two of opium consigned into her!

But just why should I expect the greedy old fart to not essay every avenue on the way to bloody showers of "blunt," he wondered? Come to think of it, if it's that bloody profitable, I wish I had a thousand pounds to purchase a share of the cargo for myself! It's nothing that evil—it's the backbone of the China trade. Twigg said so himself!

"Bide awhile, Alan," Sir Hugo bade just before he got out the door, "if you may excuse my son returning to the ship, Captain Ayscough. We have much to catch up on."

Oh, shit, Alan sighed inside. I should have known I'd not get away with a clean pair of heels.

Chapter 4

T hey repaired back to the upper level, to another room that was screened off from the dining area by a carved wood *purdah* screen that ran the whole width of the huge main salon. Sir Hugo shucked out of his regimentals, doffing red coat, waist-coat, rank gorget and neck-cloth. He kicked off his shoes and dropped his clothes willy-nilly, but there was a bearer there to catch them before they even hit the floor. The white powdered wig with the tight side-curls and short false queue went next as Sir Hugo unbuttoned his shirt and rolled up his sleeves.

"Make yourself comfortable, lad," he offered. There were no real chairs or couches in this room, so Alan wondered where he could indeed make himself comfortable. Sit on the floor, on the piles of richly brocaded pillows? On the intricate carpets?

Yes, that was where Sir Hugo was seating himself, on a Bengali *dhuree* rug that held a dozen huge pillows, while one of the younger *khitmatgars* came trotting in with a folding table support about eight inches high made of ebony wood, and a second servitor fetched a huge brass table or tray (maybe it did duty as both, Alan thought) to sit atop it.

"Oh, for God's sake, take your ease!" Sir Hugo snapped. There, that tone in his voice was more like the scheming, petulant bastard that Lewrie had grown to know and despise. "You must be stifling in that neck-cloth."

The *khitmatgars* were back with another load of goodies to set upon the tray table. Wine and spirits, clay pipes and tobacco humidor, a bowl of fruit and some candied dates. Even some Persian muck they called *halvah*. Gauzy, diaphanous insect curtains were lowered over the wide windows to the balcony, whilst from outside . . .

"For God's sake, a band?" Alan grimaced as a set of native musicians hit their stride with something plaintively twanging, ululating, throbbing and thumping on *sitars*, flutes and *madals*. "You do live well, I'll allow you that . . . Sir Hugo."

"Say 'father,' do, Alan," Sir Hugo grunted.

"Mine arse on a bandbox!" Alan snapped back.

"Have it your own way, but sit the hell down and have some wine, at least," Sir Hugo pressed in a reasonable tone.

Alan heaved a heavy sigh and untied his neck-cloth, sank down to sit cross-legged on the cushions and took a glass of claret.

There were a couple of tall candelabras made of brass between them, elaborate things fashioned from the arms and bodies of Hindoo gods and goddesses—thank the Lord most of 'em had eight or ten arms to hold that many candles. Off to either side, there were shallow charcoal braziers, now fuming with sandalwood incense amid some other aromas.

"Keeps the mosquitos away," Sir Hugo yawned. "Sandalwood, citron and *patchouli*. Christ knows what else. Better not to ask."

"If I'm delaying your retiring . . ." Alan offered, impatient to go.

"Not at all. I can still keep up with the young bucks of the first head." Sir Hugo smiled lazily, puffing on his pipe once more.

"You always could, I grant you," Alan agreed. "But then, you were damn near a charter-member of the Hell-Fire Club back in your early days, weren't you?" he concluded with a suitably arch sneer.

"And when did you become a regular churchgoer, my boy?" Sir Hugo replied. "God, if I only had penny to the pound of all the blunt I spent bailing you out of trouble, I'd still be a rich man!"

"Wasn't *my* caterwauling got you in debtor's prison," Alan sulked. "Wasn't *me* damn near press-ganged me into the Navy so you could lay your hooks on the Lewrie fortune."

"And how is Grandmother Lewrie these days? Mistress Nuttbush now?"

"Alive and kicking, spry as a pup."

"Her kind always was harder to kill than breadroom rats."

"Sounds like you considered it."

"Now you do me too much injustice, Alan m'dear."

"Oh, please!" Alan said, starting to rise, but Sir Hugo reached out and put a restraining hand on his arm.

"Bide awhile, son," he said, and for once, he sounded as if he was begging. Sir Hugo St. George Willoughby never begged. Alan made up his mind to stay for a while longer, if only to see him beg again.

"How can you call me son?" Alan shot out, sure of his superior position over the older man for the first time in his life. "Aye, you sired me, that's true, but when it came to being a father to me, you had your chance, and all I ever got from you was a cold shoulder, a snarl now and then. I wasn't a son, I was an investment! Your hole-card to take the Lewrie trick once I was of an age to inherit and granny passed over. And soon as it looked like happening, you packed me off with that crimp Captain Bevan and had me off at sea, so I'd never even know there was a Lewrie family to inherit from! You told me my mother Elisabeth was a whore, dead at my birthing, that I had no family other than you, God pity me! You and Pilchard forging documents left, right and center to get what you wanted . . ."

"Needed's more like it," Sir Hugo confessed with a deprecating shrug and a sip of his brandy.

"Yes, you always needed money," Alan pressed on harder, trying to get a rise out of him, to puncture that slightly sad, but maddeningly *calm* demeanor. Damme, he thought, does the old bastard truly not have a sense of honor to shame? "And there was Belinda and Gerald, their inheritance you squandered before they came of age, too. How was your marriage to the Cockspur widow, your second wife?"

"Bloody depressing most of the time. She was a termagant twit." Sir Hugo chuckled slightly, and gave Alan a rueful grimace and a shake of his head in less than fond remembrance. "And how are Belinda and Gerald faring?"

"What the . . ." Alan was rendered incapable of cogent speech by the man's *sang-froid*. "As if you care!"

"You're right, I don't, but I thought it would satisfy my curiosity about them," Sir Hugo replied, tippling another sip of brandy. "Bloody awful children, right from the start."

"Yet . . . yet, you treated them as the rightful heirs, and me as the barely tolerated . . . bastard!" Alan barked. "Well, Goddamn you!"

"Of course I did. Agnes' bloody sisters were still alive to

plague me, and to all intents and purposes, you *were* the little bastard, the by-blow of a youthful indiscretion. You wanted for nothing. What else did you desire? A damned pony and cart?"

"Yes, yes I bloody well did!" Alan howled with rage. "I wanted"—Alan was so full of rage, of tears, that he had to get out of the place before he killed the man!—"I wanted a father! I wanted a mother!" He shot to his feet to flee.

"You had a mother!" Sir Hugo roared, getting to his feet and seizing Alan, who struggled to get away. "She died. And, God help you, you had me for a father, such as I was."

"You told me she was a whore!" Alan screamed.

"She was!" Sir Hugo screamed back. "Know why I ran off with her jewelry in Holland? Because I caught her in bed with another officer of my regiment who'd made the crossing with us after we eloped!"

"You lying hound!"

"You've only heard your granny's side, boy!" Sir Hugo ranted. "How sweet and innocent she was. How I seduced her for her money and left her without a penny. Well, let me tell you, if she'd lived, I'd have lost count of how many times she'd have put cuckold's horns on me. God help me, I'd be here in India after all, 'cause it'd be cheaper'n trying to get a bill of divorce through Parliament! I might have ended up on the gallows for killing her and her latest! Do . . . you . . . under . . . stand . . . me . . . you little . . . jingle-brains?"

The last was punctuated with some massive shaking that almost loosened Alan's teeth in his head each time his jaw snapped shut.

"Elisabeth could be the sweetest, liveliest, most alluring damn woman ever I did see, Alan," Sir Hugo relented at last, easing his tone and his grip. "But I found out I couldn't trust her out of my sight! Oh, we went to Holland, yes. Her daddy Dudley Lewrie cut her off without a farthing. So we lived on my Army pay and what little was left of my family estate after my elder brother got through with it. Mortgaged to the bloody hilt! And do you really think I wanted to enter the Army when I was sixteen? Like bloody Hell, I did! I didn't get much of a choice, either."

"But that doesn't excuse . . ." Alan almost sobbed.

"I know, son, nothing excuses it," Sir Hugo shuddered. "I've treated you like dirt your whole life. Thought I was doing well by you, by my own lights. And nothing's going to make up for it. But I'd like you to at least understand me. If you're going to despise me to the end of time, then at least do it for the right reasons, if nothing else."

"You miserable bastard!" Alan hissed, on the verge of weeping, of falling on his father's shoulder and crying his eyes out. Either that or fetching a curved *tulwar*, a Persian sword, off the wall and hacking his head off. Sir Hugo put a hand on his shoulder and gave him a soft pat—perhaps as close as he would ever get to empathy or comforting.

"Thomas de Crecy," Sir Hugo muttered heavily, turning away. "Good, honest, cheerful, unfailing Tommy. My fellow officer in the 4th. 'Twas him arranged the minister and all for us to wed."

"Aye, I remember," Alan said with a snort and a hiccup. "But it was a false justice married you. I guess he didn't know you needed real clergy. Just a sham to get her into your bed!"

"No need of that, Alan," Sir Hugo replied, grinning. "Elisabeth had the shortest pair of heels of any girl I'd ever seen. We'd already been bedded. And I want you to know this, laddy. I loved her so dearly I was totally besotted. Money be damned, I really did want her to be my wife! Ah, but Tommy de Crecy knew what he was doing. Came over to Holland with us, brought my last installment of Army pay. Stayed with us in the same town, to see us through until Elisabeth's family came 'round and accepted the marriage. Do you see what he had in mind?"

"No, frankly," Alan replied, blowing his nose.

"Well, there we were, rapidly running out of money, 'cause your grandfather Dudley Lewrie was tighter with a shilling than a Maltese pimp, and he'd never admit the match. But there was always good old Tommy. Tommy, with his little loans. Tommy with his lord's purse. Tommy with his kind-hearted generosity!" Sir Hugo turned somber, and just a trifle angry, even after all these years as he related this. Or, as Alan suspected, he was a consummate actor and was putting on a sublime theatric.

"You mean he was the one caught in bed with her?" Alan asked, dubious still.

"He'd wanted her all along, aye," Sir Hugo grumbled, and bent over the tray table to pour them another stiff refill of brandy. His face was older, heavier, lined; the skin mottled by years of too much drink, too much tropic sun in the last few. The fine shock of light brown hair was receded, and there were liver spots on the exposed scalp. And, Alan noticed as he poured the spirit, so were the backs of his hands. Sir Hugo St. George Willoughby was no longer the fashionable buck of St. James' Place, White's, Almack's. He was a slack old man, or near enough to it not to matter, gone ropey and croupey.

"He was waiting for the moment when Elisabeth was at her weakest, I suppose," Sir Hugo maundered on. "When we both realized the enormity of what we'd done, and that things were most definitely *not* going to turn aright. Knighthood or not, she was married to a penniless captain of foot, currently unemployed. Trading down from good lodgings to the cheapest we could find, and still wondering where the next meal was coming from. I'm sure she wished she could repent and go back to her family. And she always was an impulsive girl. What I loved about her most, really. What better moment for good old Captain The Honourable Thomas de Crecy to inform her that the whole thing was a sham I'd dreamed up to get hold of her family's money, and don't ye know . . . he'd 'just learned of it' from another officer in our regiment, and he simply *had* to rescue her from me!"

"But . . ." Alan started to say, then shut his trap. He'd never thought of his father as anything but inhuman. Never allowed that he could be hurt, or feel pain (especially since he'd been so good at handing pain out to others so liberally). This brutal bastard should be incapable of sorrow, shouldn't he, he asked himself?

"Elisabeth was carrying you by then, making the whole thing worse. And Tommy swore he'd always loved her more than life, couldn't stand to see her in my brutal, callous clutches. All the *Sturm und Drang* so popular in women's novels these days, all that Gothick fright and flummery! Well, don't ye know, she spooned it up like cream. The brainless little baggage!" Sir Hugo related, sinking down onto his pile of pillows and stretching out on his side. "Probably told her he'd do right by her and the child. Maybe he really meant to; I'll never know. But he came back from Holland without her, after a few more months. After she began to show, and he couldn't trot her out to anything elegant."

"Hold on, though," Alan objected. "You still ended up stealing her jewels and abandoning her, didn't you?"

"Yes, I did," Sir Hugo nodded with not a twinge of shame. " 'Twas the only way I knew how to get back at her after I caught them. Well, I didn't *exactly* catch them bareback riding."

"Like I was with Belinda when you arranged to 'catch' me."

"Hmm, no, nothing that flagrant," Sir Hugo snickered. "She was in her bedgown. Untied, mind, and nary a sight of stockings, stays or corset to be found. Tommy'd dressed so fast he'd buttoned his waist-coat to his breeches flap! Oh, 'twas a devil of a row we had. After I'd horse-whipped him down the stairs, she lit into me. Mind you also, this was the first I knew that we really weren't married! So all I could do was rant and swear Tommy was lying, but she wasn't having a bit of it. And d'you know, lad? But termagant as she was at that moment, I had a sudden premonition of just how ghastly life was going to be with her from that moment on. No trusting her with other men 'thout a leash on. Tears, sulks and screaming fits for the rest of our natural lives. Ah, but suddenly it struck me! If we're *not* married . . . if Tommy diddled the both of us, then I was free as larks! All I could think of was 'Thank bloody Christ this is over with,' and hit the road that night. Singing with relief, as I remember."

"But you took her last money!"

"She had Tommy's money," Sir Hugo sneered, then rose up on his elbow to look Alan square in the face. "God knows I loved her more than anything or anyone else since, Alan. But I really did need the money devilish bad! And with Tommy lusting after her, he'd replace what I'd taken, and be damned to both of them—they deserved each other when you come right down to it."

"Jesus, you really don't have any shame!" Alan snapped, getting righteous again.

"Too damn poor to have any shame. You want to see shameless, you should have been in my shoes with Agnes Cockspur."

"Belinda and Gerald's mother," Alan supplied.

"Fetching enough in the beginning, 'fore she turned into this drab pudding." Sir Hugo sighed. "Chicken-chested, thick as a farrier sergeant. Rather wrestled a publican than put the leg over her. Like climbing into bliss on the belly of a bear. And her two children were rotten from the start. Still, she was absolutely stiff with 'chink,' and there I was in Bath, trying to parley what little I had left into something to live on. Had to resign my commission, don't ye know! An officer in the King's Own, Knight of the Garter or not, can't abscond with young heiresses. Not unless one's *successful*, mind, then they make you colonel of the regiment and dine you in once a year. I made three thousand pounds selling up my commission, but it was going fast. No, I may be a bit harsh on poor Agnes. Drab she may have been, dull as ditch-water and graceful as a three legged dray-horse, but she was a kindly stick. Meant well. And then she died having our child, and the child died, too. And Elisabeth had died having you. And I got to brooding on what had happened to you."

"That was after you and your solicitor, Mister Pilchard, had forged that letter of permanent coverture over Agnes Cockspur's estate," Alan accused.

"Aye, soon after that. Talented bugger, that Pilchard. What else was I to do? With Agnes in her grave, her even more ghastly sisters'd have gotten the estate and the money, and I'd be out on my bare arse again, stuck with two brats I'd never have wanted if they came with the crown of Prussia attached."

"So you heard I was still alive," Alan pressed. "And you were, as you put it . . . brooding on me."

"The only real child I ever had, Alan. I found you and took you in because I swore I'd never marry again," Sir Hugo told him. "Of course, I was just disreputable enough that the idea of me marrying into a really good family couldn't be mentioned in polite Society. Pretty much the same thing, really."

"But you didn't act like I was your only son."

"Like I said, I had to pretend to be caring for Agnes' brood. For Society. To keep the sisters shut up. After all, if I didn't have them to care for, a court would find it easier to take them away and award them to the sisters, and the money'd go with 'em. What did you want beyond what any other lad of your station got? My parents saw me at tea, perhaps at supper, once in the evening just before the governess tucked me in, and after that, it was a good public school somewhere far enough away so they wouldn't be bothered, except when term ended."

"Why did you arrange for me to get caught in bed with Belinda? Why did you exile me into the Navy?" Alan demanded, though in a soft voice as he sat down cross-legged on his pillows once more.

"The Lewrie money," Sir Hugo muttered, barely inaudible.

"And you were almost broke again, weren't you. And you needed the money, so *devilish* bad!"

After much hemming and hawwing, Sir Hugo could only nod his assent.

"Goddamn you." Alan slumped.

"Alan . . . I am truly sorry," Sir Hugo whispered. "Your father is a miserable bastard. I thought I was doing right by you, not letting you end up dead in that parish orphanage. Feeding you, clothing you, getting you a good education. You don't know how many times I was proud of you. Of how many times you reminded me of me, even when you were up to your ears in pranks that backfired to my cost."

"Fine way of showing it," Alan muttered back, staring down in his brandy and watching the candle flames dance in amber to the trembling of his fingers. "I thought you hated me."

"Alan, no! Never hated you!" Sir Hugo insisted, reaching out to put a hand on his shoulder. "Maybe I didn't show you. Or tell you. But I took you in out of guilt about Elisabeth. And about Agnes. I loved you, Alan. I love you still."

"Ah, right," Alan tossed off.

"If I seem too selfish, then that's my curse. If I treated you standoff-ish, then that's my loss," Sir Hugo insisted. "And I'm still proud of you. You've made lieutenant in half the time most people could expect. Commanded a ship of your own for a while. Made a name for yourself by being brave and clever. I read every issue of the *Marine Chronicle* and the London papers, looking for news of you. 'Came into The Downs this Sunday last, the *Shrike* brig, Lieutenant Alan Lewrie, commanding, to pay off at Deptford Hard, with a sum in excess of thirty thousand pounds prize money owing officers and men, from service with the Leeward Islands Squadron, most recently off Cape François under Admiral Sir Samuel Hood and Commodore Affleck.' I memorized it. I cut it out and saved it. I can show you."

"Maybe you could; it don't signify," Alan replied bitterly. "Your idea of affection is hellish like indifference to me. Your idea of love I could trade for two dozen lashes and stand the better, sir."

"For better or worse, I am your father, Alan. I don't expect you to ever love me. Or respect me, either. I'd admire if you could at least not despise me. Take what's past like the fine young man you are and put it behind you. Behind us," Sir Hugo implored. "I imagine that you're the best of Elisabeth Lewrie, and the best of me, with all the rotten parts cut out, like an apple only half gone-over. Lot of pith left, even so. I'll not ever expect us to be reconciled."

"That would take a power of doing. And longer than either of us have on this earth, I expect," Alan answered.

"Well, that's the way of it, then," Sir Hugo harrumphed, and wiped a tear from the corner of one eye. "Just do one thing for me."

"What?"

"Don't end up like me, will you, lad?"

"I don't know; I have a fair start on it." Alan grimaced and found himself amused in spite of himself.

"You take after me when it comes to the ladies, hey?" Sir Hugo teased.

"In frequency, perhaps. Not . . . well, I haven't cheated anyone. Not yet, anyway," Alan allowed.

"That Captain Bevan dropped me a line now and then about you. I know about the ladies in Jamaica," Sir Hugo chuckled.

"That's not the half of it."

"I thought I'd offer you a treat," Sir Hugo said, getting to his feet rather awkwardly. Part age and stiffness, Alan thought, and part being half-seas-over with drink. Sir Hugo clapped his hands and the narrow door in the *purdah* screen opened. Three girls entered the room, one dressed in a translucent *saree*, the other two in the bright gauzy skirts and tight satin jackets that left so little to the imagination, like the *nautch*-girls he'd seen in the *bazaar* earlier.

"My word!" he breathed. They were unutterably lovely, every one of 'em! *Kohl* outlined eyes, shy smiles and bright teeth, complexions clear and smooth, and as brown as pecan shells or as golden as wheat.

"This is Padmini," Sir Hugo said, indicating the one in the *saree*, who stood no higher than Alan's chin.

"Namasté, sahib," the girl whispered, though grinning with an impish expression.

"A Bengali, she is, Alan. Once you've had a Bengali woman, you're spoiled for anything else." Sir Hugo chuckled. "Draupadi. She's Rajput. And Apsara. Aptly named, too, for the playthings of Hindoo gods. Though I doubt she's Hindoo. From up north in the Oudh, I think. Maybe from the foothills. A little tigress. All can do a dance that'll set your blood to boiling. Like to see?"

"I don't know . . ." Alan sighed, feeling anything but lusty for once. All passion had been shouted or cried out of him. "Maybe some other time, sir."

Good Christ, is it *me* saying that?

"Too late to be wandering the streets, even in the English cantonments, Alan. If nothing else, accept my offer of bed and breakfast."

Draupadi was stirring slowly to the beat of the *madals* from the courtyard, smiling with heavy-lidded eyes full of promise, her extremely long, straight dark hair swishing maddeningly as far down as her fingertips, and Alan watched it sway. He transferred his gaze to Apsara, she of the dark, frizzy-curly hair and the golden wheat skin, who gazed at him with such a welcoming, open-mouthed smile.

"Er . . . hmmm," he pondered.

"Come, Alan," Sir Hugo demanded. "I know you of old, my dear son. What's worse, you know me. I'd never cut my nose off to spite my face. Nor would I turn down such exquisite quim just because I bore a grudge against my host. And I doubt if you would, either."

"Ah . . ." Alan tried to reply.

"I have a lot to make up to you for, Alan," his father said, coming close to his side to speak privately. "Maybe I never can, like you suspect. I'd buy you that bloody trap and pony, if I thought you still wanted it. But right now, this is the best I have to offer. And it may be your last chance before you sail off out of my life again. Safer than some *bazaari-randi*,* too, and won't cost you tuppence."

"Hmmm," Alan speculated at last, "don't suppose your band knows 'When First I Gazed in Chloe's Eyes,' would they?"

"Hardly!" Sir Hugo barked out a short laugh.

"Ah, well," Alan finally allowed, sinking back to the carpet and reclining against one of those impossibly thick and round barrel-shaped pillows.

With a crook of his finger, Sir Hugo summoned Padmini to join him. Alan crooked his own finger at Apsara, who beamed even wider, and seemed to slink to his side with the lithe grace of a panther, her *patchouli* and sandalwood scent enveloping him like her gauze *chudder* as she drew the headcloth about their faces to share a brief nuzzle before pouring him another full bumper of wine.

"Apsara?" he said. "Alan."

"Ahk-lahn," she breathed, taking a sip of his wine.

"My God in Heaven." He laughed with an anticipatory

*market-whores

shudder of raw lust. "Mind you, Father," he said over Apsara's smooth young shoulder, "you have one bloody Hell of a lot to make up for, y'know."

"The evening's young," Sir Hugo replied softly. "My son."

And Draupadi began her dance, her ankle bangles jangling.

III

"Divitis Indiae usque ad ultimum sinum."
"To the farthest gulf of the rich East."

—TOWN MOTTO OF
SALEM, MASSACHUSETTS

Chapter 1

Another watch with Percival, the second officer, Alan sighed as he mopped his brow. Another broiling forenoon on a deck holystoned to pristine whiteness that reflected back the heat of the sun, wondering if Percival ever felt the heat, ever grew faint and weak. Plenty of people drop dead of apoplexy back home, Alan thought; why not this bluff ginger bastard?

Bad as their relationship had been compared to the easy acceptance he'd gained with the others in the wardroom, it had gotten a lot worse after the *durbar* at Sir Hugo's house, to which even Choate the first officer had not been invited, and Alan had. Lewrie suspected Percival despised him in the beginning for rising so quickly in the Navy, and now most heartily despised him for being in the know, for being privy to secrets. For seeming so well-connected with the people who matter, here in the Far East, and back home with the Admiralty.

Yesterday's noon sights placed them exactly on the Equator, almost even with the Johore Straits, the normal passage, and by this noon, they would have made fifty leagues to the north farther on, even with fitful winds staggered almost to nothing by the heat at the Equator.

With such a late start from Calcutta, they'd be lucky to make Canton or Macao by the start of the trading season. If they arrived too late, there might not be a member of the Co Hong who would agree to be their *compradore* in their legal trading. Mr. Wythy had worried there would be so many other ships anchored off Whampoa full of cotton and spices that the value of their goods, arriving so late, would not fetch a price good enough to defray expenses.

All of which made Lewrie wonder once more if this whole

137

thing hadn't been dreamed up, this tale of piracy, to bilk the Foreign Office and the Admiralty out of a free ship and cheap goods to make Twigg and Wythy rich. If they cut up a pirate fleet or two in the process, it would make a grand report back home, but who *couldn't* find some pirates to bash out here, he wondered? It's not as if one had to go looking for them very hard. The whole ocean teemed with them like lice in a rented bed back home. Mr. Brainard the sailing master was an old China hand, along with Twigg and Wythy, in the "country trade" for years. Even Captain Ayscough had sailed in Asian waters in the last war. On the surface, it would make sense to hire their services on, but they all might be in combination to make a pile of money. Of course, Alan Lewrie had always been a suspicious and somewhat cynical observer of his fellow man. If the whole thing was so much twaddle, he hoped there would be some profit for others out of the venture. Such as himself.

"Sail ho!" the main-mast lookout hailed. "Fine on the starboard bows!"

"A little off the beaten track, surely," Alan commented. "Most merchantmen would be farther west nearer the Malay coast, I'd think."

"Say '*sir*,' " Percival demanded softly.

"Aye aye, sir," Alan picked back with a bright smile.

"Two sail! Both fine on the starboard bows!" the lookout added.

"Boy, run and inform the captain," Alan told one of the ship's boys.

"My decision to make, *Mister* Lewrie," Percival huffed. "I am senior officer in this watch, and I'll thank you to remember that."

"Aye, sir."

"Go aloft, Mister Lewrie. Report what you see. I want an *experienced* pair of eyes in the cross-trees," Percival snickered.

"Aye aye, sir," Alan was forced to reply, much as he hated scaling the masts. He'd done enough of it as a midshipman, and had been damned glad to make his lieutenancy, which at least let him stay firmly rooted to a safe and solid deck most of the time. But he slung a heavy day-glass over his shoulder like a sporting gun, went to the windward shrouds and scampered up the ratlines. Out over the futtock shrouds that inclined outward to anchor the maintop platform and the deadeyes and shrouds that held the topmast erect, hanging by fingers and toes briefly. Then up the narrower set of stays to the cross-trees where the lookout perched on slender bracing slats of wood a fat pigeon would have cast a wary eye upon.

"Where away, Hodge?" Alan asked the grizzled older man.

"Three sail, now, Mister Lewrie," the sailor replied, pointing forward. He cupped his work-worn hands round his eyes to shut out the blinding sun. "An' I ain't so sure they ain't summat up t'larboard as well, sir. Jus' a cloud, mebbe, sir."

"Cloud, Hell," Alan puffed, trying to steady his shaking limbs to hold his telescope after that grueling climb. "Four sail to starboard, and perhaps two to larboard. Tell Mister Percival. You've better lungs than I."

While Hodge bawled his report down to the deck, Alan studied the view. They were passing between a sprinkling of small islands and islets between two larger land masses—Anambas to the west of their course, and a larger island of Natuna to the east'rd. There was a safe channel of at least one hundred miles width, but littered with these reefs and islets. Perfect lurking grounds for Malay or Borneo pirates, he thought. They'd try to catch ships passing to the west of Anambas after using the Johore Strait. 'Course, they could be fishermen, Alan thought.

But, as they drew closer, hull-up over the horizon, Alan could see they were using the barest and crudest of sail rigs, and the froth about them was not a wake, but the working of many oars and paddles, far more oarsmen than any fisherman would take to sea. The hulls were blood red, winking with what he took to be gilt trim.

"Hodge, inform the deck I believe they're pirates."

Alan stepped out of the cross-trees, took hold of a backstay and wrapped his legs about it to let himself down to the quarterdeck hand over hand in seamanly fashion.

"Half a dozen to starboard, three, possibly four to larboard, sir," Alan told the captain. "Red hulls. Lots of paddlers or oarsmen."

"War *praos*," Ayscough nodded grimly. "Mister Brainard?"

"Aye, sir?"

"Any hopes the wind will pick up?"

"No, sir," the sailing master informed him. "Not with this heat, not this far easterly of the usual track. We've everything cracked on now but the stun's'l booms, and not a fraction above seven knots do we make."

"I see," Captain Ayscough grunted. "Then if we can't out-run 'em, we'll have to fight. Mister Choate, beat to Quarters!"

"What is it, Alan?" Burgess Chiswick asked as he came on deck, drawn by the drumming and fifing of the ship's small band. His lean, dark *sepoys* were struggling into their red coats below them on the gun deck, just below the quarterdeck net-tings.

"Pirates, Burgess. Maybe the ones we've been searching for."

"Subadar!" Burgess bawled, shouting for his senior native officer and clattering down to the gun deck.

Telesto mounted a light battery of two twelve-pounders forward on the fo'c'sle as chase-guns, and another two right aft in the wardroom, one to either side of the rudder and transom post to deal with ships attempting to rake her from astern. There were six more twelve-pounders on the quarterdeck, three to each beam. Each gun took a crew of seven men to operate it efficiently in Naval usage, with a ship's boy serving as powder-monkey to fetch and carry from the magazines for each one.

Her main battery was on the upper gun deck; twenty eighteen-pounders which required nine men apiece. Even in the Royal Navy, both sides could not be fully manned at the same time, so there were only eleven men per gun to share be-tween, which would require some nimble hopping back and forth if the pirates attacked from both sides at once: three men to load and charge each gun, and the rest milling about in the center of the gun deck to haul on the tackles to run the guns out and throw their weight on hand-spikes and crows to shift aim right or left while the gun-captain would adjust the eleva-tion of the guns with the new rotating screws. All were, mer-cifully, equipped with flintlock igniters like a musket, instead of the older types that required a tin or goose-feather quill priming tube and a slow-match fire.

It was on the lower gun deck, though, that *Telesto* hid her heaviest punch. Roughly amidships, behind what seemed to be unused gunports that had been expanded in size for ventilation in harbor or ease of cargo-handling, she had a battery of thirty two-pounder carronades. These were light, short-barreled guns that could be handled by only two men per gun. They threw a massive six-and-two-thirds-inch shot, not for much over two cables, or thirteen hundred feet, but when that solid shot hit at lower velocity than the conventional guns above them on the upper deck, they ravaged whatever they struck. They were mounted on slides, with a greased block of elm between two wooden rails, with an iron roller to handle the lighter recoil, and they could pivot on a large iron wheel much farther forward or aft than a gun on a wheeled truck, and had a much higher rate of fire than anything but a light swivel gun.

As junior officer, that was Alan's station; the carronades were his charge. He thundered down to the lower gun deck, passed down the narrow passageway between bales and crates of cargo, into the secret section amidships that held his battery. Four guns to each side.

"Tompions out," he ordered, tossing his hat to one side. "About ten native pirate ships. Stand ready to engage on either beam. Let's keep the gunports shut until they're close enough in to scare the bejeesus out of 'em."

"Aye, sir."

"Charge your guns!" Serge bags of mealed gunpowder came up from the magazine on the orlop and were handed over by the powder-monkeys to the gun-captains, who inspected them for dampness, weight and rips or tears. Then they were handed off to the loader, who inserted them into the short, wide-mouthed barrels. The guns had been run back to the last extent of their recoil slides so a flexible rope rammer with a wooden head could push the charges down to the base of the gun with a hard shove.

"Shot your guns!" Both men heaved up solid iron balls from the shot garlands made of arm-thick hoops of discarded anchor cable.

With a little elevation screwed in already, the balls rolled down to thump against the powder bags easily, requiring a lighter shove with the rammers to seat them firm. To cut down on too much of the charge escaping past the windage difference of ball and muzzle, thick hairy patches of raveled rope were soaked in the fire-buckets and rammed down atop the balls.

"Prime your guns."

Cartridges were pricked with the sharp end of a linstock. A measure of powder from a flask hanging from around the gun-captain's neck was dribbled into the touch-holes and pans of the flintlock mechanisms, now pulled back to half-cock. The frizzens over the pans were shut.

"Stand easy," Lewrie ordered. He wished they could open the ports. If the deck had been a roasting pan, then below decks was an oven, and the aroma of crate after crate of opium, balls of it as big as a man's head, was making him a trifle dizzy. The hatchway over his head was rigged with a grating, that grating covered with a tarred sheet of sailcloth, so there was no hope for any air.

The gun crews swayed to the easy motion of the ship, sweat running down their bodies in buckets. Shirts cast off, loose-legged slop-trousers rolled up to the knee, legs and feet bare, with only their kerchiefs above the waist, now tied 'round their heads to save their hearing once the guns began to sing.

"Stand by, the forrud chase guns!" a voice bellowed. And above the sound of the ship as she worked and groaned, they could hear drumming. Not the jerky, uplifting drumming of the ship's bandsmen, but a steady, monotonous *boom-boom, boom-boom*.

"Reckon 'at'll be th' slave-drivers, sir," the senior quarter-gunner speculated as he shifted a large cud of tobacco in his mouth. "Keep t' pace fer th' oars."

"Saints praysairve us!" an Irish loader whispered, crossing himself, and fingering a tiny silver crucifix 'round his neck.

"And good artillery preserve us, Hoolahan," Alan said with a brief grin. "Good artillery and sharp-eyed gunners."

A twelve-pounder barked from the starboard battery, then the lower gun deck drummed and echoed as the upper deck ports were drawn up and out of the way, and ten eighteen-pounders rumbled across the oak decks on their little wheels and ungreased axles loud as a cattle stampede. Alan crossed to the starboard side to peer out a slit-drain in one of the gun-ports. "About eight cables off now, half a dozen of them. I can see . . ."

He was interrupted by the blast of the forward-most eighteen-pounder as it lit off, followed in stately, controlled progression by the rest of the starboard battery. *Telesto* groaned and rocked, gun-carriages squealed as they ran in to the limit of the breeching ropes with the recoil. "Oh, good shooting! The leader's been hit hard. Dismasted. Lot of oars smashed, too."

As he watched, a gun in the bow of the *prao* returned fire, a large brass gun overly adorned with the scales, mouth and dorsal fin of a dragon. For such a large burst of smoke, the shot fell short, throwing up a huge gout of water in a tall feather of spray.

"Stone shot, sir," the quarter-gunner said. "Bad powder."

"Wind's dying," Alan whispered, and shared a worried look with the man. The ocean was flatter, hardly ruffled by wind, heaving slow and steady, almost glassy-calm farther off toward the horizon. "Do you know how to whistle, Owen?"

"I'll get on it directly, Mister Lewrie, sir."

Telesto sagged a little, heaved and rolled more gently, a sure sign that the wind was failing them, and that they would be becalmed at the worst moment in the middle of a fleet of pirate vessels that could row circles around them. It was an ancient belief that whistling aboard ship brought more wind than any seaman could handle. At that moment, Alan would have settled for a Good Hope gale.

The hatch grating over their heads was drawn back and cast aside, and Hogue, the master's mate, stuck his head down to yell at them. "Mister Lewrie, you're to try your eye once they're in your range. Both sides at once, if you please, sir!"

"Undo the lashings on the gunports and be ready to raise them." Gunfire roared out again, this time from the larboard battery. And they could hear other guns off in the distance. Pirates' guns. *Telesto* rocked a little more energetically as a heavy stone-shot struck her somewhere aft. There were some warbling sounds as hand-hewn shot crossed over her decks from either beam. But then the starboard battery crashed out its defiance once more, and men above them gave a great cheer. Alan put his eye to the vent-hole of the gunport and saw that one of the *praos* had been struck in the best English manner, 'twixt wind and water, and had opened up to the sea like a shattered tea cup!

"We've one to starboard, closing us bows-on, about three cables off!" Alan shouted. "Open the ports! Run out your guns! Take aim! Cock your locks!"

This *prao* was about seventy or eighty feet long, low and rakish. There was no deck, just a platform in the stern for the helmsman and captain, and a fo'c'sle deck forward for two guns. Between there was a walkway that ran the full length of the boat, like an etching of an ancient Roman war-galley. It bristled with flat-faced little men in turbans and printed skirts, armed with spears and swords and a few muskets here and there. There was one mast amidships, with an Arabic-looking lateen sail furled up. Rowers thrashed the water to a foam as they drove in on *Telesto*. The guns fired.

Telesto was hit once solidly, and once in ricochet as one ball splashed short and raised a great water-plume close aboard.

"Ready!" Alan called. "As you bear . . . fire!"

The carronades barked as their light powder charges went off, ran back to slam into the stops of their slides. Wool rammers soaked in the fire-buckets were swabbing out at once. As the smoke slowly dissipated, Lewrie could see that their target had been smashed! The *prao*, roped and pegged together like a *dhow*, had broken into pieces, spilling her hundreds of warriors into the water. Her bows were torn open, and she was already on her way down. Which caused the ones behind her to falter in their rowing, and turn away from a head-on attack. It was then that Alan could see the many skulls festooned on the closest one's gunwales for decoration.

"Ready, larboard!" he gulped in alarm.

"Jaysus!" Hoolahan yelped. There was a *prao* not a full cable off the larboard side. Arrows and blow-guns were working, quilting their ship's side as the little yellow men slaved at readying a pair of guns.

"Run out!"

They beat the pirates to the first shot. Four thirty-two-pounder balls hit her squarely abeam, and she shook like a kicked dog. Huge holes opened in her sides, the guns canted up and disappeared somewhere amidships, and they could hear the screams. She rolled back upright, shaking her mast down in ruin, and kept on rolling, filling with the sea and went down like a stone!

"That's the way, lads! That'll teach the heathen devils!"

The chase-guns fore and aft were firing, the upper-deck batteries were speaking now, a lot faster than those controlled, steady broadsides of earlier. Now and then there were sharper bangs as a light two-pounder swivel gun up on the upper-deck bulwarks was fired, loaded with grape or canister. To starboard, one pirate vessel was almost under the bows, too close-in to be hit with any guns. Alan could hear muskets going off in volley, and the screams of the pirates as they were scythed down. There was a heavy thump, and *Telesto*, still with a slight way on her, shouldered the foe aside with contempt. As she drifted down the starboard side, a hail of grenades with their fuses burning was tossed into her, and a couple of swivels went off, spewing death and pain down into her open hull, even as her yelling crew tried to scale the ship's sides. A pirate appeared in the foremost starboard gunport, curved sword in hand!

They had no boarding weapons on the lower gun deck. Usually they had no need of them. No pikes, cutlasses, pistols or muskets! Even Alan was without his sword. It was Hoolahan who gave a great Celtic howl of rage and rammed a handspike into the pirate's face, tearing it open and shoving him back over the side with a shriek of agony.

"Lowest elevation! Number two gun, ready . . . fire!" Lewrie shouted. The *prao* swirled on the faint bow wave and drifted off about forty feet. The carronade roared, and almost immediately, the ball hit the *prao* in the sternpost, which tied her together with the keel members. The helmsman's deck and the entire stern disappeared, and that was one less to worry about, even if half her cut-throat crew was still clinging to *Telesto*'s side. As they reloaded, it rained bodies outside the gunports as Chiswick's native troops stabbed and shot with their muskets and bayonets, and the upper-deck gun crews plied cutlasses and boarding pikes!

"Filled shot!" Alan demanded. "Give 'em grape and canister!"

Hollow iron balls were fetched from the garlands, rammed home and seated. The next *prao* that loomed up to larboard, under the guns of the upper-deck battery, got it full in the face! When they hit, they shattered into whining, razor-edged iron shards, scattering their contents of plum-sized grape and musket balls in a flash. The *prao* rocked and heaved, and her crew went down in piles, hewn down like corn stalks. She was still afloat, but she was out of the fight, bearing her cargo of dead and dying!

At that sight, the rest of the pirates bore away, paddles flashing quick as runner's heels to escape the unequal slaughter. The upper-deck guns began to bark once more in controlled broadsides. Out to about a nautical mile and a quarter, the eighteen-pounders could hurt the foe, while his weaker, older guns could not respond.

"Out of our range," Alan said finally, as their last volley from the carronades fell short. "Quarter-gunners, stand your crews easy. Sponge out, but have charges and shot ready to load if they've a mind to try us again."

"Aye, sir."

Alan was soaked to the skin, even in his lightest clothes. He wanted air, and a long drink of water from a scuttle-butt. "Take over for me. I'll go on deck where I may see the better."

He flew up the ladder to the hatch and emerged on the upper gun deck. McTaggart was there among his gun crews as they sponged out and reloaded.

"Warm enough work fir ya, Mister Lewrie?" McTaggart teased, wearing a pleased expression. "Twas a plucky pack o' rascals they sent ageen us."

"We almost had them in for tea below decks, Mister McTaggart," Alan replied with a smile, not to be outdone in calmness, now that the enemy was flying. "Shocking manners they had, though."

"Och, aye, nae the sairt ya could take tae p'lite comp'ny." McTaggart laughed, which made his gun crews respond in kind.

"Cease fire!" Choate, the first officer, bellowed from the railing of the quarterdeck. "Mister Lewrie?"

"Aye, sir?"

"Take a ship's boat to yonder *prao*!" Choate ordered. "A file of those soldiers as well! Mister Twigg wants prisoners, if there are any!"

"At once, sir!"

The pirate boat they had gutted was rocking slack on the sea, her red hull slimed with fresh crimson from all her dead and wounded. No one challenged them as they came alongside. No swords were raised as they gained her bulwarks and dropped over to the rowers' benches. Those pirates that were not incapacitated shrank away with fear as they saw European faces on their decks, followed by a *havildar*, or sergeant of Bengali infantry, and a squad of *sepoys* came on board with bayonets fixed on their Brown Bess muskets.

"My God!" Alan gasped. The smell of death was everywhere so quickly in the searing sun! Coppery odors of spilled blood mixed with spilled entrails, smashed limbs, opened visceras, loose bowels and bladders. Pirates, now looking small and wiry instead of seven feet tall and dangerous, lay quivering in their death rattles, or whimpering and crying in pain.

"Stopped their business most wondrously, sir," Twigg said as he poked and prodded the nearest corpses with his small-sword. "Aha. What have we here?"

He bent down to tear a necklace loose from a dead man who was dressed in silk. It was heavy gold links, and depended from it was a large pectoral about 3 inches across, set with emeralds and a large ruby in the center big as a robin's egg. Twigg pocketed his prize, wrapping it in a calico print handkerchief. "A bloody prince of someone's blood," he spat. "A successful sea-robber. Until today, that is. *Havildar-ji.* Disarm those men and bind them."

"Jeehan, sahib," the sergeant replied.

"What are we looking for, sir?" Alan asked, wishing he was anywhere else.

"Evidence, Mister Lewrie!" Twigg said expansively. "A bit of loot from a ravaged ship. Some clue that these might be the ones we seek. And some sign of who encouraged them. It's not often I've seen their kind take on a ship big as ours, even if the wind was against us. They're not fools, Mister Lewrie. The hope of gain would have to outweigh their fear of European firepower. Poke about. See what you may turn up."

"Aye aye, sir," Alan replied. He wandered up forward towards the fo'c'sle platform, his sword drawn and ready should one of those mangled bodies show signs of life. God knew there were weapons in plenty scattered about to use, should one of them wish to take one of the infidels with him to Paradise. The peoples of the region were mostly Muslim, he'd learned. Killing him would raise their stock with Allah.

What he found was some gold coins of Asian minting, a heavy gold ring or two. Some earrings. All useful, he thought, so he stuck them in his breeches. The muskets were chased with silver, of an ancient pattern, with long barrels and crude match-locks or even wheel-locks. The swords and knives . . . curved Eastern-looking things or wavy bladed *krees*, mottled with Damascan forging techniques.

"Profit for the morning's work!" Twigg exclaimed back aft as he turned up a small chest of treasure. The sailors and *sepoys* were not averse to looting the corpses, either.

"Sir?" Alan called. "Come take a look at this."

One of the cannon on the forecastle platform was a ninepounder. The truck had been smashed, and its crew draped about it in death. But it was not a brass or bronze Asian gun with fanciful adornments. It was a brutally plain and functional European gun, with a flintlock striker and British proof-marks. To further prove its origin, there were serge powder bags scattered about, and a flask of quick-burning priming powder hung round the dead gunner's neck.

"No way of knowing which ship it came from, but it's a start," Twigg nodded, rubbing his horny palms together. "Could have been off any of those ships reported missing. And the date is within the last two years."

"No rust, sir," Alan commented, kneeling by the cannon. "I'd not expect their sort to take this good care of an iron gun. She's fresh-painted and well-greased, still. For an iron barrel at sea to be this clean, it had to be very recent. And flints, sir. You know how often flints break or wear out. Look at this one in the dog's-jaws of the lock. That's English, too, sure as I'm born."

"Very astute of you, Mister Lewrie," Twigg congratulated. He was interrupted by the *havildar*, who had turned up several Brown Bess muskets, Short Land Pattern, also fairly new. "Now we'll have the truth out of these rascals. Fetch me that one, *havildar*. We'll find where they hailed from, and we'll go pay them a visit they'll not soon forget!"

Twigg was not too particular about how he got his information. In local lingo, he began to shout and rave in front of the first man fetched up by the *sepoys*. He made passes with one of those wavy-bladed knives. Lewrie thought he was merely threatening, until he at last made contact along the struggling pirate's bare waist. Just the slightest touch, and there was an instant line of blood droplets.

Twigg seized the man by the scruff of the neck and shoved him to the rail to look over the side, with the *krees* at his throat. The tropical sharks had been drawn by the blood in the water, the dead of the other *praos* they'd shattered and sent down with gunfire. Fins cut the calm sea, some lazy and searching, some darting and quicker on a scent. The pirate began to scream and shout, louder than Twigg and his accusations and questions.

"Look here, Mister Twigg, sir," Alan was finally forced to say when he knew the older man was dead-serious about dumping him over the side as shark-food. "He's not anybody *I'd* care to know, but damme, sir, it's just not done!"

"If you'd rather not watch, you're welcome, Mister Lewrie," Twigg replied. "Go back to the ship, then."

"It's not just that, sir. Surely there's a better way than to . . ." Alan protested. Both he and his English sailors were upset by this treatment. Try as they had not too long ago to cut these people to minced meat, once a foe surrendered, to their code, he was to be well treated. British tars had a strong sense of what was right or wrong, and were not averse or slow to voice their opinions, even under the threat of Naval discipline.

"Feeding survivors to the sharks is nothing more than they

expect, sir," Twigg argued, his blade still to the struggling man's neck. "No more than we could expect from them were we at their mercy. We are not dealing with honorable foes who've struck their colors, you damned puppy! They're blood-thirsty, murdering, piratical butchers! Look over the side! Look under their bows, sir! See the skulls of their victims? Some of those are Englishmen, sure as you're born. Aye, we can treat 'em Christian, and they'll laugh in our faces for our pains. But we'd not know where they sailed from, nor who supplies 'em. And that'll mean more English sailors murdered or tortured to death for their barbaric amusements. Now which do you prefer, sir?"

"Seems to me, Mister Twigg, that one person's barbaric amusements is pretty much like yours," Alan drawled. "Sir."

"Goddamn you, you priggish little hymn-singer! Back to the ship. I'll deal with you later! Leave the *sepoys* and fetch me when I've done."

"Gladly, sir."

They rowed back to *Telesto*, still lying slack and idle on the gently heaving ocean with her sails slatting and booming for want of wind. Hammers and saws thudded or rasped as repairs were made to what damage they'd suffered. Lewrie accosted Captain Ayscough on the quarterdeck and related what Twigg was doing.

Ayscough drew his pocket watch from his breeches and studied the face, then cast an eye aloft to the coach-whip of the long, narrow private house flag, which flicked lazy as a cat's tail in the weak zephyrs.

"Shall we allow him to proceed, sir?" Alan asked, hoping for an order from his captain to go back and tell Twigg to leave off. As he waited for Ayscough to answer, there was a shrill scream from the *prao*, followed by a splash, and a sudden commotion in the water as the sharks found a tasty new tidbit.

"I'd admire if you assisted the third officer aloft, Mister Lewrie," Ayscough grunted, his countenance dark and suffused with repressed emotions. "There's damage to the fore-topmast to put aright. God grant there'll be wind soon so we may proceed, 'stead of lying here, boxing the compass."

"But, sir . . ."

"Enough!" Ayscough snapped, then relented with a bitter

sigh. "Welcome to the mysterious, and cruel, Far East, Mister Lewrie."

"Aye, sir."

The wind came up about an hour after noon sights, and *Telesto* made her way north once more. The *prao* they burned, as a warning to the others. Her survivors, those that had not suffered Twigg's cruel attentions, hung like plucked fowl from her lateen yard by the neck.

Chapter 2

They anchored at Macao two weeks later, after riding out several heavy gales of monsoon winds and rain. Twigg, Wythy and Ayscough went ashore to the Chinese Customs House, to get what they called a "chop," which would allow them to proceed up the Pearl River to the traders' anchorage at Whampoa, an island twelve miles below the "City of Rams," China's only trade outlet to the outside world. In the meantime, they would transfer cargo.

Even before their party had returned from shore, a rickety local *lorcha* came alongside, with written instructions from Twigg that they should transship the opium to her. Reputable merchantmen could not be seen engaging in the opium trade; that was for the local Portugese, who did not require a "chop" to go up-river a short way.

The captain and mate of the *lorcha* were filthy brutes, part Indian, part Chinee and only part Portugese. Oh, they were clean enough to not stink as bad as *Telesto*'s crew, but there was about them such a nefarious and desperate air of the practiced cut-throat that no one, especially after the affair with the pirates, wanted to get anywhere near them, as though they reeked of evil. The *lorcha* was long, low, rakish and fast-looking, armed to the teeth with swivels and lighter four-pounder guns. And her crew sprouted wickedly sharp weapons from every pocket.

"They look as though they sleep armed to the teeth," Alan commented to Mr. Brainard, the sailing master. Once he was in warmer waters Brainard had shucked most of his woolen clothing for light cotton or nankeen, and looked particularly keen and energetic once more.

"If one wants to stay alive in Macao, one does," Brainard

said with a chuckle. "The most sinful city on the face of this earth, no error. Too much money to be made here, too many temptations to steal or murder for it. And engaged in the opium trade as they are, they're on the razor's edge. Who knows when the mandarins'll decide to take 'em and strangle 'em for smuggling? You can't trust anyone except the members of the Co Hong up-river not to cheat you or pirate you for your shoe buckles! Man who'll trade with you one trip'll have you killed the next, and them not a week apart."

There were eight rules for traders from the outside world in the Pearl River. No foreign-devil warships above the Bogue at the mouth of the river. No women, guns, spears or any arms allowed at the factories, or *hongs*, in Canton. All ships had to register at Macao, as well as all river pilots and ship's *compradores*. Each factory could have no more than eight Chinese working for them, so the fewest people would be contaminated by foreign-devils. Foreigners had to forego the pleasures of sailing the river for pleasure. Only on holidays could foreigners go to the Flower Gardens or the Honam Joss House, and then no more than ten at a time and only when accompanied by a linguist. They could not stay out after dark, or carouse. Foreign-devils could not present petitions to the native Viceroy; everything had to go through the Co Hong's eight members. The Co Hong could not go into debt with foreigners. Smuggling was forbidden. And lastly, foreign-devil ships could not loiter about outside the river but must go directly to Whampoa, instead of "selling to rascally natives goods subject to duty, that these may smuggle them, and thereby defraud his Celestial Majesty's revenue."

It was also, Alan learned, against his Celestial Majesty's law to teach foreign-devils Chinese, so trade was carried on in a mix of Portugee, Chinese and English called "pidgin," the closest the Chinese could come to saying "business."

Anything, anything that upset the touchy mandarins could bring a total cessation of trade, which hurt everybody, so merchantmen had to obey "tremblingly," as the Chinese officials concluded their documents. Yet, at the same time, a lively and illegal trade went on down-river at Lintin Island and at Nan'ao. Brainard had even told of mandarin boats ordered to enforce the ban against smuggling, and the opium trade, which contracted lucrative deals, and smuggled the stuff up to Canton themselves!

"Tonight, this *lorcha*'ll be receiving a government mandarin on her decks," Brainard explained. "He'll get his tobacco and wine, warn about lingering in the estuary instead of going direct to Whampoa, and then he'll get down to brass tacks. 'How many chests?' he'll ask, and we'll tell him outright. Then he'll figure out what he thinks we're worth and ask for his *sing-song*."

"He'll want a serenade?" Alan grinned. "God help him if Mister Twigg takes his bagpipers along, then."

"No, his *sing-song* is his cut. His *cumshaw* . . . his custom. 'Allee same same *sing-song*, allee same custom.' " Brainard laughed. "After he's been feted and bought off, that's the signal for the real traders to come aboard and purchase. Then the *lorcha* comes back to Macao full of silver. *Taels* and *taels* of the bloody stuff, maybe five or six *lac* with the amount of opium we have on board, young sir. A *lac*, let me inform you, is worth about ten thousand pounds."

"Merciful God!" Alan gasped in awe.

"And you'd better believe the custom official ashore yonder in Macao knows exactly what we're doing here, and our 'chop' will conveniently not arrive aboard 'til we've disposed of the opium, so we can sail up-river innocent as newborn babes. Gad, what a country!"

"So what are the chances of our suspected French privateers being at this Lintin Island, sir?" Alan asked.

"Depends on whether they've arrived or not. We may ask about, but not too much, else we'd raise too much suspicion. Might even affect the price of our cargo." Brainard frowned. "If they've looted all the ships we suspect they have, what they didn't have to share out to their native associates, they might already be up-river off Whampoa, pie-faced innocent as any other merchantmen."

"Then they'd be a big ship, like us, sir?" Alan pressed.

"Possibly. Something fast, like one of their latest seventy-four-gunned Third Rates converted to a merchantman, like us. But that pretty much describes half the ships in the world that could get here. If they came here at all."

"Well, sir," Alan speculated, "they'd have to dispose of their ill-gotten gains somewhere. Why not here?"

"Oh, I'll grant you that. Sooner'r later, they'd be stuffed bung to the deck-heads with loot," Brainard snorted. "But, they could drop it at Ile de France in the middle of the Indian Ocean, at Pondichery or Chandernargore, and ship it home on a *Compagnie des Indies* ship with no one the wiser."

"But they've taken Indiamen and country ships loaded with silver or opium. The silver they could keep, maybe load it into a second vessel. But the opium would have to be sold here. Where else is there such a market for it, and where else on the Chinese coast would the mandarins collude with 'em?"

"Which is why we're here, young sir. We may not be right, but it is a strong chance. Once we're up at Whampoa, and at Canton, I'll warn you to keep a weather-eye peeled for anything out of the ordinary."

"As if China isn't enough out of the ordinary, sir," Alan said with a shrug. "I doubt if I'd know what to look for."

"I leave that to our super-cargoes, Twigg and Wythy. They know the trade well as anybody."

"And pirates," Alan muttered under his breath.

"I know, that cut a bit rough on you, to see what Twigg did," Brainard said comfortingly. "But they'd have gotten the same after an Admiralty proceeding, stretched by the neck by 'Captain Swing.' Wish we'd had the time to hunt down their anchorage and chastise 'em just a bit more."

"I was thinking more of the way he got his information, sir."

"And not much of that, either. I've spent years out here in the Far East and the Great South Seas. It's the way of things out here. Something to leave behind you once you get back into the Bay of Bengal, or the Cape of Good Hope. Don't fret on it."

"If you say so, sir," Alan replied. "But seeing that made me feel a lot less guilty about my own faults. I don't think I could ever torture a man to death. Or feed him to the sharks for the fun of it."

"Wasn't 'fun,' Mister Lewrie," Brainard sniffed. "Just business."

Chapter 3

Whampoa Reach was so densely crowded with shipping when they dropped the hook after a four-day voyage up the teeming Pearl River that they barely had room to swing. The river had narrowed from a wide estuary to a proper river at the Bogue after the first two days. The river pilot that guided them had gone hoarse cursing the *sampans* and *junks* full of fishermen, mendicants and permanently poor to get out of their way. And the closer they got to Canton, the more it seemed that the Pearl River had been cruelly inaptly named. It stank worse than the Old Fleet Ditch, the Hooghly or the Thames, bearing as it did the ordure and the garbage of untold millions of Chinese from its mountain birthplace to their anchorage.

There were ships of every nation there, crowded into the Reach as cheek-to-jowl as the thousands of native boats that made up floating suburbs, too poor to live on land. Dane and Dutch flags fluttered above vessels so beamy they looked like butter-tubs. There were Spanish and Portugese ships, Swedish ships, and a few merchantmen from Hamburg and the Baltic, even a pair of Prussians. There were British East Indiamen as lofty and trim as the stoutest "ocean bulldogs" of the Royal Navy, and country ships looking more rakish and piratical than something from a Defoe tale. There were Russian ships, even some Austrians, and lesser nations from the Mediterranean. And there were three or four racebuilt and over-sparred vessels, a little smaller than most, flying the new Stars and Stripes of the late Rebel Colonies, now graced by the name of the United States of America. And the French, huge merchantmen of the *Compagnie des Indies*, and their own country ships.

Whampoa Island, from September and the delivery of the first teas from inland, to the first of March when the Chinese would order them out and the Monsoon winds shifted to make faster passages home, would be a floating international city of its own below the distinctive island's pagodas and towers.

Alan Lewrie reckoned it would have to do for the next few weeks. With so many strictures on merchantmen as foreign-devil barbarians, there wouldn't be much in the way of recreation, except for the infamous Hog Lane ashore in the factory ghetto of Canton. Bumboats came alongside in a continual stream offering whores and gew-gaws, but no captain in his right mind would put his ship out of discipline in such an alien harbor, outnumbered as they were.

The hands eschewed these poorer offerings and waited their turn to visit Hog Lane, where they could swill and swive, no matter that the women would probably be peppered to their eyebrows with the pox. They heeded no warnings, and no captain could enforce celibacy without having a mutiny on his hands. The men had had enough of "boxing the Jesuit and getting cock-roaches," as they termed solitary stimulation.

There were other ships to visit, if one's idea of fun was going aboard another ship after spending up to six months aboard one already. Most provided what little entertainment they could, and *Telesto* was popular since she had bagpipers, the hand-bellows organ and some accomplished fiddlers and fifers to amuse her visitors, and her own hands. But even here, they were limited by the strictures of the host nation. Once at anchor, they had put out a ship's boat so the bosun could row about to see if the yards were squared away properly, and a mandarin's *junk* had been there in a twinkling, shouting pidgin orders against "boating for pleasure."

Alan suspected the mandarins got a cut from the many *sampans* that ruled the 'tween-ship traffic, who charged exorbitant fees to ferry foreign-devils about, their prices changing with no rhyme or reason, almost from one hour to the next.

The visiting back and forth would have made it easy to snoop and pry to find their suspected French privateers. Except that Alan wasn't allowed to. After their last encounter, he was pretty much in Twigg's bad-books again, and idled aboard ship most of the time. There was work to do, and he was made aware that he was, indeed, the fourth officer, the most junior, therefore the one most liable.

Twigg and his partner, Wythy, were thankfully out of his hair. They had gone ashore to take borrowed or rented "digs" at one of the established *hongs* in the factory-ghetto, doing arcane trading things, such as turning their *lacs* of silver into checques for safer transport, arranging the purchase of teas, silks, nankeens to be woven by hand from Indian cotton, and showing patterns for sets of china and lacquerware, and diagrams for the latest styles in furniture wanted back home in England so they could be manufactured in time for departure.

Their cargo of opium, the officers were informed in the captain's quarters, had fetched over eighty thousand pounds sterling above what they'd had to pay out to customs officials and mandarins as bribes. Which sum made every officer lift his eyebrows and make small, speculative, humming noises. "Hmmm, damn *profitable* work, for Navy-work, hmmm?" Made them wonder just what percentage would be Droits of the Crown, what part Droits of the Admiralty, and what precedent there would be about shares after the expense of the voyage was subtracted. In peacetime, there was no prize-money for fighting and taking a ship in combat, and there never was much profit in taking a privateer, which was why they flourished so easily. Made them wonder if anyone from the Crown would mind if they laid a few thousand guineas aside . . . "for contingencies" . . . and never reported it. Never reported any profit at all, perhaps, and pocketed the sum entire . . . ?

Lewrie finally got shore leave after a couple of weeks. In company with McTaggart again, he went over the side and took his ease in a large bumboat, a scow or barge practically as wide as it was long, for the twelve-mile row to Canton. They were ensconced in capacious chairs on the upper deck, while seamen had to idle on the lower deck in a herd of expectant and recently paid humanity. They sampled *mao tai* brandy and lolled indolent as mandarins, though the fussy, and Presbyterian, McTaggart had some qualms about being *too* comfortable in this life.

They wafted up the narrowing river between the mainland and Honam Island, a faerie-land of willows, delicate bridges, parks and ponds, where the Joss House was, and the homes of some of the richest Chinese merchants of the Co Hong. But Honam Island, to larboard, was not their destination. They were landed at Jack Ass Point, next to one of the customs houses. The sailors from several ships gave a great cheer and dashed to the right of the huge square for Hog Lane, leaving McTaggart and Lewrie to descend and alight.

"There's mair commerce in this ain place than the Pool of

London!" McTaggart exclaimed as they goggled at the piles and piles of goods, the hordes of coolies fetching and toting and the *sampans* being loaded and unloaded. On the far side of the square, there was a long row of factories, broken only by Hog Lane, China Street and a creek. On the other side of the factories, or *hongs*, there was a wide boulevard, and the Consoo House, the headquarters of the *Yeung Hong Sheung*, better known as the Co Hong, and a matching row of old and delapidated minor *hongs* of Chinese merchants, there on sufferance from the Co Hong. The whole thing was walled in from the rest of the city to prevent the natives from being disturbed or corrupted by the barbarian traders. But the Consoo House and most of the *hongs* on that side of Factory Street, as they'd been warned, were off-limits for them, except for a few shops in Old Clothes Street, and Carpenter's Square at the far right-hand end of the ghetto.

Feeling naked without a pistol, sword or even a clasp knife, they made the best of their time ashore. First stop was at the Chun Qua Factory, third building east of China Street, to their far left, where they'd established headquarters. Conveniently right next door to the French *Compagnie des Indies* factory!

"Ah, welcome ashore at last," Tom Wythy grated, sounding anything but welcoming, as he sorted through packets of tea on a table. "Have an ale. Chinee muck, but not as bad as some."

He had a large tub near his feet, filled with ice and rice chaff, from which he drew two stone bottles and proferred them.

"Cold ale?" Alan frowned.

"Aye, ice comes all the way from Siberia, far's I know, run by some poor coolies, an' God help 'em if it melts on the way. The way they like it." Wythy belched. "No accountin' fer taste among savages. Refreshin' on a hot day, though, I must admit."

"Mm, not bad at that," Alan commented after an appreciative eructation of his own. "Close enough to home-brewed."

"Mm, if the inn's common-rooms'r chilly as most back in England. Let it stand awhile if it's too cold fer ye, Mister McTaggart."

"What are you doing, sir?" McTaggart asked.

"Gradin' tea, such as I may. Sit ye down to see."

As they quaffed their ales, Wythy laid out samples, explaining their grades and desirability. The smaller the leaves, the better the tea. There was coarse black Bohea, from late in the growing season, worth something in trade but not much: a poor man's tea. Another black tea was Congou, what the East India Company bought in quantity. The best black teas were Souchong, scented with flowers, and Pekoe, which was only of the best young spring buds, delicate and very dear.

Then there were the green teas: Gunpowder and Pearl Tea, and Yu Tsien, which were the choicest spring pickings, and in descending order, Hyson skin, and Twankay, which was mostly used to adulterate batches of the better pickings.

"Yes, I've always found the younger the bud, the more fun to pick as well, sir," Alan grinned, unable to contain himself as the lecture ran on, and on, and *on*.

"More like deflowerin', Mister Lewrie?" Wythy rasped. "Ye'd be the best judge o' that, I'm sure. Ye mind my warnin' about the local lasses, both o' ye? 'Twas Macao'r nothin'. No women in the factories, ye know."

"Yet there are women in Hog Lane, sir, for the sailors?" Alan inquired. "Do the Chinese mean no foreign women, or no women at all?"

"Aye, fer a whiff o' silver, ye may find custom, though I warn ye both, they're sure to be poxed so bad even the surgeon's mercury cure'd only slow it down," Wythy allowed.

"But something more discreet . . . uhm, more select for senior traders, sir?" Alan pressed softly, and was pleased that Wythy gave him a shrug and a sly wink. So the man's not a total lout, he thought!

"A *tai pan*, head of a trading house, well, there are places . . ." Wythy grunted. "Not at this time of day. The Chinee is a hard-workin' bugger. The day's fer making profit. If the humor's on ye so devilish hard, Mister Lewrie, I'll give ye the fairest wind to steer y'er course by, but 'pon y'er head be it, mind."

"Aye, sir," Alan agreed. "I'd expect nothing less."

"Well, be off with ye. I've work to do. Sup here with us at seven o' the evening. In the meantime, enjoy the sights. Take a peek about. Go visiting," Wythy enjoined, winking once more and jerking his head over his shoulder to indicate the French *hong* next door. "I spotted some nice bargains along China Street."

They finished their ales and went outside into the heat of the day. After a couple of cold ones, it didn't seem that bad any longer, and there was a decent breeze to keep the hordes of flies at bay and cool the air. At least it wasn't Calcutta, or the Equator.

"I despair o' your immortal soul, Mister Lewrie," McTaggart sighed with a long-put-upon air. "Wenching. Is that all ya hae on your mind, sir?"

"If left to my own devices, yes," Alan confessed willingly.

"You're as much a heathen as een o' these yellow fellas! A bluidy . . . pagan!" McTaggart spat. "I doan know why I abide your comp'ny!"

"Church of England, actually, not pagan," Alan corrected.

"Same bluidy thing," McTaggart sighed.

They shopped in China Street, running into Burgess Chiswick, who was out browzing in company with his native orderly Nandu, both wearing civilian clothes. Burgess was loaded down with packages—or at least his orderly was.

"The most unbelievable things, Alan!" Burgess enthused. "Laces as good as any from Flanders or Holland, and damn-all cheap, too. A whole tablecloth for the price of a man's shirt, can you credit it?"

"Hollo, what's this? In need of fanning, Burge?" Alan teased.

"For mother. And for Caroline. Even one for Mammy."

"Your grand-mither?" McTaggart inquired, somewhat confused.

"Family slave. Been with us for years," Burge informed him off-handedly. "Couldn't bear to sell her off at Charleston, so she crossed to England with us. Practically raised me. Those smaller bundles are silk shawls for all. Can't go to a drum or dance without a fancy shawl and a Chinese fan, now can they?"

"Slavery." McTaggart shivered, and wandered off on his own.

"What the devil did he mean by that?" Chiswick huffed. "By God, if he's slurring my family because we . . ."

"No reason to take offense, Burge," Alan said, grinning. "Between my morals, and you a slave-owning Carolinian, he's having a hellish hard day of it."

"The devil take him, then, him and his blue-stocking airs."

"My dear Burgess, the devil wouldn't dare!" Alan drawled.

After plunging into the market, Alan was entranced all over again, just as he had been in Calcutta. There was so much to see, so many new aromas to savor, so many goods in so many shops that would have gathered mobs of oglers back in London, though most of them could never afford most of it, as novel as any raree-show on earth. And once more, he was glad he'd sailed halfway round the world to see it, hard as the sailing was between ports. This experience was something he'd never forget.

As mementoes, he bought a fiery-red silk dressing gown for himself, all figured with dragons in green and iridescent blue that leaped off the cloth. A small carved ivory *junk*. Some marble models of temple dogs for his mantel, wherever that would be once he was home. And, with mention of the lovely and gentle Caroline Chiswick, he purchased a pair of earrings and a necklace made of jade, ivory and silver beads, to go home to her on the first Indiaman clearing port for England.

They loaded Nandu down like a pack-pony and sent him trotting off to the Chun Qua Factory, while they took a stand-up repast of hot soup and noodles from an open-air vendor, and strolled the square. Most particularly that part of the square behind the French Factory.

"Now what the devil . . . ?" Alan mused aloud as they saw some of the items being carted up to the factory from the docks and customs house on the quay. "Can you tell me what these are, sir?"

Alan had inquired of a man dressed as a European seaman.

"*M'seur?*" the man replied, turning to face them.

"*Parle vous l'Anglais, m'seur?* Can you tell me . . ."

"*Ah, mais oui.* Zose, *m'seur*? Ze shark feens," the man said.

"Well, now I've heard just about everything," Burgess griped.

"Whatever are they for?"

"*Pour ze potage, m'seur*," the sailor explained. "*Pardon, j'sui* Marcel Monnot. *Notre* ship *La Malouine. Et vous?*" After they had introduced themselves, Monnot went on. "Ze shark feen soup, *m'seurs*. Zese *Chinetoque*, zey *manger* zese *potage* . . . mak zem . . ." He could not think of the English word, so he rammed an expressive fist at them, grasping his arm at the elbow. "Pour ze old *homme* wiz ze *fair jeune fille, n'est-ce pas*? Mak *'l'verge' formidable*, ha ha!"

"Like oysters!" Burgess cried in delight. "For renewed vigor with the ladies. God, as many sharks as we saw on the voyage here, I wish we'd known of it. Do they pay dear for them, then?"

"*Ah, mais oui, m'seur!*" Monnot agreed heartily. "*Un* feen, zey pay *trois, quatre livres!*" he told them with an expansive Gallic shrug. "Vee 'ave *beaucoup* feen, mak *beaucoup livres*, hah! *Bon!*"

"Well, damme," Alan commented. "*Merci*, M'seur Monnot."

"Vee 'ave also ze ginseng, *m'seurs*. Vair good. Same, *aussi*."

"Monnot, allez vite! Revenir aux travaille!" some petty officer barked, and the man bowed his departure, leaving Chiswick and Lewrie to stroll among the boxes and crates as he went back to work.

"I never heard that ginseng was a restorative in the Carolinas," Burgess said. "Made a good, healthful tea, was all we used it for. Mother swears by it, but it's hard to find. Maybe I should buy her some and ship it home. Well, there were some slaves who said it was an aphrodisiac, but you couldn't put much stock in some of their tales."

"And furs," Alan pointed out.

"Oh, yes. Mister Twigg said the Chinese don't have many good furs. Have to come from Russia or somewhere. Ermine, sable, glutton, mink or such'll sell dear here in Canton. I met one of those Yankee Doodle skippers this morning. Said he'd been to the Nootka Sound on the Bering Sea. He was trading furs. Quite profitable, he told me."

"My, you have been busy this morning," Alan snickered.

"Them that had a little English," Burgess allowed with a shrug as they idled against a stack of crates to watch the coolies and the French crew unload a *junk* that had lightered their cargo up from Whampoa Reach. "Rest of it was way over my head. Never thought I'd have to learn anything more than a little Cherokee back home. I'm lucky I can savvy just enough Hindee so Nandu and my *subadar* don't cock their heads and look at me queer. I say . . . good pelts, those. That Yankee captain didn't have better."

"What do they sell for?" Alan asked idly, finding the spying business a dead bore as the hot afternoon wore on.

"He told me he'd get almost one hundred of their dollars for a pelt," Burgess informed him.

"Hmm, wonder what that is in real money?" Alan mused aloud.

"I think it's somewhere between five and six pounds sterling. But here's the profitable part, Alan. The Nootka Sound Indians'll swap you a prime pelt for one four-a-penny board nail!"

"S'truth!"

"Can you credit it? 'Course, you were among the Creeks and the Seminolee."

"Well, we weren't doing much trading. 'Cept for my wife."

"Your *what*?"

And on their way back to the Chun Qua Factory, Alan regaled Chiswick with the tale of impregnating the Cherokee slave-girl Rabbit and being forced to purchase her from her owner for a dragoon pistol, a cartouche pouch, a shirt and a pair of deer hides.

"And there you are, paying court to my sister Caroline, and you a married man," Burgess japed. "I should write and warn her how fickle your enthusiasms are!"

Chapter 4

Their supper that evening at the factory was another of those marvels to a palate ruined by ship's rations. Or by the blandness of English cooking, Alan thought, except in the rarest instances. Oh, there was lots of rice, but, like the supper at Sir Hugo's *bungalow* in Calcutta, it seemed that hundreds of dishes made their appearances as removes. Some fiery hot, some crunchy and only mildly spiced, some almost recognizable and some that could only be identified by comparing them to puppy-spew, or one of William Pitt's hairballs. The lone Chinese table-servant announced the name of each dish, with Wythy translating—pork, chicken, beef, lobster bits, shrimp, oil-fried omelets and such. Lewrie decided they could call 'em devil's turds, 'long as they kept them coming.

Wythy alone of their company ate with chopsticks in the native manner, and put away as much as two of them together with a frantic neatness. Not a wasted motion when he was at table.

"Ah!" Wythy said at last when the final dish, and the gigantic bowl of rice, had been removed. "Perfection from the soup to the nuts!"

"Speaking of soup, Mister Wythy," Alan asked, attention fixed on the port decanter that the servant placed by Twigg's elbow. "Do these Chinese really eat soups made out of bird's nests and shark fins?"

"Oh, aye they do. Daft on 'em, they are," Wythy rumbled with a laugh. "Bird's nests . . . well, that's the mandarin's style. Eat such exotic shite such's their Emperor's court can obtain. Like the old Romans. Lark's tongues, mouse cheeks an' such."

"To show off how wealthy they are," Twigg commented.

"The rarer the victuals, the better show they put on for their guests, to flaunt their wealth."

"An' ye'll have noted, no doubt, how most o' the really nabob-rich Chinese traders'r fatter'n Falstaff," Wythy added.

Alan hadn't noted any such thing, but he gave the comment a sage nod of agreement. Wythy had fed himself into such a good mood, and Alan wanted nothing to upset him. Wythy hadn't told him where the safer brothels were yet.

"Peasants in the countryside are one crop away from famine," Twigg said. "And it's short commons for most of 'em. Just take a look at the people who live on all those *sampans* we passed on the way up-river for comparison. Poor as Irish crofters, and about as starved, most of the time. It's a virtue to the Chinese to get rich, and set a table such as a duke could afford back home."

"Er . . . about the shark fins, though," Burgess pressed. "Does this soup really restore an old man's vigor?"

"Well, I'm nowhere near needin' restoration yet, sir," Wythy boomed with amusement like a thumped barrel, "but there's more wonders in this world'n ye could shake a stick at. I've heard tell it works. Mind ye, that was from Chun Qua himself. Who knows? Where'd ye hear o' shark fin soup?"

"Oh, there was a French mate on the customs dock this afternoon," Alan replied, finally getting his hands on the port and pouring himself a full bumper. "They were unloading bales of the damned things. Strung together like fish on twine. Must have had thousands, and getting three or four *livres* apiece for 'em, too, he told us."

"A French ship," Twigg commented, raising his eyebrows to Alan to start the decanter leftward down the table to his empty glass.

"Aye, sir."

"And what else did they land on the docks?" Twigg inquired.

"Furs, sir," Burgess supplied. "Nootka Sound pelts. Quite a lot of 'em. Uhm . . . bird's nests. All sorts of stuff. Right, Alan?"

"Well, most of it was crated or bundled. I did see the furs, and the shark fins, though," Alan allowed. "I'd have to take your word on the bird's nests, Burge. That, and the ginseng."

"Ginseng!" Twigg barked, and set the decanter down on the table with a loud thump. "Ginseng, d'you say, sir?"

"Oh, yes." Burgess bubbled on. "Their mate . . . what was

his name, Mon-something . . . no matter. Said they had ginseng aboard. I believe he said it's about as good as shark fins to aid old men in passion. Our old slaves back home in North Carolina said . . ."

"Mister Wythy," Twigg interrupted, almost shushing Chiswick to silence, "correct me if I err, but ginseng is primarily a Chinese herb, is it not, sir?"

"Aye, 'tis," Wythy agreed.

"But is there not another source in this world for ginseng?" Twigg pressed. "I speak of another member of the Araliaceae family, the *Panax quinquefolius*, which produces the same five leaves, scarlet berries and succulent root. And is not North America, the Colonies . . . former colonies, now . . . the only other known source of ginseng?"

"Ah ha," Wythy grinned slowly in confirmation.

"Tell me more about this ship, sirs," Twigg demanded.

"Well, she's the *La Malouine*, sir," Alan stated.

"Ah ha," Wythy said once more, maddeningly obtuse to them.

"Do you think she might be the Frog privateer we seek, sir?" Chiswick asked.

"She very well might be," Twigg replied, nodding grimly.

"Well, she stands out, compared to those ships we've snooped around so far," Wythy informed them. "Most of 'em seem fairly innocent, see. Sailin' outa Pondichery'r Chandernargore. Isle of France, or all the way from L'Orient or Nantes on the French Biscay coast. May not signify, but . . ."

"Yes, but for several intriguing 'buts,' Tom," Twigg rasped.

"Such as, sir?" Alan inquired, by then totally mystified.

"To have furs, a ship must sail to the Bering Sea to trade in Nootka Sound," Twigg said, beginning to tick points off on his long, knobbly fingers. "Then trade among the Sandwich Islands, Cook Isles, Otaheiti and all to get the bird's nest, sandalwood and shark fins. But for even the smallest crew to sail that far and live among the Polynesians for the duration of that voyage, they would have to forego much cargo on the way outward for supplies to keep the hands fit. Now tell me, young sirs, were they landing anything else? Indian goods, perhaps?"

"Aye, sir. Cotton bales, brassware, spices. Crates of silver."

"Well, now, that's an extremely odd mix of cargo. Far out of the ordinary for most French Indiamen, or country ships," Twigg mused, tenting his fingers under his cadaverous chin and gazing at the ceiling. "And I need hardly tell a seafarer such as yourself the near impossibility of that, do I, Mister Lewrie?"

"Uhm," Lewrie commented, stalling for time and wondering what in hell Twigg was talking about. Twigg dropped his gaze from the rafters to Alan's face, like a tutor expecting him to recite.

"Have to go to Nootka Sound early in summer, late spring, sir," he began, grasping for ideas. All the plum wine he'd put down with supper didn't help that process. "That means they'd have to leave Pondichery or wherever even earlier, in the . . . oh!"

"Oh, indeed, sir," Twigg said, grinning a little.

"The Monsoon, the summer Monsoons are out of the sou'west as early as they'd have to leave," Alan continued. "And about the time they're changing from the winter nor'east winds. There's violent weather then. No one in his right mind would try that. And then they'd have to sail clear across the entire Pacific, maybe a three or four month voyage to be first in for the furs, as early as May, when the ice melts. And then to gather all the rest on the way back . . ."

"Maybe they have an arrangement with some o' the Polynesian islanders t' arrive an' pick up shark fins an' all on the way out, or don't have t' spend too much time on the way back," Wythy added. "So they might save a full month all told."

"Already loaded to the deck-heads, though, with cargo!" Lewrie beamed. "Where's the room for food, water, firewood?"

"Loaded with what?" Wythy snorted. "Cotton? Sure t' take fire if ye close it up too long. Get a seepage an' watch it swell like a hundred tons o' sponges an' break yer hull? By God, opium don't keep that well that long, either. Either lose yer ship, get marooned with the savages, or watch yer best cargo spoil on ye."

"They could leave here in March and go direct to Nootka Sound," Twigg prompted. "Or make a round voyage every two years, instead of the one, like some of those former Rebel skippers do."

"Then they would have to spend their time fighting the nor'east Monsoons east and north of Guinea," Alan said, remembering his *Falconer*'s. "With the same storms when the winds shift out of the sou'east, about . . . six weeks later than the Indian Ocean, as I recall. It would be impossible to make much headway, tacking close-hauled into a nor'wester. And if they went directly from Macao to Nootka Sound, where'd they get all the Indian goods, then?"

"Excuse me, sirs, if a landsman sticks his oar into the water," Burgess chuckled, "but what if they go to India in March, *thence* to the Nootka Sound, riding the favorable winds. And only do the two-year round voyage?"

"Money, Burgess," Alan replied, smirking. "They ain't Navy. Who could afford to pay a crew for twice the work and only once the profit? And there is the matter of spoilage, like Mister Wythy said."

"Fascinating speculation, is it not, sirs?" Twigg said happily. "And finally, there is the matter of this ship's name. *La Malouine.* We may deduce that her master could possibly be a Breton. We may further imply that he is from St. Malo, on the northern Brittany coast. Who else would name a ship *La Malouine*? Bretons have been pirates, privateersmen and ship-wreckers since before the times of Caesar. Ideally placed to play merry hell with Channel commerce, an activity in which they've indulged since the last Legions marched out of England and France. They're some of the best sailors France may boast of. As good as any Liverpool or Bristol privateer, and twice as bloody-handed."

"Bit obvious, though," Alan said in the long silence that followed. "I mean, the name of the ship. Too . . . I don't know."

"Pass me that bloody port, lad, there's a good feller," Wythy said, "while you cogitate on't."

"There's closer places to get bird's nests, spice, brass and shark fins, you know," Twigg told them. "A lot closer to Canton or the Bay of Bengal. The Malay pirates. Even from Mindanao. They hate sharks so much they go out of their way to kill them. Catch them and force spiny sea-urchins down their gullets so they'll take days to die a painful death. Make them suffer for every one of theirs the sharks take or mangle."

"Best lead we've turned up yet," Wythy summarized.

"Yes, Tom," Twigg agreed. "We must look into this *La Malouine.* Find out if she's *Compagnie des Indies* or a country ship. Where she's home-ported, where she's been seen the last year or so. Have any of us paid her any mind yet? Is she a tubby little merchantman, or is she a converted warship? Small crew, large crew. How well armed, who and what are her officers."

"How much opium she sold at Lintin Island, too, if she's payin' her way, same's us," Wythy stuck in. " 'Course, if she's the one we're lookin' for, ye may count on looted opium, an' pure profit."

"Damme, I wish I'd been on the customs dock this morning," Twigg rasped. "One sight of those shark fins, and that ginseng, and I'd have tumbled to 'em a lot sooner."

"Speaking of, sir, where would they get ginseng? Sail all the way to Boston for it?" Burgess inquired.

"The ginseng, aye, Mister Chiswick. I suspect there's a Yankee merchantman gone missing. We shall have to ask around among our dear divorced cousins. They may have over-reached themselves in that matter. Maybe they took it, maybe their native confederates took it and handed it over for arms, thinking it might be worth something. Either way, they've blown a hole in their cover. A small hole, but a hole nonetheless."

"And what may we do to help, sir?" Burgess asked, looking as tail-wagging eager as a fox-hound pup about to be let out with his first pack.

"Not a blessed thing," Twigg replied quickly, and with some affrontery. "You two leave this part of the business to them that won't give the game away. I'll not have these Frogs put on their guard by a mistake by some cunny-thumbed, cack-handed *amateurs*!"

"Oh, but ye've done grand 'nough, so far, lads," Wythy interceded. "We'd not know anythin' but fer yer observin', and bringin' up the subject of that ginseng. But remember, we're trying to pose as innocent as the Frogs are. Yer not practiced at this. So ye go on with yer duties, and yer sight-seein', same's the French'd expect from ye. Do keep yer eyes peeled, though, on the sly. Don't go too sneakin'r actin' suspicious, but just idle about and take note."

"I see, sir," Burgess replied, still in a bit of a pet after Twigg's scornful dismissal of his services, no matter how Wythy had softened the blow.

"Circulate. Act the calf-headed cullys. But watch when ye may. Not a sharp watch, mind, but *watch*," Wythy concluded.

Chapter 5

They waited, and they watched.

In fact, once *Telesto* was totally unloaded and riding high in the water, there was very little else to do. Whampoa Reach was the place to idle from September to March. Their cargoes of tea were not in Canton for quick loading; they had to come down from the hinterland. What they had purchased were only sample packs of the year's pickings. The lacquerware, furniture and china had to be manufactured during the winter season, then loaded lot by lot. It took Chinese laborers time to weave nankeen cloth, silks, ribbon and fancy goods. Wallpapers had to be made first, then meticulously, and slowly, printed by Asian methods, or painted by artists by hand with their bamboo pens and brushes.

"Rope-Yarn Sunday, thank God," Alan muttered to himself as he emerged on the quarterdeck. It had rained during the night, and the masts, sails and rigging overhead dribbled fat, cool drops of water from aloft as if it rained still. There was a slight fog over the Pearl River and Whampoa Reach, a fog that amplified the creaking of the myriad of vessels as timbers and planking settled anew, as rigging slacked tension and the masts worked against themselves. As thigh-thick mooring cables groaned against the hawsehole timbers, and tinny watch-bells tinkled like a forest of windchimes, all set on chronometers that would never agree with each other.

Telesto had been a scene from the ancient Egyptian Pyramids the day before. Gun-drill, repel boarders drill, striking the upper masts and yards down to the lower fighting tops and gantlines, only to hoist them aloft once more and re-set the

170

standing rigging. Starboard watch against larboard watch. Anything to keep the men from going stale with idleness.

Today, though. Today was "Rope-Yarn Sunday," a day to celebrate idleness, a day of make-and-mend. Bedding and hammocks could be aired and re-sewn. Personal clothing could be washed and darned. Those intent on their carvings, their scrimshaw, ship-models and hobbies could indulge themselves. There would be music, a time for dancing, napping or pleasant conversation. Sailors could "caulk or yarn" to their heart's content if they stayed aboard, or go ashore and sample the dubious pleasures of Hog Lane once again.

A member of the sailmaker's crew would get rich today; he had found a source for sheep-gut, and would exhaust his stock of condoms among his shipmates. After the first few days, and the first hands had wept in agony each time they made water off the beakhead up forward, the surgeon had made a good living, too. Fifteen shillings per sufferer was the tariff for the good doctor to administer the mercury cure. A sheep-gut condom, sewn up by a trusted shipmate, was only eight shillings, which left money for enough rum to allow a man to forget *Telesto* for a while. *And* avoid the pox!

"Morning, Mister Lewrie, sir," young Hogue, the master's mate said, doffing his hat in greeting. Hogue looked ill enough to be already counted among the dead. He'd been one of the surgeon's first customers, and the mercury cure was no stroll in the park on a sunny day. He'd lost fifteen precious pounds, had gone by turns white as a ghost or grey as old linen, and even now, freed from his sickbed, looked about as cadaverously deceased as Zachariah Twigg.

"Anything stirring, Mister Hogue?" Alan asked.

"Nothing yet, sir. Though 'tis hard to tell with this fog."

"Let's be at it, then," Alan sighed. He handed Hogue a large mug of sweet, hot tea, taking in exchange a brass-bound telescope as large as a swivel-gun, and they mounted to the poop deck above the captain's great-cabins, went aft to the taffrails over the stern and lashed the telescope to the barrel of a swivel-gun to steady it.

Alan swept back the sleeves of his fiery red silk dressing gown and bent to study their quarry, *La Malouine*, as they did every morning.

Naming that ship *La Malouine* was about as top-lofty as calling Tom Turdman's scow, the flagship of Dung Wharf, HMS *Victory*, Alan thought sourly. *La Malouine* had turned out to be a rather old, rather shabby East Indiaman. In fact, she was so old, she still sported a lateen yard for a spanker on the mizzenmast over the poop, rather than a more modern gaff-rig. Inquiries had revealed that she was of about nine hundred tons burthen, short, bluff and beamy as a Dutchman's wooden shoe, and had been a familiar sight in the Far East for years. She had at one time (long before he was born, Alan suspected) been a *Compagnie des Indies* vessel, but had been discarded and gone independent once newer construction became available. As her Adriatic oak had succumbed to rot and teredo worms, she'd been re-scantlinged with teak until she could truly be said to consist of teak almost totally. Teak lasted damn-near forever, even in the tropics, and, with new coppering on her quick-work below the waterline, *La Malouine* might aspire in future to that full century of service Mr. Brainard had spoken of.

Her home port was Pondichery on the southeast Indian coast. Her master, M. Jacques Sicard, was a delightful little gotch-gut with a waggish sense of humor, a sharp nose for trade and a repute as a moderately honest man.

"Bloody waste of time," Alan grumbled, standing back up to sip his own tea.

"Seems to be, sir," Hogue agreed glumly. He gave a great yawn from being up all night in the middle watch to spy on their neighbor. Being newly returned among the healthy didn't help, either.

"Anything occur during the night?" Alan inquired, setting his mug down and taking a fast-paced stroll round the confines of the poop deck, swinging his arms to dispel the sluggish night-humors from his blood. Hogue almost had to trot to keep up with him.

"There was some visiting, sir. Off a couple of French ships," Hogue related, puffing a little. "Music and dancing. Some breastbeating saint's day, I think. St. Vitus, by the looks of it. But all quiet by ten of the clock. I say, sir . . ."

"Oh, sorry, Mister Hogue," Alan relented, slowing his pace as Hogue almost sagged to his knees. "I forgot you're light-duties yet. Still, nothing better than to be up and stirring. Good for you."

If left to himself, Alan Lewrie would be anything but up and stirring at that ungodly hour, and well he knew it. But there were certain platitudes naval officers were supposed to mouth to juniors, certain examples to set for their edification.

"Aye, sir," Hogue replied, looking a trifle dubious under his firm nod of agreement.

"A captain of Marines once told me to stay fit," Alan related. "Aboard ship, if one's aft on the quarterdeck, it's too easy to go soft and potty. Gets you killed in a fight. Never gets you the ladies," he concluded with a knowing wink.

"After the mercury cure, sir, I hope I never cross the hawse of another woman in my life!" Hogue groaned.

"Nonsense. Just fother a patch over your hull before you hoist battle flags, Mister Hogue. See Archibald and buy yourself an eight-shilling condom. Good as any from the Green Canister in Half Moon Street back home."

"Well, 'cept for being poxed to her eyebrows, she *was* a cunning little wench, sir," Hogue had to admit, albeit sheepishly.

After four more circumambulations of the deck, they returned to the telescope and made a great dumb-show of studying all the ships within sight through the thinning fog, always coming back to *La Malouine*. Nothing stirred but the crewmen of her night anchor-watch. Alan saw a French master's mate take off his hat, scratch his scalp and give out a great yawn so wide it was almost painful to watch, which made his own jaws ache at first, then yearn to gape in boredom as well.

"Doesn't much resemble a pirate, does she, sir?" Hogue whispered as he sat down on one of the signal-flag lockers to enjoy his tea.

"Can't imagine her *catching* an Indiaman, much less cowing one with her little battery," Alan agreed. They'd been rowed past the ship several times on errands or visits to other vessels farther down the Reach. *La Malouine* mounted eight-pounders fore and aft as chase-guns, and iron twelve-pounders on either beam—only sixteen of those in total, too. There were no secret lower-deck gun ports such as *Telesto* had, either. And *La Malouine*'s waterline was so bearded with marine growth the tendrils seemed to wave at them in passing, no matter that she was coppered to slow the weeds down. Flying everything but her master's shirt and breeches, it was doubtful she'd attain nine knots in a full hurricane.

"Hmmm," Alan muttered as a native *sampan* came sculling out of the fog behind their quarry. "Damn early for a social call."

Hogue took the eyepiece while Alan retrieved his own mug

of tea and sipped it with pleasure. The wardroom servant had made it almost boiling hot, and thickly laced with molasses.

"Sir," Hogue hissed. "He's bound for her. They're hailing the anchor-watch now. Hollo, here's a new'un!"

"Let me."

There was a European in the *sampan*, dressed in white shirt and black breeches, white stockings and woven sennet hat. As Lewrie watched, he stood up, grabbed the man-ropes and ascended the boarding ladder battens with a lithe, easy grace. Alan got the impression at that range of reddish hair, remarkably pale skin and a faint smudge of beard on the stranger's lean face.

"Yes, he is a new visitor," Alan mused. "Do you keep an eye on him, Mister Hogue. This fog should blow off soon. Perhaps by the time he departs, we may spy which ship he came from. I'll be below shaving. Sing out if you discover anything."

"Aye aye, sir," Hogue replied with a small nod, and the sigh of the permanently put-upon. Well, bedamned to him, Alan thought, as he made his way forward to the ladders that led to the quarterdeck; he's a midshipman, even in disguise. Hogue ought to know by now to expect the shitten chores! Snot-nosed younkers, he sneered. God save me from lazy midshipmen!

Hogue was waiting upon him when he returned to the deck, as were the rest of the ship's officers. Eight bells had rung, ending the middle watch, and "All Hands" had been piped to begin the ship's day. "Rope-Yarn Sunday" or not, the decks still had to be scrubbed down.

Wash-deck pumps were being rigged, and the hands were milling about, rolling up the voluminous legs of their slop-trousers above their knees, holystones ready to begin wet-sanding the decks. The captain, Twigg and Wythy, Brainard and Choate were all present on the quarterdeck. Percival and McTaggart were forward, supervising the bosun and his mates.

"A good morrow to you, Mister Lewrie," Ayscough grunted, looking no more thrilled to be up and about at that hour than anyone else.

"Captain, sir," Alan replied, doffing his hat.

"Yon visitor aboard *La Malouine*," Ayscough continued, sounding hoarse as a bear with a head cold. "Seen him before, have you?"

"No, sir."

"Well, Mister Hogue informs us he departed not a quarter-hour after he came aboard her," Ayscough harrumphed. "Went back down-river to another vessel. Still foggy, but she seemed to be about the fourth or fifth, somewhere thereabouts."

"That would be either *Salem Witch*, or *Poisson D'Or*, sir," Alan said, recalling the rough chart of the anchorage they'd sketched over the last few weeks. "A Massachusetts Yankee. Lots of them were privateersmen during the war, sir. Maybe this one's not yet given up the trade."

"And what of this *Poisson D'Or*?" Twigg demanded.

"Newly arrived, sir," Choate stuck in. "She's a small three-master. About six or seven hundred tons burthen, she looked to be. Arrived just at the end of September, sir. Suppose she got her name from her paint-work. Ochre hull picked out in white along the bulwarks and gunwale. Black chain-wale, same's most ships. *Poisson D'Or*. Gold Fish, d'you see?" He concluded with a sharp laugh.

They did, but didn't find the play on words as amusing as Choate did, which forced him to utter a cough and harrumph of his own to sober his thoughts.

"You're the only one that's seen her so far, I take it?" Twigg pressed. "What did you think? How was she built? Manned and armed?"

"Well, Mister Twigg, sir, she's about the same size as one of their new frigates," Choate continued. "Were she a French royal ship, I'd take her for a thirty-two-gunned Fifth Rate. Pretty fine-cut entry and fore-foot, so she's not that old. Some of their latest construction. She had what looked to be eight-pounders for chase-guns. What else she mounted, I couldn't tell; the ports were shut. But when I was rowed past her, she was unloading cargo, and I didn't see over one hundred hands, all told."

"Were she a civilian ship, she'd not need sixty hands in peacetime," Mister Brainard speculated. "In these waters, that'd be about average for a crew. And, if Mister Choate says she's fairly new, she'd be fast as the very devil, just like most Frog ships that're frigate-built. Outrun pirates faster'n you could say 'Jack-Ketch.' "

"What else did you espy, Mister Choate?" Twigg grunted. "What impression did she make upon you?"

"Well, sir, she was set up good as 'Bristol Fashion.' Looked to be a pretty ship." Choate shrugged in confusion. "Saucy, sort of. Hands were dressed neat. Hull was coppered and her waterline was pretty clean, like she was recently careened and breamed."

"I see," Twigg rasped, pulling at his long nose in frustration. "Odd, though, for visitors to come calling so early in the morning, even before M'Seur Sicard could be expected to have his breeches on."

So far, Twigg's enthusiasm about *La Malouine* had seemed to be sadly misplaced. Although the ship had a larger than average crew, that would be only as expected in a country ship that had to face the danger of piracy on her lonely voyages. She was slow as Christmas, couldn't outrun a well-paddled *prao*, so those extra hands would be necessary to man her guns, repel boarders if necessary or deal with the natives on those mysterious islands far out in the Great South Seas where *La Malouine* traded for sandalwood, bird's nests, furs and shark fins. What made *La Malouine* at first suspicious could be explained away easily, and after a time, had been.

There were at least ninety French ships in Whampoa Reach, and all during September and October, they had speculated upon all of them. Now it was nearly mid-November, and they still had no solid leads, no standout suspect to bait.

Alan felt a twinge of sorrow for Twigg and his eternal suspicions about even the most trivial thing. But only a slight twinge of sorrow, he had to admit. So far, this adventure was a dead bust, and they knew no more today than they had the morning they'd sailed from Plymouth. Perhaps their disguised foe hadn't come to Canton at all, and was lurking somewhere far out to sea, outfitting to begin another season of piracy once the opium and silver began to flow outward from India the next summer.

Twigg and Wythy were from some shadow-world, anyway, Lewrie sighed as he watched their lanky secret agent pace deep in thought. God knows, HM Government *paid* the bastard to distrust everyone! Show Twigg an entry hall back home, point out the black-and-white marble tiles, and the bloody wretch'd see grey between the cracks, get out a crowbar and have 'em up to see what's underneath! And I'll bet that Ajit Roy of his tastes his food and drink first, too, Alan suspected.

"Might not have come off this *Poisson D'Or* at all, sir," Alan said, hiding a wry grin of almost cruel amusement at Twigg's expense. "I mean, this fog hasn't burned off or blown away. Who's to say what ship he really was from? Once near *Salem Witch* or *Poisson D'Or*, he could have doubled under their sterns and gone somewhere else. And neither Hogue nor I recognized him. Could have been anyone, sir."

"Why the covert visit at such an hour, then, sir?" Twigg said, turning to stamp back to them. "Why double under another ship's stern or bow to throw us off, as you put it, unless there was a good reason? I'd not expect even a blind man could miss our continual observations by now, Mister Lewrie. Should never have entrusted spying-out duty to you or any of the ship's people in the first place. I . . ."

"Sir!" Hogue intruded on the beginning of Twigg's latest tirade against amateur sleuths. "Damme if this ain't the same bugger to the letter, sir!"

"A little decorum, if you please!" Twigg snapped. "None to take notice but us. Be about your regular duties. Tom?"

Wythy went to the starboard rail with him, and they proceeded to stroll the gangway as innocent as newly risen babes. Alan went back up to the poop deck to supervise the scrubbing, jiggling and thumping the mizzen shrouds and backstays with a belaying pin to test their tension, as a ship's officer or mate would every morning.

There was a *sampan* coming by, and a European sailor sat almost in the bows on the squarish bow thwart, a man dressed in tan canvas trousers, faded blue shirt and dark blue sailor's jacket, with a red kerchief about his neck. His feet were bare and horny as any sailor's and he looked sublimely at ease to ride without labor for a change, leaving the poling or sculling to the Chinese at the matching stern platform. A clay pipe fumed lazily in his mouth.

Just forward of amidships, not quite under the thatch-laced "cabin" of the *sampan*, sat another European, though. And damned if he wasn't the same man Alan had seen scaling *La Malouine*'s side not half an hour earlier! Closer to, when he could steal a glance at the *sampan*, he could espy a very slim young man, perhaps only a few years older than himself. There was that same dull red hair, pale skin and a slight, very tenuous attempt at a beard, which was the same dull ginger, a beard-lette which followed the line of the jaw very low down. Perhaps the man's essay at hiding what seemed a rather slack chin, or drawing the observer's eye upward from a prominent Adam's apple.

"Well, I'll be blowed!" Alan whispered. "They come calling?" The *sampan* was not exactly aimed at *Telesto*'s main chains and boarding ladder, but she was tending slowly enough in that direction to give the impression that that was her destination. "What the Hell."

Alan strode to the rail to look down upon them directly as the *sampan* got within good musket shot, about 75 yards off.

Since no one else seemed ready to do their duty, or even take outward notice of the *sampan* as they so-studiously avoided eyeing it, someone should do the normal thing.

"Damme yer eyes, bosun!" he shouted to the quarterdeck below, then turned to face the boat and cup his hands to shout "Ahoy in the boat, there!"

"Passant!" the sailor on the bows replied with a wave of his pipe, jabbing the stem up-river in the vague direction of Jack Ass Point. *"Bon matin, m'seur!"*

"And a good morning to you as well, sir!" Alan waved back. *"Bon matin a vous, aussi?* Off to *cherchez las putain* in Hog Lane?"

Which raised a great Gallic shrug and laugh from the sailor.

"If you are, I hope your weddin' tackle rots off," Alan muttered, still smiling. "You poxy Frog bastard."

The sailor waved back once more, as did the other man, and then they were past amidships, on their way up-stream. But damned if they weren't swiveling slowly on their seats and eyeing *Telesto* devilish sharp!

I do believe they're spying on us! Alan thought. What a lot of sauce these bloody Frogs have!

Chapter 6

"Choundas," Twigg told them a week later. "One Guillaume Choundas. His ship, *Poisson D'Or*, has been out here in the Far East for the last two years. Coincidence? I think not. That's about the time the first ships began to disappear."

"I see, sir," Captain Ayscough nodded. "Awfully young to be a ship's captain, though. What more do we know of him?"

"Come now, Captain Ayscough," Twigg sneered, "how many fond daddies get their sons made post-captain at the same age most young officers could only expect their lieutenancy! Admiral Rodney made his sixteen-year-old boy post into a fine frigate soon as he arrived in the West Indies on his last commission."

"Let me ask again, sir, what do we know of him?" Ayscough retorted with a growl. Twigg had not become any easier to swallow in the past months, and his harshness grated upon their captain most of all, forced as he was into the closest familiarity with him.

"I mean, damme, sir, what a *few* Royal Navy officers do for their own don't mean this pop-in-jay benefits from someone's 'interest' in the same manner," Ayscough went on. "Who and what the hell is he?"

"He, like your officers and senior hands, Captain Ayscough, is reputed to have been an officer in the French Royal service," Twigg replied snappishly. "Well thought of at one time, I'm told by certain informants. Commanded a sloop of war, what they call a *corvette*."

"To be well thought of in their fleet, he'd have to be royal himself," Choate pointed out, snuggling deeper into his coat. Despite a coal-fired heater in their captain's quarters, it was a

179

cool night, and a stiff wind on the Pearl River made it seem even chillier. "Some duke's by-blow, at best."

"Not titled," Twigg supplied. "A commoner's lad. From Brittany. Perhaps from St. Malo. I believe his father's family is in the ... uhm ... fishing trade."

"Wi' the profit from his voyages sae far, sir, he could buy any bluidy title he desired once he's hame," McTaggart chuckled.

Twigg glared in McTaggart's direction, shutting him up. Alan was glad he was seated on the stern transom settee, out of range of Twigg's considerable amount of bile.

"Yet he rose in the French Navy," Twigg went on.

"Only because he couldn't get into their Army, most like," Alan said in spite of himself. "Never made officer with hay still in one's ears. That takes both a title, *and* lashings of *livres*."

"Quite right, Mister Lewrie," Twigg allowed, sounding almost pleasant for once. "So why did they not send one of their titled, and successful, frigate captains on this mission?"

"For pretty much the same reason they sent us, sir," Brainard the sailing master griped. "We're nobodies. Expendable and not much loss to the Fleet if we fail."

"*Thank* you, Mister Brainard. I didn't know you thought so well of us!" Ayscough laughed bitterly. "If you're correct, though, one begins to wonder in what repute you were held to be part of our band, eh?"

"Ain't we a merry crew, Alan?" Burgess marveled with a cynical shake of his head.

"Burge, there's so much brotherly love and cooperation in this cabin, I feel positively inspired!" Alan whispered back.

"Back to the subject at hand, please," Twigg ordered. "And if you two could hold down the school-boy twitterings over there? Yes, Mister Brainard, the French sent this talented young peasant to do their dirty work for them. 'Cause they can't sully their limp little hands at it, for one. For a second, they're not ruthless enough to deal with native pirates and prosper. And perhaps, because they knew if they held out enough promise of reward to this wretch Choundas, he'd leap at any opportunity for continued employment."

For a summary, it still sounded hellish like the reasons *they* had been called to service themselves, to Alan's lights.

"He's an aspiring brute from Brittany. Clever enough in

his own fashion, I'm sure. Perhaps, like I said, a St. Malo corsair."

"So was this Sicard, sir," Percival stuck in, breaking his usual silences. "Sicard has the large crew in *La Malouine*; this Choundas of yours has a small crew."

"Damme, he'll fry his brains if he keeps that up," Alan muttered to Chiswick.

"Yes?" Twigg rapped out, impatient to go on, and a bit surprised to hear from Percival after all these months.

"Well, sir, seems to me Choundas has the ship made for privateering, Sicard has the perfect old tub to act as the cartel for all the loot," Percival stammered out, turning red from being on the spot, from the effort of erudition and from the possible fear he was making a total ass of himself. "They could both act innocent . . . or something."

"The two of them working in collusion?" Alan blurted, unwilling to see Percival take a single trick. "Well, damme!"

"We have no proof of that, Mister Percival, though the connection is tempting," Twigg allowed. "Sicard seems honest enough, and he's never been in their Navy. Been out here for years. Dabbled at privateering in the last war against our trade, but then, what French sailor didn't, at one time or another."

"Cargoes, Zachariah," Wythy rumbled. "Where'd Sicard get his bloody odd cargo, then? Furs from Nootka Sound'd tie one ship up fer a tradin' season. Take two of 'em t'do all we suspect. Mister Percival may have a point, at that. R'member, there's no sign this Choundas put into Macao, nor traded opium fer silver with the mandarins. Come straight up-river, an' what he's landed so far's general run-o'-the-mill Indian cargo."

"What if it's this Sicard who's the leader, and Choundas and *Poisson D'Or* are merely his bully-bucks, sent out to enforce what he's arranged?" Choate enthused. "Look, Captain Sicard has been in the Far East and the Great South Seas for years. You said so yourself, Mister Twigg. He'd be the one most like to have contacts in past with native pirates. This Choundas is a newcomer, with a new ship. What connections could he establish with 'em on his own?"

"Gentlemen, this idle speculation . . ." Twigg gloomed, those lips growing hair-thin in dislike at the direction his conference was going.

"You suspected Sicard and *La Malouine*, for good reasons, sir, in the first place," Alan pointed out, not without more than a slight amount of glee. "Maybe Choundas is just a messenger from France, a catch-fart from their Ministry of Marine. And a bloody pirate who needs his business stopped. But not the leader—merely a henchman."

"That means we got two ships t'keep an eye on," Wythy added relentlessly. "That's all right, long's we're anchored here in Whampoa Reach. Damme, we'll need a second ship t' follow both of 'em in the spring. If they stay that long."

"And two captains to shadow, now," Ayscough said, smiling thinly.

"Ajit-ji," Wythy instructed as they stood near a stack of cotton bales ashore in Canton. "Nandu-ji."

"Jeehan, Weeth-sahib?" they chorused.

"Piccha karna Fransisi havildar-sahibi vahahn. Ajit-ji, neela koortie, milna? Nandu, vo admi lal gooluhband, milna? Piccha karna, jeehan? Hoshiyar! Khatrah! Badmashes!"

"Aiee, jeehan Weeth-sahib. *Ek dum!"** Nandu and Ajit agreed, and walked away into the mob of sailors and traders milling about as Hog Lane got into full motion for another night.

"That takes care of the bosuns or cox'ns," Wythy sighed as the Indians put on a remarkable performance of two revelers wandering around in a daze, but following the two sailors from *Poisson D'Or* and *La Malouine* who had come ashore with Sicard and Choundas. They had come in separate *sampans*, but even so, their movements would be covered closely, and hopefully, surreptitiously.

"We'll take Sicard," Twigg whispered, and he and Lieutenant Percival went in one direction, leaving Wythy and Lewrie to loiter by the cotton bales until Choundas dismissed his cox'n, the same sailor they'd seen giving *Telesto* the eye the week before in the boat with him. A handful of coins changed hands, then Choundas clapped the fellow on the shoulder and barked a short, humorous comment before the sailor departed on his own errand, or amusements.

"There he goes. Nice an' slow, now, Mister Lewrie," Wythy instructed. "No need t' trod on his heels, nor breathe down his neck. Just keep the bugger in sight. Mister Cony, is it?"

*"Follow the French mates there. Ajit, [the one] in the blue coat, see? Nandu, that man [in the] red scarf. Follow them, yes? Careful[ly]! Danger[ous]! Thieves!"
"Yes, lord. At once!"

"Aye, sir, that's me name, sir," Cony whispered, a trifle nervous.

"Ye know what's wanted?" Wythy inquired. "You go on ahead of him, stroll along at a fair clip like ye know where ye're goin', an' if this Choundas bugger veers off from behind o' ye, don't worry 'bout it, 'cause we're still followin' him. If he gets outa sight, try an' spot where he went t' ground, an' come back t' join us. Right?"

"Right, sir," Cony said with a deep sigh of commitment.

"*Achcha*, Cony-*sahib!*" Wythy praised. "*Chabuk sawi! Ijazaht hai! Daro mut!*"*

"*Jeehan*, Mister Wythy, sir." Cony essayed a brief grin before he took off on his dangerous chore.

"He'll be safe enough, should he not, Mister Wythy?" Lewrie asked.

"Aye, he's a clever'un. Picks things up quick as a wink, like he's learned more Hindee'n most Englishmen out here ten years. It's us that's in more danger. Those Frogs know we're officers off the ship that's been payin' close attention to their doin's. And ye'll mind how they've been givin' us the eagle-eye the last few days."

"Aye, sir," Alan replied, feeling absolutely naked among the throngs of drunken, reeling sailors in Hog Lane. "God, I'd give my soul right now for the feel of a little rigging knife, though!"

"And it's *be* yer soul, if the mandarins' soldiers caught ye armed," Wythy warned. "One of their eight bloody rules ye never violate, not if ye know what's good fer ye. Applies t' the Frogs same's us, thank the good Lord."

Choundas wandered Hog Lane for a while, strolling into Thirteen Factory Street at last, and wandering right past the factories to the bank of the foetid creek, and across the plank bridge to the front of the King Qua Hong. He looked to be in no hurry to get where he was going, but there wasn't much down that way: Mou Qua's Hong, a wide lane that did little business that late in the evening, and then one of the large customs houses, which would be shut.

"Clever bugger. Clever as paint," Wythy commented, taking Lewrie by the arm and steering him back the other way. "He'll turn about and come right down our throats, t' see if anyone's

---

*"Good, Cony-lord! Clever fellow! You may go now! Don't fear!"

tailin' him. Not the skills ye expect t' see in a French naval officer, damme'f they ain't!"

Choundas did reverse his course and struck out west once more, making a beeline for the bridge. Cony had already crossed over, and was across the street from him. There was nothing for it but for him to turn into Carpenter's Square, and try to look as innocent as he could. Wythy and Alan turned their backs on him and suddenly got interested in an open-air grog shop that spilled out into Hog Lane, with all evidence of nothing more important in their lives than a mug of rum and hot water.

"Sorry, Mister Wythy, sir," Cony apologized, once he had rejoined them. Alan offered him the rest of his grog. It was far below the standards of Navy Issue from the Victualling Board—the rawest stuff he'd tasted since leaving the West Indies. "God, that's awful, sir!"

"You stay here, Cony. We'll follow him now."

"Headed for the French factory, Cony?" Alan asked.

"Nossir, 'e's on t'other side o' the street. Just goin' into Old Clothes Street now, sir," Cony related.

"Dead end, else he'd get into the city proper, an' I doubt he's got that much clout with the mandarins." Wythy grinned. "No, our lad's off t' put the leg over some Chinee lass. Better cut o' bagnios lays in that direction. 'Bout a dozen of 'em. Co Hong quality stuff."

"Aha," Alan commented. Wythy had at last informed him where he could get some quim.

"He'll be in there 'bout an hour'r so," Wythy said, pulling out his pocket watch. "If the brute has any taste, that is. If he's the peasant Zachariah thinks him, I'd make it a quarter o' that. Let's be meanderin' so we may keep a sharp eye peeled for when he comes out. Cony, ye want the rest o' my rum, as well?"

"Well, h'it ain't so bad, once ya gets some down, sir, thankee right kindly," Cony agreed.

They strolled west, past the Chow Chow Hong, the East India Company Factory, the Swedish, to take guard across the street from the entrance to Old Clothes Street.

"Well, damme," Percival said as he and Twigg heaved into sight.

"Sicard?" Wythy asked.

"In there," Twigg whispered, pointing with his chin.

"Same fer Choundas," Wythy snarled. "Now what's so all-fired secret they gotta do their talkin' in a brothel? Ain't their ships good 'nough?"

"This may be some theatric, to keep us off-balance," Twigg sighed with the exasperation of a longtime expert at the art of tailing a man. "Unless there's someone they're meeting in there, someone they wouldn't want even the Chinese, or the Co Hong, to know about."

"A Chinese pirate, maybe, sir?" Percival asked. "Or do these Malay or Mindanao raiders ever come up the Pearl to trade in Canton like anyone else?"

"How many brothels in there, Tom?" Twigg asked.

"Only four I know of that cater t' Western custom. Rest is fer the Co Hong, 'r the Chinee exclusively. There's touts enough in the street if ye wish t' ask about. If they went t' one of the best ones, ye can wager the pimps'r still pickin' their chins up off the street at the novelty of it," Wythy imparted with a soft laugh.

"Well, I need some volunteers, then," Twigg demanded. "To enter those brothels that accept Europeans."

"I'll go, sir," Alan piped up. It had been a long time since Calcutta—and Padmini, Draupadi and Apsara!

"Speak fluent French, Mister Lewrie?" Twigg simpered. "Speak Chinese, come to think on it? Would you know what to look for?"

"Would you, sir?" Alan shot back without a pause.

"Most probably I would not, sir," Twigg smiled. "But I would know most of the French *Compagnie des Indies* officials by sight, and more than a few of the notorious Chinese coastal pirates as well. Tom, we're in your hands now."

"Aye, Zachariah. Look, you an' Percival try the last two on the left. Lewrie an' I'll look into the others. Hope the pimps speak pidgin at the best."

The pimps did, though it didn't do much good. Old Clothes Street was full of European barbarian foreign-devils that night, and to the Chinese, they all pretty much looked alike, so even the offer of some *cash* didn't get them any useful information.

"Ever'body got a condom?" Wythy asked. "Just in case."

Percival didn't. He was relegated to street lookout on the other side of Thirteen Factory Street. Percival was *very* put-out.

"We can use yer services again, Cony," Wythy said.

"Aye, sir, though ... uhm ... I h'ain't got much money, sir."

"I didn't come prepared for sport, either, sir," Alan said, "Not in the financial sense, anyway. Do you think the tariff would be dear?" he asked with an innocent expression.

"Well, damme!" Twigg griped, but dug out his purse and handed over enough golden guineas to pay for their socket-fees, an act which half killed his soul, and made Alan delight in the prospect of getting the leg over at Twigg's expense.

They saw Cony into one of the brothels, assuring the warder at the door that Cony was a minor *tai pan*, no matter that he was dressed as a sailor.

"Ye want this'un, then?" Wythy asked. "An' I'll take the last but one on the right. Meet us at the Chun Qua Factory whether ye learn anythin' or no. Don't dawdle, Mister Lewrie. Half an hour, shall we say?" Wythy grinned.

"The things I do for King and Country, sir," Alan smiled back.

"An' not a jot on what I've done in the King's name, boy."

"Aye, sir."

The expedition took a lot longer than Wythy's stricture of half an hour. And, Lewrie suspected, if his own experience was anything to go by, none of the others would be getting back to the Chun Qua Factory before he did—might not even get back before dawn!

First, he had to pay the warder to get into the bloody place. It was nice to learn that the bobbing little weasel could speak pidgin, no matter what the mandarins' laws had to say about limiting the number of Chinese exposed to foreign-devil barbarians, their languages and alien ideas. It did, however, cost him six pence, which was not so nice.

He was lit into a small alcove through a semi-circular archway by a giggling little maid-servant. There were several of the alcoves along the main hall, screened off by folding rice-paper screens painted with some truly awe-inspiring Oriental pornography. Try as he would, he could not overhear any French being spoken, nor did he see either Sicard or Choundas in any of the alcoves.

"Wythy must be right," he muttered to himself. "The man's not here, or he's a damn quick worker. On, off and 'Where's my shoes.' "

The maid-servant seated him on pillows before a very low black-lacquered table, and began lighting lamps. Another maid came trotting in with a serving tray, offering steaming-hot towels, steaming-hot tea (an excellent early-spring picking Yu Tsien, he noted) and plates of tiny dumplings called *dim sum* for an appetizer. The first little maid returned with a straw-wrapped bottle of *mao tai* brandy and delicate little paper-thin drinking cups.

An older Chinese lady entered, dressed in a black silk robe all figured in gold-and-silver thread birds. She looked hard as flint and twice as old.

"You wan' guhl?" she began. "One guhl? Two guhl? Wan' see? Mak choose?"

"Have you any French customers, Mother Abbess?" Alan asked.

"No got French guhl. China guhl, got."

"No," he reiterated, speaking slowly as possible. "Have any men who are French come here in the last quarter-hour?"

"Ho, you wan' boy!" The madam comprehended. "Eeeh, got China boy. French boy, no got."

"Good Christ, I didn't go to Oxford!" Lewrie shot back. "You misunderstand me. Me want girl! No want boy. I look for friends here. Red-haired man. Man with beard? He come here?"

"Wan' guhl wi' *beard*?" she gasped. "Aw fo'n debbil ... loony!"

"Want girl," Alan sighed, giving it up as a no-go. "You bring girl? Me make choose, right?"

"W'y you no say so? Wan' guhl? Yes, I b'ling," she huffed.

"I fear this is not going to improve my conversational skill," Alan commented to the little fourteen-year-old maid as she poured him a revivifying cup of brandy. She covered her mouth and giggled.

The girls arrived, four of them at once, and they didn't titter or giggle, thank the good Lord. Hair black as ink and elaborately coiffed, stuck through with long decorative pins—hair as lacquered and shiny as polished ebony wood. Faces painted bolder than any English whore's, with pale powdered faces and bright rouge and lip-gloss, their eyes and lashes outlined and brushed so that they loomed enormous, upper lids brushed with powder so they seemed like almonds enameled in blue and black. They talked among themselves, waving the huge sleeves of their intricately designed and figured silk robes.

"I've died and gone to heaven," Lewrie breathed at the sight of them. Choosing could be a hard process, for they were as lovely a quartet as any he'd ever suspected existed. And this was one of the brothels that specialized in Europeans—surely these would be thought of as mundane, with the absolute very best saved for the Chinese as too-precious pearls to be cast before foreign-devil swine!

They enveloped him, one seated to each side, one seated by the doorway to play a stringed instrument for his enjoyment, while the fourth began to sing, lolloping out some horribly off-key (to his Occidental ear) nonsense in a quavery, breathy voice. The one to his right plied chopsticks to feed him bites of *dim sum*, while the one to his left kept the tea and brandy flowing. And after each song, they would trade places, to introduce him to all their accomplishments.

"Speak English?" he asked each of them as they settled in at his side. "Speak pidgin? French? Bloody Latin?"

Sadly, three of them could not, but Wei Yen could. She was youngest of the four. It was hard for him to judge just how old she really was, but he guessed around sixteen or seventeen. Her skin was clearer, her features more delicate than the others', her mien not as artificially gay and "cherry-merry" as the other three, either.

There was more tea, more *dim sum*, some more appetizers fetched out, another bottle of *mao tai*. And then the madam was back, with her hand out for more silver, to pay for the treats supplied so far.

"You mak choose, now," the woman said, making it sound like a demand more than a request. "You wan' one guhl, two silla. Two guhl, fo' silla. Wan' keep aw fo', ten silla."

"One girl. Wei Yen," Alan replied, forking over two shillings for the girl and another six pence for the entertainment. The others bowed their way out and tripped down the main hall, toward the front of the establishment, their services already in demand.

Wei Yen beamed at him with a maidenly little smile, then took him by the hand and led him in the other direction, towards the back.

"Give bath," she promised.

A steaming wood tub sat sunk into the floor of each bath cubicle, some already full by the sounds coming from them. Lewrie took his time dawdling on his way to his, trying to peer into each one or linger long enough to listen to see if he could hear French being spoken. He shrugged, thinking Choundas either not there, or long gone by this time.

Wei Yen hung up his garments, wrinkling her pretty little

nose each time and sing-songing something in Chinese, laughing softly as she did so. Lewrie preferred to think that they
were jokes. When he was bare to the world, she indicated that
he should get into the tub. He slid down into the extremely hot
water, wincing on his way down, and found a bench to sit on
by the side.

Wei Yen walked with mincing little steps to the other side
of the tub and disrobed down to a very thin nankeen under-
grown, which she slipped back off her shoulders as he
watched, entranced.

She was a little bit of perfection. Middling shoulders, slim
neck, creamy skin the color of pale ochre wheat. The silk robe
she had worn had concealed the springy young bounty of her
breasts that stood up firm and proud and straight-ahead together, shadowing a dark cleft he wanted to dive into. There
was the slightest bit of stockiness around her rib cage, but the
waist was wasp-thin as a doll's, and her belly was so firm and
flat, with a ridge of what he hoped would prove to be damned
talented muscle down the center, leading to . . .

"Shaved?" he asked the room as she came toward him. She
slid down into the tub with him gracefully, and came to his
side. If she had seemed maidenly shy and tender before, it had
been a theatric, for she became an unleashed tiger. She sat
straddling him on the bench seat, reaching down to seize his
member, which sprang awake as the Brigade of Guards in a
twinkling. They slopped around in the tub, splashing water everywhere. She almost let him enter her, then slid away from
him until she had him roaring in frustration.

But no. He had to leave the tub, sit on another damned stool
while she soaped him from head to toes and scrubbed him
clean with a sponge, sliding away from his soapy embraces
and laughing all the while. Back into the tub for a cleansing
soak, and then she was toweling him dry, letting him towel her
dry. Then they gathered up their clothing and went up a back
stairway to a private chamber.

He came to his senses just long enough to remember his
condom, and then they were delightfully engaged, at long last,
both making noises more usually associated with Iroquois mas-
sacres. "Father's wrong, ya know!" he said between gasps.
"Bengali women have nothing on you, my dear!"

He lay utterly spent at long last, used up far further than he
could ever remember, while the girl stroked him and kissed

him, working him over with a small towel, and loosing her long dark hair that spread like a cloak to cover them both. She'd come unpinned somewhere in the second bout whilst teaching him an entirely novel manner, wrists and one ankle behind his neck as he sat on the edge of the bed clasping her small bottom like holding two small melons.

Her teasing fingers, and the moist warmth of the towel, strayed to his member, and it flickered with renewed interest.

"You wan' 'gin, *qua*?" she said with a gasp of wonder.

"Again? After that?" he chuckled. "Well, in a few, perhaps."

"No wan' 'gin, soon you go, *qua*," she said in a soothing whisper. " 'Nudda man, he wan', I got go. You stay, 'nudda one silla. You wan' *chai*, *mao tai*? Wan' eat 'gin? Allee same silla."

"I stay," Alan replied. "*Mao tai*, you and me both, right?"

She gave him a kiss and slid out of bed to slip on her undergown, open the door and call for one of the maid-servants.

While they drank and recuperated, he quizzed her as much as he was able. He learned that she had once been one of those little maids, purchased from a peasant family far to the north when the crops failed. Girl children could always be sold to support poor families. It was a prime reason to keep them, instead of putting them to death at birth: as a hedge against an uncertain future.

They were just about to partake of another spell of amour when Alan got down to his real questions, and the reason he had chosen her instead of one of the others who had no pidgin or English.

"Does a red-headed man ever come here?"

"Red? Wha' red?"

"Like this pillow tassel. Red," Alan prodded. "Dull, like ginger."

"Aw fo'n debbil red ha'," she tittered.

"Pale skin, like yours. He has a thin beard." Alan had to make a partial mask over his lower face with both hands. "Not long. Short, ginger-colored beard."

"Him debbil!" the girl shuddered.

"He comes here?" And she nodded her assent. "Did he come here tonight?"

"Him mak nudda guhl 'night," Wei Yen said, looking thankful. "Debbil, him! Mak wan' li'l guhl, no wan' ollo guhl, my. Las' yea', him wan' my, no so ollo. 'Night, him wan' new li'l guhl Yi."

"So he did come here tonight!" Lewrie exulted. "And is he still here? Right now?"

"Him heah. Him ba' man debbil! Hu't, my! Hu't Yi allee same!"

"What does he do?"

The girl could find no words, so she forced him onto his back and began to slap the air over his chest. "Dat!" She bit at his nipples. "Dat!" She pretended to slap and choke him. "Dat!" Teeth took hold of his shoulder and neck. "Dat!" she told him, biting lightly.

"Jesus Christ, what a monster," Lewrie agreed as she sat back up.

"Whi' lak dead, him!" Wei Yen shuddered once more. "Bear' mak sclatch. No wan' guhl, wan' bebbee. No wan' bebbee guhl him on top! Him wan' . . ." She slipped off to one side of the bed, knelt with her head on the pillow, arms held behind her back as though they would be tied if with Choundas, then slapped her rump. "Wan' go ba' place, allee same guhl place."

"The pervert!" Lewrie growled. "What an utterly rotten bastard!"

" 'Otten bassah'?" Wei Yen said, sitting up once again.

"Rotten," Lewrie corrected.

"Lotten bassah," the girl parroted, then said it to herself several times, trying "pervert" on for addition to her vocabulary as well.

"Well, you're not with him now, you're with me. And I'm not a rotten bastard, or a pervert," Lewrie assured her, drawing her down to him. "Well, not much of one, anyway."

Then there came a muffled scream from down the hallway, and a series of yelps. Wei Yen stiffened in his arms, burying her face in the pillows. "It him, red ha' fo'n debbil!"

"He's still here!" Lewrie said, starting off the bed, almost dragging the frightened Wei Yen with him. "Oh, what luck!"

More wails of terror and pain, hiccupy little strangling wails such as a very young girl, one even younger than Wei Yen, would make. The sound of cuffs or blows, perhaps, preceding each new outcry.

Lewrie went to the door and opened it to hear better, even as Wei Yen tried to drag him back. He saw another door open, saw Captain Jacques Sicard lumbering to the noise as the madam and one of her bully-bucks came up the stairs from the front of the bordello, their sing-song voices sounding anything but musical. Sicard was rapping on the door, whispering "Guillaume!"

Lewrie ducked back as Sicard began to remonstrate with the madam, opening a purse to pay her off for whatever damage or harm his man was causing. Another door opened, only a couple of rooms beyond his own, and a distinguished Chinese gentleman emerged, drawn to the commotion. He stopped in his tracks, though, and squinted his eyes, when he saw Lewrie, just shutting his door.

"You no go, him hù't!" Wei Yen rasped, dragging him back into the room completely and slamming the door with her behind. "Ver' ba' man, him! Wei Yen mak you contentee, no silla, you stay 'way!"

"What are they saying?" Alan asked, trying to shake the little baggage loose from her death-grip on his body and find his stockings.

"Him pay muchee silla, muchee *tael cash* fo' Yi," Wei Yen translated. "Ollo woman Ma she say fo'n debbil go, him, no comee back. Is good!"

Doors opened. Voices rumbled in Chinese, pidgin and French as Lewrie began to dress, much against his better judgement. Wei Yen was trying her damnedest to coax him back into bed with her. But he'd had his fun, expensive as it had been, even if it had been Twigg's money. He had to be ready to shadow Choundas once he left the brothel.

With his stockings and shoes on, his breeches pulled up and buckled, he heard footsteps coming his way. Ignoring the girl's protestations, he stepped to the door and opened it just a crack, standing well back in the shadows so he could see what was happening.

The shoes sounded different. Two pair, perhaps, of hard-soled European shoes with heavy heels. And the swishing sound of a pair of slippers.

Alan saw the Chinese man, now dressed in an elegantly embroidered silk robe, with a round pillbox hat on his head adorned with one coral button on the top and a long peacock or pheasant feather. The man cut his eyes towards his companions.

And there were Sicard and Choundas, shoulder to shoulder behind the Chinese man. Sicard paced on past, but Choundas slowed down to a crawl as he passed the crack in the door. And he grinned! A brief, sardonic, mocking grin, before resuming his pace and joining his companions!

The cheeky bugger, Alan thought at first. His second thought was for a weapon. For that brief glance was as chilling as coming face to face with Old Scratch himself! There was no shame in the leering grin. No fear of discovery. Only scorn for whoever it was behind the door.

I'll wager he grinned 'cause he thinks there's a poor whore in here he's tortured before, Alan thought. Gloating at her. Or maybe he was daring whoever he took me for to come out and say or do something about it.

Or, he realized with another chill of dread, that Chinee bugger saw enough of me and recognized me. Christ! "Sorry love, duty calls. Damme her eyes. This is for you," he said, handing over two of Twigg's golden guineas. "I go follow bad man. And when we catch him . . ."

He made a *scritch* sound and the motion of cutting a throat.

Alan trotted out of the door for the end of Old Clothes Street where it opened out onto the wider main road. He looked about for a sign of Twigg or Wythy, for Will Cony, but his was the only Occidental face present. And, as he emerged, the number of Chinese in the dark street melted away into the doorways and the darkness between the few oil lamps.

He was almost out of the street when something made a quick swishing noise, and his skull exploded! There was a burst of light he could taste, something brassy-coppery, and then a pain that made him wish to scream like he never had before, except that it hurt so much to draw a deep breath that he couldn't! Without knowing how he had done it, he was face-down in the dust of the street, eyes barely able to focus on a pair of bare and horny feet at the edge of his vision. They were coming towards him. A knee appeared, as if whoever it was was preparing to kneel.

Without thinking, he lashed out with his left arm and leg, and the agony that doubled and redoubled in his head was so exquisite he found breath this time, gasping for air to let out a scream of pain as he swept whoever it was off his feet.

The man went down, overturning some baskets, spilling garbage against the dingy walls. A stout stave clattered against the bricks. Howling with more pain, Alan clawed himself onto his assailant, but the man retrieved the stave and rolled over to strike him across the top of his shoulders. Alan yelled some more, though the blows didn't hurt. Nothing could hurt as bad as his skull did in comparison!

There seemed to be other cries now, stirred up by his howlings, and the drumming of feet heading toward the street opening. His foe shrugged Alan off and got to his feet to flee, but Alan got both hands around one ankle and held on for dear life, getting dragged through dirt and garbage for his pains. He could smell blood. He could smell mildew, his face pressed against the back of the assailant's ankle: the salt and mildew-moldy reek of a sailor's clothing.

The man stumbled to one knee, kicked backward to free himself as Lewrie tried to scale him, nails rasping on rough duck cloth as he got a couple of fingers in the man's waistband from the rear. More blows from the stave, one on the skull again, this one bringing back the explosion of light once more.

He couldn't hold on, and dropped away. The next blow swished past his drooping pate to *thock!* on the wall with a horribly hard blow.

"Hold on there, ye bastard!" Alan heard a voice say, and then there was a flash of light that winked as Alan tried to look up, one small glimmer of flickering oil lamps on metal. Knife!

Ignoring his skull for his life, he scuttled back against the wall, turning over more tall wicker baskets as he tried to rise and crab his way up the rough bricks. A shadow bulked from the street entrance.

"He's got a knife, Mister Wythy, look out!" Alan screamed.

Two bodies swayed against each other. Two quick blows. Two more winks of steel, and then the foe was gone, running east down Thirteen Factory Street for the creek and the plank bridge. There was a hue and cry, the babble of Chinese voices.

"My God," Wythy sighed as he stumbled to the wall to lean on it, sinking to his knees. "My God!"

Alan lurched away from the wall to sink to his own knees by the older man as Wythy pressed both hands over his abdomen. "That bloody bastard!" He grimaced, his expression turning to a cock-eyed grin of sarcastic surprise. "Think the bastard's killed me!"

"Hoy!" Alan called, his head splitting with every breath. "Hoy the watch! A man's been stabbed here! Somebody help us!"

"Oh my God," Wythy whispered as his blood flowed like a spilled bottle of claret and steamed in the cool night air.

Alan staggered to the street entrance. Yes, sailors from a dozen nations were coming on the run. He could see Twigg and Percival, with Cony bringing up the rear.

"That way! A sailor with a knife! Somebody stop the bastard!" Alan yelled, and then his own vision began to turn into a dim tunnel, pinpointing Twigg's ugly phyz. He sank to his knees again. "Oh, will no one catch the murdering shit?" he moaned.

"Oh . . . my . . . God," Wythy wept in reply.

Chapter 7

The Consoo House was crowded with traders, ship's captains and Europeans for the execution. The eight members of the Co Hong sat to one side, trade taking a poor second place to justice in this instance. The Chinese mandarin Viceroy for Canton sat on his inlaid throne on a pile of silk pillows, with his Banner Men soldiers behind him, and his linguist at his feet.

Lewrie had missed the trial, laid up with a concussion, but he had been told it was a brief affair. The Chinese officials had been highly upset that one of their strictures had been violated. There had been more than a strong rumor that all foreign-devil ships would be ordered out of Chinese waters if more of these fights between the French and English occurred.

"Fight, Hell!" Alan had protested, but Twigg had told him to stay silent. There was too much pressure from the East India Company to let it go for what it appeared to be: a bungled attempt at robbery by a drink-addled French sailor on an English trader. Trade was too good this season. The pickings coming down from the hinterland were the best anyone had ever seen, and the prices were for once reasonable.

So Twigg had to sit silent and let his friend and partner pass over as a man in the wrong place at the wrong time, who had died trying to aid an English shipmate. It had taken Wythy a couple of days to die, from the suppuration of two deep belly wounds that were untreatable and a death sentence. Lockjaw had been added to the insufferable agonies of his last night on earth.

The surgeon had shaved Alan's head, staunched the bleeding and sewn up the pressure cut. For the moment he was forced to wear a wig until his hair grew back out.

"*M'seurs,*" someone said in a soft voice from behind them.

Alan turned awkwardly. It still hurt to turn his head, so he pivoted on one heel.

"Guillaume Choundas, *capitaine, La Poisson D'Or. A votre service*," he said. "I am mos' sorry for your loss. Zat it was a French sailor who did this . . . words cannot express my sorry."

Twigg laid a hand on Lewrie's arm before he exploded.

Choundas was turned out in his Sunday Divisions best, a dark blue master's coat trimmed in white lace and silver buttons, short white tie-wig over his dull ginger hair, silk shirt and neck-cloth, dark red waist-coat and black breeches and stockings. On his left sleeve, he wore a wide black riband, tied in a bow. In mourning for the French sailor.

Choundas turned up the corners of his mouth in a sad smile. He had droop-cornered eyes, orbs of a pale, washed-out blue that were as icy as Greenland bergs, though, belying his evident sorrow.

"Zis *pauvre homme, messieurs*," Choundas went on. "Zis poor lad. what 'e did was . . ." A Gallic shrug. "But 'e was in drink, *n'est-ce pas*? A good *matelot*. One of mine, as you know. 'E is *tres* . . . so very young, *messieurs*. Surely, *Brittanique gentilhommes* such as you may find ze *Christianité* . . ."

"Not my decision, sir," Twigg said, glaring. "He killed one of mine!"

"*Ah, mais ouis, mais ouis, m'seur* Tweeg," Choundas sighed like a disappointed suitor. "Ze *Chinetoque* courts, zo, zey do take . . . uhmm . . . like ze Gauls *ancien* . . . what your Saxon ancestors called 'were-gild,' *messieurs*."

"Blood-money?" Lewrie gasped.

Amusement danced in those pale eyes as Choundas turned his slack-jawed gaze to him. "Ze lad by zis courts could be freed to return to 'is aged parents, 'is young wife and child, m'seur Looray. And you still live. 'E did not mean to 'arm anyone. 'E was drunk, in need of money. 'E did not mean to kill, 'e 'as sworn to me!"

Choundas put his hands together as if at prayer and his face became even more droopy-eyed, like a dog whose master has just yelled at him. "Your *m'seur* Weethy frighten 'im. 'E only wan' to flee. Please, *m'seur*, I beg you, as 'is *capitaine*, as a Christian *gentilhomme*. As a fellow *Brittanique* who share *l'ancestrie* with all ze sires of *notre* race . . . Celts, Gauls, hien? Spare 'im! *Mon Dieu*, in the name of God, spare 'im! Tell ze court you take ze . . . blood money, if you will name it zo. Whatever sum you wish, *messieurs*! Name ze price and I swear to pay it!"

Lewrie was shaken by Choundas' demeanor. He certainly *seemed* sincere. But then, so did Sir Hugo, when he desired something. A fine pair they'd make, he thought sourly: both of them consummate actors. And frauds! And damme, if he ain't laughing at us, even now, I swear. Standing there, judging his *performance*. Like I do, I have to admit, now and again. But, bedamned to the bugger!

Twigg took his arm and gave his elbow a squeeze.

"I could be prepared to spare the young fellow, if he was only confused and drunk, Captain Choundas," Twigg replied slowly, weighing every word. "As you say, we are of one race, sprung from the selfsame root-stock that flourished in Gaul and Brittania before the time of the Caesars . . . before the German barbarians came . . . the Romans."

"Ah, mais ouis, mais ouis!" Choundas nodded, his eyes glinting with unexpected triumph. The pious expression he wore flickered to a revealing brief smile, a smile tainted with just the faintest bit of a leer at Twigg's stupidity.

"He is awfully young, is he not, sir," Twigg sighed, and his stern visage creased into a grin. "God, I pity the poor . . ."

Surely not! Alan thought.

"But, the courts have given their decision. Death by strangulation. To put a curb on this unfortunate animosity between English and French in their port. The assault on one of my ship's officers, and, no matter the reasons, the death of my most trusted and beloved longtime partner, Tom Wythy, with a forbidden weapon, well . . ."

"Ah, but *m'seur* Tweeg . . ." Choundas floundered a bit.

"And the poor lad, when one gets right to the meat of it, *is* a lice-ridden, scurrilous Frog, ain't he now, Captain Choundas? A murdering cut-throat son of a Frog bitch, ditch-dropped by a Frog whore!" Twigg went on, those lips pursing, temples pounding, but a beatific grin creasing his lower face. "A brisket-beating superstitious slave to Rome, and, like all French of my acquaintance, born under a threepenny, ha'penny planet, never to be worth a groat!"

Choundas recoiled as if slapped, dropping his pious pose and slitting his eyes.

"If this court don't scrag him, I'll volunteer to twist the cords myself, sir!" Twigg rasped.

"You play with me, *m'seur*, you make ze sport . . . !"

"Far as I know, you play with *yourself*, you *sans coulotte* peasant," Twigg barked. "Why don't you go back to eatin' snails and catchin' an honest fishmonger's farts?"

"You insult me beyond all *honneur, m'seur*, I demand . . ."

"Try it and see whose ship gets booted out of this port, sir. Try it and see who ends up in a Chinee grave!" Twigg hissed. "Who knows, from what Mister Lewrie tells me, your demise might make a few poor whores happier'n pigs in shit! Takes more'n that pitiful excuse for a beard to make a man a real man, right, Mister Lewrie?"

"To quote the Bard, sir, 'Who is he who is blessed with one appearing hair.' Or something like that," Lewrie fumbled out.

"Only French have *l'honneur*! You English have none!"

"Perhaps, but we do have bloody marvelous artillery," Twigg simpered. "Do but give us the opportunity to prove it to you."

Choundas spun on his heel and stalked noisily away to join the rest of the French traders and ship-captains, heels ringing on marble.

"Good on you, sir," Alan said firmly. "That was bloody well said! Told that perverted monster off good and proper."

"Do but dwell upon this, Mister Lewrie," Twigg whispered, turning back to the court as the accused was led in. "We might have just struck flint to tinder, created a blaze hot enough to goad him into something rash. Like following *us* once we leave Canton, 'stead of us having to track him. The gloves are off now, ours and his. For old Tom Wythy's sake, I'll have that bastard's heart's blood. You watch your back from now on, 'cause it's war to the knife!"

The Viceroy began to speak, sing-songing formal phrases which his linguist translated bit by bit for the foreigners. "By the will of our Emperor, Son of Heaven, Complete Abundance, Solitary Prince, Celestial Emperor, Lord of the Middle Kingdom and swayer of the wide world . . . my master, Viceroy for the prefecture . . . in the City of Rams, Yu Quang Shen Wang speaks. Hear his words, make *kow tow* and obey, tremblingly!"

The eight members of the Co Hong and their creatures, and every Chinese went flat on the floor, while the Europeans performed elaborate bows, doffing hats and making legs. The British barely inclined their bare heads.

"Psst," Lewrie said, nudging Twigg when the linguist began again. "Third from the right, sir. Do you mark him?" he whispered from the corner of his mouth and cut his eyes to Twigg, who swiveled to glare at a minor mandarin in a sumptuously thick and rich embroidered silk robe and pillbox cap with coral button and feather. Twigg nodded and turned back to face the Viceroy on his throne.

". . . and disturb the heavenly harmony of our Celestial Kingdom! We tolerate the rude behavior . . . of foreign-devil barbarians who know no better . . . the export of our valuable goods . . . in exchange for what worthless items they bring to the City of Rams . . . until such time as they displease us beyond measure. You are quarrelsome slaves whose crude barbarian chieftains cannot control . . . your rustic kings have sent ambassadors to pledge fealty to our Celestial Emperor . . . made their *kow tow* to recognize the superiority of the Son of Heaven . . . made themselves subjects to the one who sways the wide world . . . the foreign-devil Louis of France . . . the foreign-devil George of England . . . so that the Solitary Prince might stay his hand and not conquer them."

"Like to see the buggers try!" Lewrie muttered.

"Hush!" Twigg warned with a hiss.

"We order that there be no more fighting!" the linguist shouted. "No more murderings! Or the Lord of the Middle Kingdom shall withdraw his *chop* for you to be here! See the punishment! Witness tremblingly, and obey!"

"Damme!" Lewrie was forced to say as he recognized the prisoner. It was Choundas' cox'n, the one in the *sampan* with him the morning they'd first seen him.

The executioner came forward with a silk rope while two Banner Men soldiers held the sailor by each arm and led him into the center of the gathering and made him kneel down. For a man about to be garroted, the seaman seemed unusually calm, gazing about disoriented but obeying the soldiers without struggle. His eyes seemed glazed and his mouth hung open slackly, with a bit of drool at one corner.

"They've drugged him," Twigg whispered. "Lots of opium. I doubt he even knows what's about to occur."

They strangled him, taking their time about it, too, applying one turn of the silk rope at a time, then waiting to see the results. The executioner looked gleeful as he readjusted his grip before taking another twist or two, which had all the Europeans muttering and shuffling, some coughing.

They continued to strangle him slowly, until the man's tongue stood out, and his face went blue. His head was so suffused with blood, his eyes almost popped, and trickles of blood ran like sparse tears until he went totally limp and ceased breathing.

Lewrie found it as satisfying as any hanging he'd ever seen at Tyburn, though the poor wretch hadn't had his wits about him enough to go game, with a final japery or two, and a crowd of fellow bucks cheering him on, the doxies throwing flowers and kisses to a brave rogue. He turned his head to look at the French, Choundas particularly. Surprisingly, for one so affected by the sad fate of one of his own crew, Choundas was remarkably blasé about it, standing slack and bored with his weight on one leg. He looked more like a man waiting for his coach to be brought round, ready to drag out a pocket watch and wonder what was keeping his ostler. Choundas looked around and shot a glare at them.

"Fuck you," Lewrie mouthed slow and silent, hoping the bastard could read lips, then gave him a sly grin.

"And just who was that Chinee you pointed out to me, Lewrie?" Twigg asked, once they were outside after the ceremony was ended.

"He was the third partner in the brothel with Sicard and our jolly friend, sir," Alan replied. "He's not one of your pirates?"

"None I recognize, no," Twigg said, pulling at his long nose. "By the color of his button, he's well-connected. One of the Viceroy's staff. Too well-connected, for my liking. Could get us sent away empty-handed, if he wishes. Or ambush us down-river between here and Lintin Island once he boots us out."

"They couldn't get away with that, sir, not with so many ships in the Reach, armed as they are," Lewrie protested. "Why, we'd blow their city to flinders if they tried!"

"Nothing official," Twigg replied, frowning. "Set upon by . . . pirates . . . if you will. So sorry. Nothing to do with his Celestial Emperor's glorious navy, or his crooked mandarins. And trade is too good for anyone to protest too much, not this year. Just a country ship, not 'John Company,' they'll say back in London. Anyone wish to dispatch a fleet and army to Canton? No? Any questions for His Majesty's Minister? End of session, then."

"Arrogant shitten bastards," Lewrie spat.

"Who, Mister Lewrie?" Twigg asked lightly. "The Chinese and their arrogance? Or Parliament?"

"Little of both, maybe, Mister Twigg."

* * *

"Excuse me, sir, you're wanted on deck!" Hogue said, bursting into the wardroom like a bombard. "All officers to the quarter-deck."

They grabbed their swords on the way, sure it was the suspected attack by pirates, or a demand they sail away at once.

"Surely they wouldn't dare, not in the middle of Whampoa Reach?" Burgess Chiswick panted as they dashed topsides. "Should I muster my half-company, d'you think?"

Ayscough and Twigg stood together by the taffrail of the poop, and they ascended in a thundering pack to join him aft.

"Just got a note from the Superintendent ashore at the 'John Company' *hong*," Ayscough explained, mad as any time Alan had ever seen him. "Seems we have to go ashore tomorrow and entertain more questions from the mandarins about the murder. And look yonder."

"The bloody bastards!" Percival shouted, quite beside himself and ready to tear up a section of taffrail to shred in his bare hands.

"*Poisson D'Or*'s been ordered out of harbor," Ayscough grunted. "For the sake of the rest of the traders," he continued, the sarcasm hotly dripping. "Her *chop*'s been withdrawn, and her cargo's been impounded."

"By the same mandarin Choundas and Sicard dealt with," Twigg surmised. "You may lay any odds you like there'll still be profit enough paid to Sicard to reimburse Choundas for this . . . penalty!"

Poisson D'Or had already gotten her anchors up, and was paying off from the land breeze with foresails and spanker, her hands aloft ready to let fall her tops'ls once her stern was clear of the American trading brig *Salem Witch*.

"Damme, to hell with the mandarins!" Alan cried. "Let's be after them, then! We'll never find the bastard until next autumn, else!"

"We'd be fouled by every mandarin junk in the river, Mister Lewrie," Ayscough snarled. "To keep us here for more 'questioning,' see? Might even touch off a war, them and us alone. Goddamn and blast that poxy French bugger! Goddamn him to the hottest fires of hell!"

"Smarter than I thought," Twigg sighed, sounding sadly amused. "I underestimated them, d'you see, gentlemen. Which mistake I shall not make again. They could have gotten Choundas' cox'n off with ten pounds' bribe paid to the court, but I suppose they thought it was better the poor wretch got scragged, so he couldn't talk. Now we know we're dealing with craftier foes. Choundas gets clean away, kicked out of the port, while we have to wait here for our cargoes to arrive. And Sicard stays here, ever the innocent, to keep an eye on us. After murdering the one man who knew most about the native pirates and their lairs. I hate to admit it, gentlemen, but they've made fools of us. And of me. This whole thing was planned long before we tailed them ashore the night Tom Wythy was knifed."

"They lured us, sir?" Mr. Choate asked.

"Aye, lured us. Gulled us, more like it," Twigg snorted. "One of us . . . Tom or I was to die that night. Perhaps both. To cripple our endeavor. Why else meet with a mandarin on the Viceroy's staff so openly? Trail their colors before us like a false fox? Then pin us in port with more questions, and boot *Poisson D'Or* out, freeing her to continue her plans for the next season's raiding. But before the next year is out, we'll have them, you mark my words!"

Damme, another year out here, Alan groaned to himself.

"Choundas might be waiting for us to sail in the spring," Ayscough said. "His ship and Sicard's combined against us."

"Ah, but for now, Captain Ayscough, our crafty little peasant has left something of great value behind in Canton," Twigg spat. "An item he cannot do without, or threaten us with such combination."

"And what is that, sir?" Ayscough wondered gloomily.

"Why, *La Malouine*, Captain," Twigg almost chuckled. "Sicard and *La Malouine*. Mister Percival said something a few weeks ago that set me to thinking. I believe he was correct."

"Sir?" Percival gawped, swelling with pride, but unsure about what he had done in spite of himself.

"Who has the largest crew? Sicard. But who has the frigate-built ship with more gunports? Choundas. Somewhere out at sea, in the islands, perhaps among the native pirates, I believe these two ships trade hands back and forth. Perhaps there's more of his fell crew waiting with the Mindanao pirates or the Sea Dyaks even now for his return for them. Well, at the moment, he's a little short of the wherewithal, and shall be for some months, if *La Malouine* will play the innocent here in Canton."

"No point in her not, sir," Ayscough agreed. "There's little profit in taking an outward-bound vessel, 'less he's willing to give up hands enough to take her all the way back to France. Better he lays low until the opium and silver start heading for Canton next summer."

"Then once Sicard sails, we follow him, and he leads us to Choundas, sir?" Choate asked. "Then it's two ships against our one."

"Aye, he'd like that, I'm thinking," Twigg replied, nodding. "In fact, this departure could be another ruse to draw us out, with Sicard in pursuit a few days later for just that purpose. Well, we shall not be drawn, sir. Truly, we shall not."

"It occurs to me, though, sir," the first officer went on. "Surely, if we know who he is now, sir, and may lay this plot to our government officials back in Calcutta, there'd be a stiff note to the French ambassador, and the game's blocked at both ends for them. And they know who we are, more's to the point, Mister Twigg. Surely, this Choundas'll haul his wind and cut his losses. Go back to France."

"And go home a failure?" Twigg barked, rounding on Choate. "I think not. That wouldn't show him clever enough to remain a secret. And if we did send a 'stiff note,' as you say, it's fourteen to eighteen months before a reply could be sent out here from London or Paris. Once they'd wrangled over where the commas go. And who'd take his place, sir, soon as we're called home? How many more ships'd disappear the next time? Well, we're here now, and we have a chance to stop this bugger's business so thoroughly the French'll give up on the whole bloody idea. Wrap things up neat and proper before we lay eyes on the Lizard."

Poisson D'Or let fall her tops'ls as she took the night wind abeam, drifting slantwise away from her anchorage. Her taffrail lanterns were burning, as were many smaller work-lights to illuminate her crew's labors. They could espy Choundas by the quartermasters by her wheel on the quarterdeck. They could watch him stroll over to the starboard bulwarks to look back at them as his ship's bows turned down-river.

There was just enough light, for those with telescopes, to see the smug sense of victory on his face.

IV

"*Nunc Iove sub domino caedes et vulnera semper,*
nunc mare, nunc leti mille repente viae."

"But now that Jupiter is lord, there are wounds
and carnage without cease; now the sea slays,
and there are a thousand ways of sudden death."

"The Poet Sick—To Messalla"
—TIBULLUS

Chapter 1

In March, the trading season ended in Canton. Whampoa Reach emptied slowly, as ships drifted down-river to Macao, at the mouth of the Pearl River estuary. For many traders and merchants, their families awaited them, and for a time, Macao rang with balls and parties in celebration of a successful season. For some ships, there was time enough to celebrate their freedom from the strictures of Chinese law in one of the most sinful seaports known to mankind, then hoist anchor and hope for the best in the South China Seas as the winds shifted more favorably for Calcutta, Pondichery, Chandernargore, Ile de France in the middle of the Indian Ocean or all the way to the Cape of Good Hope to begin the long voyage home laden with the treasures of the Far East.

Telesto was one of the first ships to put to sea after two perfunctory days of revel and refit in Macao, bearing south for the Johore Straits and the Straits of Malacca. And in her wake, sure as Fate, another ship dared the changing Monsoon winds—Sicard and *La Malouine*. They could recognize her, hull down over the horizon, during the first day of passage. And though she fell back until only her tops'ls could barely be espied as the days passed, she was there every morning, the sight of which tops'ls made Twigg almost hum a snatch of song now and again in sheer delight.

"Ship's company, off hats!" Lieutenant Choate commanded. The hands, brought aft by the summoning call from the "Spithead Nightingales," the bosun's pipes, took off their flat-brimmed dark tarred felt hats, or the tarred woven sennet ones, and stood swaying and shuffling in a dense pack.

Perhaps they thought it was a call aft to witness punishment.

The sight of their officers and mates wearing steel on their hips was rare. Rarer still was Chiswick's half-company of native *sepoys* clad in *dhotis*, red coats and cross-belts, tricornes and *puggarees* for the first time in over six months, drawn up like a Marine detachment on a proper warship with their muskets held stiffly at shoulder arms, Chiswick and his native *subadar* and *havildars* before them.

"Men!" Captain Ayscough began in a rumble that could carry as far forward as the fo'c'sle belfry. "I know there have been some rumors flying below decks about just what it is we're doing out here."

Amen to that, most of the men nodded in agreement.

"What are we doing with such a heavy battery hidden away below. Why do we have Hindoo troops with us," Ayscough continued, hands in the small of his back and rocking easily to *Telesto*'s motion from the vantage point of the quarterdeck nettings overlooking the waist and upper gun deck. "Maybe you wondered why we run this ship 'Admiralty Fashion.' And, I'm sure, since poor Mister Wythy's death in Canton, you've been wondering what led to it. Well, it's come time to tell you all. It's the French, lads! The bloody French!"

Ayscough sketched out for them the fact that they were a Navy vessel in disguise. He outlined what Sicard and Choundas were up to with the native pirates. How good English sailors had been overcome and slaughtered far from home for opium and silver by not only native pirates, but by the French as well.

He drew a sheaf of documents from one large side pocket of his dark blue frock coat. "I bear a Letter of Marque from 'John Company,' lads! I hold active commission from our good King George the Third! And I have a Frog pirate lurking off my stern-quarters! They risked drawing steel on Mister Lewrie, one of your officers. They murdered an agent of the Crown back in Canton, and then their leader, Choundas, threw his henchman's life away, let him be strangled to death at the hands of those Goddamned heathen Chinee rather than let him answer questions! Choundas is out here somewhere, men, and we're going to find him and kill him, him and all his sneering, torturing, Godless Frog crew. And any pagan pirate that'd deign to shake hands with him. For now, though, the ship that gathers up his spoils, washes good English blood off their foul booty and sails the seas acting innocent as your own babies, is astern of us. Well, we'll stop this bugger's dirty business. We'll do it to save the lives of other God-fearing English seamen. We'll do it to revenge Mister Wythy's murder. And we'll do it to put such a fear of retribution into the bastardly Frogs and all their help-meets in these waters that them that survived'll tremble in their beds and piss their breeches whenever they think of it!"

There was a ragged howl of agreement with Captain Ayscough's sentiments. No fouler creature drew breath than a Frenchman, to true English thinking. No Jolly Jack would abide a pirate. Unless of course he was English, and preyed on other nations' shipping—then he was Drake and Robin Hood rolled into one. And sailors were a most sentimental lot, their feelings simple sometimes, but close to the surface, and closely held dear. Ayscough had them.

Except for one hand, speaking for a pack of whispering mess-mates. "Er, 'scuse me, Cap'um, but ... er ... beggin' yer pardon an' all, sir, don't mean ter ... uhm ..."

One of his mates gave him a nudge.

"D'zat mean we goes back ter Navy pay, Cap'um?" he finally stammered out.

"It does not!" Ayscough smiled. "Merchantman pay-rate until we pay off back home in old England!"

If anything, that raised an even greater chorus of cheering.

"Mister Abernathy, we shall splice the mainbrace!" Ayscough said in conclusion. "Mister Choate? Dismiss the hands."

"Ship's company, on hats and, dismiss!" Choate yelled. "All hands forward to splice the mainbrace!"

Abernathy and his Jack in the Bread Room, the assistant purser, went below with a bosun's mate, master-at-arms and ship's corporals to fetch out a keg of rum. There would be no debts due on this issue. No "sippers" for sewing another man's kit back up, for taking a watch, or for a favor or debt. All would get full, honest measure in addition to whatever issue came at seven bells of the forenoon watch at "clear decks and up spirits."

"Still there, Mister Hogue?" Ayscough shouted up to the cross-trees of the main-mast.

"Still there, sir!" Hogue assured him with an answering yell.

"Mister Percival, I'd admire you hoisted the cutter off the midships tiers in the day watch. And dismount the taffrail lanterns."

"Aye, sir," Percival replied.

"Mister Choate, gun drill in the day watch as well. Sharpen 'em up. Say, an hour and a half on the great guns, and then rig out boarding nettings along the bulwarks, and chain slings aloft on the yards. Strike useless furniture below once it's dark."

"Aye, sir."

"Mister McTaggart, fetch a spare stuns'l boom and a boat compass to install in the cutter, if you'd be so good, sir."

"Aye aye, captain."

"Before dawn, gentlemen, this bastard Sicard will wish he never laid eyes on our *Telesto*," Ayscough predicted grimly. "We'll begin to get some of our own back with these poxy Frogs!"

It was a nacky ruse, Lewrie had to admit as he saw it put into service. The heaviest ship's boat, the thirty-six-foot cutter, was swayed off the tiers and lowered over the side around three in the afternoon. A studding sail boom about twenty feet long and six inches thick was lashed across her sternposts. At each end of the boom, a heavy glass lantern had been lashed. The captain's cox'n was put in charge of her, given a boat compass and a small crew to set sails, a barricoe of water and some dry rations in case they were away from the ship for longer than planned, and then they were paid out to be towed astern. They were given muskets, pistols, cutlasses and a small boat-gun mounted in the bows, partly to counteract the weight of the lanterns and boom. The cox'n was entrusted with slow-match, flint and tinder, and a hope they could find them in the morning.

As the late afternoon progressed, and the armorer's whetstone competed with the fifers, fiddlers and pipers, *Telesto*'s lower courses were reduced, taken in by one reef. The stays'ls between the fore and main-mast, and the stays'l between main and mizzen, were lowered. The ship soughed a little less lively in the sea, slowing by perhaps half a knot. Just enough to allow *La Malouine* to draw a few miles closer to them before full dark, so that any lookout from her cross-trees or upper royal mast cap could just barely, with a strong telescope, make *Telesto* out as riding a slight bit higher above the horizon— enough to make out her tops'ls in full and reassure them she was still there.

Chiswick and Lewrie paced the quarterdeck, from nettings on the starboard side to the taffrail and back, each time pausing by the stern to raise a telescope, though seeing anything from the deck was a forlorn hope. The sun was westering rapidly, and the skies to the east were already gloomy, the skies to their starboard side going amber and the high-piled billows of clouds beginning to take on the colors of sunset in one of those magnificent tropical displays.

"I would suppose the timing of this is rather tricky," Burgess opined, staring down at the cox'n and his crew, lazing happily in the cutter being towed about one decent musket-shot astern in their wake. With time on their hands, one definite job to do and sheer, blessed idleness until they were let slip, they were napping or skylarking to their hearts' content.

"I've *heard* of it done, mind," Alan admitted. "Never thought I'd see it attempted. Like club-hauling off a lee shore. At least the moon's going to cooperate. Be dark as a cow's arse by eight of the clock. What little is left before the new moon'll get hidden by those clouds, too, I trust."

"What if this Frog sails up too close?" Burgess asked.

"Then we might go about and give him a sharp knock, anyway."

"God in Heaven, what if it's not him, after all?" Burgess fretted. "I mean, it could be any ship, couldn't it? This Sicard could have slacked off once he saw we were headed south, let another ship pass him, and gone off to play silly buggers with his pirate friends."

"If that happens, Burge," Lewrie assured him with a wry grin, "we'll look like no end of idiots. Or Captain Ayscough will."

That would kick the spine out of the crew, Alan thought, taking on some of Burgess' fretfulness and turning to stare at the captain and Mr. Twigg up forward by the wheel binnacle. All the spine he'd put in them that morning. It made the hands easier to control if they knew what they were about, he realized, and he'd seen enough examples of captains who explained things to their crews. Contrariwise, there was the risk of saying too much of one's expectations. And when those expectations or predictions turned out false, a captain could expect to lose renown in his own ship, making the seamen and mates, even the officers, suspect his abilities the next time.

If the ship astern of them turned out to be something other than *La Malouine*, it would be disastrous for morale. Not to mention the no-end-of-shit wrangling if they fired into a stranger, or loomed up on her beam like . . . well, like a pirate, themselves!

"Could be just about anybody back there," Burgess reiterated.

"Oh, for Christ's sake!" Alan harrumphed. "Let's not go borrowing trouble, Burge. It has to be *La Malouine*. She chanced the *taifun* weather to keep an eye on us. She's been there big as life and twice as ugly, every hour since we left Macao. Why would Sicard go off east now, when he's just as loaded as we are with profitable cargo? He has to get it to Pondichery and send it home in one of their Indiamen or lose money. I doubt King Louis could pay the bastard that much, else."

"I've been wondering . . ." Burgess began again, sounding a bit more tremulous and doubting.

"Ye-ess?" Lewrie drawled lazily.

"If Sicard is dogging our heels like this, that must mean that Choundas is somewhere up ahead. Where they could combine against us," Burgess mused as Lewrie turned to go forward again, leading the Army man with him wordlessly. "He left Canton the end of November last year. Time enough to get back to wherever he's based, re-man his ship, clean her bottom to make her faster. What did you call it?"

"Careen and bream," Alan replied. "Yes, I'd expect him in the Malacca Straits, if that's what he was doing. Narrow waters, where we have to pass. But remember, it's patrolled out of Bencoolen, and other ships'd be about. Perhaps too many for what he has in mind. He can't let anyone see him fighting us. He's supposed to remain as covert as we are, mind. Maybe farther north, on the eastern side of the Malay peninsula. Closer to the Johore Strait."

"Among the native princes," Burgess grimaced. "And pirates."

"Never let it be said that you don't give a *world* of joy to your companions, Burge," Alan moaned sarcastically.

"I only speculated to pass the time," Burgess replied, a trifle archly. "'Tis not my nature to get the wind up over nothing. Like some sailors of my acquaintance. Or is that the result of a pea-soup diet?"

"That's a natural wind," Alan told him, tapping the stiff back of Chiswick's cocked hat to tip it forward over his nose.

"I know what you and Caroline think of me, Alan," Chiswick said stiffly, refusing to be japed out of his sulk. "A calf-headed dreamer. Too starry-eyed to prosper. I heard you that day we came back from Sir Onsley's. It's because I wept in the boat when we escaped Jenkins Neck after Yorktown, isn't it? Well, what Governour did to that little shit . . . he had it coming, I know that, now. But it was against everything we'd fought for up to then. He shot him in the belly, a fifteen-year-old little hound. But a civilian hound, Alan. He wasn't even armed. It wasn't right. And I had a perfect right to be upset. Well, how much of a hard-handed warrior do I have to be before I live that down with you?"

Burgess' elder brother had put a dragoon pistol into the lad's stomach and blown it away, down low where it wasn't immediately fatal, so death was days away. Days of unspeakable agony. He'd gotten past their pickets, run all the way through the marshes and creeks to tell the French and Virginia Militia they were at his mother's plantation down Jenkins Neck. If not for him and his misplaced heroism, they'd have gotten clean away, and half of Governour and Burgess' men would still be alive; half of Alan's seamen would be home now on a pension, or enjoying life. A lot of Virginians in their Militia would still live, and the stern veterans of Lauzun's Legion would be swilling cheap *vin ordinaire*, slurping down snails and veal cutlets in some French tavern, instead of laid out in death-rows by the Ferguson rifles and his sailors' cutlasses. It had been a smoky horror, at little more than arm's reach, and when it was over, the dead greatly outnumbered the living. All for nothing. Cornwallis had surrendered and the war was to all purposes over and lost. Governour had lost neighbors and lifelong friends from his orphaned detachment of North Carolina Loyalists. He'd done what felt right at the time, yet Burgess stumbled into the boat, shaking like a whipped puppy.

"I hold nothing against you, Burgess," Alan whispered softly. "I doubt you gave the harsh side of life, and soldiering, enough thought before you took this commission. And Caroline and I were worried about you out here in the East Indies. Mind, now," he said, taking Chiswick by the elbow, "that was before I even suspected I'd be stuck out here myself!"

"You didn't volunteer to"—Burgess gasped—"to look after me for Caroline's sake?"

"Do I look that stupid?" Alan sighed.

"Yes, I thought you did. Ah, I see. Sorry, Alan. All this time, I thought you'd volunteered, for Caroline," Burgess fumbled. "I mean, the volunteering part. Not about your looking stupid, ey?"

"That's a fine relief."

"Excuse me, I've been nursing this . . . not a grudge, actually, ever since we sailed. I was rather glad to see the back of you when I went ashore in Calcutta. And here we were, together again, and I thought it was your doing. Something you said to your father, Major Willoughby."

"Burgess, you idiot!" Alan grinned. "The less I have to say to Sir Hugo, the better, man! No, I'm not your governess. And, no, I never held you in less respect because of Jenkins Neck. I think you're a glory-hunting fool sometimes, but that don't signify. You're not as brutal and direct as your brother Governour, so yes, I do think you less suited for all this death-or-glory venturing. But that don't mean I consider you soft."

He still had his doubts about that, but Burgess was a friend.

"God bless you, then, Alan," Burgess brightened, standing taller in his own estimation, and what he took to be Alan's. "Here's my hand on it. It wasn't concern for a helpless fool you felt. It was concern for a friend. A firm friend, I trust."

"Aye to that, Burge," Alan replied, shaking hands with him.

"A fellow I'd be proud to have as a relation someday."

"Thankee kindly for your opinion, Burge," Alan said, feeling cornered. Now the little oaf was buttock-brokering his sister at him! Maybe I'd be better off if he despised the very air I breathe! I'm much too young for that, sweet as Caroline is, he thought.

"Ahoy, the lookout!" Ayscough wailed upwards to the cross-trees. "Still there?" His permanent litany, it seemed.

"Royal 'bove the 'orizon, sir!" the lookout shouted back.

Just after full darkness, before the last waning sliver of moon-rise, they let slip the cutter. *Telesto* had brailed up her main course, taken a first reef in all three tops'ls and reduced her t'gallants to third reef to reduce their silhouette against what was left of the sunset horizon. From the deck, it appeared they were alone on the ocean, an ink-black shadow on an ink-black sea.

With lug-sail winged out, and a small jib set forward, the cutter paced alongside *Telesto* for half an hour, slowly drawing ahead from stern-quarters to bow-sprit. From sprit-s'l boom to larboard bows: a cannon-shot away, another spectral imagining.

"Four knots, sir," Alan reported to Ayscough after a check of the knot-log. Ayscough nodded and drew out his pocket watch, leaning over the single candle in the compass binnacle to read it. Other than that one tiny glimmer, the ship was dark as a boot.

"Eight of the clock. Sound eight bells forrud. End of the second dog-watch," Ayscough ordered.

Ting ting . . . ting ting . . . ting ting . . . ting ting, the last echoing on and on. Time to begin the evening watch. Time on a well-run ship to call the lookouts down from aloft and post the oncoming watchstanders on the upper deck vantage points. Time to recover the hammocks so men could sling their beds on the mess-decks and sleep, for ship's corporals to prowl about below to see if every last glim was extinguished for the night. Time to light the taffrail lanterns to help illuminate the quarterdeck for the watch-keepers, and warn other ships of her presence to avoid collision.

Ahead on the larboard bows, there was a tiny flurry of sparks as the captain's cox'n struck flint on steel, several times, until the tinder caught. A brief flare of light. Then the sullen ruby glim of a burning slow-match swaying about in the darkness.

"And the Lord said, let there be light," Ayscough whispered, as first one, then the other taffrail lantern began to glow their yellow whale-oil cheeriness.

"Mister Choate! All hands on deck! Stations to come about!"

Chapter 2

"If he holds his course, sir," Mr. Brainard said in the airless chart space, all ports and doors, all partitions doubly cloaked in covert canvas, "at a pace of about . . . uhm, say five knots with night-reefs aloft, he'd be *here* by now." A pencilled X appeared on the ocean chart. After a moment's thought, Brainard drew a guesstimate circle around the X. "We put about here, nor'west with the wind abeam, at ten past the hour. Held that course for one hour, tacked to east, sou'east at ten past nine of the clock. We should, if God is just, be somewhere off his starboard stern-quarters now. We should see him dead ahead, or slightly . . ."

"Excuse me, sir, Mister Choate's compliments, captain, and the hands are at Quarters," Lewrie reported, leaning through the folds of canvas that served as a light trap for one betraying lantern that swayed and winked coin-silver bright over the chart table.

"Any sign of his lights, Mister Lewrie?" Ayscough asked.

"None, sir."

"He's sneaking along to trail us like a foot-pad in a London fog," Twigg sniffed. "All the more sign he's out there. An innocent ship would be burning her running lights."

Evidently, Twigg and Ayscough had shared the same doubts Burgess had expressed earlier as to the identity of their dogged pursuer.

"As I was saying," Brainard continued, marching a brass divider across the ocean chart slowly, punching a small pin-hole in the paper and turning to protractor and rule. "Do we come about to our original course in . . . ahhumm . . . five minutes, say, and we'll be astern of him. He should be dead ahead, or

216

fine on the larboard bow. I say five minutes, so we do not overrun his track in the dark."

"Very well," Ayscough grunted, satisfied as much as he was going to be until he could throw rocks at *La Malouine* and hear them go *chunk*. "Six after ten. Mister Lewrie, let me see your watch? Ah, with mine. My respects to the first officer, and he is to lay the ship back on our original course of sou'sou'east half south in . . . four minutes."

"Aye, sir," Alan replied, stumbling out of the chart space to fumble his way to the passageway that led forward to the quarterdeck. He relayed his message to Choate.

"Now how the hell do I know when four minutes have passed?" Choate griped. Even the compass binnacle candle had been extinguished now, just in case. "Night black as a Moor's arse . . ."

"I hadn't thought about that, sir," Alan had to admit. "Perhaps if you prised the glass cover off your watch, sir? Read it by feel?"

"Not *my* watch, Mister Lewrie. My wife gave it me."

"My father gave me mine, sir," Alan stated.

"Mister Lewrie," Choate coaxed. " 'Tis for the King!"

"Excuse me, sir, I'll go aft into the passageway. Perhaps I'll find a glim there, sir."

Damned if he'd ruin a prize watch for anyone!

They were saved by Ayscough and the others coming on deck and issuing the instruction to come about. Ropes slithered and hissed through blocks. Sheaves squealed in those blocks loud as opera stars. Sails rustled and boomed, and the hull groaned loud as a storm as she adjusted to a new angle of heel, resetting her timbers in complaint.

There was nothing to see. And damned little light from the occluded stars to see by. The sliver of moon was not enough light to help pick out a man on deck were he dressed all in white.

"Keep close watch astern," Ayscough warned. "Just in case."

But there was nothing there, either. The only sign of motion on the sea were the taffrail lanterns in the cutter's stern, far out ahead of them, and those almost on the rough edge of the horizon, so low were they to the water, and so far off by now after their triangular diversion. It took a sharp eye to make out that there were two and not one, foreshortened together as they were.

"Well, damme," Ayscough muttered after half an hour had passed. "Where is that bastard? Not hide nor hair of him. Can't even smell him. Anyone see phosphorescence from his wake ahead? No? Damme!"

"Has to be ahead of us," Twigg insisted.

"Might have reefed for the night, same as us," Choate opined. "Still, even at the four knots we were doing before we turned, we'd at least be abeam of them. He'd have slowed to keep his interval."

"Or," Ayscough wondered aloud, "Sicard would have dashed on ahead. The cutter's lights are closer together than our taffrail posts by eighteen feet, and lower to the water. He might have cracked on more sail to catch up. Mister Choate, hands aloft. Lay out and let fall the tops'ls to the second reef. Loose t'gallants to the first reef."

"Aye, sir. Bosun, no pipes. Topmen of the watch lay aloft!"

"There, sir!" Hogue almost screamed from the larboard gangway ladder. "Something went between us and the cutter's lights! Two points off the larboard bows, sir!"

"Avast, Mister Choate. Quartermaster, put your helm down. One point closer to the wind. Make her head sou'sou'east," Ayscough barked. "Hands to the braces."

"Aye, sir," the quartermaster replied, spinning his spokes on the huge double wheel slowly. "Helm down a point. Sou'sou'east. Wind large on the larboard quarter, sir."

"Thus, quartermaster. Steady as she goes."

"Aye aye, sir. Sou'sou'east, thus," the man intoned.

Maddeningly, after that brief, tantalizing glimpse, there was still nothing to be seen. Another half an hour passed. They allowed the hands at Quarters to stand easy, or lay down to nap on the bare decks. They rotated the lookouts to allow fresher eyes to peer into the almost stygian blackness, searching for their foe.

Another half-hour passed.

"There!" Percival rasped in a harsh whisper. "Hear it?"

Very faint, almost like a fantasy, there came a chiming.

"Six bells o' the evening watch," Ayscough agreed. "Damme, for us to be able to hear that, he has to be up to windward of us. And not too far to windward, at that!"

Hogue with his incredibly sharp eyes was back from larboard, tugging on the captain's sleeve, and pointing to their left, over the larboard side. The captain stood behind Hogue, letting his arm be a pointer. Ayscough sucked in a quick breath, then let it out in a sigh of contentment. "Ayyye!" he whispered.

There *was* something out there. Something a little more solid than the spectral shadows that had played at the edge of their vision for the last hour, the kind that are seen but not seen, apprehended and then lost to sight the harder one peered for them. This one did not go away.

"Helm down another half a point, quartermaster. Handsomely does it," Ayscough ordered.

"Aye, sir," the senior quartermaster agreed, grunting as he put his weight to the spokes, and the steering tackle ropes on the wheel barrel groaned softly. Three, four spokes of larboard helm, and *Telesto* leaned a bit as the wind came larger on her left beam.

"Yes!" Alan muttered. "Sir, a light!"

It wasn't much. A tiny, insubstantial afterthought of a light. Not so much the light itself, but the outer glow it threw, like the glow of a seaport under the horizon reflected on clouds.

"One . . . two . . ." Ayscough counted. "Yes, one at his binnacle, one forrud, that'd be by his fo'c'sle belfry. Damme, look at that!"

A smoky brown square appeared, barely discernible from black, behind the second glimmer, an almost butcher-paper brown.

"Captain's or wardroom quarter-gallery, sir," Alan supplied. "They've some canvas screens or curtains over the windows, but there's a lantern behind."

"Aye." Ayscough was almost panting with excitement. "If he . . ." Ayscough held up his hands, calculating angles and distance. Left hand by the brownish hint of illumination, right hand and index finger aimed at the foremost glow like a gun. "Two points off the larboard bow, and I make the range to be two cables. We've got him! Mister Choate, wake the hands at Quarters. I intend to rake him in passing with the starboard battery. Boot him right up the arse. Then wear ship and give him the larboard battery from close aboard. If we take him by surprise he'll fall right down to us. To hell with the wind gauge! He'll not be expecting us to fight from leeward."

Alan dashed down below to the lower gun deck as midshipmen and ship's corporals passed their messages. He found Hoolahan, his Irish gunner, resting on a jute-bound bale of cloth bolts, silk bolts that were worth more money than his entire county back home. Owen, the senior quarter-gunner, was

napping with his back leant against a carline post that supported the upper deck, his feet propped up on a crate of tableware worth a duke's ransom.

"Stand by, men. We've spotted him. Starboard battery first,
right up his stern, then larboard guns at twenty paces."

They could hear gunports being drawn open overhead, and
the heavy, dull rumble of gun-trucks as the eighteen-pounders
were drawn foot by foot to emerge from the opened ports.
They unpegged and opened their own. Cool night air, damp
and salty, entered, making them all tremble with chill. With anticipation, and a little fear, too.

"Ah, yes," Alan said, sticking his head out a port. Once one
spotted *La Malouine*, it was hard to believe that she could ever
have been hidden by the night. There was the wash and green-
ish phosphor glow of her wake. The faintest reflection of that
phosphorescence on her lower hull at the waterline, and those
betraying glimmers of belfry and binnacle lanterns. "Can you
mark her, Owen?"

"Uhmm ... might need a set of younger eyes, sir. Here,
Hoolahan, you could poach a bunny at midnight."

"Why, so oi kin, sor!" Hoolahan grinned, ever the cheerful
one. "Jus' don't let 'im be loik t' last lot. Barely got the deck
clean."

"Just look, don't prose on, boy," Owen groaned.

"Aye, sor. Mebbe cable, cable 'un t'half now, Mister
Owen."

Telesto leaned to starboard more as she went up to windward. Gunners removed tompions, spun the elevating screws to
compensate for the heel of the ship. Greased slides whispered
as the short, brutal thirty-two-pounder carronades were run out.
Iron wheels creaked as the lay of the barrels was corrected.

"Oi kin smell 'er now, sor. Gahh, bloody Frog stink!"

"As you bear!" a voice shouted. "Fire!"

It crossed Lewrie's mind that this ship had better indeed be
La Malouine, and not some parsimonious merchantman that
begrudged even a ha'porth of whale-oil for lanterns.

The starboard twelve-pounder chase gun barked as the forecastle ranged even with the strange ship's stern, sending a hellish finger of pink-and-coral flame into the night, fuzee-flashing
just how near they were to their target, and how large she
bulked. There were not a hundred yards between them! Then
the larger, deeper-throated eighteen-pounders spoke, loud
as thunderclaps from a lightning bolt's near miss. Shot after

shot as each barrel came even with the foe, more pink-and-coral flames, more red-and-amber sparks of half-spent gunpowder. Clouds of foul-smelling smoke wafted downwind, wreathing about the other ship.

"Ready ... cock your locks ... as you bear ... fire!" Lewrie intoned. The forward-most carronade belched with a fiery eructation, whipping backward on its greased slide quick enough to shriek wood on wood, and set the grease smoking. Most satisfying deep bangs of guns going off, followed immediately by the crash of heavy iron hitting timbers, the moaning wail of oak and teak as scantlings were shattered, and the *thonk* of balls ranging down the entire undefended length of the hull inside their target. Shattering tableware and vases, ripping precious cargo of wallpaper, silks, teas apart in aromatic clouds. Ripping men apart as they hung close-packed as sausages in a butcher's window in their hammocks. Killing men with the air of their passage without making a mark upon them. Breaking at last into savage iron shards among a sleet-storm of broken beams and frames, which in those enclosed spaces below decks would whirl and maim as ruthlessly as irate, razor-tipped sparrows.

"Now, ready the larboard battery!" Lewrie yelled as the last of their carronades had recoiled inward. Ports slammed open, making space for the wide-mouthed barrels to be run out. "Hull the bastards when I give the word, Owen."

"Aye, sir," Owen replied around the stem of his pipe. "Now, gun-captains, lowest elevation, an' wait for the down-roll! Wads atop your ball, rammer-men! Don't dribble the damn things out now!"

The ship creaked ominously as she slewed about. Cargo made dry rustling sounds as crates and bundles shifted slightly against restraining ropes and baffle-boards. The helm was put over so quickly *Telesto* churned the sea to a green-white froth of phosphor and foam, being over-steered so that she would slow down and not run her jib-boom and sprit into the stern of the enemy. She went wide off the wind as her deck-hands strained to loose sail and haul the yards around to gain speed, no longer working slack with the sea but beginning to oppose its will with her own desire for a faster pace.

Then she was brought back up to the wind a couple of points, to steady on a parallel course to the stranger, to steady her own decks for a surer gun-platform.

"Half a cable!" Lewrie estimated, leaning out one of the

ports alongside the cold iron barrel of a carronade. The larboard chase-gun banged, and he ducked back inboard quickly. "Wait for it!"

Eighteen-pounders roared out their challenge, lighting the sea amber and bright red between the two ships, giving him short snatches in which to see the other ship. It *was La Malouine!* He'd stared at her long enough for seven months to recognize every tar stain!

"Cock your locks . . . stand by . . . on the down-roll . . . together . . . Fire!"

All four larboard carronades took light as one. There was some spectacular noise that had everyone's ears ringing, a brilliant burst of light worthy of a lightning strike, fading from bright yellow to a dull burgundy, and a wave of burnt powder rushed back in the ports as bitter as rotten eggs. With the wind fine on their larboard quarter once again, most of it blew away past the bows, but enough was blown back onto the lower gun deck to be-fog them and set them all wheezing.

Damme to hell, but I love artillery, Alan exulted silently! The power, the noise, even the stink of 'em! And what they can do.

"Yes, by God!" he crowed, leaning out the port once more. In the after-flash of the last eighteen-pounder, he could see large ragged rents in *La Malouine*'s lower hull, one right on the waterline that sucked and blew spumes of foam as the waves rushed past the hole, the other three higher up in her chain-wale. They'd nailed her 'twixt wind and water, shattering her main-mast's starboard chains, that complicated array of dead-eyes, shroud-tensioners, heavy horizontal timber through which the stays for the lower mast threaded and terminated. "Reload!"

La Malouine was not as asleep as they had thought. Her side lit up in flashes as well, her twelve-pounder cannon returning fire, but not as organized as the ship-killing broadside they'd just delivered. Here a forward gun, there a piece in her wardroom aft, then two guns from her waist together.

"Musta kept 'alf their hands at Quarters t' fire that quickly, sir," Owen guessed. Usually it took ten minutes for even a Royal Navy vessel to clear decks, load and run out their batteries. "Mighta been plannin' on doin' the same for us this night."

"There's a biter bit, boi God!" Hoolahan whooped.

Then the gun-captains were standing back from priming

their carronades, fists in the air while their excess hands tailed on the tackles to haul the guns up to the port-sills once more. The upper deck guns began to howl again, and it was time for another crushing broadside.

Five, six times, they fired—about ten minutes of battle at the hottest pace the crews could sustain for a short time. Slowly, the return fire from *La Malouine* slacked off. She was not built to take such punishment. She was a merchant ship, with wider-spaced timbers and lighter scantlings of perhaps no more than six inches thickness. Strong enough to protect her in storms, against rocks and shoals, and to stiffen her when she was laden with cargo, but not enough to guard her vitals when heavy iron was flying. Even the toughest oak or teak gives way when hit with eighteen pounds of metal at twelve hundred feet per second at such short range.

Telesto had been built to bear twenty-four-pounders on her lower deck, twelve- or eighteen-pounders on her upper deck, and her sides were ten to twelve inches of seasoned English oak laid over much heavier and thicker framing spaced closer together. She had been laid down for warfare. Some of *La Malouine*'s twelve-pound balls hurt her, even so, but she was built to take much heavier battering and live for hours in the line of battle.

La Malouine had drifted down closer to her, as Captain Ayscough had predicted she would. Perhaps her helmsmen had been scythed away by the quarterdeck twelve-pounders, the two-pounder swivel-guns, and the muskets of Chiswick's *sepoys*. Perhaps her crew had been so decimated that no one could tend her braces, or be spared from the gun battery to go aloft and loose more sail. Now the range was almost hull-to-hull, and when the carronades erupted, shattered wood came flying in the ports at once, making more hazard for Lewrie's crews than anything that the French had done yet.

"Mister Lewrie!" one of their midshipmen yelled from the after companion-way. "Close your ports, secure your guns, and come on deck for the boarding party, please sir!"

"Aye aye!"

They gained the upper deck, dug into the open weapons tubs at the base of the main-mast and fetched cutlasses and pistols. This time, Alan had his own pistols: the small pair he'd purchased long ago in Portsmouth when he first kitted out as a midshipman, and a brace of dragoon pistols he'd carried away from Yorktown. He checked the primings and stuffed them into the Hindoo *cummerbund* he still wore, drew his sword, and led his party to the larboard gangways where Chiswick's troops were still firing away with their muskets

"Grapnels, bosun!" Choate was yelling. "Form up, lads! Stand ready! Lower the boarding nettings. Now, *away boarders!*"

With a concerted howl, they were up and over their own bulwarks, leaping onto *La Malouine*'s bulwarks across the gap created by the tumble-home of the two hulls. There was an irregular volley of pistol and musket fire as the French met them. Men shrieked and clawed at sudden hurts, lost their footing or their handholds and fell into the narrow tide-race between the ships to be crushed to death as the hulls ground and bumped together every half-minute or so. Pike-heads stabbed up at them, stopping leapers in mid-air. One sailor screamed as sharp iron found his belly, his weight dragging the shaft of the pike down atop the bulwark. The wielder must have been a strong man, for he held the sailor there, kicking wildly and vomiting blood and half-digested rations before he slipped off and fell howling between the hulls.

Lewrie leaped, banging one knee on the ship's side, getting one foot on the Frenchman's bulwark, and a precious handhold on a loose stay that felt like it was half shot-through and ready to come free at any second. He had a brief glimpse downward at the bloody water foaming between *La Malouine* and *Telesto*, saw a man's head crushed as flat as a frying pan, an imploring arm and hand waving madly at him as another drowned below the surface, trapped by untold tons.

He hauled hard on the stay to throw himself forward out of danger, and stumbled to his knees to the deck. Ignoring the pain in his knee, he rose up and started swinging his sword for his life! A man tumbled into him from behind, knocking him flat once more. Then there was a volley of shots that cleared the deck around him for a moment, allowing him to get to his feet.

"At 'em, Telestos!" He yelled. A French sailor came at him with a pike leveled like a charging cavalry lancer. A quick move to parry from left and below, pushing that wicked pikehead away to his right and past his shoulder, then a riposting thrust at the belly.

The Frenchman screamed almost in his ear, a foot of Gill's best English steel in his entrails, lost his grip on the pike, and dropped away like a spilled sack of meal, almost dragging

Lewrie with him as his ravaged stomach muscles tried to clench around the blade. Alan had to plant a foot on the man's chest and thighs to drag his sword back out, bringing forth the slithering horrors contained within.

Dark faces with swarthy mustaches and whiskers came raving on La Malouine's gangway. Chiswick's sepoys, less practiced at boarding and slower to cross over. Now that the seamen had cleared them some room, they were trotting forward and aft, bayonets fixed, and their havildars shouting encouragement.

"Maro, maro ghanda Fransisi!"*

Percival and McTaggart were headed forward with a large pack of seamen, teetering their way over the boat-tier beams to get to the larboard side as well. Alan spun about and led his men aft. Where it came from, he had no idea, but there was now some light on deck, enough to see the party of Frenchmen rushing to defend their quarterdeck. It was disconcerting to see Marcel Monnot in their lead, the sailor he'd spoken to on the docks one morning. But Monnot had a cutlass in his hand, and he began hacking away at an English sailor.

Lewrie let his hanger dangle from the wrist-strap, pulled out his first dragoon pistol and pulled it back to full cock. Stepping forward with his men, he took aim and let fly. The fight with Monnot swirled out of his aim, but another Frenchman was struck by the ball in the chest, plumping a sudden burst of scarlet on his white shirt front and dropping him out of sight. He drew his second pistol and shot a hulking French seaman right in the face, who gave a great howl and flipped over backward, making a gap for more English sailors to dash forward and crowd the French back. Cutlasses sang and whished in the air, ringing steel on steel. Pikeheads and bayonet points stabbed out in short thrusts.

Then there was Monnot again, leaping back into action and hewing a sailor down, pushing forward and leading more of his hands with him against everything.

"Vous!" he exclaimed, spotting Lewrie. "Espèce de salaud!"

"Strike, Monnot! Throw down your sword! It's over!"

"Va te faire foutre!" Monnot cried, throwing himself forward.

Lewrie jerked his wrist and brought his sword into his palm,

*"Kill, kill the dirty French!"

leading with a thrust that Monnot beat aside, but the speed of it made him drop back a pace. Alan stamped forward, countering a hard counterswing of Monnot's cutlass blade. They were too hemmed in by struggling bodies to do anything more than beat at each other vertically after that. Bayonets stabbed on either side, and Frenchmen were dying, going down as the *sepoys* loaned their strength to shove their foes backward and upward to the quarterdeck, beginning to thin them out enough for Lewrie to have more fighting room.

It was disconcerting to fight a man he knew, even slightly. He had nothing against Monnot personally, so it felt less like a duel. A stranger he could have crossed swords with gladly. But it was his life to not kill him. Monnot was monstrously strong. A bit unskilled with a more gentlemanly smallsword, perhaps, but ruthlessly competent with a cutlass, his wrist hard as an iron anvil.

Monnot fetched up against the ladder that led to the quarterdeck, last of his men still standing on the gangway, and he howled in glee as he swung his sword in the full cutlass drill. There!

An opening, as Monnot swung backhanded, fumbled backward to take a step up the ladder, still facing his foes. Lewrie leaped for him, raising his sword to block a further swing, but ramming the lion-headed pommel of his sword into Monnot's mouth!

The man stumbled onto his back, one hand grasping at the rope balustrade of the ladder, thrusting with his cutlass, a thrust which Lewrie parried off low, and then he was inside Monnot's guard with a backward slash of that superbly strong and razor-honed hanger across the man's belly and chest.

Monnot howled again, reaching upward to take Lewrie's throat in one hand, drawing his cutlass back with the other. Alan started turning purple as he reached out to take Monnot's sword-arm wrist in his hand and hold off a killing blow, drawing his hanger back behind his knee to turn it upward, and thrust the point into the Frenchman's jaws. Up through throat skin, through the tongue, into the sinuses and the brain! Monnot grunted and twisted like a piked fish, bumping down the steps of the quarterdeck ladder one at a time, dragging Alan with him with one hand yet gripping his throat in a final, inhuman spasming strength!

Sailors and soldiers dashed past them while Alan was dragged to his knees, gasping for air and watching the world go dim, until at last Monnot's heels began to drum on the deck, and his hands lost all strength. His eyes flared once more with anger, then rolled up into his head and glazed over unblinking. Alan rocked back onto his heels and gulped great lungfuls of air, massaging his throat with one hand and tugging his sword free with the other. He felt like shooting the man, just to make sure he was dead, not shamming until he'd stepped over him to ascend to the quarterdeck, then strike him from behind!

He settled for a slash across Monnot's throat as he sprang up and rushed aft, getting away from the brute as quick as he was able.

"Jesus Christ!" he muttered, once he'd gained the deck. No wonder it was light enough to see! *La Malouine* was on fire! After lights-out aboard any ship, it was the officers aft who could keep a lantern or two burning past nine P.M., and their gunfire must have overturned a lamp, killed a gun-captain who had dropped his smoldering slow-match onto something flammable. Smoke drifted and curled from between the deck planks. Pounded tar to waterproof the joins was running slick and hot, sticking to his shoes. One corner of the poop deck farther aft already showed gaps through which tiny flames licked. He turned to see if *Telesto* was safe, and saw no sign of fire. But amidships, in *La Malouine*'s waist, there was a bright red glow under the tarred canvas that covered the midships cargo hatches and companion-way hatches. Even as he watched, the tarred canvas took fire with a sullen *whoomp* and disappeared in a sooty shower, and long, licking flames leaped aloft with a roar like a bellows had been applied to a forge!

"Back to the ship!" Choate was yelling, waving their men back to *Telesto* with his sword. "Move, lads, if you don't want to burn!"

There was no greater fear for a sailor than fire aboard ship.

Once it got a good hold on the dry timbers, the tarred ropes, greased running rigging and canvas sails, a fire was almost impossible to extinguish. In the blink of an eye, a ship could flash into a ruddy horror, roasting her crew, who would be fearful to abandon her until the last minute, for most sailors could not swim.

"Back!" Alan yelled. "Back aboard our ship, stir yourselves!"

They were lucky to make it, for the small crew that had stayed aboard *Telesto* were chopping and sawing at the grapnel ropes even before everyone could reach the rails to prepare themselves for the leap.

It was a panic. *Sepoys* crowded the rails, their eyes rolling in fear, ready to abandon their weapons in their haste to flee. Chiswick was raving back and forth, shouting at them in Hindee and pushing muskets back into their hands, arranging a party of some of his largest men to literally throw some of the others across to *Telesto*'s bulwarks, to be caught by seamen.

La Malouine was keening as the flames began to roar in earnest, the sound a soaked river rock makes when placed in a camp-fire. Men wounded and unable to move were screaming and gibbering in terror.

"Damnit!" Alan sighed, sheathing his sword. He picked among the bodies, searching for his own. The dead he could do nothing for, but there were surely some English wounded that simply could not be left behind to suffer.

"Oh, God, sir!" Archibald, the condom-maker, keened shrill as a frightened child as he lay on the gangway with blood soaking his leg. "Help meeeee!!!"

"I'm here, Archibald, Let's go!"

He got him to his feet, an arm around him, and half-dragged him to the rail, yelling for help. Hodge, the topman, came swarming over to them with a free line, and quickly whipped a loop in it. They got Archibald seated in it and let it swing. Even if he bashed his head in on their ship's hull, he was away. Cony returned with it as they began to search.

"Telestos!" Lewrie called, almost choking on the stink of burning cargo below decks. Singed tea leaves swirled around him like a plague of locusts. "Hoy, Telestos! Sing out and we'll save you!"

A gut-shot French seaman raised an imploring hand from the deck, terror in his eyes. They passed him by. He was not one of theirs. Hodge drew a heavy belaying pin from the railing and did the man the favor of knocking him senseless so he'd know less about his immolation.

"Don't think they's any more of our'n, Mister Lewrie!" Cony said, tugging at his sleeve.

"Lewrie, leave it!" Ayscough called from their ship. "Leave it or die over there! I can't keep station on her any longer!"

Flames were shooting up the main-mast now, furled sails bursting alight, standing and running rigging covered with tiny shoots of fire like some expensive holiday illumination.

"Good enough for me," Lewrie responded, climbing over the rails.

They threw them lines, and they swung across, suspended from gant-line blocks and yard-tackles. Lewrie thrust out his legs to take the shock of impact, but it knocked the wind out of him anyway. He dangled for a moment against the hull by the gunports until someone reached over and grabbed him by the collar to haul him up.

He landed in a heap on the larboard gangway, almost getting trampled by sail-trimmers as they heaved on the yard braces to get the ship underway. He could barely hear the shouted commands over the roar of the fire aboard *La Malouine*.

"Ya awright, sir?" Cony asked, helping him to his feet, and disentangling him from the gant-line block and three-part loops of line. "Christ, wot a mess!"

When he had a chance to look back at their foe, once *Telesto* was far enough to leeward that she wouldn't catch fire herself, he could see that the French ship was alight from taff-rail to the tip of her bow-sprit. Her upper yards were raining down in chunks like dripping embers. No matter that they were heavy, they were almost floating against the fierce, roaring up-draft of the fires. Now and again, there was a bright, blue-white flash and dull *thud* as a powder cartridge burst, or a loaded gun took light. Sparks would fly against a yellow-white cloud of powder, making *La Malouine* look even more like carnival fireworks.

Men dribbled from her, too. Men whose clothing, whose very flesh had caught fire, and swarmed staggering and blind in unspeakable agony, swathed from head to toe in greedy, gnawing flames like animated torches. They keened and howled, reeled and dropped out of sight. Or tumbled over the bulwarks of their ship to raise great splashes in the water alongside, where only a greasy smoke and a circle of foam marked their passing.

They dropped into the water beside others who floundered and thrashed in the glowing amber water, thrashing clumsily for any bit of flotsam to support them before they drowned. Pleas for help went unnoticed, cries to God went unheard, amidst all the screaming and wailing, amidst the crackle and roar of the flames.

La Malouine had had four ship's boats, all nestled on the tiers that spanned the waist between the gangways over the up-per deck, and three of them now roasted like unattended steaks on a grill. The fourth was in the water, one side charred black and half sunk, reeking with smoke. Half a dozen men clung to her, and two sat on her after-most thwart, fighting the others to prevent them climbing in and swamping her. There was one large, grid-worked hatch cover in the water, and more men clung to the sides, while others who could swim splashed in its direction. Out of *La Malouine*'s crew of roughly one-hundred-fifty men, not thirty could be discovered alive now.

"Oh, Christ, sir, look!" Cony shuddered.

Dark, triangular fins cut the glassy, illuminated red-and-amber waters. Sharks! Lewrie winced with a sudden cold chill as a fin went underwater just behind a struggling man. That man suddenly shot out of the ocean as if he'd been tossed by a bull, screaming louder than he could have thought possible from anyone's throat, setting off more panic among the survivors. Pale white fish bellies rolled with him as they seized upon his flesh, bit and shook like bulldogs to tear off huge chunks of living meat! More fins darted in from nowhere, summoned God knew how from the depths. More men thrashed and wailed as they were taken. The survivors who had been clustered around the half-sunk boat swarmed up on it in a wave, climbing over each other in their haste, as the boat rolled on its beam ends and capsized.

There was no time to put boats down. *Telesto*'s crew lifted up their own curved, grid-work hatch-covers and tossed them in as Ayscough had her steered through the thickest pack of Frenchmen. The tail-ends of halyards, lifts and braces were slung over so that those that could might reach them and climb to safety, and life.

But it was futile. Three French sailors who could swim climbed aboard, shaking in terror. Perhaps three more made it to the floats. By the time *Telesto* had sailed on past, wore ship and came back into the area, there was no sign of living men around the overturned boat, and not seven altogether on all the floating hatch-covers, girded round entirely by circling fins and face-down bodies that one by one were taken under. There had to be a thousand sharks by then around *La Malouine*, striking at anything whether it moved or not—paddles, broken oars, charred flotsam or discarded clothing—it made no difference to them.

La Malouine burned for two hours before she went under, still a spark on the horizon by the time *Telesto* found her cutter and took her back aboard. She finally winked out around two in the morning, about the time Mr. Twigg finished interrogating the shattered remnants of her people.

Chapter 3

"I should think we've done rather well so far," Mr. Twigg said somewhat smugly as they held *durbar*, or conference, ashore at Bencoolen on Sumatra. They'd run into port before a punishing South China Sea *taifun* that had loomed up above the Johore Straits, and *Telesto* had been lucky to make a safe harbor before the full fury had broken upon them. The storm had passed, ravaging the settlement, but sparing the well-anchored ships. In its aftermath, a crushing humidity had settled in, along with steady rain and choking heat, and not a breath of breeze. If Bencoolen had been the arse-hole of the world before, the *taifun* had done nothing by way of improvement.

"And what is to be done with our French prisoners, sir?" Captain Ayscough inquired as he poured himself another healthful mug of lemon-water and brandy. "The men don't much care for having them around, you know, pitiable as they are."

"Perhaps it'd be a kindness to leave them here at Bencoolen," Twigg said with an idle wave of his hand. "A passing French ship may take them eventually. Them that survived, that is."

They'd picked up ten terrified Frenchmen. Some had been bitten by sharks, and their wounds turned septic immediately, and the gangrene killed them. Not five lived now, and two of those were in precarious health. Lewrie suspected Twigg's penchant for cruel interrogation may have hastened the departure of some of those from life.

"Leaving them here in Bencoolen is no kindness, sir," Lt. Col. Sir Hugo Willoughby grunted. Alan's father had grown even older since he'd last laid eyes on him: his hair thinner and greyer, his face more care-lined and leathery. "Hasn't been much of a kindness for my battalion, either, let me assure you."

"You agreed it would place your troops closer to the action, I might remind you, Sir Hugo," Twigg said, frowning. The vilely hot weather had not improved anyone's tempers, but it was almost too hot and humid to argue. "As for the Frogs, I care less if all the buggers succumb. No real loss, is it, though I would wish for one or two to survive to bear the tale back to Paris. The effect would have been welcome."

"And do you feel that same impartiality to my men, sir?" Sir Hugo snapped.

"Sir Hugo," Twigg drawled. "Colonel Willoughby. Unlike my utter lack of sympathy for piratical Frenchmen, I feel most strongly and deeply for the plight of the men of the 19th Native Infantry. And I assure you, I shall be most happy to extricate them from this hellish stew at the earliest opportunity. That moment has almost arrived, sir, but you must bear the deplorable conditions here for only a few more months. Soon, I promise you."

"It had best be soon, sir," Sir Hugo replied evenly, controlling his own temper with remarkable restraint, as Lewrie could attest. "We arrived in mid-February with a grenadier company, eight line companies, one and a half light companies, and the full artillery detachment. And now, with Captain Chiswick and his half-company returned to me, I may only field eight. Eight, sir! Allow me to protest most vigorously that if this battalion is not removed to a more healthful climate, I won't have a platoon of men available to you by autumn! I demand of you, if you have any estimate of when we may depart this reeking cesspit, pray inform us of it."

"I quite understand, Sir Hugo," Twigg replied, on the edge of an explosion of his own temper, no matter how much the weather might dampen his fuses. "Two months. Three months at the most, weather permitting, and you shall be out of here, at sea and in action."

That created a stir of interest among the army officers seated behind Sir Hugo, and among the naval officers as well.

"You see, sirs," Twigg continued calmly, getting a smug look on his face. "I know where this fellow Guillaume Choundas is. And where he shall be in a few months' time." Twigg looked about the damp and gloomy room, a wood and thatch imposture of a proper building, letting the stirring and chattering of their excitement swell and recede like a breaking wave of adulation before continuing.

"Shaken as the French survivors were, it was fairly simple to play upon their fears, catch them out when they were at their weakest," Twigg explained. "Have we a good chart of the South China Seas, Captain Ayscough? Could it be hung where all could see it? Good."

"Here, gentlemen. In the Spratly Islands." Twigg chuckled.

"Pretty far lost and gone from anywhere," Ayscough commented.

"But located so nicely for piracy, sirs," Twigg informed them. "Flat, tiny, and worth nothing to anyone. As our sailing master may attest?"

Brainard stood to address the assembly, flushing a bit at being before so many people. "There's water enough, wild goats and pigs to eat. Sea-birds and their eggs. Nobody lives there, though, not permanent. Too small to farm. Too low to make 'em safe durin' *taifun* season, 'cept for the highest hills inland. Good anchorage, I'll admit. Chinese pirates sometimes shelter there, same for other pirate bands like the Sea Dyaks. Have to bring in salt-meats and such if you plan on stayin' there a long time."

Brainard shrugged and reddened, trying to think of what else he might impart, but Twigg waved him off, which Brainard accepted with a whoosh of relieved breath.

"The Spratlys are two-hundred-fifty miles southeast of the Annamese shores, three hundred miles northwest of Borneo, right in the middle of the mouth of the South China Sea," Twigg related. "A ship, or ships, working out of here could control the shipping trade in time of war, especially if one were to be allied with native pirates who could patrol in their *praos* for likely pickings. Too far west for the Spanish in the Philippines to worry about. Too far north and west for the Dutch or Portuguese to deal with. Too far north and east of even this poor trading settlement of Bencoolen for England to look in on. I'm told a man named Francis Light may develop trading stations on the Malay peninsula soon, so that situation may change, but properly fortified and garrisoned, this little group of islands would be a hard nut to crack, even in time of war when a fleet might be available. This is where Choundas shall be. This is where he is based during the summer months. Where the pirates meet him. Where captured ships are looted, and their crews taken."

"And did we discover with whom Choundas and Sicard were in league, Mister Twigg?" Lieutenant Choate asked. "Would some of our prisoners be there still that we might rescue?"

"As to the last part of your question, I'm afraid the answer is no, Mister Choate," Twigg replied, frowning while rubbing the bridge of his nose as though in pain. "There is little chance that any Englishmen survived capture for very long. Especially if it was the native pirates who did it. Should they have, they'd have been taken east to Sulu Island and sold in the great slave markets there. And it would take a fleet to sail in there and free those unfortunates. As to the first part, we now know that the French are allied with the blood-thirstiest of the lot. The Lanun Rovers, from the Illana Lagoon on Mindanao."

"Oh, stap me!" Brainard hissed with alarm. "More likely, our people are skulls adorning their bloody *praos* by now!"

"Goddamn French!" Ayscough spat. "Trust them to take hands with those devils. Not just as allies, but friends!"

"Well, not for very much longer, sir," Twigg said, chuckling dryly. "I propose we strike the Spratlys sometime after mid-June. When Choundas and his piratical crew will be there. When the Lanun Rovers will spend the summer with him. We may catch them all in one fell swoop!"

"And just where is your pirate now, sir?" Sir Hugo asked.

"He left Canton in late November, Sir Hugo. As I told you, I suspect he waited downriver at Macao for at least a week or so, to see if we would pursue him. When we didn't, he most likely stopped in at the Spratlys, then sailed for the French possessions in the Indian Ocean. We have information that his first stop would be Ile de France, to have a refit in the yards there. Those same yards service the Royal French Navy, I might remind you. His usual course of action, his *modus operandi*, if you will allow me"—Twigg sniffed loftily, but gave them all a brief smile to remind them that he was human, after all—"would be to sail on for Pondichery, where he would load a cargo of Indian goods destined for Canton in the fall. A cargo that he would land at the Spratlys, since the goods would prove a liability to a privateering cruise. He does not load opium, only run-of-the-mill wares that will not spoil during storage ashore. The opium comes from our ships."

"And he didn't sell any out of Macao, as I recall, sir," Captain Ayscough stuck in.

"Indeed not, sir," Twigg agreed. "Part of his innocent pose

is to deplore the opium trade. And a man so high-minded as to forgo the profits of opium could never, ever be suspected of anything so vile as piracy, now could he, hmm?" Which set them all into ironic laughter. "Then, he and Captain Sicard of *La Malouine* would meet in Pondichery."

"To put the bulk of their combined crews into *Poisson D'Or*, so he'd be as well-manned as any royal frigate, sir?" Percival asked with a hopeful expression.

"Exactly so, Mister Percival." Twigg beamed at him like a fond daddy. "Exactly as you surmised. Right, then! Here's Choundas, waiting in Pondichery for Sicard and *La Malouine* to arrive by at least the first of April, but she won't this year, nor next year, either, ha ha! By mid-April, he'll have smelled a rat. What's worse for him, Sicard was to bring the profits from both ships to him. He lost no money by having his cargo confiscated by the Viceroy in Canton. Their arrangement with that particularly corrupt mandarin made sure he'd get full value from it, and give him freedom of action to boot. But suddenly, he's starved of operating funds. There's nothing to purchase a cargo with in Pondichery. No money to buy arms and powder for his piratical allies. And, more importantly, no ship such as Sicard's to serve as his cartel for all the loot he expects to take this year of our Lord 1785. We've limited his options to an early raiding summer. Here!"

"It strikes me, though, Mister Twigg," Lewrie spoke up, "that even the most valuable goods such as silver and opium take up a fair amount of cargo space. Surely, *La Malouine* could not carry all of it. If only a quarter of the booty ends up in Canton, there must be some other ship, or ships, involved with Choundas yet. If he has, as you say, a full, believable cargo stashed in the Spratlys for his appearance in Canton in the fall, where does the rest of it go?"

"A great deal of it would end up in the market at Sulu, sir," Twigg countered. "Brasswares, copper, Indian cotton goods, all of it would be just as valuable among the pirate bands as it would in Canton. No, it'll be Choundas on his own this year, I'll wager. Driven by desperation to take more risks than before."

"If he's any brains at all, he'll know the game's over, sir," Lieutenant Choate insisted. "Time to lay low for a season. Or sail home for France and let someone else take over for him for a while."

"Ah, but he can't do that, Mister Choate," Twigg insisted.

"If he leaves the Indian Ocean, he loses everything he's built up out here. No rendezvous with the pirates in the Spratlys, say. Then what pirate would ever trust another Frenchman to keep his word? He'd not only be discarding his present alliances, he'd be ruining a chance for anyone who follows. The French Ministry of Marine who dreamed up his dirty business would never stand for that, oh no! Why, they'd break Choundas to common seaman if he simply sailed away. And, I don't think our lad is the sort to cave in so quickly. He's an ambitious little Breton peasant, a jumped-up *fisherman* who has no desire to end his days netting sardines in a filthy little smack. Pride goeth before a fall, and our boy has an ocean of pride. No, he might be late for the rendezvous. He may come empty-handed, but he'll be in the Spratlys by June."

"So we should get *Telesto* back to Calcutta as soon as possible," Captain Ayscough surmised. "After a year in Asian waters, and all that time idle in Whampoa Reach, we have to careen and bream her bottom. The weed on her quick-work looks like the Forest of Dean. Land our cargo, unload the artillery first, then refloat her and outfit her for battle."

"And be back here toward the end of May, to pick up Sir Hugo's battalion and escort the *Lady Charlotte* transport to the Spratlys," Twigg said bouyantly. "Sail into harbor, land troops and guns, and blow Choundas, his ship and any pirates clean off the face of God's seas!"

There was a lot of cheering that ringing speech. Cheers for a chance for action after festering at Bencoolen in sodden heat and agues, for final retribution against the hated French who had outmaneuvered them during the winter, for a chance that this whole affair would end and *Telesto*'s flexible term of commission could end snug in some English harbor by early 1786. They would be two years away from friends and family by then, two years gone from their homes, and did not relish the prospect of a third.

Lewrie was not enthused, though. Troubling questions had their way with his imaginings. While he was most junior naval officer there, he knew he had to speak them aloud, before the conference ended. Later would look like croakum, and Twigg would not change his mind once they had settled on the plan, unless forced to, and afterthoughts would not be force enough.

"Excuse me again, Mister Twigg," he said, clearing his throat to draw silence enough in which to speak his piece, "but Choundas has had four months' freedom to refit. He's lost profits from this year's work, but there's no telling how much they earned the first two years. He could outfit another ship to work with him, hire a new crew to replace what he lost aboard *La Malouine*. And there's nothing to prevent him from *already* being in the Spratly Islands. We didn't peek in to see if anyone held the islands for his return, or if these Lanun Rovers were already there waiting for him. We have no idea what we're to sail into, really, and he has all the time in the world."

"Because I did not want to alert anyone who might have been in those islands until we were in all respects ready to strike when the basket was full, so to speak, Mister Lewrie," Twigg sneered in objection. "And, as I have just related, I have it on the very best authority that Choundas will sail to Pondichery first, waiting for Sicard to return and join him. That is his usual wont."

Twigg looked as if he'd enjoy picking up a "barker" and firing a pistol ball right through Lewrie's heart. The *durbar* had been going so wonderfully well, and his plan had carried, when up popped Lewrie with his morale-eroding carping!

"His *usual* style, sir," Lewrie replied, smiling. "But things aren't the usual this year. He has us to worry about. What the survivors of his crew remembered him doing in the past don't signify. He could have looked into the Spratlys and left some men behind as a garrison this time. Hired hands to man *Poisson D'Or* with the hopes of meeting us on our way back to Calcutta, with *La Malouine* tailing us to make it two against one. He could be up in the Nicobars or the Straits of Malacca waiting for that this instant. Or rush back to the Spratlys ahead of last year's schedule while we have to sail for Calcutta and back, to gain a march on us. Seems to me, sir, if we wait 'til June we either hit an empty bag, or walk right into a bloody fleet of pirates and wide-awake Frogs."

He turned to his father, who was scowling at his audacity to speak to authority like that. "As my dear father may tell you, sir, his troops would do us no good aboard their transport if Choundas is ready for us. His men would stand no chance at all."

"And what would you suggest, my lad?" Sir Hugo inquired, stifling any objections that Twigg was more than ready to raise.

"That we hit the Spratlys now, sir," Alan stated. "That we do not allow Choundas to form a combination against us, with pirates of another cartel ship. Or hire another French captain to side with him. We're here, even against the nor'easterlies, two weeks' sail away, with nearly a full battalion of troops trained for shore landings and equipped to fight. Land our cargo here in Bencoolen for the nonce if we have to. Even if you have to sail to Calcutta and back afterward, we would hold the island before Choundas even knows Sicard is lost."

"Oh, God," Twigg sighed, shaking his head as though at the fire-eating impetuosity of youth. "Mister Lewrie, I thought better of you. If we do take the Spratlys, and Choundas arrives earlier, as you say, then he escapes before we're ready to strike him, and God knows what secret lair he establishes next. I'll not spend all this summer and all of '86 chasing him 'round the Great South Seas! And if we do take two precious weeks to delay our refit in Calcutta, we lose any chance of pursuing him."

"The Spratlys are a healthier climate for my father's men than Bencoolen, sir," Alan rejoined. "And we would not have to depend solely upon *Telesto* for support. If you could dispatch another well-armed country ship to our aid, once we're ashore . . ."

"And where, pray, do we find funds enough to do that, sir?" Twigg fumed.

"Why, from the profits of this year's trading season, sir," Lewrie responded. "That's what they're for, surely."

Twigg's jaw dropped open for a brief moment at the suggestion. And before he could put a refuting argument into play, Sir Hugo stood up and cleared his throat, wandering to the map to peer at it.

"Sounds like a good idea to me," he announced. "Does it not to you as well, as the senior Navy man, Captain Ayscough? Does your sailing master think a battalion could find decent provender there for a period of some months? Would it be healthier for my men?"

"If the place may swarm with pirates and Frogs, Sir Hugo, it'd support them decent enough," Brainard allowed. "And you have salt-meat and such for rations here, and in the transport. You could hold out long enough for us to get to Calcutta and back with more. And there's goats, pigs and fowl enough here in Bencoolen to take with you. As to the climate, it's be not near as hot, and a lot drier. Sea breeze'd make it seem ten degrees cooler."

"And there is the possibility that this Choundas fellow's pirates might already be there, could they not?" Sir Hugo speculated. "I don't know much about 'em, but it seems to me it'd be better to fight them now, before they could ally with French artillery and trained gunners. A battalion of well-drilled troops'd make mincemeat of 'em once we're ashore. Why wait until your foe is lined up and ready to fire, I say? My officers'll agree with me; the way to defeat a larger foe is chew 'em up into penny packets first. Then boot hell out of the remainder. Knacker the buggers bit at a time."

"Gentlemen, we . . ." Twigg tried to object.

"Lewrie's right, I think," Ayscough stuck in, enthused from his torpor. "As you are, Sir Hugo. Take them on in manageable portions, is the best way. Let's also allow as how Mister Lewrie could be correct in thinking that there's much too much booty for only one or two ships to carry. We might discover another Frog cartel ship such as *La Malouine* there. Hamstring the bastard even more."

"I might point out," Twigg griped, "that it is nearly two thousand miles back to the Spratlys, sirs. Fifteen days' sail against the prevailing northeasterlies at this season? Say three more to load the troops aboard the *Lady Charlotte*. Then nearly a month from there back to Calcutta. 'Tis the third week of March, now. First week of April would put us here, off the Spratlys. Then three weeks back to Calcutta would be the first of May. Not enough time to refit *Telesto* and clean her bottom, *and* make it back to the Spratlys before Choundas arrives. It simply cannot be done, sirs. But from here to Calcutta is only *ten* days! A week to unload cargo, lighten ship and careen her, a week to set her to rights again, and be back here to escort *Lady Charlotte* and the troops to our destination. By the end of May, sirs. By the first week of June, at worst. When Choundas most certainly shall be there, and may be confronted. And defeated."

"Then by all means sail to Calcutta direct from here," Sir Hugo said. "But let me take my battalion north now. The same argument obtains. We take the islands and the harbor, defeat what pirates we encounter, destroy or commandeer what works the French have built and await your return, snugly ashore and entrenched, as soldiers best understand, sir. And you don't wait until your ship is ready to put to sea. Do what . . . do what my son suggested. Charter or purchase a fast, well-armed ship and crew to come reinforce us."

"There'll not be half a dozen suitable vessels in the Hooghly to choose from, sir. The bulk of the country ships and

East Indiamen will still be in Macao, or on passage still," Twigg snarled.

"The slow ones will, sir," Lewrie stuck in. "But we don't want anything to do with a slow ship. Like that Rebel privateer John Paul Jones said, 'Give me a fast ship, for I intend to go in harm's way,' did he not?"

"And what's even harder to find in the East Indies than trained European soldiers, are trained European seamen and gunners," Twigg said in reply.

"I . . ." Captain Ayscough began, "that is, you and I, Mister Twigg, have writ from the Crown to commandeer or recruit as we will. The *Lady Charlotte*'s crew for one. The crews of the patrol cutters and small brigs here in Bencoolen. Why, they'd trample each other to get out of this pesthole and see some action! A fair amount of any merchantman's crew have Navy experience. Who knows what loot there is to be found among those pirates? Enough *lure* of loot, anyway, to get any number of hands to sign aboard. It's not like we were meant to show a profit out of our voyages. The earnings were to help support our work, not line our pockets, or end up surplus Droits of the Crown. And here's another thought for you. If you gentlemen would join me here at this window, such as it is?"

The assembly of infantry officers, Navy officers and civilian experts was drawn by Ayscough's prompting away from the table and the maps, to gather by the window and stare out through the rains and the water guttering off the thatch and bamboo roof.

"I conjure you to feast your eyes on the transport yonder, the *Lady Charlotte*," Ayscough directed. "For the benefit of you Army lads, she's the shabby old bitch on the left, not the splendid 'Bristol Fashion' lady on the right, ha ha!"

Lady Charlotte was indeed shabby, an old, neglected dray-horse of a ship, of about eight hundred tons burthen. She mounted some six-pounder chase guns, and sixteen twelve-pounder great guns on her upper deck, but had the gunports of a better-armed ship.

"My bosun may give up what paint we have," Ayscough told them merrily. "And he will, if he knows what's good for him! *Lady Charlotte* may be transformed into the very image of the stoutest fifty-gunned two decker as ever swum! A proper ocean bulldog!"

"Or, sir," Choate snickered, "she could end up looking remarkably like *La Malouine*."

"Why, bless my soul, you nacky young bastard!" Ayscough said with a booming laugh, the first anyone had heard him utter in months. "I do believe you've been conniving with Mister Lewrie. Yes, with a lateen yard on her mizzen for a spanker, 'stead of yon gaff and boom, she could be laying at anchor in the Spratlys, waiting for Choundas to return."

"Imagine the consternation he would feel, to expect her lost, and there she is, big as life, sir," Lewrie chortled. "He'd have to sail into harbor to speak her. Close enough for us to hull him with artillery. He might sail right into a trap. Oil or varnish to darken her upper works and she'd resemble *La Malouine* well enough."

"He'd never fall for it," Twigg carped.

"One never knows, sir," Ayscough sniffed. "He might. He just might. And, if *Telesto* and the second vessel Lewrie suggested that we hire were to be lurking off-shore, somewhere to the north . . . yes, to the north would be best, I believe . . . a shore party could send a signal to alert us as to the best moment to fall upon the harbor."

"I most strenuously object to this . . . dribbling of our assets into . . . into"—Twigg spluttered—"penny-packets! As Crown representative, Captain Ayscough . . . damme, sir, any delay in getting to Calcutta, and there will be no second ship dispatched from there to succor Colonel Willoughby's troops. And there will be the transport, in harbor and defenseless. Her loss would destroy any hope of pursuing Choundas, should he not fall for your ruse in disguising her. And strand our troops on this island a thousand miles from nowhere."

"She could be escorted north by one of the patrol vessels here in the harbor already, sir," Ayscough allowed, turning to peer out the open window once more. "There's a ketch-rigged ship out there that's suit. See her yonder? And if not her, perhaps the brig lying farther out. That might be best, after all. In addition to whatever vessel we may send out from Calcutta before *Telesto* is ready to rejoin our endeavor."

"Little better than fishing smacks and packets," Twigg scoffed.

"Some fresh paint, the proper flag flying, and at a distance who may deny they are not well-manned warships?" Ayscough shot back. He was in a fine and confident fettle now, and would not be gainsaid. "Were I a pirate, I'd not wish to fight one of them. One hard battle yardarm to yardarm would cause so much damage the raiding season would be over right there.

That's the risk a privateersman takes. I doubt if this Frog
Choundas wants to fight a real battle against a flotilla, after all.
Overpowering one weak merchantman at a time is more his
style."

"Even more reason for him to turn tail and run for God
knows where as soon as he spots strange ships in his harbor,"
Twigg gloomed.

"They might look like early captures," Lewrie suggested.
"If they were in harbor, sirs. Even more reason to enter and
moor, to see what the booty amounts to so far."

"And should Choundas arrive early, enter harbor," Twigg
carped, "and *not* be utterly destroyed, then *Telesto* hits that
empty bag you spoke of, with him days' gone and free to plunder still!"

"Come, Mister Twigg, you cannot have things both ways,"
Captain Ayscough smirked. "Either he will arrive early, as
Lewrie suspects, or he shall keep to his previous schedule, as
you believe. Either way, sufficient force shall confront him."

Twigg opened his mouth to make further objections, but
Ayscough raised a restraining hand and cut him off.

"You, sir, have fulfilled your brief. You were charged with
an investigation into the disappearance of so many of our merchantmen, of identifying which native pirates were responsible.
And that you have done. You were further charged with the
task of unmasking the French behind their activities. And that,
too, you have accomplished. You have found their base of operations, when to expect their arrival to launch more depredations against English shipping and have raised a naval and
military force to destroy them."

"Yes, but . . ."

"But now, sir," Ayscough hammered on, "the said destruc-
tion is a naval and military matter, the proper use of those
forces allocated to you. And that use, Mister Twigg, is my bail-
iwick at sea, and it is Sir Hugo's on the land. From here on
out, sir, allow other batsmen to have their innings. Now, you
may hold *our* coats."

And about bloody well time, too, Alan thought! Damn all
civilian meddlers. Especially the ones that dreamt this horror
up in the first place.

"Are you familiar with the vessels in harbor, Sir Hugo?"
The captain asked.

"Hmm, I fear it's my son who understands things nautical,
Captain Ayscough," Sir Hugo replied, chuckling. "The brig, I

believe, though, is a Macao packet. I've heard tell the . . . what-you-called-it . . . a ketch? . . . is the local supply ship from Calcutta or Madras. I've met their owners."

"I shall wish to speak to them about hiring or selling us their ships, should they prove suitable," Ayscough said decisively. "I believe that we have sufficient funds aboard *Telesto* at present to do so, and pay a guinea joining-bounty for every hand that signs into service. Do we not, Mister Twigg?"

"Aye, sir, we do," Twigg nodded, all fight blown out of him.

Sir Hugo took Alan's arm and steered him out to the verandah as the details were thrashed out. It was a little cooler, but not much, out of the overcrowded rooms. They could hear Twigg, still insisting they sail for Calcutta as soon as the weather moderated.

"Thank you for that back there, Alan."

"Oh, you're welcome, sir."

"I'd have done just about anything to get my troops out of this malaria-ridden sink!" Sir Hugo said with some heat. "Do you always up and speak your mind like that? Can't promise you an ambitious naval career if you keep that up. But for now, I'm grateful. And for what you said. About 'your dear father.' "

"Well, about that, sir . . ." Lewrie cringed. "It was the only way to get your support, you see. Get you to listen to what I had to say and back my play. I expected you wanted to get your arse out of Bencoolen, before you went under to some sickness, so what you want, and what I thought needed doing, could work together."

"Damn you, you little shit!" Sir Hugo stiffened. "Get mine *own* arse out of here? Do you think what I said about my men was so much moonshine?"

"I've never known you to care very much about anyone. I don't know what to believe," Lewrie replied evenly.

"By God, Alan, you may think me the biggest sinner you'll ever meet, but you'll not lay that on me!" his father growled. "Before I wasted seed enough to quicken your miserable life, I was a soldier! May not have been a great one. May not have been a *glad* one most of the time, but I was good enough. Think what you will of me, but by God above, this battalion is mine. I fought with it, marched with it, killed with it and bled with it. We've cracked lice together, eaten the same rotten food, swilled the same filthy water, and they look to me to do what's right by 'em! And I will, no matter what you think. You may sneer at 'em. Sneering's a thing I remember you're quite good at. So they're not a fashionable English regiment! Think they're not good soldiers just because they're Hindoos? Think it's a come-down for me ... all I can command is a tag-rag-and-bobtail pack of bare-arsed Bengalis? Well, let me tell you, even when they were at their worst, they're the best troops I've ever seen, Goddamn your blood! And now they've been fleshed out and equipped proper, I could take them through the Brigade of Guards like suet through a goose. Something else I'm prepared to do, and they know it ... I'm their colonel—I'm ready to die with 'em, if it comes to that. Aye, you sneer all you bloody well want. Maybe you were born a bastard after all!"

Sir Hugo reset his waist-coat, the hang of his smallsword, and thumped down the steps to the muddy yard, leaving Lewrie at a loss for words, red-faced with sudden shame.

"Sir?" Alan called out, stepping down into the mud and drizzle. "Father?"

Sir Hugo halted and turned around, squelching mud on his boots.

"Yes?" he snapped.

"I'm sorry. I didn't know," Alan admitted. "I didn't even know there was anything you really cared about. Except for money and quim."

"Well, they still rate pretty high on my list of favorites," Sir Hugo confessed. "Doing what I'm best at, horrible as it can be, is on that list, too, you know."

"I most heartily apologize, Father."

"Apology accepted. Son. To be expected, I suppose. You know very little about me. Part of that's my fault. Come to my quarters."

"You haven't brought your band with you, have you?" Alan smiled.

"No, and the girls are in someone else's *bibikhana* now. Still, I never travel without a decent wine cellar. There's some claret you might appreciate." Sir Hugo laughed.

"I'd admire that, thankee ... Father."

"You know," Sir Hugo commented as they trudged across the muddy *maidan* of the military cantonment, "I don't half trust your man Twigg."

"I've yet to know what to make of him, yes."

"What bothered me most was what you said about scouting out the islands we're to capture. He sounded more eager to get his precious goods back to Calcutta. First ship in would reap a fortune. Fortune to fund your expedition out here, yes. And fortune enough to line the pockets of a *palatikal* with what's left over."

"He knew!" Alan spat out. "That's what surprised me. Right after we sank *La Malouine*, he knew. By that morning at the latest. And yet he kept it to himself, told no one, didn't suggest we look in on the Spratlys. If that *taifun* hadn't forced us down here to Bencoolen for shelter, I expect we'd be halfway up the Malacca Straits by now, your battalion be damned, and he'd sit on his news until we'd crossed the Hooghly Bar. Probably wanted something to impress Warren Hastings with."

"Ah, well he'd better be quick about it, then. Hastings is under a cloud. There's talk from home of him sailing for England to face impeachment charges with 'John Company.' Might have someone new in the Bengal Presidency soon."

"Someone who doesn't know a bloody thing about our mission?"

"That could make things *very* interesting." Sir Hugo frowned. "Damme, here come the bloody rains again! I assume a sailor can run? Run or get soaked."

"This sailor can," Alan said, matching the older man's stride easily.

"One thing to expect," Sir Hugo puffed.

"What?"

"Twigg probably cares for you now ... as much as cold, boiled mutton," Sir Hugo replied between breaths. "Look for a spell of the dirty."

Chapter 4

It didn't *seem* like a spell of the dirty, even if Twigg had a hand in influencing the captain's decision.

Ayscough had explained it to him. Lieutenant Choate, as first officer and his most reliable man, would be the one first in line to take the job, normally, but he would be needed to take command of whichever suitable vessel they hired in Calcutta while *Telesto* was refitting.

To fill his vacancy, he had to draw upon his next-most experienced and skilled officer, Lieutenant Percival, to remain aboard *Telesto* to advance to first officer in Choate's absence. Lieutenant McTaggart had to remain aboard *Telesto*, at least to Calcutta, and go as first officer for Choate in his new captaincy.

Captain Ayscough could advance the midshipmen-in-disguise now serving as master's mates to Mr. Brainard into acting lieutenants, but they would be slender reeds upon which to depend to command the escort north with *Lady Charlotte*.

"As I said in my journal about this matter, Mister Lewrie," the captain had told him, "that leaves only you, but you have shewn yourself to be more than reliable, competent and daring, but not *too* daring. I also made note that you only of the remaining commission officers, had, no matter your lack of seniority, commanded a King's ship even briefly. The chore is fairly simple, if you do not exceed your brief and go off chasing pirates too rashly. If they don't kill you, then I shall."

Lewrie got command of *Culverin*.

She had started life in 1778 as a bomb-ketch, laid down in Calcutta once the last war had spread from the Colonies to a world-wide conflagration against the Spanish, the Dutch and

the French. To be a bomb-ketch, she had to be solid and heavy
enough to absorb the kick of two twelve-inch mortars firing at
high angle, so she was made of teak, as overbuilt as a 1st Rate
line-of-battle ship, though her sides did not need to be as thick.
She would never have been required to stand in the line of
battle, anyway. She was further stiffened with riders that were
scarfed from her frames as cross-members, to the keelson up to
the deck beams, making her interior a maze totally unsuitable
for large cargoes, with much of her centerline length taken
up below deck as magazine and shot racks for her former
weapons.

The huge mortars were gone, though the wells where they
had sat remained, one forward of her main-mast, and one forward of her shorter mizzenmast. *Culverin* had been sold out of
naval service once the war in the Far East had ended in 1783.
Bombs were too easily replaced if war broke out again, the
Admiralty decried the expense of maintaining many of them
in-ordinary and their usefulness was limited to those occasions
where high-angle explosive shells needed to be hurled into harbors and fortifications along a hostile coast.

She would have seemed like the perfect answer to an enterprising captain for coastal trading. About ninety feet on the
range of the deck, roughly the length of a trading brig, about
twenty-six feet in beam, and shoal-drafted to let her get within
firing range of coastal forts. Her rig was only two masts instead of three, making for less crew, and ketches sported large
gaff-rigged fore-and-aft sails on the rear of her masts, making
sailing, tacking and wearing ship even simpler.

All of which—her ease and cheapness of operation, rigidity
and stout construction, and shallow draft—had convinced
young Captain Dover to buy her and put her to work on the
Bencoolen-Calcutta run, contracted to service the needs of that
fearsome settlement, with the occasional jaunt to Macao running opium lurking somewhere in the back of his mind as
well.

The only trouble was that she was not particularly weath-
erly; even with fore-and-aft sails she could not go close-hauled
against the wind. She could point closer to the wind, yes, but
her shallow draft made her slip to leeward too much, unlike a
deeper-bellied ship with more grip below the waterline. And
then, there were those riders in her innards, that limited the
amount of cargo she could carry. They could not be removed
without dismantling *Culverin* completely, bolted as they were

from the outside of her hull, right through planking, her beams and frames, keelson and futtocks. But at four thousand pounds sterling, she had seemed a bargain, so he had bought her, and had been losing money on the deal ever since, scrimp as he might to make her pay.

Which was why Captain Dover had leaped at that chance not simply to hire her out, but sell her outright, even if Twigg had only offered three thousand pounds. Neither was the enterprising Captain Dover quite so enterprising or ambitious as to remain aboard as part of the venture, so he took passage for Calcutta aboard *Telesto*, along with his first mate and four of his small crew that hadn't decided to cut his gizzard out yet.

Most of the remaining crew were just as happy to see the last of Captain Dover, though he left their pay in arrears, so when Ayscough harangued them to sign on at civilian pay rates, with a golden guinea for a joining-bounty, and the promise of untold loot, they had agreed to stay with her.

He would have no surgeon or purser, no sailing master—none of those excess warrants who made an officer's life easier. Lewrie suspected he'd have to swot up on how to lance boils, issue biscuit and rum, do his own navigation and almost serve as his own bosun. He did get Mr. Hogue, promoted to acting lieutenant, to serve as his first mate, which helped immensely. And Ayscough gave up Hodge and Witty as senior hands, Owen, the quarter-gunner, Hoolahan and some of the lower deck carronade gunners, Murray, the forecastle captain, to serve as bosun, and Cony, to come along as cabin-servant/cox'n/seaman. All in all, he had, including himself, only sixty-five people aboard, thirty of them her original crew. Not exactly inspiring circumstances, but she was a command, and she was all his. And once Ayscough had delivered new paint and bosun's stores to put to rights the neglect she'd suffered, he had to admit that *Culverin* looked almost saucy.

Fresh red paint inboard, bright blue upper bulwarks and the rest of her hull freshly varnished, and some yellow paint to touch up her transom, beak-head, entry port, quarter-galleries and railings.

And fresh black paint, grease and varnish for her guns. She had once been outfitted with ten six-pounders, in addition to those two monstrous mortars, but they were gone now. They had been replaced with ten twenty-four-pounder carronades, another sign of her recent civilian nature. The carronades were lighter to mount, only took two men per gun to fight them (which required fewer paid hands) and their recoil was lighter. Most merchantmen were switching over to carronades for those reasons, and Captain Dover had swapped the original battery for them in Madras.

Finally, four days after her purchase and refitting, with her new crew sorted out into a semblance of naval discipline, her holds, former magazines and shot-racks crammed with edibles and her mortar wells so crowded with livestock that she resembled the original Ark, they got under way.

Chapter 5

"This ain't all claret and cruising," he sighed to himself on the sixteenth day of passage. Trying to take *Culverin* north was a thankless chore. With fore-and-aft sails hauled in close, square-sails furled, and flying all her stays'ls and jibs, she would point within 55 degrees of the apparent wind, a whole point of sail higher than a square-rigger. But she made so much leeway! For every two feet gained forward, it seemed she slipped 1 foot sideways.

So for a course of roughly nor'west, she had to make a long board on the starboard tack to make progress, then come about and do a short board on the port tack headed almost due east to correct her drift. If not, they'd have ended up somewhere in the Gulf of Siam!

And, for a vessel with such a wide beam compared to her hull length, she obstinately refused to put her shoulder to the sea on either tack, never heeling over more than 15 degrees or so like a proper ship with more-rounded chines.

"You say something, sir?" Hogue asked, turning his head.

"I said, it's not all claret and cruising, Mister Hogue," Lewrie repeated, louder this time.

"Well, sir, it is to me," Hogue smiled, still be-dazzled by his sudden advancement to part-sailing master, part-lieutenant. "For myself this couldn't be a better day. We're roaring along like a whale!"

They stood aft on the miniature quarterdeck, which did not measure twenty-four feet by twenty, out of the way of the long tiller bar by which she was steered, and the bulk of the after capstan. It was more like a poop deck, steeved higher than most to give almost-standing headroom below in the officers' and warrants' quarters under their feet.

Culverin was bucketing along ahead of *Lady Charlotte*. They had decided to keep station up to windward, where their little ship might have room to point up higher, and slide sideways quicker, without ramming the slower but better-behaved square-rigger. The winds were quite fresh, trending more easterly than when the voyage began, as the Monsoon breezes shifted to their summer direction of sou'easterly.

Culverin rattled and banged, her rigging sang to wind-song and her wake spread out wide and white behind her, creaming down her sides and frothing into a huge mustache under her bluff bows. Up she'd ride, on a long Pacific swell, then down she'd swoop, sedately cocking stern or bow into the air. Now and again, when her bowsprit rose up to the blue skies, she'd fling a cloud of salt-spray droplets around herself. And, now and again, a fleeting rainbow would form across her fo'c'sle, and shimmer in the slots between her jibs where air was compressed and sped along, imparting drive, those sails bedewed with atomized ocean nearly to the main-course yard.

"Well, I'll be damned!" Lewrie breathed, taking in the glory of it. "Don't know as how I've ever seen *that* before!"

" 'Tis lucky, sir," Hogue laughed out loud. "We've a lucky little ship here. Now she's back in proper hands, that is, and I think she knows it."

"Captain," Murray said, raising a knuckle to his brow. "Nigh to seven bells o' the forenoon, sir. Permission t' pipe 'Clear Decks an' Up Spirits,' sir?"

"Aye, Murray, on the bell. How are our hands doing with their merchantmen counterparts below?"

"Main well, sir," Murray shrugged. "They've heard tell o' all our ships disappearin', an' most o' them had mates aboard some. So they're rarin' t' have at the Frogs, sir, an' the pirates, too. An' the booty's got 'em pretty keen-like, sir. No problems so far."

The deck angled a bit more to leeward, the starboard side going about six inches higher than before, and Lewrie turned to look at the helmsman at the tiller, then at the long coach-whip at the peak of the mizzenmast truck.

"Wind's backing on us, at last!" he cheered. "Put your helm down to larboard and keep her full and by."

"Aye, sir!" the helmsman agreed. "Full an' by. Now she lays nor'nor-west, half north, sir."

"We'll make that bloody island by sundown, if the winds

will only cooperate, sir," Hogue stated. "We won't have to jog to the west so far now, nor do a board back."

"Excellent. If the wind does indeed stay backed," Lewrie said, fretting for a while at the pendant. Seven bells chimed. Murray put his bosun's pipe to his mouth and blew the call for labors to cease and rum to be issued.

"Look, sir!" Murray exclaimed, pointing over the windward bow to starboard. "Dolphins, sir. Come t' play on our bow wave!"

"And flying fish, too," Hogue added, as a school of the fish broke the surface and began to beat their "wings" to race alongside *Culverin*, leaving a tiny frothing wake behind each.

"Dolphins, *an'* a rainbow, captain," Murray sighed happily. "I b'lieve ever'thin's gonna turn out aright this time!"

"The island is occupied," Chiswick stated once he was back aboard *Lady Charlotte*. They had fetched the low-lying island just before sundown, and had laid off-shore out of sight, sending a cutter in with a party of scouts from Chiswick's light company.

"Then should we risk entering harbor and landing troops?" Captain Cheney of *Lady Charlotte* asked. He was not a Navy officer, merely a civilian transporter of military and naval goods and people, and had never been called upon in a long career to do anything really risky.

"Any ships in the harbor?" Lewrie asked, leaning over the chart he'd obtained from Mr. Brainard before *Telesto* sailed for Calcutta.

"Aye, there were, Alan," Burgess nodded. "You'd have to ask Lieutenant Hogue as to what they were, though."

"One small trading brig, sir. Anchored here," Hogue said, tapping the chart of the harbor with his finger. "And a slightly larger three-masted ship . . . here. We landed here, on this narrow peninsula to the west of the harbor. There's quite a good beach on either side, and the ridge down the center is just high enough to screen anyone from view who lands on the seaward side."

"There's not much vegetation for cover anywhere that I could see," Chiswick added, looking up to match gazes with his colonel. "But these rocks were pretty jumbly. The main encampment is farther along, in the center of the curve of the harbor beach, here."

"So we could land troops here, at the base of the peninsula,"

Sir Hugo said, humming to himself. "Set up artillery atop the ridge here, and advance down the beach, and from slightly inland."

"There's a flat place perfect for artillery, sir," Chiswick agreed.

"What about the ships, Mister Hogue? Could their guns interfere with a landing, once they were over the harbor-side of this peninsula?" Lewrie inquired.

"They're moored fore-and-aft, sir. Sterns to the peninsula, starboard beams facing to seaward and the harbor entrance," Hogue went on. "The small brig is a Yankee named *Poor Richard*, out of Boston. I think she might be a prize. T'other is French for certain. *Stella Maris*. I couldn't make out her homeport."

"Gad, what eyes the lad has!" Sir Hugo chuckled.

"They were unloading cargo, sir. Lots of work-lanterns on both ships, and long torches stuck into the sand. A bonfire or two burning ashore as well," Hogue explained. "No Mindanao pirate boats about yet. I heard no English spoken, though, aboard *Poor Richard*. That's why I think she was a prize. Just French was all I heard."

"You went aboard?" Captain Cheney gasped.

"Well, I swam out as close as I could, sir," Hogue grinned, making a night approach through a shark-infested lagoon sound like nothing much, but secretly pleased with his own fortitude. "As to guns, they've no springs on their cables, sir, none that I could see. There was too much light on the water between ships, so I could not approach *Stella Maris*, but it didn't look as if she had springs fixed."

"What about artillery ashore?" Sir Hugo pressed.

"They've a log and thatch fort, sir, rectangular, with one long side facing the sea and the beach. There are what look to be storage buildings inside the compound," Chiswick replied. "Where they got the lumber, God knows. Probably from looted ships. They've four guns on that seaward side, and two each on either shorter end. Light stuff, by the look of the platforms they were mounted on. Four-pounders on naval trucks, not field carriages. And there was a lot of drinking going on."

"And I suppose you snuck up to the walls like a Red Indian?" Sir Hugo snorted.

"Well, yes, sir," Chiswick smiled, proud of himself as well.

"Well, then!" Sir Hugo beamed, clapping Chiswick on the

shoulder. "That was bravely done, sir! Now, Lieutenant Lewrie. Just what do we do about this?"

"I defer to your military prowess, Colonel Willoughby," Alan said in return. "When would you like to land your troops for an assault?"

"Now," Sir Hugo purred. "Right bloody now, while their attention is elsewhere, and their bellies are full of piss-poor brandy."

"Any lookouts watching to seaward, Burge?" Alan asked.

"None that we found. There's a start on a four-legged tower in the palisaded encampment, but it's too low yet to even see over this peninsula. I don't think they've had this place constructed long."

"Weather's decent," Lewrie pondered. "Captain Cheney, what's the state of the tide around first sparrow-fart? Say at four A.M.?"

"About the middle of the ebb, sir. But surely, you would wait for the stronger ship to arrive from Calcutta," Cheney replied, paling.

"Since I don't know when that will be, sir, and I am here now and ready, I cannot delay," Lewrie stated firmly, not feeling quite as firm inside.

Goddamn my eyes, will you look at these fools, looking at me as if I've Moses' scrolls tucked into my side-pockets! Ayscough surely couldn't have meant this much responsibility for me. I might be going into as big a hornet's nest as that idiot Captain Nelson did back at Turk's Island, and look what a ball's-up that was!

"How long for your troops to assemble on this beach, set up artillery on this flat bench at the base of the peninsula and be ready to advance, Sir Hugo? I assume you prefer a dawn attack."

"First boat-loads on the beach at one A.M. would be better," Sir Hugo sniffed. "Takes time to sway out those guns of ours, get them ashore, mount them on their trails and carriages and man-haul them up this slope, rocky as Captain Chiswick says it is. Sure to be noisy, as well."

"Captain Cheney, could you please be so good as to provide some scrap sails and rope fragments to muffle the noises for them, sir?"

"Aye, Mister Lewrie, but . . ."

"Do you come to anchor here, about half a mile off-shore, then," Lewrie pressed on, feeling like a toddler having the pre-

sumption to purchase a house. "You have twenty fathoms of
water there before it begins to shoal: sand, rock and coral bottom. If all else fails, you are in the island's lee, and may
fetch-to without drifting too far to the west between waves of
boats. Better yet, take all of my ship's boats to help things
along. I shall then stand off-and-on without the harbor entrance, and enter harbor at . . . six A.M.? Will there be enough
light for you then, Colonel? Even at low tide, this entrance
channel shows a possible five fathoms, and *Culverin* only
draws one and a half. With luck, we shall overawe the French.
With none at all, we'll have to close on *Stella Maris* here and
get within two cables to shoot her to pieces with our carronades."

"Who shall fire first, then?" Sir Hugo asked.

"Either way, they're sailors, mostly," Lewrie schemed.
"When things go to Hell, they run for their ship first. You
open fire at six A.M., or when you see me enter the harbor
channel. Captain Cheney, I'd admire if you had *Lady Charlotte*
somewhere well in sight and close astern of me as you are able
around that time. You may, at long range, resemble a warship
just enough to take the stuffing out of them."

"I shall try, sir, but should I enter harbor?"

"Block the entrance channel if all else fails."

"Aye, sir," Cheney said, looking squeamish enough that
Alan knew he'd be nowhere near the harbor entrance at six
A.M., for all the best reasons. He'd not risk his thin-sided transport at the behest of some jumped-up junior Navy lieutenant!
Well, just as long as he may land the troops and stand seaward
where he can be seen, Lewrie sighed, that would be good
enough.

"Here's to victory on the morrow, gentlemen," Sir Hugo
proposed, as glasses of wine were passed around by Cheney's
steward. "Confusion to the French!"

"And clear heads for us!" Lewrie chimed in.

The rest of the night was Hell. Lewrie went back to his ship
and went below to sleep. Her former master had had a large
berth as big as a double-bed back home built into her stern
quarters, widening the transom settee into a solid bedstead. Instead of hay or corn-shucks, the mattress was stuffed with Indian cotton, which wicked up any night sweats one would
suffer below decks in the sweltering tropics. He had come to
enjoy the berth, with both stern sash-windows open for a sea

breeze to cool him well enough to sleep undisturbed in those hours that a ship's captain could expect to find rest.

But this night would not pass, and he could find no ease. Not even a stiff glass of brandy could numb him into true slumber. And there could be little of that, anyway. *Culverin* stood off-and-on, reaching across the easterly winds. First north toward the island, until near enough to see the hint of bonfires, then tacking out to sea once more, always clawing in her tacks up to the east to correct drift to leeward. Every two hours, he was summoned to the deck to supervise the maneuver and lay the course he desired.

In between, below decks, he would shuck his clothing and attempt to sleep. But then, "What if?" he would think, and his mind would go galloping off on a flight of frenzied imagining. Had he foreseen all that could go wrong? Had he forgotten anything vital? And then those possible disasters would play themselves out in half-nodding nightmares from which he would snap awake, only to slip into another.

"Goddamn, I'm only twenty-two years old!" he muttered aloud. "Who in their right minds'd ever give a twit like me this much to be responsible for?" He might get people killed on the morrow. He *knew* some people would die. For him. What if they died for nothing?

Like the Battle of The Chesapeake. Like Yorktown. Like Jenkins Neck. The expedition into the barrens of Florida, or trying to retake Turk's Island.

He'd go back over his plan once more, finding gaping flaws in it. Would shiver with chill and bolt upright, suddenly finding need to speak to *Lady Charlotte* or his father, now ashore, just one last time. But that was impossible. Would pore over his one poor chart searching for omens, for portents of victory or defeat.

They came about for the last time at four A.M., just as the last of eight bells chimed, ending the mid-watch, and the bosun's pipes sang to summon "All Hands" to scrub decks and stow their hammocks in the bulwark nettings for the day.

Time, too, to prepare for what the dawn would bring. Lewrie dressed in one of his Navy uniforms, spurning civilian clothes for the day's bloody work. The coat and waist-coat were badly wrinkled from being pressed to the bottom of his sea-chest, mildewy, and stiff with salt crystals from being so long at sea.

"Ready about, Mister Hogue?" he asked.

"Aye, sir."

"Helm alee!" Lewrie shouted. With nothing aloft but fore-and-aft sails on both masts, there was little of the usual heavy labor involved. Except for the jibs up forward, they almost tacked themselves.

"Should be here, if we maintained an easy four knots during the night," Lewrie said, peering at the chart tacked to the traverse board. "A little east of north would put us here, even with the harbor entrance, by half-past five. Perhaps that would be even better than waiting until six, and full dawn."

"And if we have slipped to leeward that far during the night, we may harden up to the wind and make it good, sir," Hogue added.

"D'you want t' inspect the decks, sir?" Murray asked, coming aft from the waist of the ship.

"White decks are not the greatest thing on our minds this morning, Mister Murray," Lewrie replied, unable to suppress a smile. "Hands to breakfast. Then douse the galley fires soon as they've eaten."

"Aye, sir," Murray replied, knuckling his brow.

"Got some 'ot coffee, sir," Cony offered. "An' wot'll ya be 'avin' fer yer breakfas', sir?"

"Just the coffee, Cony, thankee," Lewrie replied, taking the mug in both hands to savor its warmth and its aroma.

"Land ho!" the lookout called.

"Where away?"

"One point off the starboard bow, sir!"

"That should be the central hill, the highest point above the sea. And a little to the left of a direct line for the entrance," Alan surmised, bending over the chart again, then straightening. "Quartermaster? Larboard your helm, half a point, no more. Pinch us up to windward a mite."

"Aye, sir."

"They should be able to see us by half-past five, sir," Hogue prodded.

"Aye," Lewrie nodded. "Bows on, coming into harbor like we're expected, with no flag flying. Now who, I ask you, would be stupid enough to enter a pirate's lair but another pirate, Mister Hogue? They might go on their guard, but they don't know what a surprise we have ashore already. We shall have to chance it from here on."

"Aye, sir," Hogue shrugged with him.

"You get below and eat if you've a mind. I have the deck," Lewrie said. "Spell me when you get back so I may shave. And then, Mister Hogue, we shall beat to Quarters."

Chapter 6

"We're going to be damned early," Lewrie groused. The winds out of the east were beginning to blow more freshly, and *Culverin* had the bitt in her teeth, cleaving the early morning at a pace he did not like. "Hands to the braces! Ease her sheets!"

They winged out the big gaff sails until they luffed and fluttered, then hauled them back in until the luffing eased, but *Culverin* was still making a rapid five knots. Too fast! They'd arrive in the middle of the narrow harbor channel not a quarter of an hour past five A.M.

"Lower the outer flying jibs!" Lewrie commanded. It made little difference, as if their little warship had a will of her own! She slowed by perhaps half a knot, and the shore loomed closer.

"First reefs in the mains'ls, sir?" Hogue suggested.

Lewrie took a look at the chart once more, gnawing on the inner side of his lips in frustration and worry. Last of the ebb, still at least five fathoms in the entrance channel, he told himself. Narrow entrance, but widening once we're in. Calmer waters once inside, and the eastern peninsula will partially block the winds; we'd have to shake out our reefs once we're in harbor, and we'll be too busy for that!

And gun-batteries, he almost gasped! Something else I didn't consider, but only a fool would not have a battery on the tip of the western peninsula, to guard the entrance. Speed's the thing. Get past them before they could get off more than a couple of broadsides.

"No, Mister Hogue. Stand on as we are," he ordered. "I think a certain amount of dash is necessary this morning. Leadsmen to the chains now. You take the gun deck."

"Aye, sir."

"Sail ho!" the lookout called from aloft, making Lewrie feel like his bladder would explode. "T' the larboard beam!"

Lewrie seized his telescope from the binnacle, raced to the larboard mizzen shrouds and scaled them until he was about twenty feet above the quarterdeck. Thank God!

It was only the *Lady Charlotte*, standing sou'east from her night anchorage after disembarking the troops, fulfilling her role as a possible threat. She was deliberately being placed too far down to leeward to make the harbor entrance against the prevailing wind. But at least she was obeying his command even in part.

It was getting light now. Light enough to see details on the island, now not two miles off *Culverin*'s bows. Suddenly, Lewrie was glad the wind had freshened. Now came the time when the plan lay at its most exposed. Troops *possibly* in position, artillery ready for firing, *perhaps* . . . and *Culverin* and another strange ship racing to enter harbor. Let's get it over with, he thought eagerly.

He descended to the deck and stowed his telescope away, trying to show that great calm which was expected of naval officers, the calm which he had never quite achieved before. Things always seemed too urgent and desperate to him at moments like this to walk instead of run, to keep a gambler's face instead of cheering his head off or cursing Fate.

"And a half, two!" a leadsmen screeched from the fo'c'sle.

Lewrie could not stifle a yelp of alarm. Where in hell was *that* shoal sprung from? Was it charted? Were they about to wreck this fine little ship? He bent to the chart and sighed heavily. It was marked. An outer reef wall that lay tumbled like those the Romans had built in the far north of England centuries before. Some island-to-be, an outer harbor that might have existed long before a *taifun*'s fury had shattered it.

Coral heads and breakers to starboard, two cables off, thank Christ!

"And a half, two!" the other leadsman shouted. *Culverin*'s keel was now skating across razor-sharp coral with about six feet to spare. If the chart did not lie, please God, he prayed.

"Three!" the first leadsman yelled. "Three fathom!"

It sounded like a winter wind, to hear all the people on the quarterdeck sigh out in blissful relief at the same time, and *Culverin*'s captain the loudest of all.

"Six fathom at low tide from here on to the entrance," Alan

told them, once he had got his breath back. "We'll see breakers to the west on the shoals off the peninsula, and a long line of breakers to east'r'd. The entrance is a cable-and-a-half wide, gentlemen. And the main channel will be dead in the center, right, quartermaster?"

"Aye, sir," the man replied, chewing vigorously on a plug of tobacco.

"Hands to the sheets. Harden up, Mister Murray."

"Aye, sir."

One mile to go, with *Culverin* gaining speed once more. Dull grey light of false dawn. Twelve minutes past five in the morning. *Culverin* sailing almost flat on her bottom on a reach, a soldier's wind across her beam. The shore nearing, the breakers crashing and foaming above the sound of her wake, the rush of ocean round her cutwater and down her sides. Foaming up in low water-dunes on either side of her bows, sucking low amidships, hummocking under her narrower stern-quarters before spreading out into tumbled briny lace in her train.

"Artillery!" Murray gasped.

Yes. Over the sounds of *Culverin* as she sprinted, over the hiss and roar of the breakers, there came sharp little flat bangs. Tiny tongues of flame on the base of the western peninsula lit up the pre-dawn. The 19th Native Infantry had seen *Culverin* rushing at the entrance like a cavalry charge, and had opened fire!

"A point to windward, quartermaster, put yer helm down!" Lewrie commanded, eyeing the disturbed water of the channel. Breakers abeam, the tip of the peninsula to the west and the jumbled sucking shoals even with the main-mast. *Culverin* staggered as she met the breakers, cocked her bows high as she was for a moment checked by the mass of water, then surged onward, surfing atop a great growler of a wave with spray flying over the quarterdeck, and the long, curved tiller bar almost alive and kicking with two quartermasters throwing their strength on it to keep her from broaching sideways onto the next wave astern.

Then she was through, into calmer waters!

"Hoist the colors!" Lewrie shouted. "Let these bastard Frogs know who they're dealing with!"

The battery of guns on the peninsula fired once more, and they could see tiny little white-and-red ants rushing forward to the attack from the jumbled rocks of the headland.

Squeal of a metal sheave as the Navy ensign soared up the

gaff on the taffrail and cracked in the wind. And the sun rose. A tropic sun that exploded over the grey horizon like a bomb, as blood-red as roses!

"Larboard battery, stand by. Open the gunports and run out!"

There was no battery of guns on the western peninsula. Some men running along the strand, back toward the palisaded encampment, or back to the safety of their ship before all Hell broke loose, but no guns to threaten his vessel!

"Harden up! Helm down a point more!"

Hogue was chanting instructions to the gun-captains as they cranked in elevation with the rear set-screws, as they wheeled their long recoil slide carriages, pivotting on the mounting bolt at each gunport, the rear iron wheels rumbling as the carronades were aimed as far forward in the ports as they would bear.

"We'll give yon brig the first taste, Mister Hogue!" Lewrie shouted forward through a brass speaking-trumpet. "Fire as you bear!"

"Aye aye, sir!"

A long minute's wait as *Culverin* ghosted forward, more slowly now that she was winded by the eastern headlands, the wind snaking its way across the breakers where it found no resistance, creating a little river of air more from the southeast than the east.

"One more point to windward," Lewrie said. "Close-haul her."

"Stand by!" Hogue shouted. "As you bear . . . fire!"

Five terrifically loud explosions, spaced evenly as a fired salute. One splash close aboard *Poor Richard*, two strikes on her lower wales, making her rock and splatter hull-shaped rings about herself. Two more strikes that struck her upper works, twenty-four-pounder solid shot creating whirling clouds of dust and debris, and shattered planks flying as high as her maincourse yard to splash down alongside!

"And again!" Lewrie shouted.

More abeam this time instead of aiming far forward. Now the range was under a cable and they couldn't miss. *Poor Richard* heeled over and shivered with each hit, her masts whipping across the sky and shedding rigging. There seemed to be no resistance aboard her.

"Cease fire!" Lewrie ordered. "Aim forward for the next ship, and stand by!"

Stella Maris was a different breed of cat entirely. Her ports were opening. Men swarmed aloft to loose canvas, and axe-heads glinted in the sunlight as they tried to cut her bow and stern cables to escape.

A ranging shot howled over the quarterdeck from one of her after-most gunports. And other gunports were opening!

"Luff up, quartermaster!" Lewrie snapped. With the tiller hard over, *Culverin* turned parallel to *Stella Maris* to bring her guns into bearing, her sails now pointed straight into the wind and flapping in thunderous disarray.

"As you bear, fire!" Hogue obeyed.

"Goddamn my eyes!" Murray howled with glee. "Oh, bloody lovely!"

The trunk of *Stella Maris'* mizzenmast was sheared in two, and the upper portion of the mast came down like a giant tree to drape in the water over her stern, ripping all the standing rigging and running rigging to shreds aloft. Her transom and rudder post shattered into a swelling maelstrom of broken timbers and planks. Part of her upper bulwark on her quarterdeck disappeared, and star-shaped holes burst into existence in her hull.

"Again!" Lewrie raved. "Hit the bitch again!" He went to the larboard side, climbed up on the bulwarks, gripping the mizzen stays, and spread his arms wide as *Culverin*'s guns belched fire once more.

"Eat it, Froggies!" he screamed across at them. "See how you like the taste of that!"

"Another minute an' we'll be in irons, captain!" Murray said from below him.

"Helm up to starboard. Keep a way on her, slow as you like, but keep a way on her."

"Larboard battery . . . together . . . fire!" Hogue screamed as the ketch bore off a little, getting some wind in her sails once more to skirt down toward the French ship.

It was a blow right under the heart! *Stella Maris* shook like she had an ague as the weight of that broadside lashed her. Pieces of her whined through the air, making Lewrie jump down from his vantage point and go back to the binnacle in the middle of the quarterdeck.

"Close and board her, sir?" Murray asked.

"No. Mister Hogue, cease fire! Hands to the sheets!" Lewrie called. "Stand by to come about! Stations for stays! We'll make too much leeway if we continue on this tack, Mister

Murray. Better we sail up to windward on the larboard tack, then wear ship and come back to give her the starboard battery with the wind up our stern. No reason to board her and get our people cut up when we can lay off and shoot her to pieces, if it takes all morning."

Within half a cable of the stricken *Stella Maris*, *Culverin* showed her her stern as she tacked across the wind to run south at the wall of breakers. But long before she got anywhere near them, they tacked her again, and drove her toward the eastern shore, the leadsmen chanting out the depth once again.

"Three fathom!"

"Hands to the braces! Helm alee! Wear ship to larboard!"

Culverin came about, across the eye of the wind, then farther, taking the wind across her stern at last, steering back down to the west with the beach on her starboard side and the wind on her larboard quarter.

Stella Maris had by then cut her cables and was underway, of a sorts, if one wanted to be charitable about it. She had paid off from her head-to-wind anchorage somehow, pivotting off her fallen mizzenmast, bumping against *Poor Richard* astern of her, and was aiming for the harbor entrance. Hands were laid out on her tops'l and course yards to get sail on her, but there was no wake after her yet; slow as she was, her ravaged rudder not yet getting a grip on the water.

"Aim right for her bowsprit," Lewrie said. "We'll round up as we close to fire broadsides, then point at her directly to make less of a target before the next is ready."

"She'll make a lot of leeway, sir," Murray warned. "If they ain't careful, they'll have her on the beach o' that western headland sure as Fate."

"Even more reason to stand off and shoot her to ribbons at a safe distance," Lewrie chuckled. "Once we strike three fathoms, back we go onto the wind. Let's take the first reef in the gaff sails on main and mizzen. We're much faster than she is now."

"Aye, sir."

Culverin came on like Doom, implacable and menacing for all her saucy handsomeness, her gunports open and carronades cranked forward ready for another broadside. *Stella Maris* began to slide across her bows as her crew got a stays'l and jibs set, and a fore-tops'l let fall at last to give her some steerageway.

"The troops ashore have the palisade, sir," Murray pointed out. "An English flag's flyin' on that tower o' theirs."

"Three points of larboard helm, now, quartermaster. Stand by the starboard battery! Fire!" Lewrie shouted, oblivious to what was taking place on the island, almost lost in blood lust to finish off his part of the day.

The carronades roared out their challenge one at a time. *Stella Maris* quailed and cringed at each hit, shying away downwind. *Culverin* went back onto a westerly course, pointing her jibboom and bowsprit right at her until the guns were loaded once more. When they rounded up the next time, the range was just about 200 yards.

"Take your time with your aim, sirs!" Lewrie told his gunners.

Hogue brought down his arm, and his voice was lost in the howl of the guns. More shattered wreckage soared about her as the iron shot ripped her open. Masts quivered and shed blocks and cordage in a rain. The men at her helm were scythed away by a ball that struck on her quarterdeck bulwarks. A quarterdeck gun and its carriage took to the sky, tumbling over and over before splashing into the water to the downwind side!

Stella Maris, no longer under control, sagged down off to leeward, presenting her stern to them, listing noticeably to starboard where their first broadsides had punished her. Already, men were tossing over hatch-covers to escape another volley of shot.

"She'll go aground on the beach!" Lewrie shouted in triumph. "Cease fire! Cease fire! Mister Murray, round us up and let us get ready to anchor. About there, I should think. Springs on the cables."

Before they could lower their sails and drop their bower, the French ship struck. By then, she was well heeled over and sinking, low in the water. With the wind behind her, she hit the shoals and sand, the savage coral heads of the harbor's western shore, going at least 2 knots per hour. Not enough forward progress to tear her open, but enough to jam her onto the coral heads and pound and pound, so that she came apart slowly. Her masts stayed erect for a time before the strain on the larboard rope stays became too great and they popped, one at a time, to lower her masts yard by jerking yard until they groaned and split to topple into the sea.

* * *

They got *Culverin* anchored by bow and stern, springs on her cables so she could swing in a great arc to aim her guns at any ship attempting to enter the harbor. The gun crews were stood down, and Lewrie ordered the mainbrace to be spliced in sign of victory. He even took a mug of rum and water himself, suddenly reeling with exhaustion, with relief that it was over and that not a man-jack of his small crew had even been wounded. With the lack of solid fare in his belly. And with the shuddery weakness he felt at the conclusion of a battle.

"Sail ho!" the lookout called from aloft.

"Oh God, what next?" Lewrie asked the heavens. "Where away? What ship?" he shouted back.

"*Lady Charlotte*, sir! Bearin' fer the harbor mouth!" came the reply.

"Whew," Lewrie sighed, laughing at his own fear. "Whew!"

Chapter 7

"... *Stella Maris* wrecked on the shoals and her surviving crewmen made prisoner."

He wrote in his lieutenant's journal, which would also be a first draft for his report to Captain Ayscough when he came to the island, and the official account of the venture someday in far-off London and the Admiralty.

"We discovered storehouses ashore in the palisaded fortress."

"Hmm," he speculated. It wasn't exactly a fortress, now, was it? A bamboo log palisade with ship's planking for reinforcement, and built so amateurishly one could have hurled a large dog through it anywhere one wished. Still, "fortress" would read better back in official circles than "armed cattle pen." He dipped his goose-quill pen in ink and continued, more than a little tongue-in-cheek.

"The goods amassed were considerable, both gen'l trade goods to an estimated value of £50,000, & quantities of Gangetic Opium & Silver rendered into 1 oz. bars (Chinese *taels*) to a value of £200,000. Also discovered were stands of arms (French Mod. 1763 St. Etienne Arsenal muskets with all accoutrements) cutlasses & pole arms (boarding pikes & espontoons), powder & shot, six 4-pdr. French naval carriage guns, powder & shot Ditto & twelve 9-pdr cannon un-mounted, Do."

He leaned back and took a sip of a rather good Bordeaux that had traveled exceptionally well all the way from its point of origin to this dry and rocky Hell halfway around the world, and outlined to his superiors what a clever little fellow he had been.

How he had dismounted some of *Lady Charlotte*'s twelve-pounders and sited a three-gun battery on the point of the western peninsula to protect the harbor they now occupied. How they had finished the observation tower in the "fort" to an advantageous height, giving them a thirty-mile radius to espy the arrival of their foes, or the relief ships. How the captured guns with carriages had been sited to scour the harbor should any ship get inside, and the crew of the *Lady Charlotte* had been "commandeered" (he preferred that word to "press-ganged") into serving as gunners.

Stella Maris stripped of all her fittings and useful articles, her artillery and powder that had not gotten soaked employed in further defensive positions atop the high ground of both headlands before she was burned to the waterline and the ribs and carcass towed off the shoals to sink, out of sight, in deeper water.

"*Stella Maris* provided material with which to refit *Poor Richard*. This American Whaler was restored to her Capt. one Lemuel Prynge & such of her crew as survived their seizure & cruel enforced Servitude, their rightful Cargo put back aboard & *Poor Richard* allowed to sail for Manila, the closest Port where they could hope to meet up with other Yankee vessels & a snr. Owner & Master bearing dipl. title of Consul, with whom Capt. Prynge assured me the most strenuous Representations against the French Govt. would be presented."

He concluded by listing the very few dead and wounded among the Native Infantry, the utter lack of hurt to his ship or his men, the great number of French dead and wounded, the names of the Americans who had died or been hurt by capture or captivity and strong praise for those of his warrants and seamen he thought deserving.

"What else?" he muttered, leaning back in the rattan chair that creaked and gave most alarmingly as he did so. The table, the very walls of this shore house were of the same material, fetched from God knew where. Surely not from anything that grew on the island, that was for certain. Even the thatch of the roof was of palm fronds, and fairly fresh, too. So it had been a recent import to Spratly Island. He thought about putting down his suspicions that the Illana pirates had already come to visit, but decided against it. A lieutenant's journal was for wind, tide and sea-states, for weather or ship's routine. For a different slant on events—not for idle musings.

He closed the ink-pot, sluiced his pen-nib off in a cup of water and blew on the pages he had written to dry them. A slow process, that. Mr. Brainard had promised cooler climes at Spratly, but if this was in anyway dryer, or cooler than Bencoolen, it was a matter of degree only.

They had had several spells of freshening weather as the winds shifted more sou'easterly to the seasonal norms of the summer Monsoons. Wind, lashings of rain, cool, blustery half-gales that so far had not swelled to ship-threatening storms. The cisterns and rock-pools had filled with water, and *Culverin* and *Lady Charlotte* had caught hundreds of gallons of fresh water in canvas chutes. Enough to succor the men and animals brought to the island, enough to support all the livestock running wild or penned up for slaughter the French had brought.

Frankly, they had enough livestock to start a well-run estate, and that was just the imported animals. What ran wild on the island could keep one awake at night with their miniature stampedes and alarums. Everyone had been eating well ever since they arrived.

He finally got the ink dry enough to roll up the pages and tie them with a hank of thin rope, then went out to check on his latest project. Rather, his father's latest project, for which he was giving up a few crew members.

No ship could take being fired upon with heated shot. Once a red-hot iron ball lodged in a ship's timbers, the tinder-dry wood took fire like fat pine-shavings. Lt. Col. Sir Hugo St. George Willoughby had suggested a battery for that purpose, and Lewrie had concurred eagerly. Said battery was now installed above the "fortress," halfway up the rocky slopes of the central hill. He toiled up the rough path to the battery to take a look at it.

Two twelve-pounders sat in a hollow partially dug into the slope, screened from view by a shielding wall of boulders laid loose against each other and some dry brush. There were two wide embrasures through which they could fire, and cover the entire harbor. And, being about sixty feet higher than the beach, gained an advantage in range over a ship-mounted artillery piece that might try to return fire. There was a magazine dug into the back slope, and off to one side where it never could threaten the powder supply, was a rock forge where iron cannon balls could be heated before being carried to the battery and loaded down the muzzles of the guns.

Firewood should have been a problem, except that *Stella Maris* had provided tons of scrap lumber, and enough bar-iron to make the cradle-sized carrying tools for heated shot. *Poor Richard* had also gladly sold several barrels of whale oil with which to ignite the forge. And Alan had an idea lurking in the back of his mind about the rest of the whale oil.

"Good morrow to you, Alan," his father said as he reached the battery.

"And to you as well, sir," he replied. "Are you ready for a test of this contraption?"

"Just about," Sir Hugo nodded. Several of his *sepoys* were hacking hull and deck planking from the unfortunate *Stella Maris* into kindling. "Ever used heated shot?"

"No, sir." Alan chuckled. "Not a good idea aboard a ship at any time, and during battle, well . . . I'm told the French tried it but had disastrous results. Been shot at with it at Yorktown, though."

"By my calculations, I expect to be able to fire random shot to almost the outer harbor breakers along the reef line," Sir Hugo said.

"But there's only two fathoms at high tide out there. Anything worth shooting at would be aground that far out," Lewrie replied. One of his other ideas to keep his hands busy and out of mischief or boresome rumbling, was to survey the harbor at low tide and update Mr. Brainard's chart, correcting what he found mismarked or filling in a few mysterious gaps.

Those mistakes and gaps were horrendous. Taking the average of noon sights with Hogue and Captain Cheney and his officers, they found that Spratly Island itself was incorrectly charted, out of its actual location by at least fifty miles! The coastline was half imaginings, and the soundings inside the harbor seemed to be the speculations of a terribly optimistic mind. It made him cringe every time he thought about how he had trusted that chart when he sailed into harbor, over that broken reef wall and through the pass, maneuvering free as a brainless sparrow over its entire length and breadth during the fight with *Stella Maris*. In a proper ship, such as a frigate, he'd have been wrecked half a dozen times over!

"I'd admire a copy of that chart of yours, then," Sir Hugo bade. "Very useful for my *binki-nabob*. My gunnery officer."

"I shall have it done directly, sir," Alan offered.

"Sail ho!" the tower lookout screamed.

"Choundas?" Sir Hugo stiffened.

"It very well may be," Alan agreed grimly. " 'Tis the middle of April. Time enough for him realize Sicard isn't available any longer and then sail from Pondichery."

It was a jumbled run down to the enclosed fort, then up the rickety tower's bamboo ladders to the top platform. Easier to continue to the top of the hill he was already on, which was almost as high. Sir Hugo grabbed a spy-glass and they half-ran, half-trudged up the slope to the windswept crest.

"Where away!" Alan shouted down. He could not hear the lookout's returning shout, but the man pointed. To the east! "Bloody hell? Now who could this be?"

"Choundas, coming back from an early meeting with his natives," Sir Hugo snapped. "He might have never gone back to the Indian Ocean, not with us on his trail. Get an early start. And reinforcements."

Once they had gotten their breath back, and had steady hands, Sir Hugo extended the tubes of the telescope and peered at the eastern horizon.

"Here," he snarled. "Can't see a damned thing."

And, Alan noted, his hands were none too steady, either.

"If I might borrow your shoulder for a rest, sir?" he asked. "And, as the sailor in the family, I might know what to look for. A sail very much resembles what you might take for a cloud. Some . . ."

There was a sail out there to the east. In point of fact, there were a lot of sails. Dark tan, they looked, almost silhouetted by the early morning sun. And fairly low to the water. With the wind out of the sou'east now as a steady Trade Wind, he was looking at the cusps of someone's tops'ls, perhaps, angled to take the wind from the stern quarter, running almost free with a landsman's breeze. But there were so many of them! Almost as many as the first sight he'd had from the *Desperate* frigate's t'gallant yard the morning the French fleet under de Grasse sailed back into Chesapeake Bay!

"I count at least twelve, perhaps fifteen sail," Lewrie muttered. "It could be a fishing fleet, but I doubt it. They look like *praos* with their one square-sail flying. If they come up over the horizon, and don't pass on by, they're coming here."

"The Lanun Rovers!" Sir Hugo spat. "Come to meet with Choundas."

"Come to the Spratlys for whatever purpose they have, yes."

"Pray God they enter harbor," Sir Hugo snickered, shaking Alan's resting telescope. "With your batteries, your ship and my guns and my troops waiting ashore, we could make it damned hot for 'em."

"Well, let me tell you, we've tangled with *praos* before last autumn," Alan replied. "Hold still, would you please, sir? Each one carries nearly an hundred pirates. Not much in the way of artillery, but we have to be looking at . . . well, closer to fifteen boats now, so that could be a force of over fifteen hundred men."

"The more the merrier," Sir Hugo shrugged, waving the resting telescope tube about the sky, forcing Lewrie to close it and give up. "A bloody check here could ruin this fellow Choundas."

"How the devil do you come by that?" Alan asked.

"When you slap your invited guests in the face, they don't invite *you* to their house for supper any longer, now do they, lad?" Sir Hugo boomed.

"Then we'd better make sure we leave a few to carry word back to their lairs, should we not?" Alan said, getting the drift. Choundas would not know of this until he tried to meet up with his native allies. And they just might do the English the favor of cutting the man's heart out for spite.

"I wonder if those pirates yonder know the difference between a French and an English flag?" Sir Hugo speculated, humming some song to himself.

"Whether they do or not, sir, I do believe you're going to get a practical test of this battery of yours before the day's out."

Chapter 8

By God, what a fearsome sight, Lewrie thought, pacing his tiny quarterdeck as the Mindanao pirates from the Illana Lagoon came into the harbor. No matter the surprises they'd discover once they got in range, no matter the number of artillery pieces ready to lash every inch of the bay, or the troops waiting with loaded muskets and fixed bayonets to receive them, they were a terrifying spectacle.

Eighteen large ocean-going *praos*, crammed with warriors, all experts with their wicked curved swords and *krees* knives, with artillery and muskets. Warriors used to raiding cruises that the unfortunate Mr. Wythy said lasted up to three years. No shore in all of Asia was safe from their depredations, no native troops could stand against them if such troops stood between them and plunder.

"Cheer 'em, boys!" Lewrie shouted with a grin plastered on his phyz. "They're your bloody allies, damn their black souls! They're going to help you take ships and make you rich!"

"Christ a'mighty," Hoolahan whispered, crossing himself as he stood by his carronade. "But they's a passel o' the fuckers, sor."

"Not a one of 'em half the man you are, Hoolahan," Lewrie assured him with a clap on the shoulder as he paced along down from the quarterdeck to the waist of the ship where the artillery waited, ready to fire when the word was given. "Got your swivel charges ready for 'em, Spears?"

"Oh, aye, sir!"

"Good lad. Now wave your hat and cheer 'em!"

The blood-red *praos* breasted easily over the harbor bar through the disturbed breaker-water and spread out, furling their single sails at long last after a long passage. They might have stopped off on the coast of Borneo, dangerous as that was even for them among the headhunters, and done the last three hundred miles to Spratly. Most of the men in the boats stood and waved back, brandishing swords, muskets or older match-locks like Hindoo *jezails*, whooping fit to bust. They had live-stock with them, crammed in any-old-how. And slaves to do the rowing at the long paddles. Yes, they must have replen-ished on Borneo, Alan decided, to have that much food aboard.

And it appeared they'd come prepared for a long stay. Every *prao* was piled high below her rowing benches with bamboo logs and palm leaves with which to make huts.

Lewrie made his way back to the quarterdeck, watching the pirate fleet advance in a ragged band, making for the beach. Steering a course for *Culverin*, and for *Lady Charlotte*. *Lady Charlotte* wore the French merchant flag on her stern, and her spanker gaff had been given a stuns'l boom lashed to its inside end, to make it look like the older lateen that the pirates would expect to see on Sicard's *La Malouine*. *Culverin*, too, flew an extemporized French ensign painted on one of Lewrie's bed sheets.

"Oh, Christ, don't beach your damned ship there!" Hogue prayed as three *praos* angled for the inviting strand on the western peninsula. There were troops there, hidden in the rocks at the crest, with some light artillery to support them. Unlike newer naval guns, those were fired with powder-filled goose quills or tin ignition tubes to ignite the powder charges in the barrels, and that required a burning length of slow-match to touch the quills or tubes off. Slow-matches which were now lit and smouldering, giving off tiny trails of smoke. If a pirate spotted that before the ambush could be sprung, they'd have a battle-royal on their hands. And the troops could not hope for total cover in the rocks. Let someone walk up the beach a few yards, and the game would be over!

There *were* thousands of the buggers, just as he had sur-mised, and even with modern weaponry, Sir Hugo's troops could be overwhelmed. The two ships could be swamped with fanatically enraged pirates with no hope of aid from shore.

"Come on, you buggers!" Lewrie muttered. "Go on and beach your silly arses by the fort, where the goodies are wait-ing!" The plan was to wait, wait until most of the pirates had beached or anchored their boats at the fort. Canvas-covered piles of what looked to be trade goods sat out in the open, delectably available. Once between *Lady Charlotte* and *Culverin*'s guns, and the fire-power available ashore, the trap would be sprung. Sir Hugo had enough men to cover the north shore around the fort, and part of the western headland, only able to spare a half-company to reinforce the heavy battery on the point. If the pirates tumbled to it earlier, it would be a near thing as to who would get the worst of it.

Praos drifted by to bow and stern, some coming very close in as they passed. It was much like being in the middle of a pack of hungry sharks.

"I think this bastard wants t' come aboard, sir!" Murray said, pointing to one *prao* that was rounding up below the entry port. "Do we let 'em, sir?"

"Christ!" Lewrie hissed. Hard as the battle to take the island had been on his nerves, it couldn't hold a candle to this. There was a person of some rank among the pirate band standing on the rails of his boat, waving and shouting, demanding entry. "Ashore!" Lewrie said, pointing in that direction. "Ashore, hey? You . . . go . . . there! No come here!" He was all but wiggling his bottom, trying to get the gist of his message across. One pirate's eyes over the bulwarks to see loaded cannon and crews at the ready, and they'd swarm *Culverin* like a hive of disturbed bees!

"He don't sound too happy about it, sir," Murray warned. The pirate, clad in a cloth-of-gold turban, green silk skirt, jewels and weapons, was gesticulating and swearing to beat the band, upset that his will was being defied, that his august personage was being waved off instead of catered to.

"Oh, God, look sir!" Hogue yelped.

Those three *praos* had beached themselves on the western shore and their crews were disembarking, stretching and bending to loosen muscles kept taut at sea, and were spreading out in a dense pack over the peninsula's beach.

"Stand by with those grenadoes, Mister Hogue," Lewrie warned. "Well, if you want to come up, who am I to stop you, you little bastard?" he relented, waving and bowing for the pirate to scamper up. "All hands, stand ready! Ready to hoist the proper colors!"

The pirate took on a smug look, having gotten his way with the infidels at last, and began to step up to the main-mast chains. The rail of the *prao* was not so far below *Culverin*'s bulwarks.

"Most of 'em past us?" Lewrie asked, going to the starboard gangway to greet his unwelcome visitor.

"About half, looks like, sir," Hogue shuddered, like to faint with anxiety. "Only 'bout half, so far."

"Best we'll do, then," Lewrie sighed, his own nerves twittering like a dropped harpsichord. He stood and waited for his visitor, a smile on his face. The pirate stepped up on the bulwarks and frowned when he saw what waited him. He opened his mouth to yell.

Lewrie drew his hanger and lunged. He put the point in just around the navel and sank an unhealthy foot of steel into the man's belly. Before he even had time to shout or draw breath, he was over the side, tumbling back into the water between the ships!

"Grenadoes!" Lewrie screamed. "Open your ports and open fire! Get English colors aloft!"

The signal for the opening of the battle. Even as the pirates were beginning to realize their captain was dead and starting to howl with rage, empty wine bottles went over the side, with wicks burning.

Some were filled with whale oil, some with gunpowder and cut up scrap-iron bits. When they shattered, they burst into flames among the densely packed pirates, among their galley-slaves at the rowing benches. Those that did not shatter, those wrapped about with cloth to protect them, exploded as their fuses burned out and reached the powder. They caused more panic than casualties, but it didn't do the pirates' nerves any good.

And then the ports were open, and the carronades were firing. The light two-pounder swivel guns were spewing lethal loads of canister or grape-shot down into the boats closest alongside, scything howling pirates down in mid-cry. *Praos* farther off rocked and came apart at the touch of solid shot, spilling their crews into the water.

Once the *prao* alongside was fended off and allowed to drift shoreward, on fire and already sinking, Lewrie ran back to the after deck where Cony waited with his personal weapons. He took the time to see *Lady Charlotte* blazing away with her remaining heavier long-barreled twelve-pounders, ringed with boats. The shore beyond her was almost lost in the crackle of musketry and the clouds of gunpowder produced by the infantrymen, and the firing of the light artillery. There was a blast of smoke high up the hill, as the first of the hidden battery up there fired, and a great feather of spray sprang into being next to a pirate boat farther off.

Lewrie went to the rail with the Ferguson rifle he had obtained at Yorktown and began picking off those pirates who seemed to be leading in the nearest boats. Cony was himself a fair shot as well, and he used a .65 caliber fusil to snipe at helmsmen and gunners.

"Aft!" Lewrie shouted. "Hands aft! Get a swivel-gun here!"

There was a *prao* out there, not two hundred yards off, that was being turned with its oarsmen, aiming its two fo'c'sle-mounted guns at *Culverin*'s unprotected stern!

Hands came running, bearing the weight of one of the portable swivels, dropping the long spike on the base of its mount into one of the holes along the taffrail as Lewrie fired again. Bullets sang in the air as pirates let fly with muskets at impossible ranges, only a few being able to reach him.

Lewrie sat down on the flag lockers to one side of the tillerhead, braced himself on the railing and aimed for the foredeck of the *prao*. He pulled the fire-lock of the Ferguson back to full cock and bent to sight on one of the gunners. Holding a little high for drop at that range, he let his breath out and pulled the trigger. There was a respectable *bang* as the piece discharged, a *whoosh* of burned powder in his face from the pan.

But he had struck his man! At nearly two hundred yards. There were only two weapons in the world that could fire that far: the American Kentucky rifle, and the Ferguson. And the Ferguson was a proper military piece. He cranked the lever under the stock one turn, dropping the screw-breech out of the way, pulled the dog's-jaws back to half-cock and bit the end off a cartouche, priming the pan with some of the powder inside. Rammed the rest into the rear of the rifle's breech, screwed the breech shut with one turn of the lever, full-cocked the weapon once more and aimed.

Another shot, and another pirate down with a ball through his back! And then another, and another, and the pirates began to shrink away from their guns. No one could kill at that range that quickly!

The swivel-gun went off. Spears had aimed just as carefully, and put a solid two-pound shot into the pirates' forecastle, where it shattered and crazed the air with savage shards of itself, flinging pirates right and left. That was one vessel that had lost interest in trying to rake *Culverin* up the stern.

"Make it hot for 'em, Spears," Lewrie ordered, getting to his feet.

"Bow, sir!" Hogue was shouting and waving for Lewrie to join him. And off Lewrie went, racing forward up the narrow path between the guns on the main deck, to the fo'c'sle to face another hazard. Here, he found a *prao* almost under their jib-boom, with a horde of raving pirates ready to board.

"Grenadoes here! Swivel-gun with canister!" Lewrie snapped, taking a deep breath to steady his aim. He loosed a shot from his Ferguson, splattering the leader's brains on his minions, then dropped the rifle and pulled his pistols. A shot from the right weapon, then a shot from the left, while Cony lit fuses atop wine bottles and got them ready to hurl.

"For God's sake, Cony, get rid of those damned things!"

"Don't wan' these buggers a'throwin' 'em back, sir!" his man replied, tossing one to soar end-over-end, quickly followed by a second. Two explosions and the whining of broken glass, bent nails and musket balls, quickly followed by wails of alarm. Then Cony was up and throwing the flammable variety, which he had purposely lit and set aside so they would be going nicely when he needed them. These burst with softer *whoomps* as they shattered and the whale oil splashed on the boat and its fell crew and took light, turning the wails into impassioned screams.

The swivel-gun lit off, scattering death almost within touching distance, and pirates melted away from their own forecastle to shrink back amidships. Muskets banged, and the swivel-gun man by Lewrie's side screamed as he was flung backward as if hammered with a heavy sledge.

Lewrie bent to pick up the dropped canister bag. He tilted the long barrel straight up, dropped it down without taking time to ram it firmly home and stuck the sharp end of a lin-stock into the vent to puncture the powder charge in its flannel sleeve. He had to bend to the deck once more to retrieve the fallen sailor's goose-quills and slow-match. More shots sounded, and musket balls flailed the air over his head, thudding into the fore part of *Culverin*'s bows like hammer blows.

Cony was still heaving away with grenadoes, ducking and weaving through a sleet-storm of lead. More sailors were coming forward to return fire with their Brown Bess muskets.

Lewrie blew on the slow-match, stood up behind the swivel-gun and aimed at the thickest part of the throng. He touched off the quill and the world was blotted out for a second or two by the dense blast of powder smoke. When it cleared, there were no more pirates on their feet anywhere aboard the *prao* except a few stunned survivors in the sternposts, who were cut down with musket fire even as they stood there stupefied.

"Cony, do you take charge of the fo'c'sle and keep 'em off us!" Lewrie shouted in his ear before gathering up his rifle, dropped pistols, and moving back amidships to reload where it wasn't so dangerous.

Carronades to either beam were firing every few seconds. The swivels along either bulwark were blasting away, as were the ones aft. *Lady Charlotte*, he could see, had cleared the waters around her with her high-velocity guns, and Lewrie could spot the half-sunken wrecks of at least three *praos*. No *prao* would venture within range of his own carronades, for once hit, they were shattered like tea cups by the heavy shot. *Culverin*'s guns had done for three more of them already.

Lewrie regained the quarterdeck, puffing and blowing to get his wind back, and to get a sense of the battle from the higher vantage point.

The battery on the point was blasting away steadily, one gun at a time of the three, firing on pirate boats that were making their way for the harbor entrance. The ambush had been badly sprung before every victim was in the killing zone. At least ten boats were off on their way to escape.

Those three that had landed on the peninsula were still there, their crews just falling back in disorder from a charge against the troops on the crest. He could see red-coated soldiery rising from the rocks and beginning to advance in two lines with their bayonets winking in the sun. And all the while, their light guns were spraying canister and grape-shot into the pirate band.

Ashore by the main encampment, it was impossible to tell what was going on for all the smoke, but he thought he could espy at least four *praos* grounded on the beach, one of them well alight and pouring out greasy black smoke. There were three more boats that had sailed for the far eastern headland, and were mucking about in a quandary of doubt: flee for the harbor entrance against those guns on the point, rejoin the fight ashore or tackle the ships again?

A glowing ember dashed from the rising pillar of smoke ashore, soared in a sinking arc and struck one of the *praos*, making her shake like a kicked kitten. Within half a minute, the boat was aflame and her crew abandoning her! If it accomplished nothing else this day, his father's heated-shot battery had proved its worth!

"There, sir!" Hogue shouted as some *praos* came reeling out of the smoke from the shore, bent on escape.

"Larboard battery, load and stand by!" Lewrie shouted through his brass speaking-trumpet. "We clear aft, Spears?"

"Aye, sir, fer now!" the man shouted back as he reloaded the now-hot swivel-gun for another shot.

"Clear forward, Cony?" he asked.

"Fairly well, sir!" Cony said with a fierce smile.

"Bloody hell, what does that mean?" Lewrie fumed.

Whatever it had meant, it would have to do, for there were now six *praos* headed their way, rowing madly to get out of the gun-arcs of *Lady Charlotte*'s twelve-pounders. Between *Culverin*'s anchorage and shore there was a half-mile of water. With careful aim and gun-laying, Lewrie could expect his carronades to scour only half that distance, for a carronade was a very low-velocity gun for all its hitting power. The "Smashers" were close-in weapons.

"Here they come!" Hogue yelled. "Stand ready, gun-captains! Aim for the two lead boats! One and two, take the one on the right! Three, four and five, take the one on the left!"

Good for Hogue, Lewrie thought! A sensible young man who could see that the lead boat to their right was poorly manned and not much of a threat, while the one to the left had so far missed out on what horrors they were dealing out this day. Lewrie traded his Ferguson rifle for his telescope and saw that the boat on the left had what looked to be eight- or nine-pounders on its foredeck, and the pirates were swarming over those guns, readying them for firing.

"Fer what we're about t' receive, may the good Lord make us joyful," Murray sighed as the *prao* got her guns into action. A ball hit *Culverin* low on her larboard side, making her shudder heavily, while the second struck the bulwarks between number 4 and number 5 larboard guns and turned the wood into a burst of flickering teak splinters, cutting down the gun crews and raising a great howling among his crew.

"Fire!" Hogue shouted once the *praos* were within their limited range. *Culverin* lurched sideways as the guns lit off. The first boat on the right almost leaped out of the water as she was struck, mast and large, leaf-bladed paddles flying in all directions, along with some of her hull. Arabian building

techniques with rope and butt-joined board could not take such
punishment, and she dropped back into the sea with a great
splash as she came apart like an artichoke, spilling her crew
into the water.

The second boat to the left had her foredeck cleared by a
hit, guns and men flying as the heavy twenty-four-pounder ball
shattered amongst the barrels. Her mast came down and some
powder cartridge bags went off with a great burst of dirty yellow smoke and flame. She came to a dead stop and began to
sag down off the wind toward the western shore, right into
Lady Charlotte's guns.

"Well, damn them," Lewrie spat. The other four *praos*
were now bearing off under human power, their paddles or
oars slashing the sea as they fled east, out of range of the carronades that had smashed up their leaders' boats like a giant's
fist.

Lewrie turned to look seaward once more. The battery on
the point had sunk one *prao*, but it looked like at least four
would get out through the channel. And the two surviving pirate boats to the east were working their way along the line of
the breakers in shallow water beyond the reach of even the
high battery's guns. Which was where the four that had challenged him were going.

"Mister Murray?"

"Sir?"

"They're going to get away from us if we sit here," Lewrie
said, feeling grim about it and more than willing, if given any
kind of excuse, to let them do so. But it was his duty. "Fix
buoys to the anchor cables and prepare to let slip. We'll pursue
them."

"Aye, sir," Murray said with a sharp intake of breath.

"Mister Hogue! Secure your guns for a while. We shall
hoist sail, let slip the cables and get underway."

"Thank God for a simple rig," Lewrie said scant minutes later.
It would have taken a square-rigger half an hour to hoist sail,
but little *Culverin* could simply hoist her jibs and gaff-sails,
haul in on the sheets to angle those sails to the wind at the
proper angle and she was moving ahead and under control. It
made him wonder if a way could be found to rig a larger warship so simply, even if it took four masts instead of three. A
fore-and-aft rigged ship with a deep, full-run keel for a good
grip on the water so she could go to windward like a witch,

with no courses . . . well, maybe a forecourse to lift the bows, and nothing higher-mounted than large tops'ls. Armed with carronades for the most part, with a few long-ranged muzzle-loaders amidships for . . .

"Course, sir?"

"The mind can do the oddest things at the worst moments," Lewrie murmured, laughing at himself. He might not be alive half an hour from now if he took *Culverin* into that desperate pack of bloody-handed murderers now intent on escape, and even more dangerous than before. And here he was speculating on naval architecture!

"Close-hauled on the larboard tack for the harbor," Lewrie said. "We'll have to tack east or end up running aground, but that'll give us a chance to fire into those boats running along the reef line."

Culverin could point high, but the wind was solidly out of the sou'east, and the best she could do was a little west of due south to approach the harbor entrance on a long board. Leadsmen swung chains to sound the depth ahead of her as she clawed her way seaward.

"And a half, two!"

"Helm alee! Off fores'l sheets!"

Culverin tacked across the eye of the wind, onto a short board back to a heading of about 1 point, about 11 degrees, north of east. But she had gotten close enough to threaten those fleeing *praos* along the reef line inside the breakers.

"Ready, sir!" Hogue called to him. "I make it about two cables."

"Try your eye, Mister Hogue!" Lewrie nodded. "Blaze away!"

The guns on the starboard side came reeling inboard one at a time. The heavy balls, fired at maximum elevation and laid so close to the edge of the port-sills they almost singed the wood, failed to hit. They landed short, raising great feathery plumes of water into the air. But the *praos* checked their frantic pace and paid off the breaker line, stymied by fear.

"Hands to the sheets! Ready to come about? Helm alee!" Alan commanded. He did not want to get too far to the east inside their harbor, for that would put him too close to the reefs to be able to tack to windward to reverse course. To wear ship downwind would lose him every inch of ground he had gained south for the entrance channel.

"Now we shall try our luck against yonder bastards."

"Jesus!" Murray yelped, ducking into a half-crouch as a solid shot moaned overhead. "Where'd they get such heavy iron, sir?"

"That was our battery on the hillside above the fort, Murray," Lewrie commented, standing erect from his own crouch. "I pray those gunners know what they're about with that heated shot."

"Didn't miss our masts by a boat-length, sir," Murray carped as *Culverin* sailed right through the ring-shaped splash of the spent shot half a minute later. "An' they haven't got the range for very much longer. Cain't we signal 'em t' stop, sir?"

"Ah . . . uhm, I'm afraid that's one signal we didn't discuss, Murray," Lewrie confessed, suffering another qualm at all he had *not* considered once again, and feeling the lack of prior planning acutely. "We shall have to trust to their good judgment."

"Good judgment from *soldiers!*" Murray gaped with a sour look.

"Ready the larboard battery, Mister Hogue! Fire as you bear!"

"And a half three!" the leadsman chanted.

"As you bear . . . fire!" Hogue screamed, his voice cracking. Now the larboard guns lurched back on their recoil slides and a harsh, stinging cloud of powder blossomed forth, checked at the bulwarks by the winds and wafted back over them, blanking out the world for a minute. When the smoke cleared, the hands cheered at the sight of a pirate boat that was rocking keel-up about two hundred yards away, with survivors struggling and wailing about her.

"And a half, two!"

"Ready to come about!" Lewrie called. "Helm's alee!"

One more close-hauled short board on the starboard tack to the east, perhaps the last they could make as they neared the harbor entrance and the line of breakers. The next larboard tack would take them through the main channel and out to sea. Hogue let loose with a broadside from the starboard guns, once more hitting nothing, but the pirates trapped in the lagoon were too rattled to notice, and shied off again.

Back on the larboard tack. Breakers growling and fuming. The battery on the point firing at a boat ahead of them and straddling it with two shot-splashes, hitting it amidships with the third ball and shattering it so quickly that it jack-knifed like a paper boat, broke in two and went under.

"Two more hands to the tiller, Murray!" Lewrie snapped. "Stand by to pinch her up as we cross the bar."

There was more depth in the channel this time of day as tidal flooding rushed into the harbor, softening the shock. But *Culverin* could still broach on that deceptively calm-looking swell if she hit it wrong.

Culverin rose, soaring up on the swell, with a line of spume racing down past her sides, her bow cocking up for the skies.

"Helm down!" Lewrie shouted. "Luff up square to the wave!"

Four men threw their sinewy strength to the tiller to keep it from lashing to either side or throwing them overboard. *Culverin* lay on the tip of the swell, sails luffing and thundering, then began to fall as the wave left her behind, bow dipping until it looked as if she'd bury her bowsprit into the trough and keep on sliding down into the depths. She then began to gather speed after being checked in her slide.

"Helm up and give us way, close-hauled!"

It was like rowing a boat across the surf line without going arse-over-tit or being rolled like a stranded whale. *Culverin* paid off and her sails filled with wind as a second swell gathered her up out of the trough where they could find air, thundering and flapping, then taking shape once more with a series of loud boomings.

"Hold her no more than a point west of south, quartermaster!" Lewrie turned to say. *Culverin* soared upward once more, almost forcing him to his knees in her hurry to ascend to heaven, but she was halfway out of the wicked harbor entrance now. Even with her hellish tendency to go to leeward like a wood-chip, they would clear the western shoals under the point if they could only make this course good. To have to tack while fighting those entrance bar swells would be disastrous!

"Two fathom!" the starboard leadsman howled.

"Hold her!" Lewrie growled. "Pinch her up as you're able, but for God's sake, hold her head!"

"And a half, two!"

The point was astern, the shoals left behind in her wake. He breathed out as the leadsman found "three fathom" then "four fathom." The broken reef wall would be no threat, not on a flooding tide that would put six fathoms over those tumbled ruins. They were beyond the threatening swells, too, out on the open sea.

"Damn fine, damn my eyes if it wasn't!" Lewrie said to

his shaky helmsmen as they eased their death-grips on the tiller bar.

"Thankee, sir, thankee right kindly," they mumbled, working on their cuds again in mouths gone dry as desert sand.

"Now let's get after our pirate friends!" Lewrie exclaimed, beaming. "Mister Murray, they seem to be trending east, running for home and mother."

"Aye, sir. Want t' tack an' pursue 'em now, sir?"

"Wait until we're safely over this broken reef first, then lay her on the starboard tack," Lewrie replied. "Break out the water-butts for anyone as thirsty as I feel for now. Gun crews stand easy."

"Aye, sir."

"Sail ho!" the lookout called.

"Where away!"

"Due south, sir!" the man replied. "Four points off the larboard beam! Full-rigged ship, sir!"

"Damme, d'you think Mister Choate finally got here, sir?" Murray asked. "Now between us, we'll put paid t' these motherless buggers!"

Lewrie took up his telescope and went up the mizzen shrouds to almost the top platform. He raised it to his eyes once he had an arm and leg threaded through the ratlines and stays to keep himself from falling, and took a look for himself.

Three masts, pale tan sails, coming on for the island from the sou'west with the wind large on her starboard quarter. Already almost hull up. Good lines. Frigate-built, he thought. Ayscough chose well.

A large swell over the broken reef wall lifted *Culverin* higher for about half a minute. Far off, another swell raised the stranger as well. Lewrie could espy a pale ochre hull with what looked to be a wide white gunwale stripe.

"*Poisson D'Or!*" he cursed. "Choundas!"

Why did he have to arrive now, of all times? Huge clouds of gunpowder hung over Spratly Island. Artillery still fired on those *praos* yet trapped in harbor or trying to run the gauntlet to sea.

To see a strange ship giving chase to a pack of pirates fleeing to the east would be the final straw. They could not lure *Poisson D'Or* into harbor. Choundas would be wise to the game, and sail off for parts unknown, as sure as Fate!

"Goddamn your bloody luck, you rotten shit!" Lewrie almost wept with frustration. Here he'd just won two battles in a fortnight, done away with pirates by the battalions, had sunk Frogs left, right and center, and all for nothing!

What to do now, he pondered. One course of action was to go back to seal the entrance to the harbor, so most of the pirates could end up slaughtered. Or, he could pursue the eight who were getting away. If he did continue the chase, he might be able to lure Choundas into action, but the man had long-ranged guns to his short-ranged carronades. Stout as *Culverin* was, she'd be pounded to bits while he would be lucky to inflict even minor damage to Choundas.

He raised his telescope again to peer at his foe. *Poisson D'Or* altered shape. She was turning north, putting all her masts in line, heading somewhere to the east of Spratly Island. To interpose between *Culverin* and Choundas' fleeing allies.

"Bastard!" Lewrie growled. For little danger, Choundas would appear to have saved that terrified remnant, driven off an English ship and restored his luster among the Mindanao pirates. And, he would end up escaping, after all, to some port where they had no hope of finding him. "Bastard!"

Chapter 9

"And you could not pursue him?" Mr. Twigg demanded, sounding as if he did not believe one word of Lewrie's report.

"Once we'd convinced the rest of the *praos* to surrender, sir," Lewrie replied, striving to keep a cool head in the face of Twigg's unspoken sneering, "after I had returned to harbor and blocked their escape, I did sail off to the east'rd, for two days, sir, but found no sign of him or the pirates who did get out of harbor. After that two days, I felt it my duty to return to Spratly and defend it until Lieutenant Choate arrived with *Cuddalore* to relieve me, sir."

They held their conference on *Telesto*'s poop deck, under the canvas awnings with lots of liquid refreshments, instead of the airless great cabins below, for the day was sunny, hot but breezy.

"And the estimable Lieutenant Choate is where, sir?" Twigg inquired.

"Off the coast of Borneo, sir," Lewrie stated. "He unloaded his cargo of supplies, then told me to remain here as harbor-guard. He would scout to the sou'east, up to windward, from the Rajang River delta to Balabac Strait. He took along one of the captured *praos* in tow, sir, so he could go close in-shore."

"Good thinking, that," Ayscough said of his first lieutenant.

"A bit too *late*, that," Twigg retorted.

"Let me remind you, Mister Twigg, that you were still of the opinion that Choundas would be here by mid-June, and in that you were dead-wrong!" Captain Ayscough rumbled deep in his chest, arms folded over his stomach. "I also get the sense that you disapprove of Mister Lewrie's actions here on

Spratly. Well, let me tell you, I *have* read his full report, even if you have not, and as a commission Sea Officer I find no fault with his conduct of our campaign so far, nor with any decision he has made. My report shall contain my highest approbation for his actions, actions in the very best traditions of the Sea Service!"

"Hmmpf!" Twigg sniffed loftily. "Two sea-dogs whelped from the same litter. Your approval is only natural, but a chance was *missed!*"

If anything, the already strained relationship between Twigg and Captain Ayscough had grown even more testy in the weeks since Alan had last seen them, going past gentlemanly conduct to the words and sneers that back home would have resulted in a pre-dawn duel. Choate had warned him to expect the worst of them, and had expressed worries that their acrimony was bad enough to jeopardize the future conduct of their expedition. Perhaps that was why Choate had been so eager to get back to sea, so he would not be there when they arrived. They had come into port at Spratly three days earlier, the fifteenth of May. Choate had brought *Cuddalore*, a fine twenty-gunned merchantman, across the bar on the first of May, and had departed in a haste such as if all the imps of Hell were chasing him. Which, in a way, Alan realized, they were. He'd rather be anywhere than around these two headstrong men whose relationship had degraded to an open feud!

"Why, thankee, Mister Twigg." Captain Ayscough beamed. "That was a pretty compliment, to my lights, and I do take it as such! I would like to think I'd been as successful had I been in this lad's shoes. The island taken with minimum casualties, a French cartel ship captured and burned. And not just any hired vessel, but one of Choundas' outright ownership! A cartel ship, I might remind you, we were not even aware of, and she moored not a quarter-mile ahead of us for six months at Whampoa!"

"Hmmpf!" Twigg reiterated, turning beet-red from that insult to his intelligence-gathering powers, his lips going twine-thin.

"The harbor fortified and provisioned as good as any, and the encampment improved, though I am sure we have Sir Hugo's skills as a soldier to thank for that as well," Ayscough continued, inclining his head toward Lieutenant-Colonel Willoughby, who was sprawled in a canvas deck-chair with a glass of brandy in hand, booted feet up on the rickety deal table. Sir Hugo raised his glass and smiled beatifically.

Lewrie could not help but swell with pride as his praises were sung so nicely. If Ayscough were any more complimentary, he imagined they'd commission a Te Deum Mass at St. Paul's and lay on fireworks!

"An entire pirate fleet destroyed, sir," Ayscough went on, hammering gaily away at Twigg's arguments. "Ten out of eighteen Lanun Rover *praos* sunk, taken or burned, sir, and over twelve hundred cut-throats dead or made prisoner. Why, these Mindanao pirates haven't suffered such a bloody check in a hundred years! Wiped from the face of God's blue seas. As you demanded back at Bencoolen, sir."

"One might also mention the harbor properly surveyed for the first time in living memory, and the island's exact location corrected, sir," Sir Hugo prompted. "The late Captain Cook could have done no less in these waters, I shouldn't doubt."

"And that American whaler freed, too," Ayscough concluded.

"Yes, that American whaler," Twigg drawled. "Now off in Manila, shouting to high heaven. Letting the world in on our little secret! Did it not occur to you, Mister Lewrie, that our mission out here is *secret?*"

Twigg got to his feet to pace his anger off.

"It cannot be known publicly by any other power that England had disguised warships in these waters, or the recent treaty is violated, and we might face another disastrous war with France. Or any other nation that might decide to side with them. Those Yankees saw a battalion of East India Company troops, and a vessel flying Royal Navy colors, do battle with the French, sir! Now how secret do you believe our mission is any longer? You should have kept them here, found any excuse to delay their departure, until I could arrive so no one could learn of this, but no! You . . ."

"Oh, bloody Hell!" Sir Hugo snapped, slamming boots on the deck. "Did it never occur to *you*, Mister Twigg, that there may have been a tad too much bloody worry about secrecy?"

"I *beg* your pardon, Sir Hugo?" Twigg snarled back.

"Two years ago, when our first ships started going missing, it would have made eminent sense to raise the hue and cry with every seafaring nation out here and make a concerted campaign to defend trade. Not just our trade, but everyone's. Let the world know there's need to chastise every bloody pirate in the Far East," Sir Hugo went on. "But that may have been too *much* good sense for our masters back in London. Seems to me, sir, this exposure at last, with our American cousins shouting the loudest, is just the thing for us. In a year, the world'll know it was this Choundas, and the Frogs, backing these pirates. Now, our work's four-fifths done, and public pressure, and an end to all this bloody sneaking and hiding, will do the rest for us, without getting any more good men killed. I say, it's time the wraps came off this bloody business. And as for freeing those Yankees, refitting their ship and all, well, that'll stand us in good credit with those new United States. And should another war break out, we'll need all the good credit we can stand, else they'd side with their former allies."

"I would not normally expect," Twigg said after a long sigh, "such perspicacity in a military man, Sir Hugo. And in private, I might be able to agree with you. But the Crown decided otherwise. And it's not simply about piracy, you see. It's not even about this fellow Choundas, when you get right down to it, sir. It's about laying combinations out here for the next war."

"Oh, bugger," Sir Hugo growled.

"You consider another war with France inevitable, Sir Hugo, as much as I. At this very instant, there may be three dozen schemes in play such as ours, and even I have no knowledge of them, and *shouldn't* unless one of the others impinges upon mine. All to see that future foes have no strength or credit here in the Far East, nor any allies or secret bases that could threaten England. To put too much light on ours, sir, to expose any of them, would be to expose all of them, eventually. The best mushrooms, I am told, are grown in the dark."

"The best roses need the most cow-shit, too," Ayscough huffed.

"Nevertheless, sir," Sir Hugo smiled, a disarming, lazy smile that Lewrie knew of old was one of eminent menace, "I do trust that when you come to write of this campaign, you shall sound at least the *slightest* bit grateful for what we've done for you so far. And commending."

"Of course I shall, Sir Hugo," Twigg relented, obviously seeing the threat that lay behind that smile, and being enough of a political animal, with the ability to read others so he could best use them for his own purposes, or the Crown's, to know he could carp no longer.

"So," Captain Ayscough grunted. "How best to conclude

this'un? Now we've hamstrung this Choundas bugger so thoroughly."

"Have we, sir?" Twigg scowled. "And for how long?"

"Well, he's lost this island base of his," Ayscough rambled. "Lost *La Malouine*, lost *Stella Maris*, and his secret's soon to be out, thanks to those Yankee Doodle whalermen. Now he may have other cartel ships out here to serve him, but for now he's on his own."

"He still has the Lanun Rovers, sir," Twigg pointed out, with some glee. "And he has his freedom to rebuild a semblance of his web, like some noisome spider."

"Without the silver and opium we captured here, without all the arms he would have given the pirates, or the trade goods, I doubt he still has the Lanun Rovers," Captain Ayscough replied. "They lost too many of their brethren here for Choundas to hold their allegiance. Oh, he saved some few of 'em by showing up when he did, but he failed to rescue the rest. Even with that big, fine ship of his, he didn't sail up and fight us. He may have 'em in name only, but not firmly in his grasp any longer. And for the moment, he's vulnerable."

"If that's so bloody obvious, then why isn't he running home right now, cutting his losses?" Sir Hugo speculated, sitting back down and refilling his glass. "He must know this is his last raiding summer, and it's riskier now more'n ever."

"Because he is who he is, Sir Hugo," Twigg said with a knowing leer. "I've had a chance to interrogate the surviving Frogs from this *Stella Maris*. Amazing what a man will confess when threatened with a noose for piracy. The second mate told me that most of the officers thought Choundas a rather odd sort. Odder than most. Not merely in his sexual predilictions, but in his mind, sirs. Lieutenant Lewrie, do you recall that nonsense he spouted the day of the execution, what he had to say about the ancient Gauls and Celts being related?"

"Aye, sir, I do," Lewrie agreed, tensing for another lesson in just how simply clever Twigg thought himself to be. "He said that the Britons, the Gauls and the Celts were one race, sir. Damned fool."

"Us, kin of Frogs?" Sir Hugo spluttered. "I mean, the Normans aside, what a lot of ... you will pardon the play on words, but, what *gall!*"

"Choundas was born in low circumstances, yes," Twigg related with relish, "though not fishmonger poor. His father owned several boats, and hoped for better things for his son.

Education, and hopes he'd enter the priesthood. Don't have to be a nobleman to do well in France if you wear the cassock. But the boy, besides being a superb sailor, developed a bent for scholarship in history, and in Latin, of course. Why he named *Stella Maris* by a Latin name, and not *Etoile de la Mer*, I s'pose."

"Does this have any bearing on *anything?*" Ayscough groaned.

"What's the thing *all* Latin students read, sir? Caesar's *Gallic Wars*. Naturally, as a Breton, Choundas would sympathise with the ancient Gauls under Vercingetorix and such. But most specifically, he imagined himself, and his line, to be kin with the Veneti. When oared galleys daren't go five miles offshore, these Veneti in their oak ships with leather sails would roam the entire known world, much as we do today. Their strength was in their Navy. Even the Vikings of latter days didn't dare as much as they did."

"I think," Lewrie summarized for them, unable to pass up the sterling opportunity to shine, or to spill the air from Twigg's sails, "that what Mister Twigg means is that if he thinks he's the last of this noble seafaring line of Veneti, and goes on about it so much he bores his compatriots to tears with it, we may assume the silly arse will tweak our noses and raid our ships this season, sirs."

"Then why didn't you merely say so, Mister Twigg?" Captain Ayscough asked, with all innocence in his expression. "Right, then!"

Ayscough trotted out his chart of the South China Seas and laid it on the table, anchoring the corners with bottles and glasses so the wind wouldn't scud it off somewhere to leeward.

"If he thinks he's that bloody good, he can't have sailed too far to the east'rd." Ayscough chuckled. "West is out, 'cause he'd have to beat so far to windward against the prevailing sou'easterlies this time of year to get to his cruising grounds. Choate is scouting the Borneo coast now, and we may have good news from him soon. Down there is to windward, where I'd wish to base myself, were I this 'last of a noble seafaring line.' But there's a problem with that, too."

"The Borneo pirates," Lewrie interjected. "There's little love lost between them and the Lanun Rovers, is there, sir?"

"Exactly so, Mister Lewrie. He may have some relations with 'em as a hole-card, so to speak, and he may be forced to play it to allow him one last chance to go home a winner, but . . . well, damme!"

"What?" Twigg rapped out.

"Well, here's this lad Choundas, born a commoner, normally denied his chance to shine in the French Navy, but thinking himself kin to ancient sea-kings. I see why you would think he would have to do something grand against us before going home, Mister Twigg, but think on this for a moment . . ." Ayscough beamed cleverly. "The Borneo boys are river-based, and they don't go out of sight of shore too often. Who would Choundas feel the most in common with?"

"The Lanun Rovers, still!" Twigg exclaimed.

"Right, then!" Ayscough said once more, rubbing his horny palms in satisfaction. "Were I looking for prizes, I'd be far south, opposite the Johore Straits. Around Anambas or Pulau Natuna, where we met that pirate fleet last year. Here at Spratly, maybe up farther north and still to windward of the Canton run on the Tizard Bank. No shelter there, though, if the winds pipe up."

"Too close to Dutch or English patrols down south, sir," Lewrie commented. "That's why he chose Spratly in the first place."

"Yes, so we must assume that he's somewhere up to windward, but not *too far* to the east'rd. With his resources reduced, he has to be close to the scene of action and do his own dirty work for a while. So if I were constrained in such a way, I'd be somewhere around the mouth of Balabac Strait." Ayscough frowned, pacing off a divider across the chart. "I'd not be too deep inside the Philippine Archipelago. If my allies started disliking me, there'd be no escape for a single ship, even as well-armed as we assume *Poisson D'Or* to be. So he would be west of the Sulu Sea. Still allied, even tenuously, with the Mindanao pirates. And using what's left of that alliance, and their reputation, as a shield to prevent pursuit."

"Is this not a Spanish naval base, here on Palawan?" Sir Hugo asked, leaning over the chart. "This Puerto Princesa? Seems they'd have this area covered. Why let some outsider upset what arrangement they have with their own native pirates? They'd kick him out soon as those Yankees let them know of it."

"Ah, but he doesn't even know that *Stella Maris* took a Yankee as prize, Sir Hugo," Ayscough grinned, hugely enjoying himself. "It don't signify, anyway, that the Spanish would even be aware of them being there. All they have are Guarda Costa luggers and such, not ships of worth. Hell, it's two hundred miles from Puerto Princesa to the Balabac Strait. The Dons are flat-broke, and all they care about are the northern islands. Anything south of Leyte is pretty much controlled in name only. They have a loose agreement with the natives in the south—'You don't kill us, we won't bother you!' Healthier for Spanish fortunes in the long run." Ayscough chuckled with mirth. "So aspiring young Dons don't get their throats cut, or their reputations ruined, by a raggedy-arsed pack of fanatics."

"So this Balabac Strait is pretty much the King's Highway to these pirates, sir?" Lewrie asked, peering at the chart.

"Yes, just so. And I'd expect Choundas to be somewhere near the western entrance, around the island of Banggi on the north tip of Borneo, or on the island of Balabac itself," Ayscough concluded, tossing down his dividers.

"We have little time, then, before the first ships sail from Calcutta and Madras for this year's trading season," Twigg fretted. "We'll not see him playing innocent in Canton again. One raiding season, then back he goes to the Indian Ocean, leaving other ships to be his bearers for the last loads of loot, whilst he's off like a hare to France. We might be able to stymie his designs by our presence, and defeat him that way. But there's the matter of all those ships we've lost the last two years. All those murdered men. Damme if I care much for him escaping with even the slightest hint of success, sirs! I wish him destroyed, utterly!"

"Like Cato's demand," Sir Hugo mused. "Carthage must be destroyed."

"Exactly, Sir Hugo," Twigg said firmly. "For everyone's peace of mind, Choundas must be destroyed."

"Mister Lewrie," Captain Ayscough asked. "Whatever did happen to those Veneti?"

"Caesar sank the lot of them in 56 B.C., sir," Lewrie replied.

Chapter 10

To ease the overcrowding aboard *Lady Charlotte*, and not knowing how long they would be at sea, the battalion of troops had been spread out among all three ships. As had the fortune in silver, the captured powder and shot. Unfortunately, they had been forced to burn the bulk of the opium and trade goods, disposing of the remainder in the deeper part of the harbor at Spratly Island along with the cannon barrels and stands of arms. They would leave nothing behind that required a guard force to deplete their strength, and nothing for Choundas to regain should he double back on them.

The *praos* were burned as well, and the prisoners disarmed and left to fend for themselves with the wild livestock for sustenance and only the rudest remnants of the encampment for shelter.

Leaving *Lady Charlotte* to make her slower way astern, *Telesto* and *Culverin* ranged sou'east, beating up to windward, with an eventual rendezvous planned several days hence, once they had met up with Lieutenant Choate and *Cuddalore* as he scouted northward towards the Strait, too, and delivered his report, or lack of news, on Choundas' possible whereabouts.

Telesto had to stand off to seaward whilst the shallow-drafted *Culverin* did the main work closer inshore. Which arrangement was pleasant for Lewrie, since it got him out of snapping distance when Twigg and Ayscough had at each other like snarling wolves.

"And a half, four!" the leadsman in the chains said, getting bored and sunburned at his thankless task. They were skirting round the foetid, marshy tip of Borneo, near enough to a native settlement marked on the chart as Kudat (which was about all that the chart had gotten right in the past few days) to have seen several single *praos* out at sea. These at least had been peacefully fishing, but had run ashore as they drew close, leaving them sole possession of the sea.

"Time to change the leadsmen, sounds like," Lewrie said. He drew out his watch and looked at the time. "Almost the end of the day watch. Five minutes to eight bells, Mister Hogue."

"Stand off-shore once the watch changes, sir?" Hogue asked.

"I think we'll continue as we are for the first hour of the first dog-watch. After that, the light will be too far westerly for us to spot shoal-water," Lewrie replied. "We'll alter course after four bells."

"Aye, sir," Hogue said, yawning.

"And a quarter less five!" the leadsman sounded out.

Borneo reeked, as did its shoals. Rotting vegetation, rotting weed washed up on her shores, stagnant mud-flats and dead-fish odors, and the heights inland blocked a proper sea-breeze to waft it all off. Now and then a hint of cooking, now and then some gorgeous aromas from riotously thriving flowers—but mostly it stank horribly like some gigantic slaughter-house. They'd all be glad to get out to sea.

"Something in the water!" the lookout on the tall main-mast shouted. "Three points off the starboard bows!"

"Shoal?" Lewrie wondered, raising his telescope for the umpteenth time that day. "It looks low enough. No, a rock, perhaps."

"Native boat, sir," Hogue said with the advantage of his almost uncanny eyesight. "Turned turtle, looks like. God, no! It's a ship's boat!"

"Fetch-to, Mister Murray!" Lewrie shouted to his bosun. "Lead the cutter 'round from astern and call away a boat crew."

"Shall I go, sir?" Hogue asked anxiously.

"No, you stay aboard," Lewrie said. "It's not half a cable off, and we're at least three-quarters of a mile offshore. Keep the hands near the guns, though, just in case. I'll be back shortly."

They rounded *Culverin* up into the slack winds, jibs backed to force her bows off the breeze, but mains'ls still drawing and trying to drive her forward, stalling her "in-irons" cocked up to the wind and unable to go forward or back, to drift on the slow current.

Cony was already in the boat at the tiller, with eight hands at the oars, held aloft like lances as they waited for Lewrie.

"Shove off, Cony," Lewrie said, once he had taken his salute at the rail and settled himself onto a thwart near the stern.

"Aye, sir. Shove off, bow man. Ship yer oars. Give us way, larboard. Backwater, starboard," Cony instructed. "Now, avast. Now give us way t'gether!"

Once the cutter was moving shoreward with both banks of rowers pulling at an easy stroke, Cony turned slightly on his buttocks and leaned over the tiller-bar. "D'ya think them pirates got fed up an' done fer this Choundas feller, sir?"

"T'would be a fitting end for him, no error, Cony," Lewrie said in reply. "A thing devoutly to be wished."

"Boat-hook ready, there," Cony snapped, turning back to his duties. "Easy all. Un-ship yer oars . . . toss yer oars . . . boat yer oars."

It was a European ship's boat, right enough, half-sunk at the bows, and charred to crumbling cinders for much of its length, which sight made Lewrie shiver with dread that somehow it was *La Malouine*'s boat he'd seen burn and capsize, that it had drifted all this way to confront him after all those months.

"Ah, Jaysus!" the bow-man gagged as he peered down into the boat. Up forward, two men lay in the bottom, stuffed under thwarts to keep them from sloshing about in the foot-deep water that flooded her. Or what was left of two men. They had bloated and split open with rot in the cruel heat and humidity, swelled like leather-hued steer carcasses and their clothing stretched taut as drum-heads where the seams had held together. Their wounds, where exposed to the air above the water level, swarmed with flies, blue-black and festering. One man had lost his leg below the knee, and some attempt had been made to tie it off with a tourniquet and bandage the stump. The other had the marks of several bullet wounds that had also been treated with scraps of clothing for bandages. But both faces gaped wide-mouthed under the scummy water in final, ghoulish rictuses of agony, and their eyes had gone for gull-food.

"They're sailors, anyway," Lewrie coughed on his bile as the odor hit them. "But whose?"

In the stern, which was somewhat dryer where only an inch or so of water sloshed about, there was a barricoe of water, a sodden biscuit bag and many bones and feathers littering a tarpaulin that might cover other supplies.

"Looks like they mighta et some sea-birds afore they died, sir." Cony shuddered. "Mighta been driftin' fer weeks out 'ere."

Lewrie prodded the water butt with his sword, and it tumbled into the water, floating high and empty, the bung gone.

"Jesus Christ!" the bow-man screamed as the tarpaulin stirred. Lewrie felt the hairs on his head stand up in terror as a shape came up from the bottom boards of the boat, draped in the tarpaulin.

"A ghost!" one of the oarsmen keened in shrill horror.

Then the tarpaulin was flung back, revealing a ravaged face. That face also split in horror and screamed like a banshee, just as terrified as the boat crew! A bony, sun-scarred arm emerged with a seaman's knife clenched in a lean and bony fist. Lewrie put his sword forward, ready to lunge. "Hold!" he shouted.

"Oh God no don't kill me please don't kill me, h'ain't I been through enough?" the apparition managed to say through a dry throat and blistered lips. But he dropped the knife.

"Are you English?" Lewrie asked, aghast.

"Aye, sir. 'R you? Please don' be them Frog devils, oh, say yer English, please!"

"Cony, fetch the water butt," Lewrie instructed.

"Water, God yes, lord love ye, sir, *water!*" the man raved. "I h'ain't 'ad no water fer days, jus' some blood outen a gull, once't!"

"What ship?" Lewrie asked, feeling another shiver of dread.

"*Cuddalore,* sir."

"*Cuddalore!*" Lewrie burst out. "What happened to her?"

" 'At Frog ship *Poison Door* took 'er, sir. A week ago 'n more."

"Goddamn my eyes," Ayscough sighed, so pale and shaky it was as if he'd seen a ghost himself. "Is this Choundas in league with the devil? What the hell are we up against?"

"A bloody clever man, sir," Twigg replied. "A bloody lucky one, but still, just a man, Captain Ayscough."

"What else did he say, Mister Lewrie?"

"Sir, he said *Cuddalore* fought *Poisson D'Or* about a week ago," Lewrie informed them somewhat gloomily. "Close inshore of Banggi and with the help of several *praos*. They put up a good fight, the man said, but eventually they were overwhelmed. Lieutenant Choate was killed."

"Oh, poor man," Ayscough groaned. "His poor family . . ."

"Dismasted, shot to pieces," Lewrie went on. "They captured her, sir. Murdered the survivors. Lieutenant McTaggart and all the mates and warrants. This fellow Prouty was lucky to get away, sir. His mates got into the boat, cut it loose from being towed astern, but the French shot them, dropped a round shot through the bow to sink it and set it afire. Prouty went over the side and clung to the rudder where he couldn't be seen. They drifted ever since, forward or back on the currents and tides. No oars, no masts. 'Tis a wonder he lived. Had to use their corpses to staunch the inflow."

"What a gruesome experience he must have had," Ayscough said. "Will he live?"

"The surgeon is not too hopeful, sir. Burns and exposure to the sun, no food but for one gull in all those days." Lewrie sighed. "Prouty did inform us he watched *Poisson D'Or* take *Cuddalore* in tow, though, sir. Downwind to the north'rd."

"Balabac!" Twigg exclaimed. "Where else to leeward could he find harbor in which to strip her."

"And haul her in front of his Mindanao pirates to prove to them he's still worth alliance," Ayscough growled. "Aye. So, if it be Balabac, the best and most sheltered harbor is on the north end. See here."

Ayscough shuffled through several rolled-up charts to find the one he wanted, and rolled it out onto his desk. "A good channel to east and west, some small spits of land to the north to shelter against the winds when they come nor'westerly. And a village."

"A pirate village, sir?" Twigg asked.

"Not as I recollect." Ayscough shrugged. "We patrolled around here during the last war after the Spanish came in on the Rebels' side with France. Watered there, once. They were a peaceful enough lot. No big seagoing *praos*, just fishing boats and such. But if the Lanun Rovers put in, they'd have to go along with whatever those devils want, for safety's sake. Better to suffer some looting and a rape or two than end up massacred."

"Are there no better harbors, sir?" Lewrie asked, peering at the chart, which indicated several settlements and coves.

"There are others, to be sure, Mister Lewrie," Ayscough allowed. "But most of those are more suited to *praos*, which may be beached like Greek ships of old. But Choundas needs at least five fathoms of water at low tide to feel comfortable with a proper ship, and this is the only one of which I am aware. If one were to need a snug harbor for repair, and a place to strip another vessel, this would be my choice."

"And anything on the southern coast would be too exposed, no matter how tempting it would be to base closer to open water, I take it," Twigg added.

"The east-west channel leaves two avenues of approach or escape, yes," Ayscough agreed. "And open water, deep water, either way. Without having to claw off a lee shore whilst the winds are out of the sou'east each time one leaves port."

Ayscough drummed his fingers on the chart for a time, then slapped his palm on the chart, making them all jump. "My regards to Colonel Willoughby and Captain Cheney in *Lady Charlotte*. Signal 'Captains Repair on Board.' With luck, if we're quick enough, we may have this bastard at last!"

After his successful defense at Spratly Island, Captain Cheney was almost resigned to playing warship one more time, in company with *Culverin* and *Telesto*. Sir Hugo peered at the chart for a long time in silence, cocking his head this way and that. When he did leave off an irritating humming, he asked a few questions about the various beaches, what the interior was like, what Ayscough remembered from years before about the terrain.

"Do you put my troops ashore here," he finally said. "Three or more miles shy of the village. We shall proceed inland to here, where you remember crops and fields, Captain Ayscough. Open country where I may employ my troops to best advantage. That is, if you're set upon this completely, without reconnaissance."

"Oh, we'll scout, sir," Ayscough retorted. "We'll put a boat down and send her inshore once we're close enough."

"Then I should request some cloth," Sir Hugo said, smiling bleakly. "Something that could resemble yellow silk. A Navy Ensign as well, and some wood for staffs."

"Hey?" Ayscough asked, perplexed.

"I shall also have need of your pipers, sir," Sir Hugo added.

Chapter 11

Lt. Alan Lewrie, Royal Navy, paced his tiny quarterdeck as the hours dragged past. Hands in the small of his back, head down deep in thought. And in worry.

A launch from *Telesto* had assured them that there were two European ships at anchor in the rude harbor at the north end of Balabac Island: one painted a golden ochre with white gunwales and one vessel that bore no masts above her lower masts and tops. There were also at least twenty native *praos* beached by the Filipino settlement, big seagoing boats with hulls painted blood red. It hadn't been much of a reconnaissance; just a quick peek in from seaward at sundown of the second day after they had discovered the lone survivor from *Cuddalore*.

Choundas is a clever animal, Lewrie fretted to himself during his limited pacing. He's sure to have hidden batteries on the harbor approaches. Perhaps hidden batteries off-shore on those low islands that to the north shelter the harbor. His minions in *Stella Maris* had not deployed artillery at Spratly past the palisade's walls, but they could not assume Choundas would make that sort of mistake.

"God help us, it seems he never makes mistakes," Lewrie cursed in the darkness. "And sentinels all along the bloody coast, on all the land approaches to . . ."

"Did you say something, sir?" Hogue asked with a yawn.

"Making my peace with the good Lord," Lewrie snapped, driving the acting lieutenant away. Who would interfere with a man praying at a time like this, Lewrie thought somewhat cynically.

Since *Culverin* was so shallow-drafted, she had been chosen once again, that evening, to ferry troops ashore from *Lady*

302

Charlotte, which had to stand at least a mile off-shore. Three trips they'd made in all, in almost total darkness, with *Culverin*'s decks and former mortar wells packed tightly with *sepoys* and weapons, with field artillery and all the accoutrements for six-pounder carriage guns, two-pounder boat guns on low, wide-wheeled mounts and coehorn mortars with their carrying blocks equipped with four small but wide wheels like dog-carts.

Lewrie also worried about Burgess Chiswick. When he had last seen Chiswick and shaken his hand before he embarked in a ship's boat for the beach with the men of his light company, Burgess' hand had been all atremble. That would seem perfectly natural in any man, but in Chiswick he felt it a sign of his friend's unpreparedness, his weakness.

There had not been time enough to say all the things one wished at a moment like that; there never was. Perhaps that lack of time was a blessing. Burgess had given him a small parcel of personal items he wanted passed on to his family should he fall. A final word for dear sister Caroline, and a promise Burgess had wrung out of him that should he . . . *fall* (there, that platitude again), Alan would swear to take care of Caroline, and the rest of his family as well as he was able in his stead. It seemed portended, that fall, and a gruesome farewell.

Parting with his father was much easier.

"Time, damnit," Sir Hugo had snarled. "Look here, lad. If we make a muck of this, I'm much happier you're safe aboard this little ship of yours. Think kindly of me if you're able. Lift a glass and toast my shade if you ain't. Take good care of the Lewrie name today, and I'll see to mine. Right! Goodbye, me son."

They had put the troops ashore starting at eleven that night on a leeward beach on the western shore of Balabac, a little more than a league shy of the village and harbor approaches. Once that was done, the three ships had stood out to sea, *Telesto* leading and *Culverin* in last place, making a long lee-board out to sea with the wind up their sterns and all sails double-reefed or brailed up to make it a vexingly slow lee-board which would place them due west of the harbor channel just before first light. There, *Telesto* would turn east and beat up into the sou'east summer Monsoon winds, close-hauled as she would lie and with all battle-flags flying.

And Lewrie had prayed. He'd been raised Church of En-

gland, and as much a Deist as any fashionable young gentleman of his class turned out to be after exposure to the better
public schools, the classics and the latest eighteenth-century
philosophy. Lewrie had also been tended to by a steady parade
of governesses from lower stations in life who trended toward
a more personal, vengeful God. Neither curriculum had turned
him off the more than occasional venality, but when life got a
bit too threatening, and he was at the bitter end of his cable,
he found no comfort in a Deist's philosophical detachment, and
sought out the sort of God who could wake up, reach down
and pluck his arse to safety once more.

He prayed for Burgess' safety. He prayed for God's help
that this time they'd corner this Choundas bugger for certain
and carve him and all his kind into stew-meat so they could go
home. He slung in a thought or two for his father (even if he
was a rotten old bastard to me, Lord, he don't deserve gettin'
turned off today), and finally, he asked for help so that his
crew would not suffer too much, that they would win a victory
at a low cost.

"Please let the sentinels be blind as bloody bats, Lord," he'd
muttered in the privacy of his tiny cabins. "Get us past any
batteries without too much hurt. And if you plan to scrag me
today, then let it be quick and glorious. I'd rather not know
about it when it comes, so let me go like Achilles and don't let
the surgeon have me. Better I die a sinner than survive a helpless cripple, Amen."

"Bloody hell!" Capt. Burgess Chiswick swore softly as his
boots sucked and slopped in the muck inland from the beaches.
Lieutenant Colonel Willoughby had at first tried to advance up
from the strand and find cover in the forests for their forced
march. But the woods had turned out to be the ripest sort of
mangrove marsh near the shore, and the rankest, densest, slop-
piest jungle inland from that. But the artillery he had hoped to
deploy on his right flank and center could not be man-hauled
through the slop. Indeed, once deep into the over-growth, no
one could maintain a proper line of march without constant re-
ferral to a compass, and showing any sort of a light was simply
out of the question.

So it was only the first light company that made its slow
way through the jungle on the right flank, and the rest of the
battalion had to march in two company columns nearer the
beach, with the guns squeaking along the beach itself in

the firmest sand. The second light company led the advance in skirmishing pairs, as scouts, to feel out the way ahead, and silence any pickets they encountered with cold steel or a twisted garotte fashioned from their *puggarees*.

So far, thank God, they had met none, though it was impossible to know if a scout skulked in the deep jungle, spying out their march and sending reports to the village to prepare them.

Chiswick shivered with a nameless dread. Except for his man Nandu who marched alongside him, he could barely espy any of his *sepoys*. They were *jangli-admi*, used to jungle in their home territory of Bengal. Hunters, farmers, poor villagers raised at the edge of a dark green labyrinth where danger lurked. A lush green Hell full of terrors so much greater and more threatening than Carolina woods.

Chiswick asked himself for the thousandth time why he had ever thought he wanted to be a soldier, why he had thought life was better in regimental service when he could have bowed to Fate and clerked or farmed back around Guildford. What stupidity had led him to this, he trembled? He was not so much afraid of death as he was afraid of making a total, ineffective ass of himself when battle was joined! There seemed to be no steady center he could seize to calm his trembling. A mosquito whining in his ear set his heart to racing every time. He felt as if his heart wanted to leap free of his chest and escape even if he could not! And when Nandu got mired, and put out a hand on his shoulder for help, he almost jumped out of his skin and yelped with fright.

"Oh God, don't let me fail," was Chiswick's prayer.

"Come on, oh one pubic hairs!" Col. Sir Hugo St. George Willoughby rasped in a harsh whisper of near-perfect Hindee. "I've seen Rajput whores carry heavier loads. Subadar-major ji, *march* our children!"

White teeth and eyes gleamed briefly in the darkness above the white facings, the white *dhotis* and *kurtah* shirts of their uniforms. The red-faced colonel-*sahib* seemed angry, but they knew him well by now, and knew it was not true anger. They'd seen enough of that by then, as well, and knew the difference. He'd ask them to do this one last dangerous thing, and then, if they were successful, they'd all go home to Calcutta. They were soldiers, no matter what their humble beginnings, no matter how low their castes, and colonel-*sahib* Weeby treated them as such, with respect, unlike so many of the *gora log feringhee* officers. They would do this one last dangerous thing.

For Colonel Weeby-*sahib*, who threw all his efforts into their training and welfare. For this regiment of theirs that had become a haven from Indian society, and the decreed-by-birth poverty of their castes. They may have started as poor *ryots* or *zamindars*, but they were treated like all-conquering *kshatriya* now, men of the warrior caste. They had not always conquered during the war in the south against Hyder Ali and Tippoo Sultan, or against the French, but they had tried.

"God grant us a victory," Sir Hugo mumbled. "A victory that lets me keep my colonelcy so another damned fool straight out from England don't fuck this regiment up! Lord knows, it's all I've got and I'll be damned if I'll throw it away for nothing, either. So give us victory. And a Mention-in-Dispatches back to 'John Company' would go down right nice, too. A little loot for my old age, if you've a mind I enjoy one after this day's bloody work. And look after my lad. I really do mean to do right by him. A little time to do right by him would be sweet. Even if I can't, let him show well today. Carry on the family line with honor and glory. You know me well enough by now; I don't make silly promises I don't mean to keep, so I won't make any to You now. And the regiment. Lord, I know they're heathens, but they're good lads. Well, most of 'em, anyways. Let 'em carry all before 'em and not bring any dishonor to the colors."

Captain Fessenden interrupted what else Sir Hugo would add.

"Sir Hugo, sir," he whispered. "The jungle seems to be thinning out on our right flank. And the beach is bending east. I think we're getting close."

"Chandra-ji," Sir Hugo muttered, snapping his fingers at his bewhiskered orderly. "Run tell Chiswick-*sahib* to halt, then feel to his right. Major Gaunt, halt the column. Grenadier company to form on the right. Captain Fessenden, your light company to form on the left front across the beach for now, fifty paces forward."

"At once, sir."

That taken care of, Sir Hugo found himself a fallen palm log on which to sit and await the results of his scouts. He amused himself by drawing designs, which he could not see, in the sand with a walking stick.

"Sir?" Captain Chiswick whispered, having been led to him by Chandra after a quarter-hour had passed.

"Good morrow, Captain Chiswick," Sir Hugo grunted. "What have you to report?"

"Forward of where we stand, sir, the jungle continues for about three hundred yards, thinning out as it goes, and the footing is much firmer. Firm enough I adjudge for artillery. Beyond that, there are flooded rice fields and other crops," Burgess said with a shaky tone.

"Damme!" Sir Hugo spat.

"But there are some sort of firm dykes surrounding the fields, sir, that are wide enough for gun carriages, and for troops marching three abreast," Chiswick offered. "And the flooded fields are more inland, beyond our right flank. If we stay close to the beach with our left flank, we could extend across the dry fields, and use the flooded portion as a shield for our right."

"How much of a front?"

"I estimate about four hundred yards, sir," Burgess reported, his body trembling with anticipation and feeling as if he had already spent all of his strength in scouting and pacing off the area.

"Too bloody wide for eight and a half companies," his colonel muttered. "Look here, where's the bloody village, then? How much of it do we threaten if we form as planned?"

They paced out into what little moonlight was left to draw a map on the beach sand with Chiswick's sword tip, using dry palm fronds that could be more easily seen.

"Once we incline right, sir," Chiswick stated on his knees, "the beach here west of the village is rather wide. I saw what I took to be pirate boats beached, starting here. They'd have artillery in the bows that could enfilade us. Thin undergrowth and trees for cover above the beach, extending south for about one hundred yards. Open fields with knee-high plantings, God knows what, all around it. If we come in from the west instead of striking north, we'd have three hundred yards frontage before our right flank brushed up against these dykes and rice-fields."

"Chandra-ji. Summon officers here to me," Sir Hugo commanded, then rose and paced while Chiswick continued to draw out a more elaborate plan of the village and its environs. "Palisades, captain? Any batteries your scouts could discover facing inland?"

"Bamboo or palm logs for a palisade, sir, quite low,"
Chiswick replied, intent on his model that he was now adorning with fronds to represent the jungle, the dykes and the palisade. "We saw no guns on the inland wall, sir. There is a
French battery on the point."

"Right about here, where the coast trends east?" Sir Hugo
asked, using the toe of his boot for a pointer.

"Yes, sir. Dug in as a three-sided redan made of palm logs
and sand. It's been planted with bushes on the seaward side to
conceal it. Two, perhaps three guns, my scouts told me, sir,"
Chiswick went on, intent on his model. It felt so much like
playing soldier, childish and silly, to be on his knees once
again, re-creating his little fields of battle, moats and entrench-
ments out of the clay or sand soil of his native North Carolina.
He'd stolen clothespins off the lines to be "troops," and they
could be anything—Romans, Indians or Grenadiers.

"How big is the village?" Sir Hugo asked, kneeling down
slowly so his joints didn't creak and pop. "How far does it extend, sir?"

"About a quarter-mile, sir. On the far side, there is more
jungle, much thinner than here, and some dry fields. And another battery of guns, about a mile farther on," Chiswick said,
gathering more material for his construction. "There's a
quarter-mile of open lands beyond the far palisades and the last
native houses, pretty much the same as this end. The rice-fields
don't extend that far, though, sir. They approach the center of
the village's back walls."

"Which would funnel us down as we fight our way in," Sir
Hugo mused. "And if we came up from the south?"

"We'd have to split the regiment on either side of them, sir.
Or get channeled into the dykes."

"Damme if I'll play that game," Sir Hugo snorted with de-
rision as the white officers and their native *subadars* came to
hear their orders.

"Gentlemen, we shall change direction right at the halt and
go east, through the thin jungle south of these rice-paddies and
fields," Sir Hugo began. "Our ships shall be sailing into harbor
from the west, so we must attack from the east, to create the
greatest confusion. One gun battery here, Captain Fessenden,
on the point ahead of us. Have your best *jangli-admi* emulate
Kali's Thuggees and silence them. Now."

"Yes, Sir Hugo," Fessenden whispered back.

"We shall form regimental front facing west here, in the

jungle east of the village. Captain Chiswick, your light company to seaward on the new right flank. You get two of the light two-pounders. And I want you to silence this battery to your rear that your scouts discovered. Grenadier company in the center, with the bandsmen and the six-pounders spaced between companies. Coehorn mortars two hundred paces to the rear of the grenadier company and prepared to support either wing. Major Gaunt, your half-battalion shall form our left, with Captain Fessenden's light company on your extreme left. Supported by one two-pounder. The other three two-pounders placed between line companies across our general front. Be ready, Captain Addams, to shift your pieces to repel any threat. Our front shall be between three and four hundred yards, so we shall have to form in two ranks only. With the rising sun at our backs, we should have good shooting and they should not. Caught between our ships and our attack, we ought to create a little confusion for them, and their only line of retreat will be to their boats on the beach, or across our front through the paddies, then south into the jungle. Major Gaunt, you shall decimate them should they retreat south. Captain Chiswick, you shall threaten their boats. Once in position, prepare torches so you may set fire to as many as you are able as you advance down the beach. Do not allow the bastards to put their bow guns into play. There is a low palisade about this village. I shall not wish us to actually enter the damned place and get cut up in their little lanes. Better we incline right and seize the beach, though it may be necessary to at least gain control of the eastern palisade. Questions, gentlemen?"

"Once we incline towards the beach, sir, do we let the enemy flee into the paddies and jungle?" Major Gaunt asked.

"If they seem to be in great disorder, sir. You may find it necessary to torch the southern palisade and houses, then form your half-battalion as a screen to prevent any counterattack from that quarter, facing south, once we've taken the beach and the east wall," Sir Hugo stated after a moment's thought. "The fire should guard your back well enough, and discourage anyone left in the village."

There were no more questions. Sir Hugo dug his watch from his breeches pocket and held it up close to his nose, swiveling in the faint moonlight to try and read it. "It lacks a quarter-hour to three, gentlemen. And the Navy tells me true dawn is at a quarter to six. False dawn, a quarter past five. I wish to be in position at least half an hour before that. Then let the Navy have first honors. Return to your companies. Good luck, God speed and let us be on our way."

Chapter 12

"Time to do what they pay us for, Cony," Lewrie said decisively, shoving away what was left of his cold breakfast. "Damme all Banyan Days."

Gruel, cheese, hard biscuit and small beer, with a banana for something sweet in place of a duff. Several days of the week were meatless, according to the strictures of the Victualling Board, and Lewrie felt no desire to end up paying for anything he wasn't given permission to issue, even in foreign climes.

"Seems t' me, sir," Cony said with a rueful expression, "if'n they warnts us t' fight strong an' all, they'd make allowance fer a battle, they would."

"Wish to God somebody would," Alan grinned in return. He put on his coat, squared away his sword and donned his hat.

He stepped out onto the quarterdeck, just forward of the sweep of the tiller, and leaned one hip against the after capstan-head. The crew had stowed their hammocks away already, and stood swaying to the motion of their little ship. Evidently, they were not very hungry this morning, either. The cook was shoveling coals into the sea off the lee side, and his assistant was hauling up a bucket of seawater to put out his galley fire.

"Good morning, captain," Hogue said from his station to leeward.

"Good morning to you, Mister Hogue. Any signal from *Telesto*?"

"Nothing yet, sir."

But even as Hogue spoke, there was a tiny, shielded light that appeared on *Telesto*'s taffrail far ahead of them, a tiny spark from a single lantern to show them where she was, followed by another from *Lady Charlotte*.

311

"Mister Hogue, prepare to put the ship about onto the wind," Lewrie ordered. "We shall tack in succession."

"Aye, sir!"

"Second light, sir," Murray pointed out. "Her helm's down." And the two weak glims swung slowly into line as one, then ghosted to the right across their bows. A minute later, *Lady Charlotte* did the same. And when *Lady Charlotte*'s faint glimmer was directly on their starboard beam, so, too, did *Culverin*.

"Shake out our night reefs, Mister Murray. Mister Hogue, beat to Quarters," Lewrie ordained. "And hoist the colors now." Furniture, chests, provisions, livestock from the manger and any flimsy temporary partitions were struck below out of harm's way. The decks were sanded for better traction for the gunners and brace-tenders. Fire-buckets were filled, and slow-matches lit in case the flint-lock strikers of their carronades did not function properly in the damp of a tropic dawn. The guns were run in on their wooden recoil slides, the tompions were removed from the muzzles and stowed out of the way. Serge powder cartridges were rammed firm, then heavy twenty-four-pounder solid shot were trundled down the barrels and seated with a thump from the rammers. Charges were pierced with metal prickers to give vent for the ignitions to come, and the secure lashings on the gunports were uncleated. They would wait to prime their guns until they had the enemy in sight, since the humidity might spoil the powder in the pans. With the pans empty, they check-snapped the flints to see if they had a good edge that would spark well against their checker-scored metal frizzens, then covered them with leather flaps to keep them dry.

"Stand easy," Hogue instructed from the gun deck. "Mister Owen, I'll see to those swivel-guns now."

The night was still dark as a boot, with the island and its harbor a faintly heavier darkness ahead of their starboard bows. A thin line of charcoal grey heralded the false dawn to come, against which the masts and sails of the leading ships could almost be seen now and again. For a lookout gazing to seaward, they would still be invisible, their wakes lost in the general roil of offshore waves, to leeward of the rising sun.

" 'Ope this last'un'll do fer all, sir," Cony muttered, fetching Lewrie one last bracing mug of coffee.

"This coffee, or this battle, Cony?" Lewrie asked, amused in spite of the circumstances.

"Be nice t' see England agin, sir." Cony smiled.

"Be damned nice to see tomorrow's sunrise."

"The battery to our rear is silenced, Sir Hugo," Chiswick told his commanding officer, breathless from a quick jog-trot. "Mindanao pirates, mostly, with four Frenchmen to supervise. We lost four men."

"Oh, I am most dreadfully sorry, sir," Sir Hugo replied, but it was a perfunctory sort of sorrow. He dragged out his pocket watch and read the face with more ease. "False dawn. Quarter past five."

"Yes, sir."

"No enemy to our rear? No scouts or sentinels along our front, to your determination, Captain?" Sir Hugo went on.

"No, sir."

"Very well. Rejoin your company and stand by."

Sir Hugo paced out in front of his command. He could barely see most of it. The grenadier company lined up two deep, spaced out wider than he'd like, instead of shoulder to shoulder, but they would have to suit. The bandsmen with their drums and fifes, and Ayscough's borrowed pipers, tricked out in cast-off red tunics. The six-pounder field guns, and behind them, the coehorn mortar crews. The color party nearest him. The other companies were too far away, too deep in the fringes of jungle.

He could see them in his mind's eye, though. Could imagine the formed ranks standing easy with their muskets, with their officers to the front. One word of command and they would be erect as ramrods, ready for what this bloody morning would bring.

It was hot and close, the air like a steaming barber's towel, and just as moist. There was no hint of rain, and the ground across which they would advance was dry and firm. It was simply the humidity of these climes making a slight mist that tried to hide the village from them. And hid his regiment from the foe.

Willoughby paced farther out in advance, with his *subadar*-major, the senior native officer, and his bearer, Chandra, by his side, until he was about twenty paces forward of his color party.

He consulted his watch again.

"Sah!" his bearer gasped with a quick, indrawn breath.

Willoughby looked up to see a woman and a boy child, not

fifty paces off. They had arisen early, perhaps to fetch water or firewood for the morning cooking. They froze in place, almost froze in mid-step, as they might at the sight of a tiger. Then the woman gave out a shrill yelp and turned to run back to the village.

"Oh, for Christ's sake!" Sir Hugo groaned, "You brainless old bitch! They're not even friends of yours, and you'd warn 'em?"

"Mebbe jus' frighten, *sahib*," Chandra commented, outwardly calm though his luxuriant white mustaches quivered as he chewed the lining of his mouth.

"Either way, she'll give the alarm," Sir Hugo sighed. He took a deep breath and opened his mouth.

"Reg'ment!" he boomed out loud as Stentor, and could hear the bushes in the jungle shiver as his men awoke from their standing doze.

" 'Tal'ion!" came the answering shouts from Gaunt and the other half-battalion commander.

" 'Shun!" Sir Hugo roared as he drew his smallsword from its scabbard. Lush green stamping of feet, muffled by vegetation. "Uncase the colors!"

Two color parties came forward from the jungle, the flag-staffs held low like pikes, until they were out in the open. The leather condoms were stripped off, and the colors rolled out to hang limp in the light breeze. Two British ensigns, one borrowed from a warship; the King's Colors. Two Regimental Colors, one real, and one made up from light canvas and painted to resemble the pale yellow silk of an authentic regiment.

"Light companies will advance, fifty paces forward!"

The light companies left their extreme flank positions to trot out ahead of their line companies as skirmishers. Once in position, Sir Hugo turned to face the front, raised his sword on high and gave the decisive order. "The regiment will advance!"

There was a ruffle of drums, an eldritch wailing moan, a thump of a bass drum, and then came music—of a sort. It would be the first time anyone on this island, any Lanun Rover, had ever heard it—perhaps the first time French seamen had ever heard it—as the pipes began "All the Blue Bonnets Are O'er the Border."

And the regiment emerged from the jungle. Two light companies. Two color parties. What seemed to be two grenadier companies massed in the center. And two ranks of men in red coats and white *puggarees*, with their muskets held at shoulder arms, legs moving to the lilting skirl of the pipes and the crash and roll of the drummers' sticks, more urgent, more compelling than the stately one hundred steps a minute of a usual line battalion. As the ranks approached, Sir Hugo could see the expressions of his *sepoys*. First the same sort of alarm he wished to see on his foes, their eyes rolling at this strange new invention, and then the grins of delight. It wasn't *feringhee* tootles on fifes, this strange new music. It was wild, heathen, barbaric and brutally martial. They seemed to like it.

A Lanun Rover was making water off the parapet of the low palisade. He had roistered with his fellow pirates all night long, drunk deep of coco-palm arrack. Had had his way with a frightened Filipino girl, who had known better than to complain, not if she knew what was good for the health of her family, and her own life. She'd warmed from fear to resigned sullenness to his play, and he'd left her one tiny Spanish coin.

In the midst of his plashings, though, here had come a woman and child running for their lives from the forests. And he could barely see some strange men standing out in the open by the edge of the jungle. Oddly dressed men, but he had shrugged it off. There was no telling what the French would do next. And then had come a great shout. A series of shouts. And the most hideous screeching and howling he had ever heard in his life. A whole raped village or ship had never made such a noise!

And then he could see men. A lot of men, all dressed in red, with muskets at their shoulders, and between groups, he could see a cannon or two! Just like the tale the survivors had told of the slaughter on the island. He realized he'd forgotten his original order of business entirely, and had pissed down the entire front of his *pareu*. He drew a trembly breath and gave a great shout.

Capitaine Guillaume Choundas liked the Orient, liked Oriental women. They were so tiny compared to the Breton girls back home, or the languid cows he'd had in Paris, all beef to the heel as if they had to emulate some artist's reproduction from the classics. Tiny, childlike and helpless. Chinese girls were all right, he supposed, but he much preferred the fine-boned slimness of these Filipino natives. Indian whores in Pondichery were fine, but sometimes too European in their features, too wide across the beam, and cursed with heavy thighs.

Something had awakened him, and he lay there for a while, with the girl beside him. She'd fallen into an exhausted sleep after he'd used her well into the evening. She twitched and shuddered in some dream, perhaps reliving the memory of what he'd forced her to do in that endless night. As he relived it, he became prick-proud. He reached out to touch her smooth, peachlike bottom, and she stiffened, her breath halting as she awoke on the mats in his shore hut.

Tiny to begin with, not over fourteen years old and coltishly slim to top the bargain. He rolled over atop her, took hold of her wrists to hold her face-down, and insinuated a knee between her legs.

"Tuan!" she begged. He liked it when they were aware of what was in store. The first time was delicious. Whore or virgin, to be forced was outside their experience. But to repeat the act, and feel their fear, even their revulsion, that was sweetest of all. This was ancient Gallic, this rapine.

He used his thighs to part hers, to push her adolescent bottom up in the air a little so he could enter her from behind. She was panting in fear now, whining with pain as he forced his large member between the dry lips of her entrance, could almost taste the wetness waiting inside her once he was past the gates . . .

"He', merde!" he exclaimed, as he heard the strange noises, freezing in mid-stroke. *"Zut! Putain!"*

The bamboo door was kicked open and his first officer stood there, bending down. "The English are here! Troops and guns to the east, *Capitaine!*"

Choundas shoved the girl away from him and scrambled for his breeches and stockings. "From the east? And just how did they land, eh, Gabord? Get back to the ship and prepare to up-anchor. We'll have the 'biftecs' sailing into harbor with the sun behind them. I join you as soon as I stiffen our miserably blind allies. Go!"

He stood and donned his shirt, and gave the crawling girl a kick of frustration. "Goddamned useless, all of them! *Putain!*"

"Reg'ment!"
    " 'Tal'ion!" came the chorus.
    "Halt!"
Rather a lot of 'em, Sir Hugo thought, surveying his ene-

mies. The village had come to a boil, and what seemed a brigade of pirates had emerged, swords, spears and antique muskets waving, each done up in gold, silk and batik-printed cotton as sleek and shiny as an army of poisonously colorful sea-snakes.

"Reg'ment will load!" he shouted, stepping back toward his color party. "Skirmishers, engage!"

The light companies broke off into skirmishing pairs, one man standing, and one kneeling. With a howl of rage, the Lanun Rovers lurched forward, thousands of them in an avenging mob. The flat crack of muskets sounded from the light companies as they opened fire. Once a man had discharged his piece, he would retreat a few paces behind his rear-rank man, who would cover him while he reloaded, and take a shot of his own. Back they came, giving ground slowly and raking the leading pirate ranks with ball, dropping a man here, a man there. The pirates checked, shying away from being the first man to die, while their leaders urged them on.

"Light companies, retire!" Sir Hugo howled. "Reg'ment! First rank, kneel!"

Emboldened by the seeming retreat of the skirmishers, the pirates found their courage again, and started walking forward. At first uneasily, then with greater boldness. Some began to trot, to save their lungs and strength for hand-to-hand combat later. Some braver souls broke into a run.

Sir Hugo stepped forward again, to ascertain that both light companies were safely out of the line of fire on the flanks.

Brown Bess was a hideously inaccurate weapon. Massed gunfire shoulder to shoulder settled the day, delivered at a man-killing sixty yards. To strike a man in the middle, one aimed high for the neck at that range, even so. With his regiments deployed in only two ranks Sir Hugo had to wait to let them come even closer.

"Cock your locks!" Sixty yards, and mechanical crickets sang.

"Present!" Fifty yards, and barrels were leveled with sighs.

Forty yards. "Fire!"

The long line of musketmen erupted in a wall of gunpowder and the crackling reports of priming pans and rammed charges sounding like burning twigs. Pirates screamed in surprise, and went down like wheat.

"Second rank . . . cock your locks! Present . . . fire!"

He could hear the rattle of ramrods just before the second

rank pulled their triggers and the snapping and crackling rang up and down the line. More pirates howled, with pain this time, and he saw men driven backward, thrown off their feet and back into their mates by the sledgehammer blows of .75 caliber lead ball.

"Guns!" he yelled, turning to glare at Captain Addams. And the artillery went off, rippling from the center half-battery of six-pounders out to the flanks where the converted boat-guns barked and reared on their trails.

"Well, Goddamn!" Sir Hugo spat. He'd never seen the like, not in the last war certainly, not at Gibraltar for sure. The air was so moist with humidity that when the artillery discharged, those brutal barrels not only flung out a huge cloud of spent powder and sparks, they split the air with their loads, leaving a misty trail behind.

The best one could expect from any field gun loaded with canister and grape was about five hundred yards, and one usually saw the end result, but not the passage of shot. But this time, it was as if each barrel had flung out a giant's phantasmagorical fist of roiled air that went milky as the shock wave passed through it. Like a row of shotguns, the artillery cleaved great swathes from the enemy ranks. Densely packed as they were, they went down by platoons. Before each piece, there was a mown lane of dead and dying twenty yards across and three times that deep!

"Platoon fire!" Sir Hugo roared. Now for the grim business to continue in normal fashion, to create a continuous rolling volley of fire up and down the line. No one could fire faster and with more effect than an English-trained regiment.

The pipes had been skirling out something Sir Hugo had never heard before. Now, with no need to set a marching pace, they broke into civilian strathspeys and reels. "The Wind That Shook the Barley," "The Devil among the Tailors" and "The High Road to Linton." Hard-driving, frightening in their hurried pace, for all their gaiety, dance tunes turned to the Devil's business amid the rattling of musketry and the deeper-bellied slamming of the guns.

"They're breaking!" Major Gaunt shouted. "They're retiring!"

"Cease fire! Load! Fix bayonets!"

"Fix . . . bayonets!" the officers repeated eerily, and the sudden silence was broken by the slither of steel, steel that winked and glittered in the dawn.

"The 19th will advance!"

The pipers cut off their latest reel, extemporizing themselves back into a march as the coehorn mortars began to fire. Explosively fused round-shot lofted overhead to burst in mid-air above the wavering hordes of pirates, who had just begun to screw their courage back to the sticking post, and were ready to charge once more.

It was the guns that decided the matter. Slow to roll between the company ranks, the regiment had to stay to a half-step pace even with the pipes urging them on, so that they looked as if they minced forward, but with both ranks bearing musket-stocks held close to the hip, barrels and wicked bayonets inclined forward. And for bayonet work, the *sepoys* had to be closer together, shoulder to shoulder, reducing their front to a bare two hundred yards.

With an unintelligible shout, the native pirates came forward to meet them once more, sure they could sweep around both flanks and encircle them this time, and chop them to bits at last.

"Reg'ment . . . halt!" Sir Hugo screamed. "First rank, kneel! Cock your locks! We'll serve 'em another portion of the hottest curry they've ever tasted, by God!"

Chiswick pulled back the fire-locks of his two pistols, stuck his smallsword into the turf in front of him, and stood ready, with his nerves singing a gibbering song as that manic horde came on.

"By volley . . . first rank . . . fire!"

Twenty muskets discharged at sixty yards. Perhaps nine foemen went down, trampled by their fellows in their rage to get at Sir Hugo's men.

"Too damned soon!" he cursed himself. "Second rank, present! Fire!" Another eight or nine pirates were hammered backward.

Too few once more! The artillery *subadar* looked at him, and he waved his arm vigorously. Both boat-guns bucked and reared, slashing the front of that implacable mob with grape and canister, and finally they checked their headlong rush, shying away for a second.

"Goddamnit!" Chiswick moaned. He had shot all his bolts, and there was nothing left. Although his immediate front was cleared, there were at least a hundred foe sweeping his right flank. He fired both his pistols, and took down one man, then cast them aside and drew his sword from the earth. "Bayonets! Charge!"

His troops went in at a rush, weapons fully extended, to be met with shields, spears and sword blades. At first, they carried all in front of them with bayonet and musket-butt. Chiswick carved a spearman's face open, reversed and ripped the belly from another to his left. Nandu gave a great scream as he was shouldered backward and stumbled under the point of a third. Chiswick hammered the edge of his blade across the foe's back; the man screamed like a rabbit with his spine cut in half, then twitched uncontrollably.

"Dahnyavahd, sahib, dahnyavahd!" Nandu shivered as Chiswick helped him to his feet. *"Achcha!"**

"Bloody young fool!" Sir Hugo grumbled. "Captain Yorke, face right, double time and reinforce the right flank! Support the guns! Nineteenth! Charge!"

Once again, two slim ranks of musketeers had shattered pirate ambitions, and the guns had strewn the ground with howling, broken wounded. It was time to go in with cold steel, or be driven back.

"One more charge!" Choundas insisted.

"No *tuan*, boats!" his interpreter shouted back as the pirate chieftain raved and slobbered with wrath. "He want go now! No good this place no more! No good fight on land!"

"He'll sail off and leave all his treasure?" Choundas sneered coldly. "Sail off and abandon all my gifts? All the muskets and shot?"

"He say, you want, you stay and keep, *tuan*," the interpreter finally replied. "He go Illana. Steal more nex' year."

"Filthy cowards," Choundas whispered. "Filthy pagan brutes!" He turned on his heel and stalked off for the waiting launch, his face burning with anger at this final failure of his ally, this final proof of their utter uselessness. And with his own failure as well. He had no hope now of a raiding season. He'd seen the two regimental colors and the massed bands, all the artillery that only two one-battalion units could array. Where had the heretical English gotten so many ships to carry that many troops, and then land them on the eastern shore, where he had not expected them? Only an overt operation with

---

*"Thanks, sahib, thanks! Good!"

the full strength of the Royal Navy could put such an expedition at sea and support it this far from India. Something had happened to force the English to take the lid of secrecy off. Had another war broken out back home of which he was unaware?

"To the ship," he snapped at his waiting boat crew as he sat down in the stern. "And quickly!"

"He', merde alors!" his new coxswain groaned, pointing out to sea. *"Les Anglais!"*

Chapter 13

"Have we the depth to stand in closer?" Hogue asked.

"And a quarter less four!" the leadsman shouted from up forward as if in answer.

"Captain's Ayscough's recollections say we do, sir," Lewrie replied with a happy but fierce grin on his features. "Helm down to larboard, quartermaster. Ease her up as close as she'll lie to the wind, full and by."

"Full an' by, sir!"

"How we got this far, I don't know, sir," Hogue enthused as they swept into the harbor in *Telesto*'s wake. "I was sure that was a battery on the point, but nary a peep from them did we hear."

"Most thoroughly in the barrel, drunk as lords, I expect," Lewrie said, clapping his hands with anticipation as he strode to the quarterdeck nettings to look down upon his gun deck. "Mister Owen, I give you leave to open fire as you bear!"

"Thankee, sir!" Owen shouted back. "Wait for it, lads, wait for it!"

Culverin could work her way much closer to the beach than any of the other vessels, where her short-ranged but heavy carronades had the advantage. There was a mushrooming pillar of smoke coming from beyond the native settlement. He could see a coehorn mortar shell burst in mid-air, most excellently fused, against the rim of sunrise on the horizon over the trees. And on that wide beach was a gunner's fondest dreams—stationary targets drawn up with their prows resting on the sand, their guns pointing inland and useless! At least twenty blood-red *praos* abandoned by their crews engaged against the troops on the far side of the little town.

Telesto opened fire first, followed by *Lady Charlotte*. Sand

322

flew into the air as eighteen- and twelve-pounder balls struck the shore. Boats twitched and thrashed as they were hit, their sterns leaping out of the water to fall back downward and flail the shallow waters like a beaver's slap. Masts and paddles went spinning in confusion, and hulls split open as they were flayed with iron.

"Two cables, sir!" Owen shouted. " 'Ere we go, then! Number one gun . . . fire!"

Lewrie stood amazed as the flower of smoke and flame gushing from the muzzle expanded into an opening blossom larger than any he had ever witnessed, the air torn apart with weapons' song, and the twenty-four-pounder ball's progress marked by a misty trail of shock and turbulence as if they were firing combustible carcasses. The ball hit a *prao* on the beach, square on the stern-posts, ripped right through the light wood and flung a shower of broken timbers and laced-together planking into the air. There was a sudden, screeching *rrawwrrkk!* as the ball rivened her from stern to stem, to topple her in ruin.

"Huzzah, lads, do us another!" Lewrie cheered his gunners as they took aim with the rest of the starboard battery. "Quartermaster, luff us up a mite. Slow our progress to give the gunner more time to aim."

Smoky, belching crashes as the carronades spewed out their loads, thin dirty trails of roiled air emerging from the sudden mists of burned powder and then the slamming screech of ravaged wood ashore as another *prao*, then a third, leaped like frightened birds at being touched with iron, screaming their *rrawwrrkk, rrawwrrkk!* as if in their death-agonies.

"Carry on, Mister Owen," Lewrie said, picking up a telescope for a better view. In the distance, he could see villagers running one direction, pirates in their gaudier clothing falling back into the village and down to the beach to save what they could of their ships, to fall in irregular clots of terror as iron shattered and keened in clouds of sharp shards and splintered wood.

He directed his glass forward to see *Telesto* take *Poisson D'Or* under fire. The French ship had cut or slipped her cables, abandoning her anchors, and was getting underway, even as several ship's boats thrashed oars in her wake to catch her up.

"By God, I do believe that's our bastard Choundas in one of those boats!" Lewrie crowed aloud. "Can't even fight from your ship this time, can you, you pervert? Have to let some more of your people do your dying for you, you poxy whoreson Frog?"

Poisson D'Or had gotten her jibs and stays'ls set, her spanker over the stern hoisted, and had let fall her tops'ls, but they were a-cock-bill and not yet fully braced round to draw the wind. She was not yet under full control, but her larboard gunports flew open in unison, and muzzles emerged. She would fight it out.

And right in *Telesto*'s wake sailed *Lady Charlotte*, paying off the wind a little as if in trepidation of getting too close, but her guns crashed out a solid broadside, and the sea around *Poisson D'Or* erupted in feathers of spray, and several balls hit her low, "twixt wind and water."

A hefty explosion drew Lewrie's attention back to the task at hand. A ball had hit one of the *praos* on her foredeck where her guns were seated, igniting a powder store, which had blown up in a great dark bulb of smoke and flame. The *prao* had disintegrated and was cascading down in smoldering chunks onto two other boats to either side, setting them alight and scattering the pirates around them.

"A guinea for that gunner, Mister Owen, my word on it!" Alan vowed.

"And a quarter less five!" the leadsman called out over the roar of the battle.

"Damme, sir, we could get inshore even closer!" Hogue shouted. "We're dead astern of *Poisson D'Or*'s anchorage. Deep water, sir!"

"Luff up again, quartermaster. Pinch us closer inshore!" Alan commanded. "Mister Owen, load your next broadside with canister and grape-shot! Put an iron hail on the beach and skin the bastards!"

Culverin rounded up into the wind, ghosting almost to a stop with her sails shivering and thrashing, until the leadsman found only three fathoms of water. The quartermaster put his tiller over to the windward side to fill the sails with wind, and she heeled hard for a moment before riding back upright. They were now only a single cable off the beach, two hundred yards, just as the central part of the village came abeam. Pirates were falling back in disorder through the town, massing on the beach and heaving to launch their boats for an escape.

Alan could almost hear the sudden fatalistic sighs, the groans of alarm, as they saw the trim little ketch with her guns run out and the muzzles staring them between the eyes.

"As you bear ... *fire!*" Lewrie called.

Five carronades lurched inboard on their recoil slides. Five crashing bellows of noise, stink and shudders. Five great blooms of smoke towered over her sides and drifted away to leeward through her sails. Five fists of God struck the beach, hewing away everything they touched, taking down the bamboo log palisade behind the beach, scything the palms above the high-tide line, lashing the thatched rooves. But most particularly, flailing the sand into a bloody cloud and scattering Lanun Rovers, bowling them over like nine-pins. And when the smoke cleared, the beach had been abandoned by the living, with only the broken dead and whimpering wounded remaining.

"Merciful God in Heaven!" Murray whispered in awe at what they had wrought. "Bloody ..."

"And again, Mister Owen!" Lewrie bade. "Grape and canister!"

The next broadside only thrashed at the heels of the pirates, who fled that threat of death, back into the palisaded village for shelter, bold sea-rovers too afraid to save their ships.

"They're afire up yonder, sir," Murray pointed.

Lewrie raised his glass and looked toward the eastern end of the harbor. *Praos* were burning there, smudging the dawn with greasy coils of smoke and ruddy flame. "I see soldiers on the beach there!" he rejoiced. "Mister Owen, direct your fire upon the village walls and clear the way for the troops!"

"Aye, sir!"

"And a half, two!" the leadsman warned.

"I believe we may haul our wind a point or two for now, men," Lewrie told his helmsman. The long sweep of the tiller was put over to starboard, and the bows swung off the wind. Deck crew flung themselves onto the belaying pins to free the sheets and ease the set of the sails to draw more wind.

And *Culverin* slid to a stop.

"One fathom and a quarter!" the leadsman called out, much too late.

"Well, shit!" Lewrie fumed, turning red with embarrassment at running solidly aground, right in the midst of a battle. Of all the places to choose from, he'd staggered right onto an uncharted sandbar!

"Uhm, she struck mighty easy-like, sir." Murray frowned, his mouth working hard. "Prob'ly didn't do no damage t' her quickwork. Her gripe an' her cut-water is solid enough, and she's a tough old lady, she is, sir. Flat-run bottom, too. Ahh . . . er, that is, fer when the tide goes out, sir."

"Ah," Lewrie sighed, wishing it was possible to die of mortification. "Hmm. Yes. The tide. Bloody hell!"

"Aye, sir," Murray commiserated, taking a pace away.

"Well, damn my eyes!" Lewrie sighed heavily, one hand on his hip and gazing up at the masthead for clues. "Look, have 'Chips' go below and sound the forepeak to see if there's any leakage. A hand that's a good swimmer over the bows to see how hard she's . . . stuck! And boat crews into the launch and cutter to see if we may tow out the stream or kedge anchor and work her off. Before we're left high and bloody dry 'til supper-time."

"Aye, sir!" Murray replied, knuckling his brow.

"Damn all hard luck, sir," Hogue told him.

"I feel like such a goose-brained . . . *twit!*" Lewrie confessed.

"Happens to the best, I'm told, sir," Hogue added, though he had to work at keeping a straight face.

There was a shattering explosion just at that moment, which spun them about in their tracks. Something had set fire to *Cuddalore*, anchored farther to the east—perhaps a few die-hards from the prize crew Choundas had put aboard to safeguard her from being plundered by his allies. She had just gone up in a titanic blast as her magazines burst, ripping her into a plume of fragments.

Farther east, and out in deeper waters, *Poisson D'Or* was still fighting, with *Telesto* close aboard on her left beam as they fell off the wind to the north for the chain of tiny islets that guarded this harbor from the opposite Monsoons. *Lady Charlotte* had continued on easterly as she could, to cross the French ship's stern and rake her before turning north as well on the far side, to lay *Poisson D'Or* in a savage cross-fire.

"To think that but for a moment of stupidity, we could be a part of that!" Lewrie said with a bitter growl. "God, what a glorious fight they're having. And we've missed it!"

"Grand seats, though, sir," Hogue replied cheerfully. "Right in the stalls, as it were, to witness it."

Owen came up the starboard ladder to the quarterdeck and gave a cough to let them know he was there. " 'Scuse me, sir, but I've flat run outa targets, sir. No more o' those pirates t' be seen, an' half the village knocked down s' far, sir. Want me t' keep on?"

"No, Mister Owen. Continue to fire with one gun only, and I wish to have your other gunners for boat crews. We have to kedge off before the tide runs out too much."

"Aye, sir."

"Sir!" Murray called. "Those boats yonder! From Poison Door, sir! Tryin' t' land on the beach!"

Lewrie seized his glass and climbed up on the shore-side bulwark to peer at the two longboats being rowed ashore.

"Choundas!" Lewrie howled with frustration. "Can we lay a gun on him? He'll get away into the jungle, else!"

"Er, nossir," Owen almost moaned, wringing his grimy hands in frustration. "He's outa our gun-arcs, 'less we had a fo'c'sle chase-gun. An' it don't look like he'll put it anywhere close t' our poor range!"

"He'll get away at last!" Lewrie snorted in disbelief. All of their labors and suffering for nothing . . . again! "Mister Hogue!"

"Sir?"

"Take charge of the ship, sir," Lewrie exclaimed. "Keep Mister Murray and Mister Owen with you, and defend her should the pirates try to get off the beach and take her now she's aground. Use your artillery over our heads should we run into trouble on the beach. Are the boat crews assembled? Good. Arm them. Muskets, a pistol each and a cutlass. Cony, fetch my case of pistols!"

The cutter had eight oarsmen, a bow-man and Cony as coxswain. The launch had a total of eight men aboard. Instead of a kedge anchor lowered into the stern-sheets, or one of the stern cables, the men were surprised to receive arms.

"Row for the beach!" Lewrie snapped, "Row like the Devil was at your heels. I want yon bastard!"

They cast off and put their backs to it, digging in deep with their oar-blades and grunting with the exertion, Lewrie's cutter in the lead. He stood in the bows, loading his pistols.

"Not straight for the beach, Cony. Take us east up the coast for a ways before cutting in. Closer to them before we ground."

"Aye, sir," Cony replied, angling the tiller-bar under his arm to steer them more slant-wise across the lapping wavelets.

* * *

Choundas looked up from gazing at the bottom-boards of his boat with a bleak expression. The eastern palisade of the village was yet being defended, but he could see most of the pirates streaming off for safety, south through the longest wall and over the rice-paddies into the jungle. The remaining *praos* on the strand were on fire, damaged or under the guns of the ketch-rigged gun-boat. There would have been no safety aboard *Cuddalore*, minus her topmasts and rigging, so after picking up his tiny watch party from her, he had set her on fire, so the "biftecs" would not have the satisfaction of recapturing her.

"She's aground, I think," he said to no one, turning to look at the saucy little ketch. "And a dropping tide."

No means of escape there, either, even if his small party could take her.

Coehorn mortar shells were bursting farther inland, over those rice-paddies, and he could hear the muffled popping and crackling of musketry in a steady, rolling platoon-fire. They would have to run that deadly gauntlet across the paddy dykes to escape. And from the continual, thin screaming they could barely hear, that way was being turned into a killing-ground.

Choundas swiveled aft to look at his beautiful ship. *Poisson D'Or*, one of the finest thirty-two-gunned frigates that had ever swum, was almost hull-down up the fringe of islets, wreathed in a mushroom cloud of gunpowder, with two of her masts gone. As thinly manned as she was, after losing *La Malouine* and his best hands, she was putting up a marvelous fight, but she was going to lose. It was fated.

And he wasn't aboard to lead the fight in her, when she was battling for her life, as a captain, as an officer of the French Navy should be! No, he had waited too long, trying to put some spine into that churlish native chieftain. Who could have expected the damned English to land their troops on the east side of the island and march overland through all that trackless jungle, and then attack him from the *west* with their ships? Only the insane would beat against the wind and attack from leeward, when the best approach would have been to ghost into harbor with a following wind, with the rising sun at their backs to ruin his gunners' aim. Everything had gone wrong!

"What shall we do now, sir?" one of his surviving *garde de la marines* asked him in a soft whisper close to his ear. Choundas lifted his face to gaze at him. Nineteen years old, the equivalent of an English midshipman, an officer-in-training.

Choundas wondered just what sort of lesson Valmette was learning today.

"Steer for the beach, *timonier*," Choundas instructed his new cox'n. "Land us west of the land fighting, but out of range of those guns on the ketch. This side of the eastern palisade. We shall take a path through the village, go out its western side, and get into the jungle away from the 'biftecs' artillery. Then strike down the western coast and find a decent seagoing boat. A *prao*, perhaps."

"Two boats setting out from the ketch, sir," Valmette warned. "To kedge her off? Could we take her?"

"Too few of us," Choundas snapped, having already counted heads and discounted their chances. "And their boats are no better than ours for deep ocean."

Choundas took a second look. Small as his party was, he had more men, well-armed men, than what appeared in the English boats.

"Hostages, perhaps, *mes amis!*" Choundas brightened. "For safe passage out of here. *Timonier*, steer to meet them in the shallows. Men, ready your muskets! I want prisoners. An officer if we can."

"They're turning to meet us shy of the beach," Lewrie told his boat crew. "We're going to have a fight on our hands, lad. A devil of a fight! Load muskets and pistols, and lay your swords to hand."

Lewrie looked back at *Culverin*. There was not one gun barrel that could be cranked around in its port to lay on the French. Even if they could have pointed, the range was too great. He looked back to the shore, to the eastern end of the beach where the boats were on fire; it would appear that his father's regiment had been held up in their advance. There would be no aid from that quarter, either.

I could meet 'em gunnel to gunnel, he thought, but one peek over the side canceled that thought. The water may have been clear as gin but there was the niggling little matter of his not being able to swim, and boats were sure to be capsized if they meleed like miniature frigates! The water was so clear it was impossible to judge its depth but for the faint sunrise shadow of his hull on the bottom-sand, and he judged that to be over his head, perhaps a full fathom still.

"Cony, put your tiller over hard a'larboard," he ordered.

"We beach and meet them with the boats for cover and steadier aim."

"Aye, sir," Cony parroted, and shoved the tiller bar over. The second boat in his wake followed suit a moment later.

"We'll be the stone fortress, he'll be the enemy squadron, men," Lewrie told both boat crews to cover his queasy fear of being drowned. "Once ashore, get down below the gunnels and we'll skin 'em. And if they want to come to us, then be-damned to 'em, I say! Save your pistols for when they get close."

The French boats changed course once more, and the oarsmen laid almost flat on their thwarts to drive faster, once they saw their plan for a miniature naval engagement was for nought.

"Row! Row! Get us ashore, quickly now!" Lewrie urged his hands. The French were aimed right for him, trying to be upon them even before they could jump over the gunwales or get the oars shipped! Musketeers lay in the bows of the French boats, and one or two tried shots at long range. A stroke oar aft by Cony shrieked and fell back among his mates, upsetting the furious stroke, his neck shattered by a ball.

"Toss yer oars!" Cony yelped as the surf heaved them forward on a limp wave. The cutter lurched and slithered with a wet hiss as her keel ran onto the sand.

"Damn the oars!" Lewrie shouted. "Over the side and make ready!" The bow man leaped shin-deep into water and started to drag the bows farther up the beach, while the oarsmen let go of their oars and took up their weapons. The bow man was hit, flung backward with a grunt of ruptured lungs, which encouraged them to make haste and slither over the off-side gunwale instead of standing and leaping out with a care to staying erect and dry.

Muskets were popping, and bits of the cutter were flying into the air as ball splintered the wood. Lewrie had gone sprawling once over the side, and when he raised his head, there was the lead boat not ten yards off, ready to ground almost alongside!

"Cock your locks . . . take aim . . . fire!" he shouted as he drew his first pistol. Six muskets spat out a thin volley. The seventh had soaked priming and only squibbed with a dull *phutt!* But three French oarsmen had been hit as they stowed their oars and took up weapons from the bottom boards. The second French boat, the one with Choundas aboard, was landing ten yards farther up the beach. Lewrie drew back the lock of his pistol and took aim at a French musketman. He pulled the trigger and his weapon squibbed.

"Well, damme!" he spat, tossing the useless pistol aside and drawing its mate. By then, his target was kneeling out of side on the far side, his arm appearing as he rammed down a fresh load. He popped back up and Lewrie fired. This time, the weapon gave out a sharp bark and the Frenchman fell back with a shrill scream as the top of his head was blown off. "Fire at will!"

His second boat grounded, and the musketmen came running for shelter behind his cutter as four muskets fired. The French sailors were returning fire at a suicidal range.

"Cony, our crew. Steel!" Lewrie snapped. "Witty, give 'em a volley and then join me!"

He drew his hanger as the last of the French weapons popped. "Boarders! Away boarders!"

He went round the bows of his boat and ran straight for them.

Pistols were going off. A Frenchman leaped up with a musket to confront him, but was shot down. Another spun about in his tracks and fell into the surf with a great splash. And then Lewrie was upon his first man. Two-handed, he slashed upward, forcing the man's long musket barrel high, stamping forward with his left foot to get inside the reverse swing of that hard metal-plated butt as it came for his skull, only pummeling his shoulder. A quick downward slash that left him kneeling, and his foe was howling with pain, his belly laid open from left nipple to right hip.

A cutlass came probing from his dying foe's right, tangled in the man's flailing arms, and Lewrie drew back and thrust, taking this enemy in the stomach. Lewrie sprang erect, pushing himself forward to stay close, so Choundas' musketeers could not take a shot at the melee and pick out Englishmen to kill. He was met by a flaxen blonde sailor who was trying to decide if he wanted to finish ramming home a charge in his musket or drop it and draw his cutlass. Lewrie towered over him and cut downward through shoulder and collar bone, bringing a huge gout of blood that shot into the air like a fountain.

There was a volley of musketry, and two of Lewrie's hands went down as they clambered over the boat to get at the Frenchmen. From higher up the beach, there was an answering volley. Choundas had gotten his crew organized and they fired.

Able seaman Witty had taken his hands out to the right flank where they could get a clear shot.

"Pistols, Witty, then charge!" Lewrie howled. "Come on, men! At 'em, Culverins!" Without looking to see how many hands remained he waved his sword and ran for the second French boat.

Choundas waved his men on, too, so no more shots could be fired at his own hands. Those who had fled from the first boat found nerve to turn and join the charge as their gallant captain led them.

They met in the shallows between the boats, up to their knees in water with the light surf surging up to their crotches, and their feet sinking into the swirling sands as the waves lapped in and drew back. Witty's hands were coming in from the shore side, forcing the fight into deeper water. Pistols were popping, and a feather of spray from a near-miss leaped up between Lewrie and the young Frenchman he faced off with.

He's a gentleman, Lewrie thought, seeing the fineness of the young man's smallsword. They crossed blades, and Lewrie was sure of the man's background. He had a good wrist and arm, and quick nerves, meeting a direct attack with a prime movement, going to a high guard over his head at fifth to fend Lewrie off, then swinging under his blade to second before launching a thrust of his own. Lewrie let his left hand go and counter-thrust at the young man's lower sword arm, which was blocked by a marvelously well-executed circular parry to spiral Lewrie's point wide to the left. But Lewrie drew back out of range, two-handing his hanger again, and cut over from left to right, dragging the officer's blade back up to a high fifth position. As he did so, he waded forward to get inside the man's guard, feinting a thrust. The young man's reflexes, learned in an elegant sword-master's salon, made him step back, and he tripped over his own feet, bouyed free of the sand momentarily by the surf. As he came back up, spouting and blowing, flinging stinging salt from his eyes, Lewrie overhanded a thrust down like stabbing at some fish and speared the young man through the side of the neck. With a gasp of surprise, the man sank once more with bright arterial blood looping and trailing in the sea.

"*Vous!*" Choundas screamed, beating his breast and striding easily through the surf toward Alan. "*Timonier a mois*, I think 'e slay ze wrong man in zat alley! *En garde!* I eat your brains and shit in your skull!"

Lewrie waded shoreward to meet him, to avoid the clumsy fate of the younger officer, sword held at third, waiting for Choundas' first move. It was like an explosion!

Choundas had no grace, no elegance to his swordplay, coming from a rougher school. With howls he was upon Alan with his smallsword swinging like a cutlass. Blades rang, not in beat, but with the rasp of a farrier's hammer, and the shock sang up Lewrie's arm like a bell's echo with each blow. Try as he would to thrust and counter-thrust, to slash with the point and cut over from defensive guards to direct or even indirect cuts, Choundas was always there, quick as lightning, all attack and very little defense of his own.

Lewrie was forced to give ground, half a step at a time, and the sea swirled higher up his body. From the ankles to his shins to his knees, then to mid-calf.

Captain Osmonde warned me I'd meet a truly dangerous man if I kept this up, Lewrie frowned, recalling the Marine officer aboard his first ship, the one who had taught him the true rough and tumble of steel, and guided him through his first adult duel on Antigua.

Choundas was pressing forward, both of them up to their waists in salt water and being buffeted by the incoming surf. Lewrie swung down and left to ward off a chest cut, felt a leg reach out to tangle with his to bring him down and stumbled right and away, into shallow water. Choundas' sword came arcing up out of the water glistening in the dawn light with water droplets, and he met it high left, the beat of steel on steel forcing his own blade back to touch his left cheek!

A shoulder lunging forward, and Lewrie stumbled again, reaching back with his left hand to steady himself. Falling sideways into the surf, with Choundas splashing forward to tower over him, and a wicked razor-honed blade descending in a powerful two-handed overhead strike!

He got his hanger up to parry at fifth, got his left hand under his hip and swept out with his legs. Cut directly down and forward under the off-balanced Frenchman's blade to clash with the hand-guard!

Choundas reeled back, almost going down himself. Lewrie came up soaking wet with his left leg under him and thrust with all of his might to leap like a porpoise with sword arm extended as rigid as a pike-staff. And missed!

His sword's point went over Choundas' left shoulder as the man ducked. Their bodies slammed together, and Choundas was going over backward, but he hefted Alan high enough over his shoulder to heave him a few feet away, to splash into water deep as his waist!

Drowning! Lewrie's mind screamed as he tried to get his feet under him, tried to fight the rush and shove of another wave. Tried to find a breath of air for lungs thumped empty by Choundas' body!

Lewrie lurched erect, coughing on the water he'd taken in, his eyes burning with salt and his hair streaming down his face.

Choundas! The final thrust! DEATH!

Arm across his chest to defend, sword point held low at prime, the blade pointing down as the thrust came for his throat. A sting on his left hip as the smallsword's point bit him, and he was going over backward again, and could feel Choundas' feet near to his own!

He kicked with his right foot as he landed on his left hand and knee. The heel of his shoe took Choundas in the nutmegs, making him hiss like a serpent! Choundas bent over with the sudden agony, and Lewrie came up with all he had left.

Bright steel and sterling silver came sweeping up from the sea bottom, under Choundas' guard, under his upraised sword drawn back for a killing hack. Salt water streamed in a glittering arc as the hanger swept upward. Choundas flinched back to avoid it.

Lewrie could feel the shock in his wrist, up his arm, as his sword made contact, flicking point-low to point-high following the angle of the razor-sharp edge as he straightened his wrist and turned it. And Choundas was falling backward, his sword hand to his face!

A wave of surf surged high as Alan's shoulders as he got to his knees following that stroke, and Choundas was tumbling about in the water, rolling and tumbling shoreward like a piece of flotsam.

"Don't tell me I actually *killed* the bastard!" Lewrie gasped in surprise, retching saliva and salt water as he rose to his feet and shuffled onto the beach, sword ready at fourth slightly across his body should Choundas be shamming.

But there was red in the water, pink on the man's shirt.

And when Choundas managed at last to crawl ashore on hands and knees, his sword forgotten, he was screaming. Screaming and writhing like a worm in hot ashes, moaning and whimpering pitifully between his screams and patting his face. Rolling over and over, twitching like a serpent.

"Strike, you bastard!" Lewrie hissed, prodding that body with the tip of his sword. Choundas kicked out with his left leg and hit Lewrie painfully on the kneecap, and without thought, Lewrie slashed down hard into the back of Choundas' left calf, which raised another howl of pain and set him rolling and thrashing again.

"Sir!" someone was yelling. "Sir, we done fer 'em, sir! They struck, sir!"

Lewrie stepped back from Choundas and looked up to see Cony coming toward him, limping from a sword-cut across the outside of his thigh, and blood matted in his sweaty blonde hair.

The beach was littered with dead and wounded, and the most of them French, Lewrie was happy to observe. The rest were sitting in a fearful knot, covered by his men's weapons.

"You failed!" Lewrie crowed at Choundas. "You failed at everything you tried, you bloody murdering bastard! We beat you, understand me?"

"Alan, what's all the shouting about?"

"Hey?" he said, swiveling to see Captain Chiswick coming down the beach, leading two spaced ranks of his troops. His hat was gone, his sword was slimed with blood and he winced with each step, but he was whole. "Bloody Hell, where did you spring from? Took you long enough."

"Were you impatient for my arrival, dear Alan?" Chiswick said with a rasp of gunpowder in his throat. "Had to clear this damned eastern palisade first. Had a busy morning, have you?"

"Tolerably busy, yes," Lewrie replied. Now that the fight was over, now that they were safe in the hands of the *sepoys* of the 19th Native Infantry, he could allow his usual weakness to creep over him as he loosed the awful tension of mortal combat. A moment later and it was all he could do to stand.

"Much hurt?" Chiswick inquired anxiously after wiping his sword clean and sheathing it to come to his side.

"Pinked in the hip," Lewrie allowed, sinking down on his haunches to let Cony undo his breeches and take a look at it.

"Not deep, sir," Cony assured him as he laved it in the sailor's universal nostrum, fresh seawater. "T'ain't bleedin' much, neither, so 'e didn't get ya nowhere vital. Make ya stiff fer awhiles, sir. Could I 'ave yer breeches, sir, I could bind it. Er if ya got a clean handkerchief in yer pocket, sir, I could fother a bandage over'n it fer now."

"The bandage, Cony," Lewrie said with a shaky laugh. "Damned if I want to go back aboard bare-arsed."

Chiswick dug into his tailcoat pocket and offered a small silver flask, which Alan drank from gratefully. "Um, a lovely brandy you have there, Burge. I was half-expecting some of that corn whiskey I remember from Yorktown. Are those bloody pirates beaten yet?"

"Slaughtered like rabbits," Chiswick assured him with a harsh laugh, which made Lewrie look up at his face. There was something odd about Chiswick now. Some new-found brutality he hadn't had when they'd put him ashore the night before.

"And how did your regiment fare?"

"Main well," Chiswick replied, shrugging and taking a sip of brandy himself. "I got my light company in a hellish predicament. Shot my bolt a bit too soon and had to melee with the bayonet. But the boat-guns cleared the way for us, and your father sent reinforcements to our flank. We lost about fifty dead and wounded, it looks like. Fourteen of them from my company, I'm sad to say."

"Sorry to hear that."

"Aye, they were damned good lads," Chiswick added, nodding and getting to his feet. They could hear the pipes skirling as the regiment took the village at last, and the guns fell silent. They could also hear the braying of Lt. Col. Sir Hugo St. George Willoughby as he issued some new command and laughed at something that amused him.

"Seems I'm still blessed with a father," Lewrie smirked.

"Here, what's the matter with this bugger?" Chiswick demanded, toeing Choundas in the ribs, which brought on another bout of howls. "Hmm, hamstrung neat as any Indian'd do a straying slave. He'll be a 'Mister Hop-kins' from now on, if I'm any judge. Don't take on so, you bloody bastard. You'll hang before it heals!"

Chiswick used his foot to roll Choundas over.

"My word!" Chiswick gulped.

"Kill me!" Choundas pleaded in a harsh whisper. "Kill me!"

"Our captum done fer 'em, sir," one of the sailors boasted.

Choundas had taken the hanger's edge across his lips, and the hard steel had knocked out several teeth—knocked them out, or cut them out, for the upper gums were laid open on the right jaw. The right cheek was pared back to show the chipped bone beneath, and the nose was hanging free on the right side. Choundas' right eye teared blood from the slice that had chopped it in half like a grape. And a ragged patch of eyebrow and forehead hung open, matted and gory with clotted blood and sand.

"Well ain't you the pretty young buck, now, Captain Beau-Nasty?" Chiswick drawled, once he had gotten over his shock. "I say, Alan, you do bloody nice carving when you've a mind. Remind me to have you for supper next time we have roast beef!"

"Kill me!" Choundas croaked. *"Messieurs, je implore . . . !"*

Chiswick drew a pistol and checked the priming.

"No!" Lewrie shouted, reaching up to put a hand on Chiswick's wrist. "Leave him the way he is. Let him live with it."

"Yes, I suppose Mister Twigg'd prefer a hanging at that," Burgess sighed, putting the pistol back into his waistband.

"I think he'd prefer M'seur Choundas go back to France as he is," Lewrie replied. "As a warning. An example of failure. Of what the next bastard'll get should they *dare* cross our hawse in future!"

"Well," Chiswick nodded, seeing the wry sense to it, "s'pose he could always do himself in later."

"My dear Burgess," Lewrie chuckled, "the way this poor wretch's luck is going, he'd probably miss with a pistol to his skull! Failure has a way of staying with you, don't ye know."

There was a dull boom that sounded across the harbor, making them turn to look seaward. A cloud of smoke wreathed *Culverin* as she sat higher and dryer as the tide ran out. But coming into the bay was a frigate.

"Almighty God!" Lewrie snapped, getting to his feet and doing up his breeches. "Cony, get the hands back to the boats. We have to defend our ship!"

"Flag, sir," Cony said instead. "T'ain't Frogs, sir."

"What are they?" Chiswick asked.

"Well, Goddamn, I do believe it's a Spanish ship of war!" Alan blurted as the white-and-gold flag curled out lazily.

"Bet they're going to be mightily displeased with us," Chiswick prophesied. "Poaching in their private preserve and all."

"Back to the ship, anyway. Burge, I trust I'll see you later.

After Captain Ayscough and Mister Twigg talk their way out of this."

"Think you they can, Alan?"

"Burgess, Twigg is half a politician," Lewrie replied, smiling. "He can talk his way out of anything!"

V

"Iam valete, formosi!
Nos ad beatos vela mittimus portus,
magni petentes docta dicta Sironis,
vitamque ab omni vindicabimus cura."

"Now fare ye well, ye goodly youths!
We are spreading our sails for blissful havens
in quest of great Siro's wise words,
and from all care will redeem our life."

Catalepton, V 7–10
—Virgil

Chapter 1

The Board Room at the Admiralty was blessed with a huge fireplace trimmed in wooden carvings of navigational instruments. Tall candles lit the chilly chamber against the gloom of a late February afternoon. As they huddled in front of the fireplace, lifting the tail skirts of their uniform coats to warm their frozen backsides, Lt. Alan Lewrie studied the white-and-gilt ceiling, the light-toned wood paneling and the parquet floors.

He'd only been inside the Admiralty once in his life, back when *Shrike* had paid off in '83, and then only to the first floor, to cool his heels for hours in the infamous Waiting Room before going to the basement to wrangle for even more hours with a clerk in a tiny monk's cell of an office, perched on tall stools to stay out of the two inches of water that had seeped in from a recent Thames flood. All to balance the ship's books and military inventory.

"Ahem," Captain Ayscough grumbled as the double doors opened and two elderly officers entered. First was Admiral Lord Howe, First Lord of the Admiralty, followed by Admiral Sir Samuel Hood. In their retinue were several civilians. Lewrie was amazed to learn during the introductions that they were Secretary of State Lord Sydney, and the first Secretary to Admiralty, Phillip Stephens. They took their seats behind a long table, and Ayscough, Percival and Lewrie were seated on the opposite side.

"We have read your report with great interest, Captain Ayscough," Lord Howe stated. "The lieutenants' journals as well. With not only great interest, but, may I be the first to say so, great admiration for your energetic prosecution of this matter in the King's name."

"There is also, milords, gentlemen," Lord Sydney added,

"the report from Mister Zachariah Twigg, as regards the . . . uhm . . . political matters beyond the purely nautical and military scope of your recent expedition. The gentleman commends you and your officers in the most forthright manner, captain. For your zeal and enterprise, sagacity and competence. In fact, his only regrets or recriminations are the unfortunate demise of his fellow Crown . . . uhm . . . emissary, Mister Wythy, in Canton. And the untimely arrival of that Spanish frigate at Balabac Island. Had that not occurred, we might have been out and gone before any civilized nation could ever learn of our presence in those waters, assuring us total secrecy, start to finish, and then the book could have been closed shut on this affair forever."

"Well, the French know of it, milord," Admiral Hood scoffed. "To their detriment, even if the Dons did free Choundas and his men."

"There are some niggling . . . uhm . . ." Lord Sydney posed, "ramifications anent our relations with the Spanish crown regarding this expedition. Violation of their territorial waters, for one. Violation of their sovereign sanctity ashore. Some remuneration paid, *sub rosa* I need hardly inform you, to their Viceroy-General in Manila, to help restore that native village, one would assume."

"Should the moneys ever find a way of trickling down through their Viceroy's fingers," Lord Howe smirked, cracking his bleak and patrician visage for a brief moment.

"Fortunately, there was hardly any mention of the incident in the . . . uhm . . . American public notice from the crew of that whaler we freed," Lord Sydney continued. "That . . . nation . . . has more on its rebellious little mind than taking time to be in any way grateful for the lives and freedom of some of its . . . uhm . . . citizens. Gratitude to their mother country is in rather short supply on that side of the Atlantic, and most likely shall be, for a generation to come."

"Whilst gratitude here at home, for the heroes of this venture, shall have to be rather thin as well, sirs," Lord Howe intoned, turning in his chair to see if Lord Sydney had anything further to add. Lord Sydney inclined slightly towards the older admiral, allowing him to proceed. "By God, sirs, had we leave to print your reports in the *Marine Chronicle* or the *Gazette*, it would be an eight-day wonder! The populace would chair you through the streets! However"—here he sobered once more, and settled back into a strong resemblance of the rebel General

George Washington suffering an acute attack of gas—"for diplomatic reasons, none of this may ever see the light of day. I fear, Captain Ayscough, that the inestimable credit due you, Lieutenants Percival and Lewrie, shall never be adequately expressed by a grateful Crown, or an equally grateful Admiralty. Until such time as another war occurs with France, any word of this glorious expedition of yours must never pass your lips, not even to your dear ones."

"I ... that is, we, completely understand, milords," Ayscough nodded sternly. "And obey your strictures without question, it goes without saying."

"There shall be no public commendation," Lord Sydney smirked, "but that does not mean there shall be no expression of pleasure for your valiant deeds. Name the reward dearest to you, my good sir, in reason, and we shall endeavor to please."

"An adjudgment by Droits of Admiralty in the matter of prize money, milords," Ayscough said quickly. "Not for my own gain, let me assure you. But for the ship's people. Most especially for those widows left without succor. I believe the reckoning of what we took at Spratly, and at Balabac, was in excess of five hundred thousand pounds, assigned as Droits of the Crown. Even an eighth of that for warrants, petty officers, able and ordinary hands would reward them for all their magnificent courage and loyalty, even when they didn't know what we were doing out there."

"Nothing for your officers or yourself?" Lord Howe queried.

"Active employment, naturally, milord." Ayscough reddened, feeling ashamed to even dare ask for anything for himself. "The heartfelt cry one would hear from any Sea Officer."

"And do, daily, belowstairs," Admiral Hood stuck in with a short bark of amusement. "By God, Captain, your concern for your people is perhaps even more commendable than any deed you've wrought the past two years! Well said, sir. Damn well said!"

"I believe it would be impossible to deny such an aspiring and courageous officer the opportunity to ply his profession," Lord Howe assured him. "Active commission it shall be, sir, a Fifth Rate frigate at least! And your personal selection of first officer."

"Lieutenant Percival, sir," Ayscough said quickly.

"Make it so, my dear Stephens," Lord Howe told his principal secretary, who was scribbling away at the end of the table.

It would have been nice for Ayscough to have wanted a share of all the booty they'd taken from the Lanun Rovers, Lewrie thought as the praise was heaped on their shoulders. It would have been nice for him to have included his poorly paid officers in that request for reward.

But Lewrie was not as rankled as might have been his usual wont. His father had been one of the first into the chieftain's personal lair, and had emerged dripping diamonds, rubies, pearls and emeralds, with his bearer, Chandra, grunting under the strain of a small chest of more loot. What Ayscough reported as captured, thence to be given to the Crown as their exclusive Droit, was only about two-thirds of what had actually been there, the rest shared out among the *sepoys* and officers of the 19th Native Infantry.

Before *Telesto* had sailed for England from Calcutta, he'd had one final supper with his father. Lewrie had regretted that Draupadi, Apsara and Padmini were no longer in his father's employ, but the loot had restocked his *bibikhana* most wonderfully well, and it had been the grandest send-off he'd ever had. Sir Hugo had handed over certificates worth enough to pay off his creditors back in England. And, as a final parting fillip, had given Alan a little present or two as well.

A reddish gold necklace set with diamonds and rubies, heavy and showy enough for royalty. And a triple strand of pearls with matching earrings, bracelets and rings fit for a queen. He hadn't had a chance to have them appraised by a Strand or St. James' jeweler yet, but he was sure he was at least five thousand pounds richer.

"And for you, sir?" Lord Howe asked. "Lieutenant Lewrie?"

"Hum?" Lewrie said, coming back to earth from his monetary musings. Come on, you toadying wretch, think of something to ask for, a reward you really desire! No, he countered; ask for something noble-sounding, or they'll know you for the greedy swine you really are!

"Well, there is the matter of Midshipman Hogue, sir," Lewrie began, shifting in his chair. "It would be a hellish come-down for him to revert from acting lieutenant to one more midshipman, milords. If there is an examining board to sit soon, I assure you he could pass it. And were there an officer's berth come available, I know it would please him no end should he gain it."

"Acting lieutenants made on foreign stations have no need to sing for their supper," Hood stated. "Consider him a commission officer."

"And I would desire him aboard my ship, milords," Ayscough added. "As the least senior officer, to season him properly."

"Make it so, Stephens."

"Aye, sir," the longterm servant replied. "Nothing for yourself, Mister Lewrie?"

"Well, there is the matter of my father, Mister Stephens, milords," Lewrie stammered out. "Sir Hugo St. George Willoughby."

"Ah," Lord Sydney replied with a suddenly prim expression, his lips popping together. "Him. You're his ... uhm ... son, are you?"

"When we left Calcutta, the question of his brevet to colonel of the 19th Native Infantry was still up in the air, milords. And he more than proved his worth, on every occasion."

"He wishes to remain in India, in 'John Company' service?" Lord Howe asked, incredulous that anyone would want such an exile.

"He does, sir. His men adore him. And he ... well, whatever his faults, milords, he is a good soldier and a good officer, and he truly does care about the regiment."

"Hmm, s'pose that's best, after all, him to remain out there," Lord Sydney sighed. "I'm told he's cleared his creditors? And there was a Captain Chiswick mentioned in Twigg's report. I assume he is to stay in that regiment as well? A cater-cousin to you, is he?"

"A good friend, milord. We were together at Yorktown. In fact, I shall be going down to Guildford to visit his family next week, to deliver news of him, and some presents for them."

"There wouldn't be a pretty sister, would there, Lieutenant Lewrie?" Lord Sydney teased.

"There is indeed, milord," Lewrie said, blushing for real.

"Active duty, naturally," Hood intoned, lifting a wary brow. Officers of his generation were extremely leery of younger men who contemplated marriage too early in their careers— they were forever lost to the Sea Service, in their opinion, and even the hint of an imminent attachment was suspicious to that worthy. "I trust, hmm?"

"Active duty, yes, milord, that goes without saying," Lewrie answered quickly. That was the response they expected, much as he wished he were brave enough in the face of this exalted gathering to tell them what he really thought: that if he was truly as rich as he dared hope, they could have his resignation and bedamned to all the nautical deprivation he'd suffered since his father had damned near press-ganged him into the Navy as a midshipman back in 1780! After the last bit, he'd had nearly enough, and no public thanks or fame from it, either!

But that could never be said, he realized. And shaming himself before Ayscough, Hood and Howe by such a declaration was a thing he didn't have the courage for. He could only hope that they would file him away for future employment, hopefully very close to home for a change. Else they'd allow him a few months' shore leave and forget their promises, as great men were wont to do, and let him fester most happily on the half-pay list to the end of his indolent days!

"I once, milords, awarded Lieutenant Lewrie command of a small brig of war off Cape François," Admiral Hood said, turning to face his fellows. "The war ended before he could make his mark with her, but he more than made up for it with little *Culverin* this time. I am convinced he would be wasted in some other captain's wardroom."

Oh, sufferin' shit! Lewrie groaned to himself, aghast that they would send him right back to sea. It was peacetime, after all! The Waiting Room below his feet was crammed to the ceiling with half-pay officers so eager for employment they'd crawl from Whitehall to Limehouse Reach on their hands and knees, in a dog-collar, if they could crawl up a ship's gangway when they got there!

Lewrie's throat was already dry, and he essayed a cough. The artificial soon became the genuine article. Maybe, he mused, if they think I'm going to expire right here in the Board Room from the flux or something, they'll delay it, at least. He dug out his handkerchief and began to bark into it.

"Are you well, Mister Lewrie?" Lord Sydney inquired with some alarm on his face. "A glass of something, perhaps . . ."

"The change in weather, milord," Lewrie "struggled" to reply. "All this cold and rain here in England, after the tropics . . ."

He cut that statement off, paling at what they might do about it. Idiot! He could have kicked himself. No! Wrong thing to say, you damned fool! Goddamn their solicitous little hearts, they'll probably ship me right back where I just came from, and think they do me a blessing! Dear Lord Jesus, just a little help here, please?

"A small vessel below the Rates," he heard Lord Howe instruct Mr. Stephens. "In a somewhat healthier and warmer climate than the Channel Squadron, I should think. What do we have at present?"

Pray God they've all sunk! Lewrie hoped, turning a wild gaze on Stephens. Stephens had been first secretary to the Board of Admiralty for years, the Lords Commissioners for the Office of High Admiral, surviving one First Lord after another. More than any other man in England, he was the one who truly had his fingers on the pulse of the Fleet such as no senior officer or appointee had. Stephens executed more administrative power in an hour of scribbling and reading of files than most fighting admirals did in an entire career of bloody battles. He knew of every opening, every promising officer, every fool and every little scandal.

Stephens gazed back at Lewrie, sizing him up, cocking his head to one side as if reading his career file from memory. Lewrie ducked a little; Stephens most probably knew of *his* every scandal, too!

"Nothing suitable immediately, milord," Stephens said after pretending to glance through a sheaf of documents. "There is a possibility coming due in a few months, though. Lieutenant Lewrie shall find it familiar, I believe. A ketch-rigged gun-boat shall be ending her commission and returning from the Mediterranean station at Gibraltar. We had discussed sending her to the Bahamas, after her refit, you may recall, milord?"

"Ah, yes," Howe nodded. "We've need of swift, shallow-draft vessels out there, Lewrie. If it's not piracy in the Bahamas, it's our Yankee cousins, violating the Navigation Acts and stealing our carrying-trade, selling their shoddy goods without paying customs due. And the Bahamas are so temptingly close to that new nation, so easily reached from their southern ports. Rather a dull little back-water but for that, as I remember. But just the place for an ambitious young officer to show his mettle, hey? What say you, sir? Ready to conquer the King's enemies a little closer to home?"

Lewrie remembered the Bahamas as well, and none too fondly. The most fun he'd had there was watching the dogs roll over halfway through their afternoon snoozes. Well, Nassau on New Providence was sporting enough after sundown, and heaps of American Loyalist families had made the place their home after the war ended. Surely one or two of 'em'd have daughters! He swore to be more careful this time.

I really should never set foot in the Admiralty again, he told himself: Every time I do, I come out feeling raped!

With an exuberance he most certainly did not feel, he was at last forced to say, "Words cannot express my gratitude, mi-lords, sir. Naturally, I shall be delighted to serve in any capacity! Lead me to 'em!"

"That's the spirit!" Lord Howe exclaimed approvingly. "That's our sort of lad, Lewrie! I knew you'd be pleased."

Yes, he thought. It seems I'm fated to be your lad for bloody ever, don't it?

Afterword

From some of the fan mail I've received, I may have erred on the side of authenticity when it comes to ship-handling and the jargon of the sea in use in the eighteenth century.

This came from a deep-seated fear that someone a whole lot saltier than I ever hope to be would telephone me in the middle of the night and call me a lubberly "farmer" if I got it wrong. It also came from my abiding love of ships and the sea; I figured that if I was already "there" (so to speak) I might as well learn something for myself as well. And, too, there is the tendency among sailors to speak a language that most landsmen don't readily understand, a language I must admit I have to partly relearn every boating season, but one that makes me one of "the fraternity."

Ships propelled by the wind didn't deal in numbered bearings on their compasses; their crews spoke of WINDWARD or LEEWARD. Going up to WINDWARD, eighteenth-century square-riggers could not get closer than roughly 66 degrees to the apparent wind (6 points of 11¼ degrees each). When sailing as close to the wind as they would lay, they were said to BEAT, to go FULL AND BY, or lay CLOSE-HAULED.

If their destination was up to WINDWARD, it could take forever to get there, sailing aslant in a zigzag that took two or three times the actual straight-line distance to fetch a port.

They would BEAT or proceed CLOSE-HAULED on either the STARBOARD or LARBOARD tack. When the wind crossed the STARBOARD (right) side of the vessel first, and they sailed a course to the *left* of the baseline, this was called the STARBOARD TACK. When the wind crossed the LARBOARD (left) side of the ship first and they proceeded to the

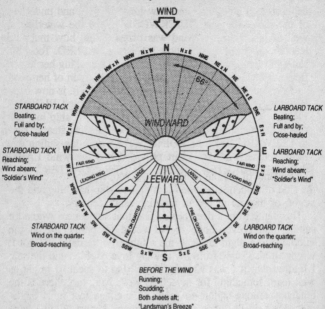

POINTS OF SAIL AND 32-POINT WIND-ROSE

right of the base course, this was called the LARBOARD TACK.

(I warn you now, sailors were, and still are, a contrary lot!)

To zigzag from one side to the other, ships TACKED across the eye of the wind, wheeling the YARDS around from one TACK to the other, shifting the fore-and-aft sails from one side to the other.

To go with the wind abeam was called REACHING. This was also know as a "Soldier's Wind," since sailors have always considered a soldier less capable and intelligent than a sailor.

The side of the ship facing the wind was referred to as up to WINDWARD, sometimes A'WEATHER, while the side away from the wind was the LEE side, or ALEE. Anything below the ship and the source of the wind lay to its LEE. And a ship made LEEWAY going to WINDWARD as well. This depended on how deep and how long the keel and underbody of the ship were, her QUICKWORK below the waterline; as well as how hard the wind was blowing and how much she leaned over from upright, how much she HEELED. Too much sail aloft could make her HEEL even more, making her less efficient through the water, as could the distribution of her cargo.

To sail off the wind, with the wind from abaft, is now called BROAD REACHING but back then was termed RUNNING FREE with the WIND ON HER QUARTER. A ship just a little off the wind had a FAIR WIND. One heading steeper down to LEEWARD had a LEADING WIND, and one sailing even more southerly on the chart provided had the wind LARGE ON HER QUARTER or FINE ON HER QUARTER.

To sail directly downwind was to RUN, sometimes to SCUD or to carry BOTH SHEETS AFT, and was also known as a "Landsman's Breeze."

Winds, by the way, are named for the direction *from which they blow*, not the direction in which they blow. The northeast trade winds in the Caribbean *come* principally from the northeast; they do not blow *toward* the northeast.

To change course while sailing off the wind is now called a GYBE but in the eighteenth century was termed WEARING SHIP. It was easier to perform shorthanded, so many captains preferred, even when going to WINDWARD, to make a complete circle in the water, falling off the wind, WEARING the wind from one quarter of the stern to the other, then hardening back up to the wind on the opposite TACK CLOSE-HAULED.

The pointy end up front is called the BOW; that is FORWARD, corrupted to FOR'RD. The wide end at the back is the STERN—AFT.

A ship has two sides. The right-hand side of the ship is *always* the STARBOARD side. The left-hand side back in the eighteenth century was called the LARBOARD side. It's simple when you're facing the BOW, but when you turn and face AFT, they don't change places!

Sailors back then were more concerned with which side was the WEATHER side and which was the LEEWARD side, depending on where the wind was coming from, anyway. Steering commands were issued with that as the prime concern.

Here we reach another of those pesky posers created by the contrariness and conservatism of seafarers. In the very old days, every ship (they weren't so big back then) was steered by a rudder that was controlled by a TILLER, a wooden bar that sticks out from the top of the rudder like a lever. You still see them on smaller boats.

Boats do not steer like a car. To make a boat turn to the right, to STARBOARD, the tiller has to be pushed over to the left-hand side, to LARBOARD. This angles the rudder so that the force of the water across it swings the stern out in the opposite direction and swings the bows the way you want to go.

That's why Lieutenant Lewrie would order "helm alee" when he really wanted the ship to head up closer to the wind. Putting the helm *down* turns the bows *up!* Putting the helm *up* turns the bows away from the wind: "helm aweather." By his time, most ships had a wheel on the quarterdeck to steer with, but the wheel controlled ropes and pulleys connected to a TIL-LER HEAD below decks that did the same thing that a small boat's tiller did. When Lewrie said "helm up" or "helm aweather," the helmsman would turn the wheel a few spokes to either the LEEWARD side to put the helm "down" or turn it to the WINDWARD side to put the helm "up" or "aweather." But even if the addition of the wheel made it seem more like driving a car, the deck officer and the man on the wheel knew what they were really referring to was what was happening with that TILLER hidden below decks and what the rudder was doing, not which way the wheel was turning.

There were no auxiliary engines back then, no motive power except the wind and sometimes an "ash breeze," when the ship's boats were used to tow a vessel in light air. When the wind came FOUL so that there was no way to work out of harbor, no matter how well drilled a crew was in TACKING, ships sat in harbor until the wind shifted. In the Indian Ocean, South China Seas, and the Bay of Bengal, the monsoon winds shifted FAIR or FOUL by six-month seasons. While it might be fine for a ship bound south and west for the Cape of Good Hope and a homeward voyage, it would be almost impossible for a ship to make a journey in the opposite direction, beating into the teeth of that same wind from the Cape of Good Hope to Calcutta, which lay to the northeast.

Further, no naval captain would willingly cede the WIND-WARD advantage to a foe. Staying up to windward and mak-ing the other fellow come to you was known as keeping the wind gauge. Choundas could not operate against the principal sea-lanes to and from Canton from LEEWARD. He had to be up to WINDWARD, from which he could strike and then dance away if he ran into some ship stronger than he was. I hope I have related the limitations and advantages of wind position in *The King's Privateer*.

The harbor I invented at Spratly Island was a right bastard—easy to get into with a southeast trade wind, almost impossible to exit—and I hope I showed how near Lewrie was to losing *Culverin* in his attempt to get to sea and chase those pirates. Harbors were always carefully selected so the entrance was not blocked with a headwind, a "dead muzzler," most of the time. A ship trying to work its way out, short-tacking across a narrow entrance channel, would end up stuck on a lee shore and pounded to bits by the waves and rocks. That's why most harbors in the Caribbean are on the lee side of the islands—not just for protection from gales.

I could get into a lot more detail shown on the sketch of a full-rigged ship—what the braces, lifts, jears, and halyards did and all that—but that would take an entire book in itself. Let me recommend, instead, "the" guide: John Harland's *Seamanship in the Age of Sail*, U.S. Naval Institute Press, lavishly illustrated by Mark Myers, Royal Society of Marine Artists, Fellow of the American Society of Marine Artists. The U.S. Naval Institute also has Bryan Lavery's *The Arming and Fitting of English Ships of War, 1600–1815* and Peter Goodwin's *The Construction and Fitting of the English Man of War, 1650–1850*. Interesting, too, is *The Fighting Ship of the Royal Navy: 1897–1984* by E. H. H. Archibald. Time-Life's Seafarers series is out of print, I believe, but most libraries should have Fighting Sail, which covers the American Revolution and the high points of the Napoleonic Wars—the Great Age of Sail.

Speaking of the Napoleonic Wars ... there's Alan Lewrie, bound for the Bahamas after a few months' rest ashore. I expect that he shall have a rather peaceful time of it during his three-year commission. That should put him back in England, should he outrun any more irate husbands or furious daddies, in 1789. Just in time for ...

... but as they used to say at summer camp when they shooed us off to our cabins so the counselors could cavort with the girls across the lake, "That's a story for another night's campfire."

Don't miss Alan Lewrie's next exciting escapade!

THE GUN KETCH
by Dewey Lambdin

will soon be dropping anchor at a bookstore near you!

For a glimpse of this authentic adventure of the late-18th-century British Navy, please read on . . .

". . . is not to be entered into unadvisedly, nor lightly; but reverently, deliberately . . ." the vicar intoned, his voice ringing in stony, rebuking echoes from the transept of St. George's of the village of Anglesgreen.

Now they bloody tell me, Lt. Alan Lewrie thought in anguish!

". . . and in accordance with the purposes for which it was instituted by God," the vicar continued, casting a chary eye upon the couple before him, which made Alan almost wilt. He directed his gaze to his right, where Caroline stood flushed and trembling, ready to faint with joy, and the smile she bestowed upon him at that moment was so radiant, so shudderingly glorious, that he found himself quaking as well, not *completely* in terror of his bachelorhood's demise.

"Into this Holy Union, Alan Lewrie, gentleman, and Caroline Chiswick, spinster, now come to be joined. If any of you assembled may show cause why they may not be lawfully married, speak now; or else for ever after hold your peace," the vicar warned, wincing at the words, as if he expected the Hon. Harry Embleton to charge through the doors at the back of the nave on horseback with sword in hand. The crowd . . . a devilish *thin* crowd, Alan noted . . . fairly bristled and stirred, and a sigh or two, a grumbly cough could be heard.

"I require and charge you both, here in the presence of God, that if either of you know any reason why you may not be united in matrimony lawfully, and in accordance with God's

Word, you do now confess it," the reverend rushed on in breathy relief.

The tiniest quirk of a smile touched Alan's lips, in spite of his best intentions, as he mulled over his passionate, albeit brief, "marriage" to a Cherokee/Muskogee Indian girl named Soft Rabbit, and wondered if it counted. No, he sighed, no benefit of proper clergy there, he thought; no way out. Damme, and my enthusiasms for quim!

How *do* I get myself into these predicaments, Alan groaned.

"Caroline, will you have this man to be your lawful husband, to live together in the covenant of marriage?" the vicar inquired, not without what to Alan seemed a cocked brow in amazement. "Will you love him, comfort him, honor and keep him, in sickness and in health, and, forsaking all others, be faithful unto him as long as you both shall live?"

"I will," Caroline declared without a pause with a tremulous eagerness and vigor, delivering upon Lewrie once more a visage of pure adoration.

"Alan," the vicar intoned, rounding upon him, and to Alan's already fevered senses seeming to frown the *slightest* bit, "will you have this woman to be your lawful wife . . . ?"

Forsake *all* others? Lewrie shivered. Bloody, bloody hell! Be faithful as long as we *both* . . . I say, hold on, there! Mine arse on a bandbox! The solemnity crushed in upon him then, and *he* like as not would have torn out the doors, if his legs would have shown any sign of strength beyond holding him shudderingly upright.

Yet found himself declaring for all time, "I will," with a force born on a quarter-deck that echoed off the ancient stones like a pronouncement of doom.

There was a tentative Giving in Marriage by Uncle Phineas, in his role of *paterfamilias* for the Chiswicks, before the vicar ordered "Let us pray" and they could thump to their weak knees upon the pad before the altar. And as the vicar recited the short prayer of blessing before the Lesson and Epistle, and the vows proper, Caroline insinuated a slim, cool and soft hand into his and their fingers entwined to squeeze reassurance and strength.

There was no backing out now, Alan thought; in for the penny, in for the pound, ain't I? Ye Gods, it may not be that bad—I do care for her, well as a rogue like me may care for anyone. I might even call it love. Much as I know what *that's* all about!

355

He returned her squeeze, and they secretly leaned their shoulders against each other, and he became enveloped in the light, citrony scent of her Hungary Water perfume again.

The Gun Ketch
by Dewey Lambdin

Published by Fawcett Books.
Available soon in bookstores everywhere.

THE NAVAL ADVENTURES OF ALAN LEWRIE

By Dewey Lambdin